Unity House

Keith Christian Milne

UNITY HOUSE
© 2025 Keith Christian Milne
All rights reserved.

This is a work of fiction. Names, characters, businesses, places, events, and incidents are either the products of the author's imagination or used in a fictitious manner. Any resemblance to actual persons, living or dead, or actual events is purely coincidental.

Versions/ISBNs
Hardcover: 979-8-9926759-9-3
Softcover (Amazon): 979-8-9926759-7-9
Softcover (IngramSpark): 979-8-9926759-8-6
ePub: 979-8-9926759-6-2
Kindle: 979-8-2646754-6-1

Cover design by Keith Christian Milne
Published by Keith Christian Milne
www.keithmilne.com

Printed in the United States of America
First Edition

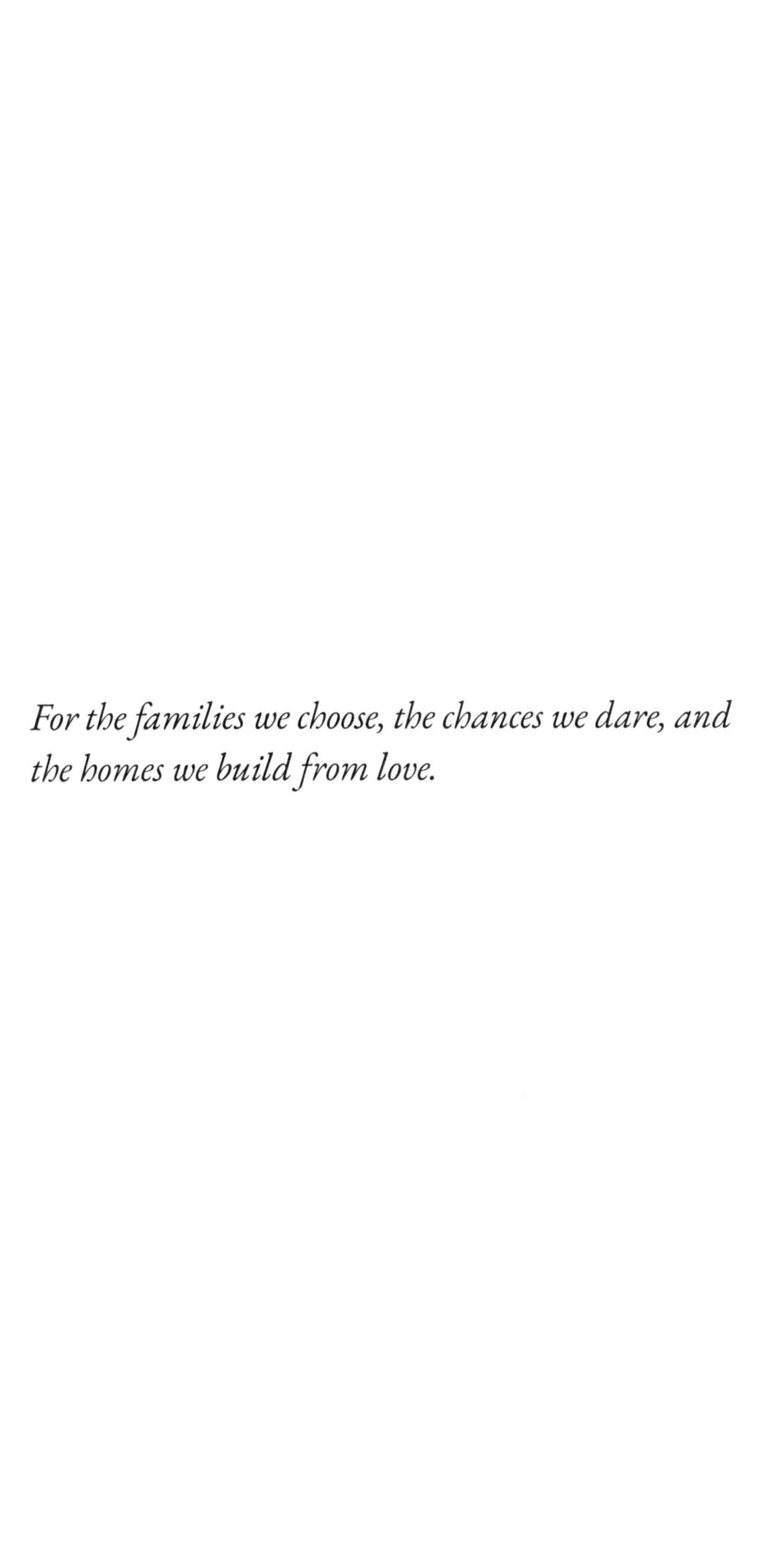

For the families we choose, the chances we dare, and the homes we build from love.

"What we focus on with intention grows. Therefore, focus on what you want — not what you fear."
—Keith Christian Milne

TABLE OF CONTENTS

1

ON DEATH'S DOORSTEP

Tanner Dalton stared down at the old woman. He barely recognized her. She was in a hospital bed at the University of California, San Francisco Medical Center. She appeared to be asleep, but in reality, she was in a drug-induced, semi-comatose state. *Pain management* they called it. He hadn't seen or spoken with her in almost twelve years. The essence of her image, the one Tanner had always seen in his mind when he'd thought of her, was still intact, but she had changed quite a bit. Tanner could have passed right by her on the street, never knowing that she was his mother, Mrs. Rachel Devon.

Her neighbor, Eda Selenski, had sent for him, promising him that nothing would be asked of him. His mother only wanted to see him one last time, she'd said. So, he'd come, as a son should, not from caring or a desire to see her one last time, but out of his sense of obligation—nothing more.

She lay before him now, dying from liver disease. Apparently, all the drinking and prescription drugs, the partying, and the strange men had finally caught up to her, and now her liver was finally calling it quits. She wasn't a candidate for a transplant due to her advanced age. A do-not-resuscitate order was in place, prominently posted on the door facing the hallway and on the wall over her bed. Now, standing over her, Tanner could barely stand the smell of her; she stank like someone with one foot in the grave

1

already. He wondered how long it had been since someone had bathed her.

Growing up with her had been a traumatic, frightening experience. Nevertheless, he'd tried to act like it was all good. But it never was, and never could be, and, over the years, they'd both come to that same conclusion. Whenever one of them would try making amends, the other would always be receptive and abide, until it all blew up in their faces, which it did *again, and again, and again.* Tanner had finally cut the cord permanently.

She had trouble accepting it, and never really did, but he'd left her no choice about it. She'd kept calling, until he blocked her number, kept emailing while he ignored them, and he eventually blocked her email address. He wouldn't hear from her for a few years, and then, out of nowhere, she'd send him a birthday gift, usually a shirt, or a pair of winter gloves, or warm socks, along with a note saying,

I know you weren't expecting anything from me, but I had to take care of myself, so I bought you this. I hope you like it. If not, then return it and get something else. Love, Mom. P.S. I know you don't want to talk to me or have anything to do with me. Fine. But, I'm your mother and you're my son and it's your birthday. I want to buy my son a birthday gift, so I did. I'm simply taking care of myself and doing what I need to do for me.

Rather than finding out his actual size, she'd buy it from a store that would likely be within a drivable distance away: a Walmart, Target, Penney's, Nordstrom, or Kohls. Tanner never responded. He knew she wanted to get under his skin, it was in her

DNA. He also knew that she hated being ignored, which he had gotten really good at doing over the years, out of necessity.

He took off his coat and hat, hanging them on the hook just inside the bathroom on the right, then sat down next to her, prepared to stay a while. He hoped she'd wake up soon and then he'd surprise her . . . likely for the last time. He pulled out his device and began checking the latest headlines.

Tanner had taken after his father in looks, charm, and build. He still had a full head of strawberry blond hair, slowly becoming gray for the first time at sixty. At six foot three, and at only two hundred pounds, he'd become nearly rock solid from working out three times per week for the last couple of years. Women often checked him out. He'd always been high energy and loved feeling that way.

He tucked his device away and returned his gaze to his mom. She lay there quietly, a feeding tube disappearing into her covers approximately where her belly would be, with a clear plastic, twin-nozzle, supplemental oxygen tube in her nose. Her heart beat could be heard on the monitor next to her, which seemed to be trying to keep time with the rhythm of her oxygen feeding system. He noticed a few silver streaks still visible in her greasy, almost completely white hair. The nurse had swept her hair upward and back in a grandiose way, making her head look like a spaghetti rack drying two different types of pasta at the same time.

Lying back against the bed had forced her excess girth outward on both sides, exaggerating it even more than normal. He was shocked by how much weight she'd gained over the years and the way her face now hung hard on her skull. He scanned her face closely, then shuddered, *misery and unhappiness—as a habit,* he thought. All the years of being miserable and unhappy, holding her mouth downward in that ugly, unhappy posture had resulted in it being left that way permanently.

After an hour, he was getting bored and hungry. Finally, he got up and went out to the nurse's station. A pretty nurse sat staring at a computer screen, seemingly hypnotized. Her blonde hair was pulled up into a tight bun, and her white two-piece top and pants, along with sturdy white shoes, were all business. Tanner stood there, ignored for a full minute, before finally having to say, "Excuse me."

Without looking up she said, "Yes, I know you're there, hang on just a second, please. After another ten seconds, she finally looked over at him and smiled.

"What can I do for you, Mr.—"

"—Dalton. Tanner Dalton. My mom, Rachel Devon, is in 3B. Any idea how long it might be before she wakes up?"

"Um, no, I can't really say. Sorry."

"Well, she actually does wake up, though, right?"

"Yes, but we never know when. We let the terminal patients sleep as much as they want, or need to. Your mother is still getting all the nutrients she needs through her tube and oxygen through the breathing machine." The nurse giggled a little, then finished, "She might end up sleeping the better part of the entire day today. We just never know."

A little exasperated, Tanner shrugged, "Okay, thank you." He nodded at the nurse and went back to his mom's room. Determined to not have had his time completely wasted, he went over to the right side of her, and got as close to her as he cared to, then took a selfie of them. "I'll talk to you later, mom, I have to get out of here, sorry," he said, looking at her face, trying to convince himself that she couldn't hear him.

Tanner drove down to Ocean Beach, and took a long walk in the sand. He rolled up his pants and let the water wash around his ankles and feet. The icy waters nearly took his breath away, bringing him back to the present in a hurry. His mind quickly ran through his situation and it didn't take him long to realize that he had nothing in Massachusetts to go back to. He tried to put it out of his mind, but he needed to make a decision and put a timeline on his expensive rental, plus he just wanted to make a choice and stick to it; was he going back there, or staying here and starting a new life? Originally, the plan was for him to be here just long enough to see his mother one last time, wrap up as much of her affairs as possible, and get her in a long-term care facility if needed.

He had been shocked two years ago when a process server knocked on his door and served him his divorce papers first thing in the morning while eating breakfast. His wife, Sheila, was supposedly spending the weekend with some friends at a beach house. Once she'd returned home, he'd confronted her and she'd confessed the entire two-year affair to him before angrily packing a bunch of her clothes and coming back several times over the next few days for more.

Her new billionaire boyfriend had a much more lavish stone palace perched on a hill in Whately, Massachusetts. Over the next few months, Tanner had purged half the contents of the house of stuff he was tired of or that reminded him of Sheila. Now, with nothing to really go back to, and despite having only visited the Bay Area a few times since leaving in 1977, he decided he was going to stay.

The next morning, he went over to mother's apartment to see what, if anything, needed doing. She wouldn't be coming back here, that he knew for sure. She needed full-time care; she had advanced dementia and had become a danger to herself, and now her liver disease was rapidly progressing. He'd been shocked to learn that, nevertheless, she still had a driver's license and had been driving, until being admitted into the hospital.

He was even more shocked by her debts. She'd rolled an unpaid car loan into another car loan by trading in her unpaid car, then having the unpaid balance added to her new car's balance. The dealer, of course, always made sure that the trade-in amount was insufficient to pay off her current car loan. She'd done this three times, and now owed $46,000 on a four-year-old Honda *Fit*. Fifteen credit cards all nearly maxed out, and only $236 in a passbook savings account. Her checking account history showed that her balance would go from $2,000 per month from Social Security at the beginning of the month, to zero, and even negative amounts each month as she paid different amounts on different cards at different times, with no rhyme or reason. Some had been forgotten for a while, others were running a credit balance, but between them all she owed $126,000. She would need to pay more than her whole Social Security check every month in order to prevent the total interest from all of those cards from growing, without ever paying any of the multiple principal balances down. She would've been evicted if her rent payment hadn't been set up to happen automatically each month after her Social Security check was deposited into her account.

Tanner was frightened by debt. He had grown up poor, and had vowed as a young man to never go back to that condition ever again. He'd made that vow to himself with so much conviction, it had stuck. Over time, he opened a self-directed IRA, and began tracking individual stocks, and followed the Warren Buffet method of wealth accumulation: buy what you know, buy quality, and then hold onto it—forever. It worked and his homework and discipline paid off, and he'd made a couple of million dollars over the last twenty years.

Then came the market crash from the Covid-19 shutdown of nearly everything and the subsequent supply chain problems and price gouging that went on. Next, Sheila took half of what was left after the market crash. Add in attorney's fees, and Tanner found himself in a much more fragile financial place than he'd been in since he was in his late twenties while looking for a job fresh out of the Navy. He'd sold all equities, and put the cash into another IRA account to eliminate losing any more to the whim of the stock market. Besides, he was too old to get back into the securities game, and he'd been thinking that he wanted a much simpler life now, without the stress of risking his financial well-being every time he bought and sold shares in the stock market.

While he was trying to map out a plan about his mother's things, Mrs. Selenski from next door must've heard him moving around, and came over.

She pushed the front door the rest of the way open and, sticking her head in but not seeing anyone, shouted, "I know you're in here. Just so you know, no one is supposed to be in here you know—whoever you are."

Tanner was just finishing up in the bathroom and hadn't heard a thing over the noisy exhaust fan. A few minutes later he came out. He immediately spotted Mrs. Selenski, who was still standing over by the front door in the living room. "Hello, I'm Tanner Dalton, I'm Mrs. Devon's, I mean Rachel's son," he said walking over to her.

"Oh, yes, pleased to meet you, Mr. Dalton, I'm Eda Selenski. I'm the one who wrote to you, and then spoke with you on the telephone. I'm so happy that you came. Your poor mother has been through so much, and she talked about you in such an endearing way. She's very proud of you, you know."

Tanner's mind was racing with his own thoughts about his mother and their feelings about one another. "Well, gosh, I never know what to say when I hear that one. My mom did like to brag about me while I was growing up, but I never felt like I had done much for her to brag about. It was always about my good grades and my athleticism. She used to embarrass me a lot then." Before Mrs. Selenski could respond, he said, "I hate to change the subject on you so abruptly but I'm wondering if you know of any plan in place for when my mother passes? I really hate to say it, but she seems to be getting pretty close."

Mrs. Selenski looked a little alarmed. She raised a brow, then started to frown, "Didn't your mother share her plan with you?"

Tanner blushed, "We . . . we really haven't spoken in a long time. I don't suppose that she happened to mention that to you, did she?"

"No, she said that you and she had many disagreements in the past, but never said anything about the two of you not speaking. I'm sorry to hear that. Well, the plan is very simple. She has already bought a direct cremation plan where, once she passes, her body will go directly from the coroner's office to the local crematorium where she will be cremated. She's already given away everything she wants others to have, with instructions for you to take anything you might want in the apartment. The rest, what little is left, is to be cleaned out by a crew that the manager uses more often than I can believe. They'll clean out the rest. It's all here in this envelope." She handed Tanner a larger manila envelope that only held a couple of pages. It was titled *RACHEL DEVON If I'm dead, then here is what happens next.* Only a couple of pages long, it specified, almost verbatim, what Mrs. Selenski had just said.

"Thank you. I appreciate that."

"You're more than welcome, Mr. Dalton. If you need me for anything or you have any more questions, I put my contact information in the envelope, and I'm right next door." She pointed in the direction of her apartment several times for emphasis. "Good luck, and nice to meet you."

"Nice to meet you too. And, thanks for the call, and the information. Again, very much appreciated."

"You're welcome, Mr. Dalton."

She retreated like a snake that had slowly slithered out from a shady cavern on a hot summer day to deliver information to a visitor, and was now slithering back to her cool cave to coil up and rest. He watched Eda shuffle back out through the door and painfully complete the six steps to her own door as the sound of waves crashing on the shoreline and screeching seagulls wafted past her into the apartment.

Tanner quickly looked around. Seeing nothing that he wanted, he locked up and left. As he made his way to his car, he thought, *So, everything's been taken care of already? What about all this money owed?* What about the credit card debt? I guess they won't have a choice, they'll have to charge it off. What the hell were those bastards thinking giving that much credit to an indigent, elderly woman in the first place? Serves them right! She has no spouse, no assets, no savings, not anything worth enough to pay off that kind of debt. All her belongings are going to be disposed of, and she's already arranged for her cremation. Awesome. Thanks, Mom. Works for me. I think this is the only time you've ever thought of others in your entire life, here at the end. I'm glad you did actually learn something in all your years. I wonder what the hell she bought to run those credit cards up so high? I didn't see much there at all. Then, he remembered what Eda had just said, *She's already given away everything she wants others to have.*

Three days later, a nurse called and woke him up to tell him that his mother had passed away shortly after 6 a.m. She said the body had already been sent to the coroner's and then it would be going to the crematorium. At that point, Tanner realized that he hadn't thought about her ashes, and hadn't seen anything about that in her instructions to the world. He asked, "What will become of them if no one picks them up?"

"They'll be put into a community ash pit with the ashes of others sharing the same predicament."

Tanner said, "Thank you very much," and hung up. *Perfect* he thought, then got up to start his day.

2

SOPHIE

Tanner was relieved that his mother had taken so much off of his plate already. Internally, he yearned to just go home to Massachusetts, but all of that had changed now, and he knew it would be easier for him to get past his divorce, psychologically, by staying here, far away and with a zillion new distractions. Now, he'd have to focus. He decided to spend time looking for a less expensive place to live, and getting a decent car. Luckily, he had driven around the Bay Area enough as a young man and, despite many changes, it still seemed very familiar to him. That would help ease the transition.

He looked at Zillow.com and saw that the most affordable rentals anywhere in the greater San Francisco Bay Area seemed to be concentrated in the east bay regions of Concord, Walnut Creek, Martinez, Benicia, and Pittsburgh. Looking at rentals in that area, he began daydreaming a little, and his mind quickly wandered back to 1975. He'd just moved out of the house at seventeen, having lied about his age to his new landlady at the Robin Lane Apartments. The rent back then was a paltry $170 per month. After moving in with furniture bought at the Salvation Army, he remained in high school, working until late each night washing dishes at a nearby steak and lobster restaurant.

Browsing through the rentals on Zillow, Tanner noticed two listings for one bedroom apartments in his old complex. Just like back in 1975, rentals in that complex were the least expensive anywhere in the entire region, and were currently hovering at $1200 per month for a 1-bedroom unit. *That used to be two-thirds my mortgage payment back in Massachusetts,* he thought.

On his way home from the local car rental office in Mill Valley, Tanner noticed a sign for Bob's Beaters—*only the best used cars available.* Once he finished turning his car in, he walked back down the road to it and found an old 1996 Toyota Camry with only 120,000 miles on it for $1,500. It seemed to be in really good condition; it had no leaks and great tread left on the tires. The paint was slightly oxidized, but Tanner didn't care. He knew how reliable Toyotas were, having owned them for years back east. After a quick drive around the area, it seemed solid, so he bought it. He filled it up and headed to Concord to check out what had become of the Robin Lane apartments.

As he pulled up, he barely recognized the place. He'd seen it in the rental listings and remembered that it was his old complex. When he arrived, it seemed oddly familiar, but he needed to check the address twice because it looked so improved, he barely recognized the place. Everything had been completely renovated. The walkway configurations seemed the same as he remembered but the formerly barren parking lot was now landscaped with small trees and shrubs planted in boxes bordered with concrete curbing, with parking spaces painted all the way around them. The entire outer part of all the buildings in the complex had been renovated using energy-efficient, dissimilar materials: cement board, brick facade, and trim board.

Parts of both the upstairs and downstairs units were bumped out, and had low-E, argon-filled windows. Also, the inside of all the units had been completely revamped bringing them up to the latest fire and building codes, making them all more fire-resistant, quiet, and energy-efficient.

Tanner went ahead and put down a deposit, and first and last month's rent, all at once. Didn't matter whether he was shocked about the prices of everything or not, the price would only go higher elsewhere, and the same format would apply. He was thrilled about getting his old place back after all these years, but not so thrilled about living all the way out here in the hot, dry, barren east bay again. He'd gone from being a long-married, just-becoming-elderly, semi-wealthy man, living in lush, green, western Massachusetts for almost thirty years, back to being a bachelor, with rapidly depleting resources, living, once again, in the brown abyss of the east bay for the first time in almost fifty years.

Indeed, he was moving back into the only affordable apartment he could find; the exact same one that was the only one he could find nearly fifty years ago. He was impressed by how improved the complex was. He was determined to make a new life for himself, and he made up his mind that he would continue to accept his new circumstances and make the best of them, while also working hard to improve them. He decided that he would continue to do the necessary work, that he would show his gratitude, and be conscious of what he was grateful for, and then give thanks for all the good in his life, everyday, just as he'd privately done his entire life.

Tanner got up and went to the bathroom again, then shuffled into the kitchen and glanced at the clock on the stove. 9:31 a.m. He picked up his phone, extra determined to actually connect with his old friend, Tammy, who still lived in the area, or at least he thought she still did. So far, she hadn't returned any of his calls, but he knew the number was valid. Every call went to voicemail, forcing him to leave a message, and today was no exception. Tanner finally decided to drive over to her house. Maybe he would catch her at just the right time and she'd want to go to breakfast with him.

Morning traffic anywhere in California is something to behold, and Tanner remembered it well from his earlier days. He finally arrived at Tammy's, a little rattled by some of the crazy commuters he'd just encountered, but it appeared as if no one was home. He double-checked the address—it was right. He had checked the town's property listings and found one listing that showed her as the owner of the same house that she lived in when they lost touch with one another.

Not only did it look like no one was home right now, it kind of appeared as if no one lived in the house anymore. The shingles on the roof looked like they were on their last leg. One of the front windows had fracture lines running from all four corners caused by a bullet, a rock, or a fist hitting the glass, which had left a small hole at the impact point. Someone had duct taped the fracture lines, and now the silver gray tape was beginning to fade, and fray badly from sun damage. The yard was overgrown with all types of weeds, dominated by dandelion-like flowers with super long stalks. They looked pretty waving in the wind . . . kind of. The whole place had abandoned property curb appeal, while standing in stark contrast to the manicured, weed-free, green lawns and rose gardens in the yards on either side, and across from hers.

Tanner pulled over across from her house, and turned off the motor. The more he focused on the details, the more details he saw, and they were ugly. The house looked like someone had gone to the worst, most crime-ridden neighborhood in the entire area, and then picked out the most abandoned property that they could find. The one where all the crack, meth, and heroin addicts go to get high, and end up lying in each other's vomit. Anyway, it looked like someone took that house, lifted it up, and then plunked it back down right in the middle of a nice, middle-class, conservative neighborhood in Concord, like a cruel and unusual April Fool's Day prank.

Tanner hadn't been sure of what he might find, but he knew without a doubt that if it was coming from, or had anything to do with Tammy, it was going to be unconventional. Now, looking out across the vast tundra of landscaping neglect, he felt her and, somehow, knew she was still around. He also found himself wondering about the general condition on the inside of any house that looked this bad on the outside. He noticed boxes, old furniture, and random junk piled high past the garage windows. *I hope Tammy hasn't become a hoarder too*, he thought.

Tanner believed that a person's yard was often a direct reflection of who or what kind of person lived there. Seeing Tammy's yard in such disarray, and her garage stacked high with stuff, he thought there was a fairly good chance that she might be struggling mentally.

Not seeing any signs of life, he slowly pulled away to find a place to eat. At the last second, he glanced over at her house one more time and thought he saw the curtain in the front left window move a tiny bit, but couldn't be sure. He wondered if it was his imagination, or if Tammy had been in there all along. Maybe she'd wanted to get a better look at the strange guy in the car across the street from her house. *That would be creepy,* he thought.

Tanner headed towards Clayton, trying to decide what his next move was going to be. He was running really low on money already. He thought about driving down to Santa Cruz to the boardwalk, but that was far away and would take most of the day and a whole tank of gas just getting there and back. He saw a Starbucks and pulled in, then changed his mind. He wanted a real restaurant or diner experience, like he'd gotten used to living in Massachusetts. Sure, they had Starbucks there, too, but they also still had many of the nation's last diners left in the country, and he missed them.

He kept driving, finally spotting Penny's Roadside Cafe. At least he'd be eating real food and not just getting a piece of sweet bread with his drink at Starbucks. Once inside, the smell of rich coffee made him feel welcome. He slid into a booth and immediately felt something brush his right knee. He looked down and saw that it was a real estate listings brochure for the local area. He ordered a cheeseburger, double cheddar fries, and a large Coke, then began thumbing through the booklet looking at all the listings, shocked and stunned by the prices of even simple, mundane homes. Suddenly, Tanner was jolted out of his momentary trance.

"Hey there, friend!"

Tanner looked up from his brochure right into the wide smiling face of a man with a tan so dark, he looked like a piece of cooked bacon, holding his hand out waiting for a handshake. He was dressed in a medium gray, pinstriped suit, a light blue dress shirt, and solid medium-dark blue tie. His matching eye color completed the package, and he exuded a positive energy that Tanner felt immediately while making eye contact with the man, but he decided to play along for now.

"Hello." Tanner responded while giving the man a firm handshake.

"I'm Steve Caldwell."

"Hello, Steve. What can I do for you?" Tanner said, slightly wary.

"Couldn't help but notice you looking at that brochure. Are you in the market for a house?" Steve asked enthusiastically.

"No, not at all. I found it here in the booth when I sat down. I didn't think they still printed these. I'm not entirely shocked by the home prices, *but I'm shocked by the home prices.* It appears that even dumpy little houses on the rough side of town cost between half and three quarters of a million dollars! That's really crazy to me, and I don't see how people here make it with housing, utilities, gas, fuel, food, insurance—everything costing more than most other places in the rest of the country," Tanner stated with a bit of authority in his voice.

"Where are you from?" Steve asked.

"California, but I've been living in Western Massachusetts for almost thirty years.

"Well, that makes sense. It sounded like you were from somewhere else where the cost of living is lower."

Tanner looked back down at the brochure for a minute, "I can certainly see that this place is second only to Hawaii in expensive states and places to live, along with New York State. I remember how much commission I paid when my former wife and I sold our first place in Massachusetts. I just realized while looking at this brochure that commissions on places with price tags this high could be a pretty lucrative career."

Steve smiled ear to ear, "Funny you should say that because that's exactly how I started my little empire. I own a company that employs a dozen realtors and four are also brokers. If you're interested in joining our team, I'm always looking for new talent."

Tanner took another sip of his coffee, thinking. Steve remained quiet, something none of his friends would've ever believed. Finally, Tanner looked over at Steve and said, "Thanks for the offer, but no thanks. I'm not looking to start a whole new career now, I'm semi-retired."

"From what, if you don't mind my asking?"

"Equity investing." Tanner smiled. He always loved being able to say that. It usually stopped all but the most gregarious types dead in their tracks. He knew that most people don't know a damned thing about the stock market or any serious investment mechanisms, and pay way too much to have a good amount of their investment dollars wasted, from inexperienced amateurs just out of college handling their accounts at one of the big firms.

Steve gave Tanner a tight smile and nodded, "Interesting. Did pretty well, eh?"

Tanner winked and nodded back, "Well enough."

Steve winked back, "Nice talking to you, Tanner. Hope to see you again, sometime.

Tanner knew that opportunities don't knock often. And choosing to ignore them was something done at one's own peril, but he already knew in his heart that he wasn't up to the steep learning curve to get licensed at this particular time in his life. He wanted to wind down, not up. He wanted to be involved in something that made people smile, not that real estate didn't, but he didn't want to have to be constantly on the job, always taking endless texts, and phone calls, and doing appointments, and showings, and on, and on, and on.

Right now he knew he needed a job, and he wanted to do something totally different—money be damned! He had been thinking in the background, usually while behind the wheel, that he might want to work at either a beauty salon, a bakery, a restaurant, or an ice cream parlor. Every time he'd been to one of those places, he'd seen people relaxing, enjoying themselves and, above all, smiling, and happy.

When he got back to his apartment, he logged into his bank and checked his balance. He estimated that, if his expense level stayed about the same, his account would be completely drained to zero in less than eight months. He dialed Tammy back up. Voice mail, again. Tanner hung up, and looked around. He decided to go back to Penny's, and this time sit at the counter, sip coffee, and look at want ads, *or* the pretty server he'd spied there a short while ago.

Back at Penny's, he took the first counter seat at the end. Within ten seconds, she appeared—the one that he'd seen earlier. She was gorgeous; he was stunned by her beauty. Her diamond blue eyes complemented her soft, milky skin. Thick, wavy, red hair seemed to flow past her face and cascade down to just past her shoulders. Looking at her standing there smiling at him gave Tanner goose bumps instantly from head to toe. There she was, the woman he had dreamt about more than once, standing in front of him holding a coffee pot and wearing a smile. He could never remember how these dreams ended, but he was absolutely certain that she was the woman in them.

"Coffee?"

"Absolutely. Thank you." Tanner replied. He noticed her name was Sophie when she leaned in closer to fill the mug she had just placed in front of him.

"I'll be back in a minute to take your order."

"Ah, actually, Sophie, could you please hold off on any food for now. I'm content to have some coffee and a piece of that delicious cherry pie I just spotted in your display case up front when I walked in."

"Sure thing. I'll leave you to it then and, no worries, I'll be around regularly to refill your cup." She winked at him before moving away.

Tanner admired her for a few seconds as she walked away, before returning his attention back to the houses in the brochure. One thing became apparent right away, the only properties listed for slightly under $300,000 were former small, one-bedroom apartments now being sold as condominiums, and they were virtually identical to the one that he was currently living in. After that, the next price point jumped right up to $500,000-$600,000 for old, three-bedroom ranches with 1,200 to 2,200 square feet, and with only spitting distance from the neighbors on three sides.

Continuing up the ladder, the prices seemed to be all over the place, but quite a few at $750,000 and a fair amount north of one million, some north of two million dollars. He was struck by the complete lack of any homes in the $300,000-$490,000 price range, and shocked by the overall cost of home ownership. He could certainly smell the money, and thoughts of all that fresh green excited him. It always had.

Sophie stopped by with a fresh made pot of black inspiration, and filled his cup. "Looking for a house to buy?" she said while pouring.

Tanner smiled and put the brochure down on the counter. "No, I'm just gauging the real estate market here. Looking to see what people are paying to own homes around here."

"Developer?"

"No, I just had a short conversation with a Steve Caldwell and was curious about what the potential earnings might be on commissions selling homes in this area. If you know what percentage your cut is going to be, then it's simple math to figure out your income."

"Oh, a real estate agent. Nice!"

"Thanks. Yeah, but I'm not going to do it. I'm going to do something else, I think.

Sophie looked impressed, "Wow, choices. Retired?"

Tanner looked down at the counter and said, "Should have been, but that's another long, boring story. I'm just not wanting to learn so many rules and regulations, building code standards around earthquakes, and radon and water testing. I'm going to do something soon. I'm good for now, but soon I'll need another job and I have some ideas. I want to do something very different this time," he said with conviction.

Sophie looked disappointed. "Well, you strike me as the type of guy that will do just that. I'm certain you'll figure out something that suits you."

"I keep second guessing myself about doing any of it. Starting a whole new career when I'll be eligible to start collecting Social Security as early as two years from now and, in another five years, full Social Security. So, that's forced me to pause and consider how much effort or learning I'm realistically going to want to actually do, when I know that all I really want to do is have some good clean fun, and live happy for the ten or twenty years I likely have left. Going back to school and learning all this stuff seems a little ridiculous to me at times. Like, why bother, you know?" Tanner looked up at her with an expression on his face like he just had some sort of revelation while sharing all that with her.

Sophie stood there studying him for more than a few minutes and, without warning, and while making direct eye contact with him said, "I get off in two hours. Would you like to come home with me and have dinner? I'll cook for you, and we can talk more about your plans."

Completely taken by her sudden invitation, but impressed with her direct, straight-forward way, Tanner stumbled, "Uh, I uh, yeah, I mean . . . sure, I'd love to go home with you and have dinner. That sounds really nice."

"Great. You're welcome to sit here and wait, or come back in two hours, and then you can follow me home." She left and went over to wait on a party of six that the greeter seated seconds before.

Tanner pulled his phone out to check for messages, but there were none. He was really worried about Tammy, but wasn't sure how long her situation had taken to manifest. Was it a long time in the making and nothing new, or did she suddenly change, and let everything, maybe even herself, go? Tanner wasn't sure about anything, but he needed to know that she was still alive and wanted more than ever to get her the help she needed, if she needed it.

He stayed and ate his pie and sipped more coffee. He was getting very alert now, not only from the coffee, but also from the new possibilities arriving just in the nick of time. Even though he'd already made up his mind to turn down the real estate opportunity, the fact that an opportunity had arisen at all was a good sign. Meeting Sophie added to his sense that things were turning towards the better, and he recognized it as something good coming into his life.

25

3

DINNER WITH SOPHIE

Tanner followed Sophie over to her place. She also lived in a first-floor apartment at the trendy, downtown townhouses known as Grant Street-Downtown. He was intrigued. Not only had he recently wondered how these units looked inside after driving by, but he now wondered how his new friend could afford to live here. He wove around inside the under-building parking garage looking for the spot she told him was marked as *Guest* spray painted in bright yellow.

He finally found the guest spot and pulled in. Sophie was already parked, and he could see her walking towards him. She waved for him to follow her, then turned, and walked at an angle towards an opening in the garage that looked like a stairwell. He caught up with her, and together they slipped inside the door which opened to a small lobby, offering a choice of stairs, or two elevators. She chose the elevator.

"Nice place. Do you own or rent?" he asked, trying hard to not sound as excited and affected as he felt; he had lived in a nice place in Massachusetts, but he wasn't used to being in surroundings that looked like they belonged on the front cover of Architectural Digest magazine.

Sophie glanced at him and smiled. "I own. We all do. We all have a signed contract with the owner's association which doesn't allow the renting of units. All the units are owner occupied, and that seems to be all that's needed to keep everything nice and kept up," she said matter-of-factly.

"Interesting concept."

She looked at him seriously, but Tanner thought he saw a hint of sly in it. The elevator stopped at the third floor, opening to a short hallway leading to two doors. 3A and 3B. Sophie's place was 3A.

Sophie's apartment seemed surreal. It was super modern. Sleek. Minimal. Stainless steel. Glass. Granite. Polished. High Tech. Her blinds were automatic, slowly opening and closing using light sensors inside the glass. As the sun moved from east to west, they'd automatically adjust in order to optimize the light without letting the sun's fading rays hit anything inside, including the occupants. Tanner had never seen anything like it.

"Have a seat anywhere you like, Tanner. I'll be right back. I'm going to change, and then we'll relax with a little wine and snacks, before I make dinner. Sound good?"

"Sounds perfect, Sophie." Tanner smiled at her watching her stroll towards the back, then disappear. His heart was pounding. He felt a little uncomfortable by his surroundings, and despite his attraction to her, he felt even more uncomfortable about being here in the first place. He thought, *I feel disingenuous.* I think she thinks that she'll have me for dessert as a reward for cooking for me, and it's not going to happen. I'm not ready for it to happen so quick. I don't know her and I'm not going to hop into bed with her after just meeting her. Geez. Maybe I should get it over with and tell her before she cooks for me? *Maybe you should chow down and enjoy it and let that be a lesson to her.*

His place was a dump compared to this place. He'd become comfortable with *modern shabby*, and sometimes experienced sensory overload about how nice some things were whenever he visited places like this—which was only when going on vacation and renting at a nice hotel, or over to a gathering at someone's house who lives in a mansion or something.

He loved the decor, but he also knew the costs involved, and knew that he would never appeal to her once she knew the truth about him. He felt himself begin to panic a little inside, and even thought about leaving while she was in her bedroom. *Just slip out and stay away from Penny's for a while,* he thought.

Instead, he decided to try and relax. He got up and looked around. He noticed there were quite a few framed photographs of what appeared to be a dancer. He went over to get a closer look. The framed black and white photos showed a woman pole dancing from various angles. He leaned in for an even closer look, and realized that he was looking at photographs of Sophie. She was the dancer.

"You like those photographs?" She said emerging out of the dark hallway from her bedroom. She was wearing black tights, a simple form fitting, pink top, pink lipstick and pink fuzzy slippers. Tanner watched her finish her walk over to him, taken back by her beauty once more.

Tanner replied, "Yes, I do. I love them. I love the way you look free and happy, and I love the photographers' angles. How long did you pole dance?"

"About five years. Martini? Up, with olives?"

Tanner was impressed. "Please."

Sophie continued. "It actually started when I was a senior at Concord High School. I almost didn't get my senior picture taken because I was late, and the photographer was about to pack up for the day. He was tired, and so was I. Jason was a senior in college doing photography, and he worked part time on Fridays. He took my senior picture, but then asked me if I'd like to pose for him in other ways. I asked what he had in mind, and he said just pictures of me from different angles. Slowly, he convinced me to keep taking more of my clothes off and going a little farther with my poses. Well, you don't want to hear all of this yucky stuff.

"No, if you feel the need, then I'm here for you. I can listen to whatever you're comfortable sharing." *I hope I'm right about that,* he thought.

Sophie smiled. "Thank you. Anyway, he paused at one point, and went and locked the two doors to the room. I was a little frightened by that. I continued anyway and, once I was naked, he continued taking pictures of me without incident, I began to feel more comfortable, trusting him even. Anyway, long story short, he introduced me to pole dancing and, for quite a while, I really loved it. I had done a lot of modern dance in school and this combined modern dance with strength training. He kept telling me that he would put me in touch with people who could use me as a model, but I was content to be a pole dancer. I loved where it took me while doing it; it took me to a place where I felt free and desired, and I didn't care about becoming anything else." Tanner stayed quiet and sipped his martini, but never stopped making eye contact with her.

"Well, you can guess the rest. Next, he wanted to take care of me and I ended up moving in with him. Later, he grew meaner with me, and everyone else. He eventually came to say that I owed him, when I complained about not wanting to do what he wanted me to do in the bedroom. He didn't care and, the next thing I knew, he had the nerve to start pimping me out. I had nowhere to go. I had no savings. I was told that all I had to do was have sex with the men he would send into my room, and I could continue living lavishly. Sex was the only direct cost to me. I learned pretty quickly how to just go somewhere else mentally while it was happening. Allowing it to happen came with everything, but it almost cost me everything too."

Hearing this was making Tanner feel sick to his stomach, and he felt fearful inside. He could really empathize with her about what happened, but it was too soon in their relationship to be hearing this now, tonight. He thought, *Holy shit! Too much information, lady! We just met. I'm freaking out picturing what you're telling me happened to you. Why are you leading with this anyway? My God!* She prattled on, telling him even more hideous details that he didn't want, or need, to hear.

Finally, sensing by his silence that Tanner was uncomfortable, Sophie stood up and said, "Anyway, enough about all of that."

Without another word, she became a whirlwind in the kitchen. Tanner watched from the tall swivel chair at the counter as she began pulling ingredients out like crazy, and putting them all around a cutting board. She pulled a big iron skillet out and a couple of stainless pots designed to work on her induction cooktop and oven.

She glanced over at Tanner, then smiled and said, "Need another drink?"

"Sure, when you get a chance. Would you like help chopping?"

"No, but thank you for asking. You just relax, and let me cook for you tonight."

Tanner said, "We don't really know each other, and this is fairly intimate for a first date, wouldn't you say?"

"Don't make too much out of it just yet, Tanner," she said without looking up from her chopping. Tanner smiled at her, then polished off the rest of the first martini. He was feeling a nice, warm glow, and was looking forward to another drink, some more conversation, and a nice meal. This was the first time he had been on any sort of date since becoming a divorced man, and moving back to California. Being in the company of such a beautiful woman who wanted to cook him dinner was exciting as hell to him right now. He was enjoying not feeling guilty for lusting for this woman a little bit, either.

While married, he'd always tried to keep his thoughts clean, so he would be better able to manage the lusty feelings that would arise from looking at and meeting other attractive women. When he got married, he was still young and full of desire. Sometimes, over the course of the decades that followed, he would imagine other attractive women as his wife, and maybe fantasize about what that might be like. Sometimes, he'd imagined making love with them in all of his favorite ways. Other times, he imagined having an affair with them, while they both remained married, and what that would be like. Sex with another married woman, as a married man, both completely committed to each other's marriage partner. He'd imagined that they would both get a thrill knowing they were doing something ultra naughty and against the rules, secretly, and it would be that primary carnal thrill that would ultimately push their illicit orgasms to new, unexpected heights, adding even more incentive to want to continue the affair and experience all of it again and again, while completely powerless to stop seeing one another.

All of these scenarios ran through his mind occasionally while married, but he never once acted upon any of them. In fact, he'd stopped entertaining those thoughts, or at least far less often as their years together became decades together, in order to further minimize entertaining any temptation to try out someone new on the side. He'd seen others go for it, and he'd seen how that had worked out for those who did—not well.

Tanner took his vows seriously. He did what he had to do to remain faithful to Sheila, which made her own deceit and ugly exit from his life all the harder to take. Now that he was divorced, he no longer had any real reason to squash those deeply passionate feelings that always stirred his embers.

He let himself fantasize now, and he could feel those intense passions stir in him while in Sophie's presence, and he was enjoying it. He was still processing being divorced, even after two years, and it was hard—something he'd never done. He'd been all set to be married for life. Now, without any choice about it, he was finally beginning to like his new freedom, and he was becoming reacquainted with his long repressed sexuality and his innate passion inside all over again.

In what seemed like only minutes, Sophie put a plate down in front of him. A beautiful, thick, center cut pork chop, browned, then finished in the oven while still in the skillet, served with roasted asparagus, and garlic mashed potatoes, then filled a large goblet with a nice fresh Merlot wine from Sonoma County. She served herself the same, but took the smaller of the two chops. She sat down, looked at Tanner, and lifted her wine glass. Tanner lifted his glass up, and they locked eyes for an extra long, lingering few seconds, before she said, "Cheers!"

"Cheers!" Tanner returned, as they clinked their glasses together and began eating.

Tanner was impressed, not only with her choices of food, but the awesome prep, and the cooking methods she used. All done so quickly and efficiently, that he was left wondering why, if it was that easy to cook so well, didn't he do it for himself? *Maybe I will, starting now,* he thought.

"Delicious! Absolutely delicious, Sophie. Thank you so much for having me. This is really nice of you. I really appreciate the last-minute invite and, I must add, that I'm astounded by your cooking ability."

She glanced over at him, blushing. She had a big smile on her face. "Thank you. It's not that big of a deal, really."

"I beg to differ," Tanner added. "I feel like I'm eating at a fancy, gourmet restaurant." He ate for another minute, then said, "How did you finally get away from Jason?"

Without hesitation, as if she'd been expecting him to ask, she quickly answered, "He overdosed. Some of his friends started mixing fentanyl with cocaine. You know the drill, the better it feels, the more you want, and many do just that, take more—for the last time. After I found him dead, and had satisfactorily answered all the questions by the police and coroner's office, I knew it was my chance to finally get out once and for all, and I took it. I grabbed some of my clothes and shoes, and the expensive jewelry he gave me, and threw them in my medium suitcase. Then, I went to Jason's hidden compartment down in the basement under some carpet in front of the washing machine. He kept the key to the lock around his neck, but I made sure that I took it off of his neck before anyone got there. I used the key and opened the compartment up. I managed to fill my suitcase with bundles of twenty, fifty, and one hundred dollar bills. I filled it to the brim, but left at least that much behind in the vault. Later, when I counted it, I had put almost two million dollars into that suitcase. It was more than all the people in my family, going back to the beginning of time, have made collectively.

I have done well since then. I invested it, wisely, and now the interest on my investments pay this mortgage. I'm just doing the part-time server gig to keep me busy enough that I don't lose my mind while I figure out my next move. Things are pretty relaxed for me right now. More so than they have ever been, and I like it that way."

She munched on some asparagus, took a sip of wine and then asked, "What's your story? I gave you a pretty detailed, and rather morbid part of mine. No need to compete, but feel free," she said with a smile.

Tanner smiled. "Nothing too weird. Grew up in this state, but then I joined the Navy, which took me out east, first to Connecticut, then to Virginia. After I was discharged, I stayed there. It was nice in Hampton Roads. Eventually, I met my wife while she was there visiting Colonial Williamsburg on a vacation with a friend from Massachusetts. We were married a little over a year later and I moved to Massachusetts, where we lived together, married without children for twenty-eight years. Unfortunately, for me, I guess she got tired of me after all those years, and tired of pretending that she wanted to have children, when she really didn't. She left me for some filthy rich guy she met at her weekly card game. We've been apart for a little over a two years now. Our divorce was finalized six months ago." He looked away for a brief second, and cleared his throat, choking back the emotion that was bubbling up from some hidden place inside him. Once back under control he finished, "For the first time in my life, I didn't get outraged and damage things. In fact I felt more numb than anything. I feel deeply betrayed. It shocked me when she finally told me. She was so good at hiding her affair. Apparently, it went on for over two years. The whole thing was surreal and completely reset my own sense of where I stood in the world."

Without saying a word, Sophie moved closer and put her arm around him, then gently rubbed her hand across his back. Tanner closed his eyes, and let out a slight groan as the palm of her hand passed over tight muscles. Seeing him respond to her touch with such pleasure, she rose and stood behind him, then began rubbing his back with one hand on each side. She used her knuckles and fingertips, forcing the muscles to relax, then finished with her elbow, using the point of it to penetrate deeper into his muscles, as he continued moaning in pleasure from the tension release.

He turned towards her, his eyes searching hers for the okay. She leaned in. They both closed their eyes at the same time, just before their lips gently touched, then stopped, briefly pausing before both of them slowly finished moving in, pressing a little harder. As their kissing continued, their passion quickly escalated, alternating between soft, wet, gentle kissing, and tongue sucking, frantic kissing, with their tongues lashing at one another madly. Determined to show Sophie that, at his core, he was a gentleman, Tanner took the lead and pulled away, still gasping with passion and desire, but glad that he had stopped short before things had gone any further. They both looked at one another and smiled, then laughed together.

Before things started again he said, "Thank you for a wonderful evening, Sophie. You worked all day, and still took a chance having me over. You cooked me a gourmet meal, really listened to me, then gave me a massage and made out with me. You've treated me like a king all night. I'm not sure why you would go to all that trouble, but I am most grateful and appreciative."

"You're welcome. I had my eye on you the first time I saw you being seated at *Penny's*. There is something about you that I feel drawn to. So, I'm welcoming that in, I'm welcoming you in essentially, by trusting my own, well-honed instincts. So far, I think my good guy radar is still working pretty darned well."

"Do you normally work those same hours everyday?"

"I work Monday through Friday from 10 a.m. to 4 p.m."

Tanner said, "Awesome. Now I know where I will come for lunch when I can." He put his drink down and looked into her eyes. "I want to stay, but I think I'd better get going."

Sophie looked at him with a caring, adoring look, "I understand completely. I enjoyed having you. It was fun."

"Yes it was. Very much so. I can't thank you enough."

When Tanner got to the door, he turned to say goodbye, but she was already there, and at point blank range. They locked bodies this time, and resumed their frantic kissing. She had him pressed against the door, her tongue probed his mouth as if searching for something left behind. Her hand fondling the zipper on his trousers. She began kneading him through his pants, which left him with a granite erection, standing tall against the door, ready to exit, but now pinned and helpless.

Tanner suddenly pulled away hard, putting his hands between their chests. "Stop, please stop."

Sophie stopped, and stood looking at him, panting hard, a semi-crazed look on her face, and hunger in her eyes.

"I'm not wanting to do this with you tonight. That's all. I want to very much, but I'd rather wait and see you some more and get to know you, so our intimate time together can be even more special, and feel even more amazing. Understand?"

"Yes, I understand. I think. It's just that . . ."

Tanner cut her off, "It'll be better later if we both wait until we can't stand it anymore. Trust me. It's worth the wait, and if we end up not liking one another before it happens for any reason, then we'll both be glad that we didn't do it at all."

Sophie's engine was still revving, but she succumbed. "You're right, and I know it, but it's been a long time for me too, and you're the first person I've ever met that I feel like I've known for a long time, or in another lifetime or something. I feel connected to you in the strangest way, yet I can't explain any of it. But tonight, once I started talking, I wanted to spill my guts to you, and tell you everything, and I wasn't afraid that you'd run away after hearing it all, either. Somehow, I knew you would listen patiently like you did, and accept me without judgement. I'm so excited by this turn of events, of meeting you. There are no accidents, you know. We were destined to meet. How long we'll be in each other's spheres is anyone's guess, but we have unfinished business with one another—*that I know for sure*. The energy I'm getting is pure, simple, clean, and trusting, which I find provocative. So, yeah, I'm having a hard time letting you walk out that door tonight because I'm afraid that, maybe our time was only this time, and after you leave, we'll never be able to finish what's already been started between us tonight."

Tanner hesitated, then said, "Wow! That's insightful, and tempting beyond imagination, but I will call you or come by the restaurant when you're normally there as soon as I can. Trust me, I don't want to go right now either, but I'm going to."

Sophie stepped back a little so Tanner could turn and open the door. Once he was finally in the hallway, he turned towards her, smiled, and said, "Bye for now," and left.

4

TOO MUCH INFORMATION

Tanner thought about his evening with Sophie. He liked her, but he felt sorry for her, although he strongly suspected that she might also feel a little sorry for him for losing out after spending his entire adult life playing by the rules, and ending up childless, followed by literally losing a small fortune.

He had always wondered what it was that he was truly meant to do, but had stayed perplexed for decades. The trouble was, he loved everything. He enjoyed being curious about everything, and wanted to try everything out at least once, including most of the numerous jobs he'd had over the years, and the numerous drugs he'd tried over the same time period.

Before discovering the stock market, he'd never owned anything of real value, accumulated any savings, stocks, or time towards a pension. A worker often has to work ten years for vesting in most retirement plans, which was something Tanner had never been able to manage with any one company. He'd constantly started over until discovering the stock market, then the market became his only passion and, over time, it showed.

He worried about being too attracted to Sophie, and concerned about the fact that she scared him, and he wasn't sure why. There was just something about her that he couldn't figure out, but time usually tells on people. He knew that if it were something he really needed to be concerned with, then more time would reveal the truth. She had quite an unsavory history, and he knew that there was likely even more that he would never want to know about.

Bottom line, he sensed that she was trouble, and would likely bring trouble to anyone willing to let themselves become entangled with her, just the sort of thing he didn't need right now. But he liked and respected her honesty and her ability to express her feelings, while being completely unafraid of what he may have thought about her past.

Finding himself lusting after Sophie tonight, despite her rather lurid past, and remembering how he felt, how vulnerable he felt after finding out about his wife deceiving him, despite their long time together, made him wonder why, and want to dig deeper into his own past. Looking back further, he realized that he'd always had his head up one chick's ass or another, going all the way back to when he was a freshman in high school, and that also made him wonder—why?

He was utterly conflicted. He loved women. He loved everything about them. But now that he was going to be a single man again for the first time in thirty years—albeit against his will, though he was surviving the ordeal—he wanted to forge a new life for himself on his own, without any distraction from an entanglement with a woman right away. For now, he wanted to remain unencumbered and free. To be able to come and go, stay over, sleep in, or study or read at will, or just go for a walk on the beach without having to check in with anyone else about what they might want to do. He wanted to make a new life for himself, all by himself, and have only himself to blame whether he succeeded or failed. He didn't want distraction, nor did he want help. He would have to let Sophie know. The more he thought about it, the more he began to see Sophie less as an attractive woman to be desired, and more as a dangerous distraction, and a real test for him.

Tanner kept mulling the evening over, *What are the odds that, at the tender age of sixty, I would meet a gorgeous woman who seems hot for me?* He thought, *Maybe I should go and buy a lottery ticket.* Tanner threw himself down on the couch, and turned on the virtual fireplace app on his Roku player. He packed a bowl of some nice Indica bud, and lit it. After several hits, he felt himself begin to relax. His body was relaxed, but his mind began wandering and he began thinking about what he might do next for work. The more he thought about having to go back to work, the more depressed he felt. He wasn't keen on having to hoop jump for another manager or boss, learn new rules and have to worry about other people again. He hadn't missed that at all.

Suddenly, Tanner sat up straight while inhaling hard, his eyes wide and alert. Had he given Sophie his number? He didn't think so. He checked anyway. Nope, perfect. He laid back down and quickly fell asleep.

The next morning, his thoughts became intense and directed almost immediately. With as much conviction as he could manage, he drove home the mantra of the new and improved Tanner, *I will remake my life and I will remake it better than ever. I will succeed, defining success in my own way, knowing that when I've achieved it, or attained it, I will rejoice in my accomplishment, and* then get the hell back to work, because my success will have come from finally discovering, and then doing what it is I was meant to be doing all along. *And I know I'll want to get back to that fun!*

After saying that to himself, he felt better and more directed, even though he still wasn't sure which direction that might be. *Self Improvement,* he thought. That resonated with him. *For once in your life, get good with yourself, so whatever you decide to do, you'll do it with all that you have, in a healthy way, and with a smile on your face.* Despite saying all of that to himself, deep inside, he felt a nagging doubt and a lack of real confidence.

Knowing he was short on money, he began to fear becoming homeless, as the realization of that possibility seeped into his mind through his pores, marinating him in negativity. He had to get a job—fast. Multiple times in his life when he'd been faced with similar circumstances, he'd always come out on top. Something in him always seemed to kick into overdrive, his own customized version of the fight or flight survival response. He'd figure it out. He had no choice.

He changed into a jogging outfit that he'd brought with him. It had been stuffed into the bottom dresser drawer, where it had been sitting since being laundered after he'd worn it for the first—and only—time, almost fifteen years ago. It still looked brand new, but some of the wrinkles looked permanent from being folded the same way for so long. Determined to change—starting that day, he was surprised that it no longer fit. It was way too tight to be comfortable. *Screw it, I'm wearing it anyway. What else do I have? Nothing.*

For the first time in at least thirty years, Tanner took off jogging down the street with no idea which direction to take. Within half a block, he came to Meadow Lane and turned right. He made it all the way down to the big intersection at Monument Boulevard and had to wait a long time before finally getting the green. Now, feeling faint just as the light turned green, he opted out, somehow knowing better, and turned back, this time walking.

He checked his map app and saw that he had jogged just under half a mile. *Not too bad of a start for an old fart,* he thought. Walking allowed him to think a little more, and he found himself wondering about getting a job again.

He thought about how his wife had taken fifty percent overnight once the divorce became finalized. *How does that work, anyway?* he thought. *She cheats for two years, lies about it, continues having sex with me while also keeping her lover satisfied.* In the end, she gets to walk away with the younger, wealthier guy, while also unhanding me of the money that would have kept me from having to go back to work. I should be retiring soon. She gets rewarded for being unfaithful and lying about her cheating shenanigans, and my reward is to lose half of all my assets? My reward for going to work everyday and paying for everything, while staying completely faithful and believing that she was, too? That's just wrong. *Well, I got a little revenge sex of my own after you left, darling.*

Shortly after finding out that Sheila had been cheating on him, Tanner had contacted a mutual friend, Margo, who is single. He met her at a party years ago, and over the years, she had let him know, in so many ways, that if he ever wanted to have some fun, or try out someone new, that she would always be available for him. She had even whispered in his ear that if he ever decided to go for it, that she would never tell a soul, and she would make herself available for him whenever he wanted her—discreetly.

Tanner had always found her enticing in lots of little ways and, imagining his wife screwing another man made him so furious, he finally did decide to go for it. He called her. Her tone indicated that she was very pleased that he'd contacted her. The next day, they met for lunch, then went back to her place, where they made hot, passionate love for several hours that afternoon, and Tanner had allowed himself to savor every single minute of it. All the years of feeling that sexual tension, that pressure, a drive towards completion had taken their act to another level—for both of them.

As he continued walking, he began to notice more shops and buildings, and little businesses tucked into and along the street, with quite a concentration of them in a small shopping center. Someone was cooking Mexican cuisine nearby, and it smelled heavenly. Even though he hadn't eaten breakfast yet, he was going to find the source of it, even if just for future reference.

5

TACOS WITH RICE AND BEANS

Tanner walked deeper into the little shopping center. It was deceptively small on the outside, but once inside it was larger than expected. The part visible from the sidewalk was only one side, and hid a network of other hallways that fanned out in different directions, all of them protected from the weather, but otherwise open to the outside air. There were several small clothing shops, two hair styling salons, and two jewelry boutiques and a funky bookstore that blended new and used books in creative ways.

Tanner wound his way through the complex following his nose until he finally found a little Mexican restaurant, *Es Picante* (It's Spicy), tucked away on the other side, well into the interior of the shopping center. He walked over to take a look at the menu.

Their sign said they were closed, but would open for lunch at 11 a.m. Monday through Friday, 11 a.m. to last order taken at 2 p.m. He could hear people inside talking and laughing in Spanish; loud mariachi music played from somewhere in the back. *Getting everything ready to open soon,* Tanner thought. The menu was basic, but that's what Tanner found so attractive—simplicity for a change. Tacos, with either beef, chicken, pork, fish, or tofu. Spiciness levels of Mild, Medium, Hot, or Super Hot. Odds and ends and drinks extra. Perfect. Tanner was intrigued. He left to continue his exercise, trying to decide if he should come back today, or tomorrow for lunch.

Just as he cleared the end of the building on the narrow street inside the shopping area, someone came up from behind him and poked what felt like a gun into his back. The man shoved him against the side wall of the nearest building. He was strong and so was his grip. He twisted Tanner's left arm behind his back, and kept the pressure on just enough to keep Tanner's face pushed up against the wall, until he searched and found Tanner's wallet.

"What comes around goes around, guy." Tanner hissed through clenched teeth. "I'm broke. I live on credit. Please. Just leave, and leave me alone."

The man put his knee into Tanner's back and held him in place while he went through Tanner's cashless wallet without saying a word. Oddly, he threw Tanner's drivers license and health care cards down, then pocketed the wallet with his ATM and credit cards still inside. He ran away so fast Tanner knew it wouldn't do him any good to give chase and risk having a heart attack.

"You'll get yours someday, punk." Tanner shouted after him. It was his first mugging, and Tanner was disappointed that Concord seemed to have a lot more crime now than ever before in its history. He dialed 911, and the police arrived and took his report. He never saw the guy's face, but at least the police knew to be on the lookout for a man who is mugging people in the area.

Once back home, he notified the bank and the credit card companies, then took stock of his situation. No money, no cash of any kind, no way to get more, or to pay for anything until his new cards arrived. Then it hit him, he could order food online with Uber Eats, *one of the benefits of living in this age,* he thought. He'd already set up an account with them, with PayPal as the payment method. He looked online and was amazed at all of the local places he could order from using it. That took care of food for the short term, but getting gas for his car without a card, or other digital means to pay, and with no cash, he'd have to wait until the new credit and debit cards came before using the car. Times like this made him want to use one of those old brick and mortar banks again. Then at least he'd be able to go and access his account by answering his account security questions after explaining what happened.

He went to his bedroom and looked around. Ah, the big jar of change. He grabbed it and poured the coins out on the bed. $46.76. Not too bad. He looked around, his eyes stopping on his closet door. He got up and opened the closet. One by one, he checked the pockets on all of his jackets. Two dollars in the side pocket of a sport coat, and a sweet twenty dollar bill from the inside pocket of his leather jacket. That made $68.76, plus PayPal online or in person at a few chains, none of which were in walking distance, though. Over all, he figured he'd be fine until he got his cards.

Thinking about everything that had happened over the last six months or so made Tanner feel overwhelmed and exhausted. He decided that, in addition to beginning a workout routine, he was going to try turning off the television and not watching the negative news any longer. He knew that Concord would never feel like home to him. Not a chance. He'd just wanted to stay far away from Sheila, but living here, in the Bay Area, this was the only place he could afford right now. He surmised that perhaps going to another, brand-new place would've been more prudent in retrospect.

The next morning, he woke up feeling motivated. He decided to work out right away. This time, he made it all the way around the block, even jogging the whole way. When he was done, he went home, finished with twenty sit-ups, twenty push ups, and then straightened up his apartment a bit—even cleaning the bathroom before taking a quick rinse. After showering, he was starving. He looked at his watch, and decided he'd put on some clean clothes and head over to Es Picante to try out their food.

Tanner was glad when he finally got to the quieter part of the shopping center; the traffic noise was off the scale today. Once he found the restaurant, he quickly stepped inside. Little bells hanging on the inside of the door jingled, announcing his arrival. A short, thick woman with jet black hair and a round, happy face stood behind the counter smiling at him. "Buenos Dias, Señor, please have a seat wherever you like. You're our first customer today. I'll be right with you."

"Thank you." Tanner replied. He walked over to a small table near the front window and sat down. The woman quickly finished rolling silverware up into napkins, grabbed a menu and a plastic drink cup. She opened a sliding panel and Tanner heard her scooping ice. She filled the plastic drink cup with ice, and brought everything over to him. She set the cup down, handed him the menu, then began filling his glass with water.

Tanner smiled at her and said, "Thank you, I appreciate that." He picked up the cup and drank some of the water immediately. Her name tag said, Carmen.

"I'll give you a few minutes."

Tanner nodded and looked down at the menu to be kind, even though he already knew what he wanted. The tiny restaurant only had room for a dozen sit-down patrons. One of the walls was a painted mural of a desert scene that looked like the Sonoran Desert in Northwest Mexico/Southwest Arizona, where Tanner had spent some time camping out. A few minutes later, Carmen came back and took his order.

"I'd like three different tacos, please, one with fish."

"Uh-huh."

"One with tofu."

"Okay."

"One with chicken, please."

"Uh-huh."

"Rice and beans, please."

"Okay."

"Oh! Could I also have a little cheddar cheese melted on top of the beans, please?"

"Yes, no problem. And, to drink?"

"Oh, right. Coke, please. Large."

"Okay. It won't take long." She said, smiling. After she stepped away, Tanner watched her thick pony tail swing back and forth as she fast walked his order to the kitchen. He looked around some more. The other walls were painted a happy yellow, and had southwest apparel— Mexican sun hats, blankets, beads, and even some maracas—fastened to them. All of the little tables had short candles in small glass goblets, and little bright flower arrangements next to them. The kitchen and bathrooms could be accessed through the doorway opposite the main entry door.

Ten minutes after he ordered, Carmen brought him his piping hot, fresh-made taco plate. It smelled and looked great! "Careful, the plate is very hot," she said, setting it down in front of him.

Tanner looked at her with gratitude, "Thanks."

She smiled and replied "De nada," setting a small bowl of sour cream and fresh salsa on his table.

Tanner ate hungrily. He hadn't eaten a thing in about fifteen hours, and working out and burning extra calories really added to the strength of his hunger. It felt far more intense and powerful than usual. At one point, with salsa and food pasted to the side of his face and still chewing, he caught Carmen checking him out from the counter. He smiled and gave her the thumbs up sign, and kept right on eating. She smiled back, then looked away, embarrassed.

Everything was perfect. The fish was tasty and flaky, the tomatoes and lettuce were fresh and just the right size and amount. The tofu was firm, but tender inside, and browned just right. The chicken was rotisserie roasted, and had a wonderful flavor. Everything seemed perfectly portioned and prepared carefully, with just the right amount and type of spices that, all together, seemed to take his tacos to the next level. The beans and rice were prepared traditionally, sans the lard, and both were so good, it would be hard to imagine them any better. Tanner loved this place. He knew this was his new favorite restaurant. He would be back for sure. He tipped Carmen well, and started to leave, when six other people in dress attire came in. They each smiled and nodded at him as he passed them on his way out.

He heard Carmen greeting them with familiarity, "Buenos Días, Señor Buchanan and Powell. So good to see you again." Please, you and your guests have a seat wherever you wish." She seemed genuine, joyful and happy. Oddly, Tanner found himself wondering if she would still be cheery and positive at the end of the day. Would she still sound joyful and happy, or be sick of the whole affair, ending the day sounding and feeling tired and bored, her voice painted with a distinct, sad, robotic quality?

Walking home, he reminisced about the many days he'd had like that over the years. On more days than he could believe, he had awakened full of hope, courage, vigor, and discipline, only to come home filled with fear, despair, physical exhaustion, and need-ing to engage in some type of self indulgence. The next day would often start that exact same way, and often end the same way too, but sometimes, every once in a while, he had caught some breaks and benefitted from the events of what he called *life's lucky days.* And when he thought of *life's lucky days,* he would always hear a little jingle finish at the end with *And you only get a handful of those, you know.* Without those, Tanner knew that he would likely have lost his mind decades ago.

Once back home, he decided to finish cleaning. After a short while, he flashed back on an incident that had happened in his first apartment. He'd returned home after being away camping for three days. He'd left plenty of food for his cockatiel, Pete, but that wasn't the issue. He'd also left a hefty amount of dirty dishes and greasy pans all piled in the sink, and on top of the counter, right up next to where poor Pete's cage sat. Tanner wasn't sure how long it had taken after he'd left, but when he returned, the sink and everything in it, along with the entire counter top was covered by millions of swarming ants. Of course, they had found their way into Pete's cage. He was dead, lying in the bottom of his cage with his little eyes closed. Likely dying horrifically, *a death-by-ants* process of slowly being eaten. His body was entirely covered by them. Tanner winced every time he tried to imagine the horror that poor Pete likely experienced the last hours of his life, all because he had been too lazy to clean up before leaving. He always felt guilty about that, and often flashed back on that memory when cleaning.

Since then, he had never allowed his apartment to get too dirty, or his dishes to pile up too much in the sink. Now, everything was cleaned thoroughly once per week, and he no longer owned pets. Besides, Tanner would wince at the thought of ever being perceived as a stereotypical older, single man living alone. You know, the single guy with the beer belly and bad disposition that, if you're brave enough to visit and actually go inside when you do, is a decision you always end up regretting. Complete disarray, stench, heavy dust, a bathroom that looks infectious at best, and a toilet that you'd better not sit down on. *Not me, buddy. No way,* he thought.

After finishing his cleaning, he went out and checked his mailbox, finding not one but both replacement cards waiting for him. *Thank you, universe,* he thought. He was back in business now. Once finished activating the cards, he went out to get a few things at the grocery store and fill his car up with gas, keenly aware of his dwindling money pot. He thought about getting a take-out pizza for supper at Antonio's, two blocks down on Monument Boulevard, but changed his mind, instead opting for a far less expensive, but highly adequate, frozen pizza from the grocery store.

Tanner felt good today, and he wasn't sure why. Maybe because the day had been good to him—so far. He enjoyed getting a meal over at Es Picante, and getting his place straightened up. Now he felt good being out and about on a beautiful sunny afternoon. Luckily, the shopping center wasn't crowded, he'd caught it just before everyone got off school and work.

The Big Food Mart was one of those big-box, semi-mega food stores that look enticing and dressy up front, but once you go inside, just past the front designer displays, the old school aisles are all still there ready to try your patience, and take you back to an era gone by. Once at the checkout, he thought about the rest of his day. He hated feeling the constant pressure of the dwindling money pot, so he decided that he would see what he could find online for local jobs right after getting home.

The checkout clerk, sporting six small safety pins piercing the outer edge of his right ear, seemed extra friendly. He gave Tanner a wide smile, and kind greeting. On his way out, Tanner slid a dollar into the paper machine, took out a paper, then slammed the door shut, tossing it into his cart. He got into his car, stopping for gas on the way home and, once there, threw himself on the couch with his laptop, the newspaper, a sparkling water, and some cheese and crackers, before settling into a focused job search.

Aside from the usual long list of medical and technology job postings, he saw jobs for part-time janitors at night to clean offices, carwash workers needed to finish drying and touching up cars coming out of the brush tunnel, office assistants needed to answer telephones, make appointments, and deal with grumpy people. Drivers of all types were needed, as were forklift operators. Auto parts counter workers were needed, as were restaurant workers across the board. Lots of retail clerk jobs were unfilled, mechanics were needed at two of the local big car dealerships, and welders were wanted down at the docks in Oakland.

Tanner found himself technically unqualified or lacking a necessary certification or a college degree that was needed for almost everything except the most mundane jobs. He decided to develop his own criteria for employment, what he wanted for pay, hours, location, tasks, etc. Then he would bounce potential jobs against his criteria to see how close they matched.

Tanner decided that, since he was poor, he'd better maximize pay, while also factoring in the distance to work in order to minimize fuel costs and, finally, the hours, because he didn't want to waste any of the precious minutes of his life sitting in traffic for hours each day. Nothing really matched too well for the pay being offered.

Tanner laughed out loud and thought, *That's what I mean. Who the hell is going to drive all the way to Oakland or across the bridge over to San Francisco, sitting in traffic everyday for at least two hours minimum, and then take shit all day from assholes for a lousy $15/hour? Someone was smoking something good when they wrote that ad!*

Hungry, Tanner took out the frozen pizza from the store and began preheating the oven to 425 degrees. He chuckled looking at the box again before tossing it into the recycling bin, *Bay Area Deluxe Pizza—Hand Tossed Goodness in Every Box.* He decided to give the job search a rest and just zone out with some more tube before bed. He was going to save some of the pizza for lunch the next day, and that's hard to do when you're emotionally eating. In the end, he almost ate the entire pizza, minus two pieces, while mindlessly transfixed first to a comedy movie, followed by a who-done-it murder mystery. He woke up at two in the morning needing to pee really bad. He jumped up off the couch, and stepped right on the two remaining pieces of pizza. Instantly, they squished outward, smearing across the paper plate they sat on. Tanner hopped all the way to the bathroom, barely making it in time, angry that he had to settle for such low-rent pizza to begin with, and now the leftovers were ruined and partially on his bathroom floor.

The next day, he slept until nine, then got up and had some cold cereal, lounging, sipping coffee, and playing his daily word games—something he swore kept his mind sharp. He let himself become fully awake, and fully hungry again, before getting dressed and walking up to Es Picante for a nice spicy start to the rest of his day.

As he approached the front door, he noticed a help wanted sign in the window next to the door. Curious, he stepped inside and said, "Hola," looking around for Carmen. It was silent except for the faint sound of a radio somewhere behind the counter back in the kitchen. Tanner looked around for a bell or something to ding, then just took a seat near the front, deciding to wait patiently.

After a few minutes, Carmen came out from the kitchen. "Hola, Señor. Como esta?"

"Hola, Señorita. If you're asking me how I am, which is what I think you are, well . . . I'm fine." Tanner gave her two thumbs up and smiled.

"Lunch, Señor?"

"Si, I mean, yes, please. Hey, um, just out of curiosity, what's the job about that you're looking to fill?"

Carmen stopped on her way to get him his menu, and turned around. "We are looking for a person to learn how to help us prep ingredients and prepare for lunch, and also to do general duties as needed around the restaurant. Eventually we may expand to a food truck, and sell our lunch down by the mall or other locations that we've had our eyes on. Why? Are you interested?"

"So far, so good. Would the food truck kind of be my thing, once trained?"

"Likely. You would come in and help us prep, and some of that prep would go into the truck for the mobile lunch. You would drive to a predetermined location, get set up and be ready for lunch. Afterwards, you'd drive the truck back here, clean it according to how you were taught in restaurant food safety class."

"Food safety class?" Tanner asked.

"We would train you while you took the class, but it's mandatory. A state law that all food service workers be trained in food safety protocols, which mostly involve keeping all food surfaces spotless and disinfected. It's not rocket science," Carmen said, half chuckling.

"Did I seem confused?"

"You had a worried look on your face when you realized that you would need to attend a class. That's all. Oh, also, you would need to satisfactorily pass a drug screening." Their eyes locked, and she let herself gaze into his eyes for a minute before asking him, "Would you like the same thing to eat as you had yesterday?" Tanner was amazed that she remembered him at all, and couldn't believe that she also remembered what he'd had for lunch yesterday. He had to really think for a minute what his precise order was.

Seeing that he was struggling to remember she said, "You had a three taco plate with rice and beans. The tacos were chicken, tofu, and fish." She winked and smiled again.

She's cute, Tanner thought. "Yes, please. Sounds perfect."

"I'll be right back, then." Carmen left, and Tanner thought about the job. He was already beginning to get excited. The more he thought about it, the more perfect it seemed. He could walk to work, and the driving and gas for the food truck would be on them. He would have something to do again, and not be sitting around worrying all the time. *This would be a perfect job for me right now* he thought.

As if reading his mind, Carmen brought him a sparkling water with a chunk of lime, along with a job application held on a clipboard, and a pen. Tanner looked into her eyes, while feeling, and holding gratitude in his heart. Without realizing it, he gently nodded his head affirmatively the entire time he spent filling out the application.

Carmen brought his food, then took the clipboard to the back with her without saying a word. Tanner ate in silence, but felt happy inside. The whole event was serendipitous. Carmen checked on him about ten minutes later. "How is everything?"

"Perfect. Just like yesterday," Tanner answered, looking up at her.

"Good. I'm glad you like it. My father, Señor Diego Esperanza, who owns this restaurant, wants me to let you know that you're hired if you want the job. He is grateful to have someone applying who has both a successful work history, and isn't right out of high school or in their twenties. He said it will be a nice, and very welcome change."

Tanner smiled. "Please tell Señor Esperanza that I accept, depending on the hours and the pay."

"He will pay you $15/hour to start, and pay for half of your health insurance premiums. He will outfit you with some shirts with our name and logo on them. The hours are 7 a.m to 3 p.m., and if you can handle eating tacos for lunch everyday, those are included too."

Tanner couldn't believe what his ears were hearing, "I whole-heartedly accept. Thank you so much!"

Carmen seemed pleased and said, "See you on Monday morning at 7 a.m. then!"

"I'll be here at 7 a.m. sharp," he said, smiling at her. Not only was the job going to be fairly simple, but the pay was a lot better than tapping his bank account for every little expense and, down the road, he would be mobile some of the day, and not just stuck in one place all the time, which really appealed to him. But the best part of all, was the close proximity to his place right around the corner. Once dressed and ready to go, he could literally be here in five minutes on foot.

Tanner finished up, cleaning up after himself more than normal, then turned, and waved goodby, "See you Monday morning!" he said stepping outside. Carmen smiled and nodded, then waved back.

He stepped into the bright light of the day and decided to check on Tammy again. He had the rest of the day and the weekend before having to report to work, and now that he had a job he was looking forward to, he was going to do a little driving and exploring before having his time monopolized by work again. After all, hourly employment wasn't something he was used to anymore. With stock investing, he'd been spoiled for years with his ability to be flexible and work from anywhere that he had an internet connection.

6

TAMMY

Tanner walked back to his place for a pit stop, then grabbed a bottle of water and a light jacket before leaving again. While he waited for his car to warm up, he started thinking about his new job and what Monday might bring, until his eyes drifted to the hood and he noticed that it had a series of dents right down the middle! He got back out, feeling his heart in his throat. Once he began to survey the damage more closely, he saw the rest of the them. The dents extended past the hood onto the roof and also onto the trunk, like someone got up on the car at at the front end, and walked or jumped their way to the other end, leaving dents in the body of his car along the entire length.

Now my beater truly looks like one, he thought. *One damned thing after another. Crime is way up here in the east bay. It used to be confined to only Oakland and San Francisco, but it is definitely here now.*

Tanner got back into his car and sat looking through the windshield at the dents. Sitting in the driver's seat, they looked extra deep, and so did his disdain for the people who did this. He waited to leave until he calmed down. He tried to put it out of his mind, but these incidents seemed to be happening a lot more frequently now. He'd only had two really bad incidents over the prior two decades, now they were coming at the rate of one or two a year. When they did occur, they always left him feeling frazzled. Each time, he tried to move forward, starting with putting it out of his mind. As always, he simply needed to keep it together, no matter what.

Tanner tried thinking back over the years about some of the bad things he'd done that would cause him to now have to suffer the consequences, these incidents that were happening with alarming frequency. But his list of bad things seemed too tame to deserve much, if any, retribution from the universe.

Tanner pulled up to the signal at the nearby Monument Boulevard intersection, wondering if it had just turned red, or was about to turn green. He'd been somewhere else, and hadn't noticed. His mind kept working overtime trying to unlock the mysterious cause of a streak of bad luck. *If luck is when opportunity meets preparation, then that must mean bad luck is when opportunity meets a complete lack of preparation? Kind of makes sense,* he thought. *I sure wasn't prepared in the case of my wife telling me she's leaving me, suddenly and unexpectedly.*

The only thing that Tanner could think of that might have added to his lifetime pool of bad karma, was the one-time, almost-affair he came close to having while working at the recycling plant. It was when Davis, who worked with him there, confided in him that he was having a torrid affair with one of their mutual coworkers, and asked Tanner to lie to his wife, Rosalee, for him if she called the plant and asked if he was working overtime. Davis was going to call in sick, while telling his wife that he was working overtime. If she called, Tanner was to let Rosalee know that, indeed, Davis was there on overtime, but was inside one of the two furnaces as a part of a furnace clean-out crew, and that he wasn't sure when Davis would be able to phone her back.

Just as predicted, Rosalee called and asked for Davis. Tanner gave Rosalee the lie, and she took it. She was so kind and sweet that Tanner felt extra bad for her. Then Rosalee had kept talking, while apologizing for running her mouth so much, and then had just verbally unleashed, rambling on, and on, and on, about everything. What she had seen on the news, what her boss did at work earlier that day, and how much she missed Davis. Tanner pretty quickly ascertained that Rosalee was extraordinarily lonely, and just needed some normal human contact.

Going against his instincts, Tanner flirted with Rosalee a little bit, and found her receptive, "I know I shouldn't say this, but did you know that you have a really sexy and provocative telephone voice? I mean . . . you could do phone porn. Hahaha." Rosalee giggled. Tanner continued, "It's just so throaty and womanly sounding, it's amazing. Very sexy. I'm sorry, I'm being inappropriate."

"Oh, I know you're just trying to cheer me up," she said.

"I'm betting that you also have the looks and the body to go along with that sexy voice, right?"

"Oh my!" Rosalee giggled some more. Then she kept giggling when she tried to explain more, each time regressing into a fit of laughter.

Tanner went on, "Hey, we've been talking for almost an hour now and we've had a really great conversation. Well, at least I've enjoyed it."

"Yes, I have as well," she answered.

"Well, I'm married, too, and it sounds like Davis isn't home very often. He and I normally work on different shifts. If you'd like me to come over and take you out for coffee or a drink, or some food or something, I guess it would, technically, be a date, but I would consider it as just two friends spending time together, getting to know one another better if you'd be interested."

Rosalee was silent for a long time. Tanner could almost hear her mind working, then he heard her take a deep, mentally conflicted breath, and slowly let it out before saying, "Uh, I don't know if we should, if I should . . ."

Tanner said, "Understood. I get it. I shouldn't have asked." *But your husband has his business inside another woman, right now, as we're speaking, in case you didn't know it,* he thought to himself. "Well, the offer stands. My schedule is just like Davis's, except he is in the A group, I'm in the B group. Look at his schedule sometime and you'll be able to see when I'm working and not. If you want to talk, I'm here."

"Thank you so much, Tanner. You've been so nice. If I wasn't married . . ."

"I know, me too. I feel it. Call me sometime."

"I might just do that."

Rosalee called another three times that week, and each time she did, she seemed a little more distraught and depressed, even a little angry. By the end of that week, she'd let Tanner know that she strongly suspected that Davis was seeing someone else. She'd said he was aloof and distant, and making excuses as to why he no longer wanted to have sex, even though sometimes a whole week would go by with no physical contact happening between them whatsoever. She wanted to meet Tanner for a drink, soon.

"Okay, how about tomorrow evening at 5 p.m. at the *Blue Light Lounge*?"

Rosalee said, "See you then," and hung up.

The next night Tanner stood her up. He knew what would happen if he met her there, and knew he'd regret it until the day he died. Oddly, he never heard from her again, and he was grateful, but felt bad that he'd stood her up, despite the lurid circumstances. It was the only time in his life that Tanner had ever contemplated stepping outside the confines of his own marriage, and ever after he was grateful that he never went through with it. Ironically, it was Sheila in the end that did all the stepping out on their marriage, then left him for her new lover.

Finishing his flashback, he realized that, hell yeah, he likely had the dents coming whether he thought so or not. He laughed softly thinking, *From now on, I won't even try to figure it out, I'll just realize that, if something bad is happening to me out of the blue, then I must have it coming. It's likely something that I can't even re-member. Then again, bad things can, and often do, happen to good people.*

Tanner headed over to Tammy's house, again. This time, he parked in the driveway, like a normal person, and got out and head-ed towards the front door using the little walkway, until he heard a scratchy voice say, "You can stop right there! I don't know what you're selling, but I don't want whatever it is, understand?"

Tanner stopped walking and stood still. The voice sounded like it had come from behind him. He slowly turned around and saw Tammy, but she was barely recognizable. She stood there in front of him, staring at him, wearing dirty, baggy pants, a huge shirt, and dirty garden gloves, and holding a four-pronged pitchfork. She was so skinny, Tanner thought she probably had an eating disorder. Her normally light brown skin was deeply tanned by so much sun, that her face looked like it had been carved out of a chunk of dark wood, with precise, deep lines forming wherever her face needed them to form as she talked. Her fiery hazel eyes seemed set back farther in her head than Tanner remembered. Her hair was still thick, but had become multicolored, and she kept her black, gray, and silver strands braided into dreadlocks, then wound up into an elaborate bun on top of her head.

"Tammy?" Tanner said gently.

Tammy replied with rapid-fire questions offered more as statements, "Who's asking? What do you want? No strangers are welcome here, you go!" She said, shaking the pitchfork.

Tanner was a little worried. It was obvious that Tammy had some mental or cognitive issues going on. He decided to play it more upbeat and see what that yielded. "Who's asking? Are you kidding me? Look at me, Tammy, it's Tanner!" he said smiling at her, and moved towards her a little closer with his arms held wide open.

"That's close enough. Tanner? Tanner? Hmm. Tanner!" She seemed to recognize something with his name. She looked at him intently, cocking her head a little from side to side, while processing his name numerous times.

"Tanner Dalton. Remember me from the late '70s those two years we were inseparable friends with benefits? Remember the nude beach, eating M&Ms, while playing a marathon of modified backgammon games and constantly listening to Pink Floyd's *Dark Side of the Moon?*" Tanner waited silently, looking at her with kind eyes. He asked again, "Remember?"

Then, as if someone had flipped on a light switch, but the electricity took a few minutes to get to the bulb and light it up, Tammy came to life like an energetic robot puppet that just had its batteries replaced.

"Holy shit. Tanner Dalton? Ha, I know who you are. I was just messing with you. Come here, you son of a bitch." Tammy dropped the pitchfork, and fast-walked a few steps before jumping up onto him in a hug, wrapping her legs and arms around him tight, screaming and squealing with delight. When he'd arrived, she'd seemed to have been ultra-focused. Now she seemed better, but just as crazy as Tanner remembered her being all those years ago. He held her for as long as he could, and ended up walking in circles a bit while holding her. No easy feat, even for a guy as buff as he was for a man in his sixties.

He finally put her back down, then stood back to get a good look at her again. She looked fierce, seemed strong and energetic. Tammy said, "What the hell? I haven't seen you for almost fifty years. Took me a while to see you, but now I do. You haven't changed that much, but your face is rounder than I remember, and you're, of course, heavier. The graying hair, that's what threw me off the most."

Tanner laughed. "Well, I wasn't sure it was you, either, with the hair. I really like it now that I've had a chance to look at it."

Tammy continued as if she hadn't heard a thing, "What are you talking about. You had the thickest strawberry-blonde hair and it always reminded me of Robert Redford. I loved it because I couldn't believe that a good-looking dude like you would want me, in any capacity. You could've gotten just about anyone, and I always wondered, why me? I wasn't cute or anything. But I was grateful for our friendship . . . and its benefits." She pulled off her gloves and smiled and winked, lightly patting his chest with both palms for emphasis.

She said, "Come on in and sit for a while. Unless you have someplace else to be?"

"No, no. I'm all yours for as long as you'll have me."

"Careful now," she said, "we're just going to sit and visit, I'm not getting married or anything."

Tanner followed Tammy inside, chuckling most of the way. Outside of her looks, she really hadn't changed that much. She was the same scrappy, fun-loving, adventurous person he had been attracted to all those years ago.

The entryway was dim. As his eyes became adjusted, Tanner noticed a coat closet on the left side of the hallway, followed by a few boxes stacked on top of each other. As they rounded the corner, the space opened up into a great room with wall-to-wall, south-facing glass and an unusual concrete floor with little nubs that would tickle your feet if you walked on it bare footed.

The other three walls were lined with low-profile, long, modern sofas. Near the kitchen a dining table with eight chairs that appeared to be teak wood, crafted in a modern Danish design, looked elegant. There had to be at least fifty original oil paintings by Tammy, and there were lots of shelves holding numerous artifacts of elaborate blown glass and ceramics, all one-of-a-kind pieces created by Tammy. Tanner recognized her style almost instantly. She adored free-form, swirling movement, and found ways of incorporating that preference into almost everything she created.

"I see you've become quite the artist over the years," Tanner said, still looking around the room.

"I hold my own now. I'm more known now, here in the San Francisco Bay Area, and I've come to know the right people so that my art can be displayed in interesting ways, and in places that people will not only have a chance to preview it up close and in person, but will also likely have the means to pay what I'm asking for my work."

Tanner was impressed: "That's fantastic, Tammy. That really must've been a lot of time, effort, and work, for sure."

"Only my entire adult life, with all that I have. Hey, would you like some tea?"

Tanner didn't have to really think about it. He loved tea as much if not more than coffee, but no one ever asked him if he'd like some. "Absolutely. That would be perfect. Thank you."

"You're welcome! I'm delighted to see you again after all these years."

Tanner chuckled, "More like all these decades."

Tammy glanced over at him smiling. She put the water on for the tea. "Black, Green, or Oolong?"

"Oolong, please. That will be nice. I haven't had any in quite a while now."

Tammy looked at him with a perplexed look on her face, "Why?"

Tanner sat and thought for a second, staring at the coffee table. After a few seconds he looked up at her and said, "I really don't know. How silly is that?" Tammy tossed him a little catalog. The cover showed small, perfectly placed piles of tea next to each other sitting on top of a brick colored counter top for contrast. Across the top the catalog title said, *Sun and Moon Teas.*

"That's the place where I get my tea. I order it online. I don't know why they send me a catalog through the postal mail, but it gives you an idea of their offerings. Excellent teas. That's how I discovered Oolong tea. I had never heard of it before seeing it on their website."

"Thanks. Now I won't have any excuses!"

Tammy said, "Let's go out back and sit on the patio. It's nice out there." She grabbed the tray with the teapot, two cups, a bunch of green and red grapes, a hunk of gouda cheese, and some multigrain crackers, and headed to the sliding glass door, which Tanner opened for her. He followed her a short ways out onto a beautiful stone patio under an electric, retractable canvas canopy.

Tammy set the tray down on the round, frosted glass table top, while Tanner chose one of the padded rocking chairs placed around the table.

The yard was very private. There were two small walnut trees, one in each of the inside far corners of her yard, set out a little from the redwood fencing that bordered the entire perimeter. There was a small Koi fish pond in the middle of the yard, surrounded on all sides except the side closest to the house, with flower beds. Lots of sun and shade shrubs planted in various locations around the yard, and a lovely, mature, three-stem river birch to the right of the Koi pond. The river birch provided the pond with some nice shade, keeping it from overheating. Again, Tanner could see, and almost sense, the intelligence in the use of colors, contrasts, and placement. The landscaping seemed well planned, and in an obviously artistic and creative way.

"Tammy, I must say, you've done a great job making this place almost magical. You've got a really nice place here."

Tammy smiled, "Thanks. I like it. It's my oasis away from the world. I think everyone should have one." She finished with a little uncertainty in her voice, and seemed a little nervous all of a sudden.

"So, now that I've seen the main floor and backyard, I have to ask, what's up with the front? Not that it's any of my business, but I am curious."

Tammy sipped her tea and looked down for a second, with a Mona Lisa smile on her face. When she looked back up she said, "Well, that's what remains of my *project rebellion* effort. Let me explain. I was so pissed off that this town seemed so quick, and out-of-control with tax hikes based on unfair and inflated assessments, that I decided to make my house the scary one. The house no one would want to live in, or buy, based on its lack of curb appeal. I'm not going anywhere, so I figured to hell with them. I'll give them something to reassess. I apologized to the neighbors, who loved my plan, at first. But one by one they all abandoned me in my effort, and now they all hate my guts for letting my place look so run down."

"Did it work?"

"Sort of. They reduced my taxes by 12 percent over the next five years, but, again, it cost me my former friendships in this neighborhood. They no longer exist. Now, people seem to think that, since I obviously don't care about my yard's appearance, then it's okay to dump their trash and let their dogs shit in my yard all the time now, without ever picking it up. Coffee cups, plastic ware, used napkins, cigarette butts, and beer cans are also regular visitors to my front yard on a regular basis."

"That's awful. So, sounds like something else is brewing now?" Tanner asked.

"Yep, doing it all over again. Ripping out the whole she-bang and starting over again."

"What are you going with? Conventional grass and bor-ders?"

"Nah, you know me well enough to know better than to think I would ever do something conventional." Tammy laughed so hard she had to quickly put her tea down before she spilled it all over herself. "No. Have you ever heard of a xeriscape?"

"Can't say that I have," Tanner replied.

"It's landscape design that incorporates plantings and other elements that work together to be visually and aesthetically pleasing, without requiring any watering aside from what falls from the sky. Essentially, lots of rocks and gravels of different grades and colors, planted with desert cactus and other succulents that require little to no water, and can sustain that stance for long periods of time. It will save me effort in the yard, prevent me from having to mow or fertilize, and almost takes care of itself entirely. Plus, it will more than pay for itself in a few years as I save a ton on my water/sewer bill."

"Is water and sewer expensive here now?" Tanner said with concern.

"When has anything not been expensive in this state?" Tammy said with exasperation.

"Good point, and fantastic idea."

She smiled at him, patted herself on the back before bursting out laughing, which Tanner got caught up in too and, for a short while, neither of them could stop. When one of them would look over at the other, and the other noticed, it would start all over again.

Tammy looked down at her watch. Then said, "Hey, I go skydiving every Friday afternoon, wanna go with?"

"Skydiving eh? Sure." Tanner smiled wide. He had already been five times before, but not for twenty-five years. Tammy looked surprised.

"Sure? *Sure?* Wow. I almost always get *hell no,* or *you're crazy* and, *not for me, no way.*"

Tanner laughed, "I wanted to try it out a long time ago, and did two static line jumps from 3,500 feet. Even though I had to get out of the small plane by myself, in a ninety-mile-per-hour head wind, before signaling that I was okay, and that I was ready to let go. But with the chute opening simultaneous with me exiting, all I did was float back down, and then attempt to do a stand up landing, which I did manage to do both times.

But I wasn't satisfied with those. I ended up going to Skydive Turners Falls, in Massachusetts, near where I lived for all these years, and did three free falls from 10,500 feet. So, yeah, I'm into it, but since I never finished all seven jump levels to get my USPA jump license, and it's been a long time, I guess I'll have to do a tandem jump today."

"I'm impressed, Tanner. So you know the deal about height, and velocity, and the adrenaline rush that comes with them. There is no way you couldn't."

Tanner looked a little perplexed, "Yeah, I know the deal alright. After my first free fall, I had so much adrenaline after my 2 p.m. jump that I found it difficult to go to sleep that night, even at midnight."

"Yep, that's what I'm talking about. Why did you stop?"

"Money, and then, when I finally had enough to do it again, there was a plane crash that killed all the jump masters at that jump school. The Queen Anne airplane they went up in had engine problems at 500 feet, not enough for anyone to be able to use their chutes to escape with."

Tammy was shaking her head, "No, unfortunately not at that altitude. No time for the chute to deploy and get fully opened before a body would be hitting the ground." Tammy looked away for a minute, still shaking her head in disbelief. She looked back at Tanner and said, "Um, yeah, you know, I'm likely going to be only one of three showing up today, so I can just act like nothing's up and get you in just fine, if you want. I know everyone, including the pilot, and we all go together all the time. If asked, I'll just say you left your jump license at home because you didn't anticipate going today if that's okay?"

Tanner smiled and said, "Nah, don't fib on my behalf. Just tell them the deal. I know how to free-fall skydive. I remember it like it was yesterday and, if I have a good time today, I'll work towards getting it finished up finally, so I can go up legit. I really hate lying, and liars. I'm excited about this today, though. I hope I'll be able to."

Tammy smiled. "No worries. You'll be going, I promise. You're for sure good with this? I mean, you can reimagine it in your mind, and remember all the things about it, including the things you found scary, and you're confident that you'll be fine? And, also, you do remember the free-fall position, and how to get into it quickly after leaving the plane, right?"

"Yes, on all counts," Tanner answered enthusiastically, "I remember it all as if I had just done it yesterday."

Tammy smiled and gave him a thumbs up, then stood up and gathered the tea things together. "Cool. I'll pack you a chute, and get you a jumpsuit when we get there. This is great. It'll be fun!"

He was really looking forward to doing this again. It had been so long that he didn't think he'd ever go up again, even though he often fantasized about free falling, usually while driving on the highway.

Tanner left his car parked in Tammy's driveway, after moving it over so she could get out of her garage. The striking, blood-red-metallic color looked stunning on her truck, catching the low-angle, late afternoon sun as she slowly backed it out of the garage. Tanner hadn't seen a blood-red shade like that since the 1970s, especially in a metallic, and he felt himself get goosebumps seeing it again, now. He'd always loved that deep, blood-red color.

7

SKYDIVE BYRON

The drive to SkyDive Byron took about 45 minutes. Tanner had hardly come out this way when he'd lived here growing up, but he could still remember how desolate it used to be. Long stretches of brown tundra and rolling hills, with waterways and marshes interacting with the brackish, tidally-influenced Suisun Bay. Indeed, the area had changed almost beyond recognition. He was shocked by the vast tracks of planned neighborhoods, roadways, and shopping centers. Only the rolling brown hills seemed unchanged.

Tanner began daydreaming, mentally contrasting the seemingly endless brown landscape against the lush green hills, valleys, and mountains of Massachusetts. Despite his excitement over finally getting together with his old friend, and getting ready to do another skydive—which he never thought he'd do again—he found himself really missing the lush greenery of Massachusetts for the first time since leaving.

Tanner answered Tammy's inevitable questions as well as he could, but he was already weary from thinking about his former life in Massachusetts, and he really did not want to discuss how much things had changed and grown worse for him over the last several years—his personal fall from grace. Despite being honest, doing the right thing, and playing by the rules, nothing ever seemed to work out too well for Tanner in any kind of lasting way. He'd come to believe that his marriage had been the exception, and he'd finally broken that spell. Then, he made a small fortune while married to her, and here we are.

They finally arrived and parked in front of a building with Skydive Byron tacked to the top of the porch entrance. Despite the small footprint, inside it had a gathering room for watching and reviewing videotaped skydives. In the middle, a payment terminal sat on top of it; a stack of waiver forms and half a dozen SkyDive Byron t-shirts with different colors and designs sat next to it on the far side. There were only a few chairs and, luckily, a bathroom with warning stickers on the wall above the john, warning men to mind themselves because ladies also used the same toilet. When Tammy spotted the bathroom, she excused herself and shut the door.

Tanner looked around at all of the photographs of students doing their practice skydives, and pictures of professional skydivers doing group formations that covered most of the walls. Tanner felt goose bumps form on both arms while looking at many of them. Some of the formations were quite large, and Tanner knew they likely had gone up four miles high, nearly double the altitude of his former free falls at Skydive Turners Falls.

He heard Tammy finish up in the bathroom and come over to him, "Ready?"

Tanner nodded and started to follow her, "Where is everyone?"

"They're out in the hangar over there," Tammy said, pointing to the small aluminum building about 50 yards to their south. "It's Friday, and we're the only ones who are going to be here. It's not open to the public except on Saturdays and Sundays."

Tanner followed Tammy to the hangar. A minute later, she opened the side door and stepped inside.

"Hey, hey. What's up, Tamboni?" asked the blonde guy with a thousand-watt smile and teeth so white they looked like a bright white glow stick stuck sideways in his mouth. He quickly stood up from the chute he was packing, and began walking across the hangar to meet Tammy. When he got closer, Tanner saw that he was stocky, slightly muscular, with chestnut brown eyes. He looked really fit, and was very happy to see Tammy. He met her halfway, and gave her a big hug.

"Not doing too much, Doug. Looking to get my juices flowing with a late-day jump, that's all."

"I heard that," Doug said. He looked at Tanner, "Doug, man," he said, offering a handshake.

Tanner took his hand firmly and looked him in the eyes, "Tanner. Nice to meet you, Doug."

"Likewise."

"Going up with us?" he said enthusiastically, still smiling.

Tammy cut right in, "Tanner's done a couple of static jumps and three free falls at Sky Dive Turners Falls, in Massachusetts, but still hasn't got his license."

Doug looked at her a little funny, then smiled and laughed, and looked back at Tanner, "If you want to go up with us today, then I'm good with it." He looked towards their plane parked inside the hangar and shouted, "Stanley, you okay with Tammy's friend, Tanner, coming up with us today?"

A lanky man with dense freckles on his face, arms, and neck, thick auburn hair and beard, stepped out from behind the small plane enough to be seen. He looked over at the group and said, "Glad to have you. Tanner, is it?"

"Yes, good to meet you, Stanley."

"Likewise. Well, let me finish up so you guys can get up there and soar with the eagles for a while." He turned back to the plane to continue prepping it for the flight.

Tammy looked happy. Okay, let's get started getting our chutes packed. Since you've never done it before, you can just observe this time."

Tanner was grateful for the reprieve. Luckily, they all seemed to know what they were doing, and also seemed to be all about safety, so Tanner was able to relax a little.

Doug went over to a table by a line of lockers along the same wall as the hangar door, and turned on some music. A couple of seconds later, ACDC's *Back in Black* began blaring loudly. The sound of that thumping rock echoing off the walls and bouncing off the high ceiling inside the hangar gave the song an extra surreal quality, effectively turning the entire hangar into an eery, thumping, hard rock echo chamber.

Both Doug and Tammy were rocking out to the music, but Tanner also noticed how extremely focused they'd become, and how they were making steady progress at getting the chutes packed.

He was impressed at the methodology and precision they exhibited while quietly and efficiently packing all four chutes: one for the pilot, one for Tanner, and the remaining two for themselves.

The sun was beginning to get lower in the sky, but there were still three hours of adequate light left, with at least another half hour of sunlight before dusk. Already, the late-day, lower sun angle had turned much of the lower third of the sky varying shades of orange and pink.

They packed tightly into the little single engine Cessna like sardines. The plane had a single pilot's seat. The rest of the seats had been removed so up to four jumpers could fit inside. As they taxied down the runway, Tammy let Tanner know that he would be the second one out. The order would be Doug first, then Tanner, then her.

Doug, Tammy, and Stanley were all very relaxed and talkative on the way up, smiling and laughing a lot, and keeping the atmosphere light. Tanner played it cool, but as the plane ascended, he could feel his internal paralysis growing by the second, and he had to fight from panicking.

He looked outside. The sky now looked like a giant hand had smeared it with dark rainbow sherbet. Suddenly, he began to smell the strong odor of pine, apricot, and a hint of French perfume. He looked over at the others, and saw Stanley pass a joint over to Doug. Doug took a few quick, but hard, drags on it, then handed it to Tanner. Tanner held it for a couple of seconds, then took a couple of hard hits off of it, and handed it to Tammy, who did the same. Around that fat joint went, until everyone was smiling wide, and giggling like they were all little kids again.

Tanner was a little worried that he had just made a huge mistake. After all, he hadn't skydived in decades, and now he was older. He was still confident that he remembered exactly what to do to get into free fall position. He knew he would need to check his altimeter every few seconds, and to pull his ripcord at 5,000 feet. He was all set. The strain they'd just smoked was already kicking in harder than Tanner had anticipated, and that began making him feel a little paranoid and worried that he might forget something critical with his life on the line.

He briefly imagined himself not going through with it. Then, as if reading his mind, Tammy looked at him and shouted over the sound of the plane, "You can fly back to the landing strip with the pilot if you're having second thoughts."

Tanner wasn't going to change his mind; he decided to adjust his attitude a bit. He started to get angry at himself for letting those thoughts into his mind at such a critical time. He took several deep breaths, then gave Tammy the thumbs up. She returned the gesture.

About halfway up, a calmness seemed to envelope the cabin. Tanner was excited, perhaps too much. Just like the first time he went up to free-fall, he had to fight the hyper-vigilism he felt growing inside him. Then he realized that, if today was his day to die, then it was unlikely that he would be able to do much about it; the opposite also held true. If it wasn't his day to die, then he had absolutely nothing whatsoever to worry about. That idea expanded, becoming even bigger in his mind. He realized that the control we all think we have over our lives is only an illusion and he never really had anything to worry about; worry itself was a huge waste of his time. It was an incredible insight, and was driven home by the colorful setting, the heightened mood, and what he was about to do.

The tone of the engine deepened, becoming quieter as they leveled off. Doug began actively looking out of the passenger hatch. Eventually, he shouted, "Cut it!" Stanley slowed down to 90 miles per hour, just slow enough for everyone to safely get out of the plane, but fast enough to keep it aloft.

Doug looked around and shouted, "Ready to skydive?" Everyone nodded affirmatively. He unlocked the latch and slid the door all the way open. The air seemed to explode as the cold air rushed in, filling the inside of the small cabin, dramatically changing the atmosphere. Doug finished negotiating with Stanley, helping to guide him to the exact spot they needed to be, so that they would be downwind from the landing zone. He looked around at everyone one more time with a huge grin on his face. "All set?" Everyone nodded.

Doug was the first out. Tanner was blown away watching him exit. Watching him reach out and grab that wing strut while a 90-miles-per-hour headwind blasted away at him, trying to peel him off of the plane entirely, was impressive. Doug's physical strength, courage, and tenacity were very apparent, and Tanner respected those traits deeply. Doug turned, reached out with his right hand, quickly followed by his left, leaning hard into the wind, making his move so quickly that the whole sequence happened as if done in a single motion, and then he was on the wing strut. Once there, he quickly continued hand walking all the way out to the end of it, feet flying out behind him, then once at the end of the strut, he looked back at Tanner, nodding for him to exit.

Tanner had already moved himself into position close to the hatchway, so that he would be able to exit quickly, shortening the amount of time Doug would have to hang onto the strut. Once at the hatch, Tanner sat with his feet facing forward. The ninety mph blast was mostly moving past him, but it was just outside the hatchway, only inches away. He briefly placed his left foot onto the hatchway step, while pushing off to the wing strut, grabbing it with his right hand, then his left, and hand walked himself to the middle of it until he was next to Doug.

Tanner took a look down at the two miles of air between himself and the earth. Manmade objects, moving vehicles, and the SkyDive Byron building looked far away, and very tiny. He felt his heartbeat in every cell of his body, and fought to keep from freaking out. Once again, Tanner was walking the line between fear and ecstasy, but he loved how alive it made him feel, and he welcomed it, like an old friend he hadn't seen in a long time.

The 90-miles-per-hour blast seemed much harsher and stiffer than he remembered. Nevertheless, he was very pleased with his exit. No mishaps, slips, falls, or mistakes—nothing.

Tammy exited quickly and efficiently, grabbing the wing strut on Tanner's left. Now all three of them were on the outside of the plane, holding onto the right wing strut. Tanner made eye contact with Doug and nodded. Doug nodded back. Tammy nodded okay, and all three of them began a three second count by pulling themselves up and down on the strut in unison, and on the third down, they all let go at the same time.

Just like he remembered from his first free fall, Tanner felt the sudden acceleration only for a split second. He arched his back with all he had, keeping his hands horizontal to his head on both sides, with his arms bent 90 degrees at each elbow, and his legs spread, and bent 90 degrees at the knee, while also pushing his abdomen out and arching his back until finally straightening out. He was now looking down and facing the earth, nice and steady, free falling at 120-miles-per-hour, all the while feeling as if he were floating, and almost weightless.

Across from Tanner, Doug was smiling at him as he fell at the exact same speed. Tanner could see the air pulling and tugging against Doug's jump suit, trying desperately to rip it off of his body. Seeing that, was all the visual indicator Tanner needed to re-inform him of his own speed of descent, as they both continued plummeting towards the earth at terminal velocity. The realization shocked him, *My body is falling towards the ground at 120-miles-per-hour,* he thought.

In the short time he had, he was initially high enough to be able to see the slight curvature of the earth as he looked towards the distant horizon. The manmade structures and roadways looked fragile compared to the earth around them and it appeared as if their thin walls were all that kept nature at bay. Tanner checked his altimeter; he was fast approaching 7,800 feet.

In another split second, everything became gray steam, and the humidity went off the charts as the group fell through one of the larger clouds Tanner had spotted during their ascent. A second later, they were back out in the bright sunshine. He could still see Doug, but he had drifted a little farther away, and now resembled a plastic military action figure dressed up in a skydiving outfit.

Shortly after clearing the cloud, the group reached the magic rip-cord pull altitude of 5,000 feet. Tanner pulled his rip-cord, then looked up to ensure that it deployed properly. He felt the jolt of the chute rapidly unfurling as it ascended above him perfectly, catching the air and opening up without incident. After several minutes of slow descent, Tanner managed to position himself pretty well, relative to the landing zone in front of the clubhouse. He flared his chute by pulling his steering cords down and forward as fast and hard as possible, which slowed him down enough for him to execute a perfect landing.

Tanner was amazed by what he'd just done. He kept replaying the experience over in his mind. He felt thrilled inside, and was completely jacked up by adrenaline just like he'd experienced when he went decades ago. He felt young again, and he immediately wanted to go up and do it a second time. The entire group had landed within fifty yards of the windsock at the far end of the runway, right in front of the main SkyDive Byron building. Everyone began gathering up their chutes for the walk to the hangar in silence, as they individually replayed the movie they had just stored in their minds.

Tanner savored the experience, keenly aware of the cortisol and endorphins coursing through his veins, buzzing from having just survived a life-threatening activity, and living to talk about it.

8

THE FIVE-YEAR PLAN

After the jump, Tanner was hoping that everyone would want to do dinner together, and maybe engage in some story swapping, but Doug had somewhere to be, and Stanley was expected home soon, so that he and his wife could attend their son's high school football game. Tanner thanked them for the awesome time, and promised to come out and do it again, then he and Tammy left to head back to her place.

Less than a mile down the road, Tanner looked over at Tammy and said, "Thanks for suggesting that we do this today. It's just what I needed right now. How did you know?"

Tanner watched her, waiting for her answer. Tammy smiled without looking over at him and said, "Easy, I need to do it every week. It's how I stay in touch with what's important in life. Besides, I could see the stress, former defeat, and fear in your eyes the whole time we talked on my patio earlier today. I remember thinking to myself how perfect it was that we finally connected on the day I go skydiving every week and, apparently, just in the nick of time for you, too, my man."

Tanner thought for a moment then answered, "True. And I realized that, had I not gone skydiving before, I would not have been able to go. I also realized how serendipitous it was that neither of us knew that the other had ever skydived."

Tammy looked over at Tanner. Her eyes grew wide as her own realization sank in about the true odds against this coincidence. "You're right. I wonder why our paths have crossed again after all these years, too. No coincidence. Hey, I'm starved. Let's eat. Any ideas?"

Tanner thought for a moment then said, "How about Mexican?"

"Sounds good. If you don't mind, can we get it as take-out and then go back to my place to eat? I want to take a shower."

"Sure, no problem."

"I have a surprise I think you're going to like for after dinner. No hints. You'll just have to wait," she said with a devilish look on her face.

Tanner knew her well enough not to ask anything more, so he nodded and left it at that. Tammy pulled her sleeve back and half shouted, "Hey, Siri," Siri popped up. "Call El Toltec." After a brief pause, Tanner heard Siri say *Calling El Toltec Mexican Cuisine.* There was a short period of no sound, then a phone began ringing. After the third ring someone picked up, *El Toltec Cuisine, how may I assist you today?* Tammy placed a quick order for a lot of food, so fast, it almost seemed like she worked there; she rattled the order off without even asking Tanner what he wanted.

"I hope that you'll be able to find something in our order to your liking."

Tanner smiled, "Absolutely. I love everything you ordered! Make sure I settle up with you later okay?"

"Nah, my treat, Tanner. I've had such a good time today. I still can't believe it's you sitting next to me. I look over at you and it seems so strange to me because I had long ago come to the conclusion that I would likely never see you again."

Tanner cleared his throat, then said, "Just the opposite for me. I mean, it's strange for me too. But, honestly, I thought about you quite a bit over the years, and wondered how you were doing. I was worried for you when we last saw each other all those decades ago. I thought you might die from an overdose." He paused for a second, feeling emotions well up inside him, then continued, "I wanted to stay in touch with you because we always got along so well and had so much fun when we were together. I missed the fun, and I missed you more than I could believe. My heart actually ached about it at times, but being married, I didn't feel that I could still maintain a friendship with another female without my wife getting very upset and jealous. I let everything stay the way it was to honor my vows in a very narrow and strict interpretation in order to fit her comfort zone. After a while, the years—then the decades —stacked up, and went by quicker than I could've ever imagined. In the end, she left me for someone she'd secretly been seeing for a couple of years, then took me to the cleaners financially. Stabbed me with a knife, then twisted the blade around a few times."

Tammy looked concerned, "I'm so sorry, Tanner. It got quiet for a few seconds before she said, "I never knew you had any real feelings of the romantic type for me. How'd I miss that?"

"You didn't, and I'm certain you'd tell me the same thing you told me back then, that you wanted to always remain single."

"Well, I didn't stay single," Tammy confessed. I married a guy that I met skydiving about ten years ago. His name was Rodney, and he was a cutie with his blonde curls and green eyes. So kind, so loving to everyone and everything. He died in a car crash nine months after we got married. Some drunk hit his driver's side door going almost sixty miles per hour, in town. I doubt poor Rodney saw that one coming. At least I always hoped and prayed that he didn't."

"Damn. That's really tough. I'm sorry for your loss, Tammy. I know what a big deal getting married was for you. The fact that you married Rodney says a lot of amazing things about him. I wish I could've known him."

Tammy said, "Thanks. Yeah, I think you guys would have hit it off pretty well and got along great. I think about him all the time. I still talk to him. Like, if you weren't here right now, I'd likely strike up a conversation with Rodney on my way home tonight. I'd tell him about the jump and how it felt, how much I wish he'd been there to share it with me, and how much I miss him." her voice quivered the longer she spoke so that, by the end, she was in tears.

Once she had mostly regained her composure, she continued with a shaky voice, "One night, a couple of months ago, I was right here, driving home, talking to Rodney and I got emotional, and the tears welled up in my eyes and started streaming down my face. I started wiping my eyes with the back of my palm, then my fingers, and the next thing I knew, I couldn't see anything except blurriness. I didn't realize that I had drifted over, and now occupied a good fifty percent of the on-coming traffic lane. I kept driving, even though I couldn't see properly. Rounding a long, semi-blind curve, a tractor-trailer appeared out of nowhere, and came right at me. Somehow, I managed to move over just in time to miss being hit head-on by that massive truck. It was moving so fast towards me my brain barely had time to process what was happening. I thought that Rodney missed me so bad he was trying to get me into an early grave so he could have me by his side again."

Tanner stayed quiet for a few seconds, then added, " Obviously, it wasn't your time to go; someone higher up must've superseded Rodney that time around."

Tammy laughed. "That's awesome, Tanner. I like that."

"Hey, it's a possibility," Tanner said, laughing along with her. It was obvious that Tammy frequented El Toltec; she knew how to get there like she was going home. She turned left onto Little Prairie Road, drove two blocks, turned right on Lizard Lane, then half a block down, made another quick left onto Turnpike Avenue north, for approximately 1.3 miles, and, there it was, the first building on the right, just after the statue of a cactus dressed in clothes, holding a guitar and wearing a sombrero.

Tanner stayed in the truck while Tammy went in to get the food. It was quiet here. Tanner rolled down his window. He could barely hear the sound of a tractor trailer driving on the main road far off in the distance. A dog barked twice, before everything became silent again. A chorus of crickets made their white noise in the background, singing their hearts out for all who could hear them.

A couple of blocks away, a car crossed the intersection loudly. The driver and two passengers were shouting, talking, and laughing over hard rock music blaring from the stereo inside their top down convertible. As soon as the car cleared the intersection and drove away into the darkness, the loud sound of their music rapidly diminished, and seemed to take a hard bend in tone just before the night swallowed the last audible remnants, once again restoring the silence.

Tammy came out of the restaurant carrying two big brown paper bags folded at the top and stapled shut. When she opened the driver's door, Tanner leaned over and took the bags from her so she could get in more easily. Immediately, the truck cab filled with wonderful, complex odors of meat, spices, oils, fruits, and vegetables. "I got us some chicken finger thingies to hold us over," Tammy said. "And, there should be a couple of styrofoam cups in there. That's the dipping sauce, one for each of us so we can double dip without concern," she added, smiling wide.

Tanner found the cups and took the top off one of them. The sauce looked and smelled like good old-fashioned barbecue sauce to him. He dipped the tip of his little finger in and tasted it, *Yep, barbecue sauce. Nothing too special about that,* he thought. He put one of the sauce cups in Tammy's drink holder and took the lid off for her, then laid out half the container of chicken fingers on several napkins for her.

"Thanks!" she said before snatching up one of the chicken pieces, dipping it in the sauce, and eating it. "Yum! Oh God! I was so ready to eat something. I had lunch at like eleven this morning, and nothing since.

Tanner was surprised: "Wow, I guess you're hungry, I would be too. That's a long time to go without eating."

"Just an oversight today. It's your fault for distracting me, you know."

"Is it now," Tanner said smiling wide. "So, question, and not to pry, please tell me if I am, but how do you manage to live like this?"

Tammy seemed surprised. "Live like what?"

"You know, the house, the nice ride, skydiving every week, no husband . . . how do you manage to pay for it all without working or living with someone who is?"

Tammy darkened, but only a little. She looked over at Tanner intensely for a second before returning her gaze to the road, "None of your business, Tanner."

"Okay. Just wondered. I have always wondered about people who find a way to live without working, especially in such an expensive place as anywhere within 60 miles of San Francisco."

Tammy said, "Yeah, I get it. It's not that big of a deal. For your information, I worked in the Benicia Mothball fleet of ships as a welder for years. Welders make pretty damn good money as you might already know, and I managed to pay my rent and still have plenty left over. I used to spend it all up every two weeks, drinking and what not, then I decided to start saving, and eventually got into buying stocks. I made so much money by buying stocks and holding onto them that I was for sure going to be able to retire ear-ly." Tanner's ears perked up.

"Then I got married and, when Rodney was killed, I hired a good attorney and received a really big settlement for his wrong-ful death, plus, he had taken out a huge life insurance policy to pro-tect me. That paid me a huge sum on top of all the rest of it, as well as the mortgage being paid off by the mortgage insurance he took out when we bought the house after we got married. So that's how I manage to live like this. Not that it's any of your business. I miss that man something terrible. I'm so very grateful for his thought-fulness in making sure I'd be taken care of in case something should happen to him. Now I no longer have to breathe toxic gases all day, and I have plenty of money to do what I want. I'm already wealthy, and Social Security starts for me in only a few short years. That will add even more to my security blanket."

Tanner added, "And your Medicare premiums."

"So, what's your five-year plan, Tanner? I know you lost your wife to another man, I know you retired early, and I know that your wife took half of what you thought you had to retire on when she left, forcing you back into the workplace just when you were psychologically ready to put down the gauntlet. I know you're living in a small apartment in Concord, and you are no longer do-ing stock investing. So, again, what's your five-year plan now?"

Tanner hated that trite statement or question. A few times when he was younger he had been asked by a prospective employer, *So, where do you see yourself in five years, Tanner?*

"You mean what's my plan from here?" Tanner asked, a little perplexed.

"Sure, what's your plan?"

"Well, I was having lunch not too long ago at *Penny's Roadside Cafe*, and long story short, met this guy, Steve Caldwell who owns Caldwell Realtors LLC."

Tammy said, "Yeah, I know of that guy. A real shark. He buys up foreclosures and re-sells them for a profit, and he buys up land and develops it into more shopping centers and malls, and he buys apartments, condos, and townhouses, then rents them out for an exorbitant amount of money and fees. He's been in the paper. He's been taken to court for not keeping his buildings up, and using the monthly maintenance fees for his own personal purposes."

"I didn't know all of that. Anyway, he seemed like a nice enough guy, and I was looking at a booklet of real estate listings. He noticed me looking at it, and asked me if I was in the market for a house. I said no, that I was curious about the pricing and features of the local market. He said he was always looking for more talent if I wanted a chance to come on board etc., and I told him I wasn't interested in learning all the ins-and-outs of real estate and starting another new career, but thanked him."

Tammy said, "Do you have enough coming in to live on?"

"Nothing coming in yet, and I'm still over six years from full Social Security, two for minimal Social Security, and what I have left after the divorce is rapidly dwindling."

"What are you going to do now?"

Tanner knew it was coming, and fired back, "Well, I had lunch the other day at a local Mexican restaurant around the corner from me, and they need someone, so I'm starting Monday."

Tammy looked shocked, "What? At a Mexican restaurant? What the heck are you going to do there to make it worth your time?"

Tanner was reluctant to answer because he knew she wasn't going to like what he said next: "Dishwashing, prepping, cleaning to start, then a food truck to oversee later if I end up worthy enough to be trusted with one."

Tammy just stared at the road, saying nothing for a good five minutes. Tanner found it extremely unsettling, especially after she was just being so reactive and vocal.

"So, that's your plan for now, then what? See, this is how planning out a five year plan works, you actually think it through and actually plan it so that you can steer your life where you want it to go, so you can experience the things you want to experience before dying. But this is the process. It's actively writing your own life story by deciding what comes next, and after that, and then . . . in five-year blocks, planning the next block near the end of the current one."

Tanner thought for a moment and said, "It's bullshit, just like everything else. I've seen and heard it all, over the years. Do a five-year plan, do a paleo diet, then a vegan one. The TQM or To-tal-Quality-Management method of leadership, process teams, logical flow dynamics, and on and on and on. All promising increased wealth, or better health, or better relationships, or better workflow, or better manufacturing processes. But they are all there to increase someone else's wealth to a high degree, while most of us really don't grasp or truly understand science, nutrition, personal inter-dynamics, or nearly pure, logical thinking, so we rely on others to inform us. They come along with their claims, we buy their snake oil, they make their money, and we are left with high hopes that quickly fade back into the gray of reality, and the DVDs, books, charts, smartphones, and other assorted plastics and props to help us with our lives all eventually end up in the landfill. Rinse and re-peat with each new generation coming along."

Tammy looked a little pissed off now, but remained calm and seemed pretty centered. "Tanner, no offense, but if you'd had a five-year plan you wouldn't be where you are right now."

He turned and looked at her, "Fuck you, Tammy! I have had plans throughout my life, and they were going along just fine, and working out well. I was supposed to be happy, once retired, and going on cruises with my wife. She screwed that all up, not me." Tanner's voice wavered with emotion, even though his anger resonated and punched through the sadness with enough convic-tion and pain for two people. "She had to go and screw it all up by screwing someone else, and then taking my five-year plan apart, piece-by-piece, until it made me see that our lives, and all the stupid fucking rules we all play, and dance by, are just pure bullshit. All that planning, and saving, and investing, and risk taking, to make that huge chunk of money that, in the end, came apart all at once, like a bomb going off. Then she added to that darkness by taking half of my lifelong plan. I'm old now, and I want to retire like I planned to, not come up with another stinking five-year plan."

Tammy looked over at Tanner. As they passed a streetlight, his face lit up enough for her to see that he had tears streaming down his face. "I'm sorry, Tanner. I'll lay off. Maybe we'll talk a little more specifically about that later, or not. I didn't mean to pick on you, or be mean to you. I'm sorry."

Tanner looked over at Tammy without bothering to wipe the tears from his face and said, "Thank you." Tammy kept looking straight ahead.

After a few minutes of silence, she suddenly came to life again like someone who woke up late for work, and blurted, "You know, I almost think that, even though Caldwell is such a shark, that you could still go that route, learn on his dime, get your license, then go elsewhere after working with him long enough to pay back the training or something. You'd earn so much more money over time, you'd be able to dress professionally, and you'd be out and about, seeing, marketing, and selling awesome properties, making more off of one sale in commission than you would likely make at that restaurant in months. It's really something to consider. I thought about doing that for a while. I had a friend who was a freelance real estate agent, before her and her husband moved away last year. She made between $100K and $150K in commissions per year while setting her own schedule. She loved it."

Tanner slowly, but surely, tuned Tammy out while looking out of his window. She still didn't get or hear what he just said, about being ready to retire. When he heard her pause, he felt compelled to respond, so he muttered, "Something to think about for sure," with an uninspired tone.

9

TRIPPING ON YOURSELF

When they arrived back at Tammy's she said, "I'm going to make us some special tea, we'll have it after dinner. I think you'll like it. It's very expensive compared to most teas. It will help you relax and can help you figure out where you need to go next."

Tanner was a little confused, but smiled and said, "Sounds good. I'm looking forward to it now that you've given it such a positive endorsement."

They decided to sit at the kitchen table to finish eating all the food. Tanner was so preoccupied mentally with reliving his earlier jump, he barely noticed all the food varieties in front of him, each with their own beautiful colors and aromas. The jump seemed surreal to him, now; he'd jumped out of an airplane only an hour or so ago. In his mind, he kept reliving that thrilling exit and the sudden acceleration, each time getting goosebumps from head to toe.

But the extra spicy flavors from the food quickly pulled him back to reality and, as if seeing them for the first time, his eyes grew big as he focused on the enchiladas, the beans, the rice, the chips and salsa, the tamales, and the chile rellenos spread out before him on the table. Only then did he realize that he had been daydreaming while eating, his mind somewhere else the entire time.

Despite being preoccupied with his amazing skydiving experience, he still managed to listen and respond to Tammy well enough to satisfy her; she kept talking and eating, obviously still really happy, and high on her own post-jump adrenaline, seemingly oblivious to Tanner's quiet contemplation and distance.

After they finished eating, they chatted for a while. For now, Tanner was enjoying her talking. She spoke with such confidence, and no fear—always positive, and always with a smile. After a pause in their conversation, Tammy said, "Tanner, why don't you head into the living room and I'll join you shortly."

Tanner got up, "Thanks for dinner. That was really good."

"You're welcome. Glad you liked it. I'll be right back with the tea."

Tanner found his way into the living room and slid down into a big, squishy, bean-bag chair that was made of a warm, fuzzy material that covered the orb in slices running from top to bottom, like a basketball. Alternating red, white, and black, colors that grew wide at the center and tapered to a point at each end, giving the orb an almost three-dimensional look. Tanner found the thing utterly irresistible, and moved it closer to the couch and the coffee table, where he was sure that Tammy would park herself, and the tea.

Tanner felt the fuzzy orb mould to his body. Immediately, it began lightly reflecting his body heat back at him, leaving him comfortable, and mentally reflective. His gaze wandered around the room. He looked at the walls, absorbing the multitude of photos, original drawings, and paintings. One picture showed Tammy smiling at the camera at the top of a mountain with some friends.

In another, Tammy held a dog she used to have. A photo of a sunset over the Himalayan mountains, with both the mountains and the clouds reflecting the low-angle sun, showing lots of pink and purple, adding to the magic and majesty of that moment. A painting of a mountain pond surrounded by green grassy meadows full of wildflowers on a sunny, partly cloudy summer day. *So many instants to capture during our lifetime,* he thought.

Tanner heard the sound of modern, electronic, ambient space music slowly enter his awareness, just as Tammy came back with the tea. She had a complete tea set on a bamboo tray. It held a small, white porcelain pot with a lid, and two small white porcelain drinking vessels. Tammy gently set the tea down and then went around the room lighting various candles. Once eight or so were lit, she turned off the lights, and the entire room changed into a warm, cozy, chamber.

Tammy looked at Tanner. "Are you comfortable?" she asked him. "You might want to take your belt off and put it with your shoes over by the door before we have our tea."

Without saying a word, Tanner rose from his fuzzy orb and pulled his black leather belt out of the belt loops of his jeans, then hung it on the coat rack by the door, before resuming his former position back in the fuzzy orb.

Tammy said, "Tanner, have you ever taken psilocybin mushrooms or magic mushrooms before?"

Tanner said, "No, but I have thought that I would like to try them after seeing some documentaries about them on PBS. He stopped for a second, then said, "Why? Is that what the tea is? Some kind of mushroom tea?"

"Yes, it is. I've made it before, many times now. I've tried all different amounts, and have really dialed in how much to ingest to get the desired effects."

"Which is how much?" Tanner asked.

Tammy smiled, "Well, once you take enough to actually experience a full-blown trip and hallucinate, you'll realize that it's the only way to let the psychotropic ingredients in mushrooms work their magic, and take you to a place where you'll be able to look at yourself from the outside, looking back in. It lets you see what has impacted you, and what's shaped you into who you are, then will show you where, and how, you can change and know a better life."

Tanner said, "Okay, this time I'll give you a little bit of a break because of what I've read on my own and seen on educational television, otherwise I would say that this, too, smacks of being just another bunch of bullshit, just like I said earlier tonight."

"So, are you up for it? Want to try it? I think you'll benefit from it. I really do."

Tanner thought about it some more. He was scared, there was no doubt about that, but he was equally curious, and had been for years now. More than one article he'd read about mushrooms stated that they have the power to cure alcoholics from drinking, sometimes in as little as one trip or session. The findings were equally amazing regarding overall mental health improvements. Tanner had been astounded how the healing occurs in a short period of time. Many participants involved in studies reported conversing with, or listening to, a guide who points to their core issue preventing them from actualizing and becoming their true selves. That one fact had fascinated Tanner enough, at the time, that he wanted to try it the minute he read about those findings.

"What have you gleaned from taking it, thus far? You said you've done this a bunch in the past."

Tammy said without hesitation, "Freedom from fear. Freedom from fear about everything. I used to fear everything, and all people. In my trips, my spirit guide showed me how silly it was, and what a waste of my life's time it was. It allowed me to feel confident and strong in spirit, and then I became exactly that—confident, and strong in spirit."

Tanner said, "Let's do it. Why stop the fun now?"

Tammy said, "I've added enough mushrooms to this pot so that you're roughly going to get the equivalent of one gram of dry mushroom per cup. Seeing the second coming of Christ can happen to someone with only five grams in their system, but I've found that drinking three is the sweet spot. You will be taken to a place where your animal spirit, or shaman guide, will be able to find you and help you through your journey, perhaps showing you a better way to proceed."

Tanner said, "That's what I'm talking about. That's what I've been curious about."

Tammy filled the two vessels with the tea. It had a strange, complex green, brown, gray tint to it, and an odd odor that Tanner didn't recognize. He took a sip. It had an ultra earthy, bitter, horrible taste. Tammy said, "Hang on, let me get some honey for you, it really helps cut that taste."

Tanner fast sipped his first cup, then a second, and then waited about ten minutes before having one more. Tammy smiled at him and said, "Just relax and let it happen. Expect to hallucinate and go with it. Don't resist what happens to you. It's better if you don't."

Tanner smiled and said, "Okay, but will it be okay?"

Tammy said, "For sure, but you need to loosen up and listen to the soothing music and quiet your mind of thoughts that use spoken words. Quiet the voice and let the imagery that enters your mind begin to flow from the music. Remember, you are the master of your fate."

Tanner closed his eyes. Almost immediately, the ethereal music began to elicit images in his mind: seagulls flying along the seashore at sunset; pink and purple clouds against a dimming blue sky; walking hand in hand with Sheila through a sunlit meadow, dense with wild flowers; floating on the ocean and feeling the rise and fall of his body as swells passed under him, before his body liquified and became one with the ocean.

Tanner opened his eyes and slowly looked around the room at all the lit candles. *The candle hierarchy,* he thought. He focused on the flames, noticing the variations in color between them, which seemed to be a function of the length of the wick. *How the hell did that pop in there?* Tammy sat catty-corner to him on the couch. She had her eyes closed and appeared to be far away and very relaxed.

The electronic synth music changed to a more intense, repetitive, heavy percussion sound. Tanner could feel the vibrations from the bass and the drums all the way into his bones. He could feel every fiber of polyester on the fuzzy orb vibrating to the music, and, little by little, he began to notice that every single object in the entire room, including the room itself—the walls, ceiling, and floor—were all vibrating to the exact same beat of the music in perfect unison. Slowly, the vibrations began to merge until parts of the room had become undulating regions, that were still keeping time with the beat.

One by one, individual fiber vibrations began merging with wood particle vibrations, which were merging with pillows, and the couch, until the entire room all merged into one, unified, liquified space that morphed, and stretched, and distorted perfectly in-synch with the beat of the music.

Tanner was transported to the center of his entire universe, and he gained insight from the information that began manifesting in his mind at an accelerated rate. Effortlessly he learned that each person has their own unique universe for their entire life. It can grow or diminish depending on the number of positive or negative life choices made. Each individual universe is part of a much larger universe containing all of the individual universes in existence. Tanner's thoughts became a high-speed stream-of-consciousness: *The God server!* All of us with our individual universes are part of God's database, or all of the knowledge of mankind since the beginning of time collectively, and it can be accessed in real time like the ultimate Google or ChatGPT AI machine. It is also the reason some people have such a hard time getting along with one another, because they each have different universes that have taught them different or even conflicting things about reality and, therefore, have come up with different truths that can, and often do, cause much conflict between people who simply experience the reality of life completely differently from one another. Tolerance, empathy, and love, are the keys to solve it, but those feelings and modes of being—tolerant, empathetic, and loving, all require a strong will. *Without that, all the tools, and all the help in the universe won't matter.*

The music stopped for a moment, and Tanner saw only blackness. A minute later, the music began playing again. This time it was electronic space music. The kind of music that would be in the background in a scene where an observation probe was traveling through the darkness of space towards some unknown destination. Tanner became the probe. He felt the void and iciness of space, yet he was still alive. He was impervious to the negative effects of anything: gravity, sub-zero temperatures, one thousand mile-per-hour winds, heat that could melt titanium almost instantly, were all things that Tanner could touch, sit on, pass through, or just observe without any impediment whatsoever.

Tanner's thoughts raced. *I am God. We are all Gods.* We just don't realize it yet. We are God trainees. Our lives here on Earth are given to us so that we will experience things in order to develop a deep understanding about our own existence, as well as humankind's existence. Once that is achieved, we will become privy to the revelations of our entire universe. *Not anyone else's universe, just ours, and only if we're lucky.*

He felt himself begin to spin while he was still in the sitting position. It was as if there were a small, significant force field around his body that insulated him from bumps, cuts, bullets, welding torch flames, lasers, and just about anything imaginable. His body floated inside a bubble of magnetic insulation, his entire body spinning in random directions inside it.

The speed of his rotation increased; when Tanner closed his eyes he had to fight hard not to vomit. Finally, the nausea abated and he reopened his eyes. Now, he was his own spaceship. Not in a spaceship, he was the spaceship. He was naked, and sitting with his legs crossed with his arms resting on the top of his knees. He was in deep space and hurtling at an extremely high rate of speed. He could see stars zipping by, just like in Star Trek when *Enterprise* is traveling at warp speed.

Then, as if someone snapped their fingers, Tanner was sitting in blackness again. No sounds, no lights, no stars. A large circle of light appeared, illuminating him from above and below, and he could see that he was sitting in a circular room, or a court. As he looked around the perimeter, he could see countless stars off in the distance, through a window that spanned three hundred and sixty degrees around the room.

A blurry figure appeared at the edge of the perimeter, where the lights intersected with the vastness of space. The blurry figure had a shape that resembled a fox wearing an overcoat and a fedora, while perpetually standing on his hind legs. He always stood at the perimeter's edge, looking down, and along that line, always away from Tanner. Tanner sat in the middle of the lit, bottom area, looking at this blurry figure in total apprehension about what might come next.

The voice from the blurry figure came to Tanner telepathically: Tanner Dalton. *I see you at birth, I see you as a baby and as a little child. I see you now, and I see you at death's door.* You are not your past. However, you are your future, but you must make it yours and shape it to your liking. There is nothing to fear, ever. Even death is not something to fear. Don't wait any longer. Don't keep living like you have all the time in the world, because you don't. If you still have things to accomplish then do them. Once you set the path for yourself, no one else can take it from you. Your experiences in the past have served to teach you about people and living. You have seen the faces of love, hate, anger, defeat, lust, angst, happiness, ecstasy, joy, fear, and so many more. Choose one and make it yours. Choose wisely, because you will become what you choose. Don't think about anything except choosing what you wish to become. If you choose happiness, then pay attention to what gives you joy, and be guided by the actions that manifest more of it. It is imperative that you do not wait for others; they are all on their own paths. *Don't let others keep you from your duty to become all that you can be within your own universe.*

Tanner sat very still while taking in all of the spiritual energy and wisdom that seemed to be coming at him from all directions simultaneously. Now, he was back in Tammy's living room watching everything in it move, morph, or vibrate. Everything responding to everything else; simultaneous and continuous domino action, with all of the movement from everything bumping into something else, some of it bouncing away, the rest morphing into and becoming one with the other.

Tanner felt as though he were being allowed to know about the part of living that is always going on, but that we don't notice or cannot normally see due to filters in our thinking, perception, and vision. He looked down at himself undulating in the fuzzy orb. He looked at his left palm and noticed the geometry in the molecular structure of his skin. He felt calm and reassured, and very comforted to have been made privy to so much information that seemed so simple and so achievable.

He could feel the wisdom in the words, their meaning passing through his physical body, briefly joining with his spiritual self, leaving him a copy in the form of a spiritual imprint that would be instantly recallable, and useable going forward.

Tanner opened his eyes, and found himself looking right into Tammy's eyes at nearly point blank range. Without a word, she slowly lowered herself down into his lap while facing him. She looked as if the spiritual entity had passed her the same message, or something very similar. She leaned forward, giving Tanner a long, slow, sensuous kiss. She stopped and smiled at him, then she stood and took his hand, helping him up off the orb, before leading him to her bedroom.

10

BACK TO WORK

Monday morning, Tanner walked into the Es Picante Restaurant at 6:50 a.m. after his whirlwind weekend with Tammy. First, a nice visit. Next, an extreme physical event, followed by an extreme spiritual one. All since Friday. Now, as he stood before Carmen and Señor Esperanza waiting for instructions, he felt refreshed, and had the strangest feeling that, despite this humble beginning, he was closer to his destiny than he had ever been.

Carmen gave him a quick, gentle smile, looking directly into his eyes, "Did you bring anything you need to refrigerate or stow away?"

"No, I didn't."

"Okay, please follow me, Mr. Dalton."

"Tanner. Please call me by my first name, Tanner."

Carmen stopped in front of the walk-in refrigerator and looked at him without saying anything for a few seconds, then said, "In here, you can stow any food you bring."

Carmen pointed to a stainless steel rack on the right side of the refrigerator. "The right side of the second shelf down from the top is yours."

Tanner smiled, "Thank you, I appreciate that."

She closed the door, and Tanner followed her into the kitchen where Señor Esperanza was filling a large pot with water to begin preparing the Spanish rice. He noticed both of them coming into the kitchen. He wiped his hands on his apron before coming around to greet Tanner."Hola, Señor Dalton. I am so glad to have your help. Carmen will show you the ropes with what you'll need to know to help us out while you complete your studies and get your food service certificate." Tanner could tell that it was difficult for him to find the right English words, but gave him points for his effort. Diego quickly looked at Carmen and asked her in Spanish whether she had informed Tanner that he could now take the class online and that it costs less doing it that way, and to please start calling him Diego.

Carmen looked at Tanner and said, "My father wants you to know that you can take the class online to get your food service certificate and it costs less doing it that way, and he wants you to start calling him Diego."

Tanner looked at Diego, "Thank you, Diego. I'll look into the class tonight."

Diego smiled and nodded before looking at Carmen more seriously, firing off more to her in Spanish, a language Tanner never learned, despite growing up in southern California.

Carmen giggled, "Come on, we need to get started with the chopping."

For the next two hours, without stopping, Tanner chopped tomatoes, onions, and lettuce. Next, he grated thirty pounds of different kinds of cheeses, followed by shredding cooked chicken and, finally, draining and crumbling the hamburger meat. At first, he stood, but after only forty-five minutes, Carmen brought him a bar stool to sit on.

Tanner was surprised by how much he felt the need to sit. After the food prepping, he had an early lunch that Carmen put together for him. She made him a plate of his three favorite tacos, with a little cup of refried beans on the side to which she added a couple of spoonfuls of Spanish rice, and then mixed together. Tanner was grateful. He was a lot hungrier than he realized, and ate quickly.

Diego finished cooking all the meats, then made the beans and the rice. Then the food was lined up in a row along a counter that was already sterilized, and ready for meal prep.

After his meal, Tanner took out the trash before the restaurant opened for lunch. It was the first time he'd seen the light of day since arriving that morning and, after spending hours in the kitchen, he welcomed the chance to get some fresh air.

The fiery scintillation of light emanating from the sun stretched out across the sky in all directions. Tanner had left his sunglasses inside the restaurant in his locker, so he had to squint hard to be able to see anything with that sudden, intense brightness.

He dragged the heavy, circular 30-gallon plastic trash can over to the big rollaway bin outside, grabbed it by the handle, and tilted it forward a little so he could get underneath it with his other hand. It was heavier than he'd estimated, and he was barely able to lift it high enough to catch the lip on the dumpster, which was even with his eyes. After considerable struggling, he realized that he would need to be on a ladder or stool, or at least on his tip-toes to get the bottom of the barrel high enough up to finish dumping the putrid contents.

As he struggled to maneuver the heavy, slippery cylinder into a better position, he could hear the sound of the nasty, viscous liquid hitting the pavement and spattering. He almost dropped the can when he first heard it, because his natural impulse was to look down at the source of the sound. Luckily, he was able to hang tight and finish the task, vowing to never let the container get so heavy that he would need to go through this a second time.

When he finally finished dumping the main contents of the can, what he saw confirmed his worst fears. A lot of the liquid muck had ended up spattering all over the pavement and his feet, and now a disgusting, putrid, vomit stench could not be avoided. Tanner slung the empty container against the fencing that enclosed the big bin, and took stock of the mess. Watery grease all over the side of the big bin, the ground in all directions, and his trousers from the knees down, with his shoes catching the worst of it.

Tanner went back inside to ask where he could get some grease cutter, and a hose. Carmen was rushing around because three people were already sitting at one of the tables ordering food. Diego was already putting some of their order together. He seemed totally preoccupied until the vomit odor hit his nose. "What the hell? Get out of here with that mess. What's the matter with you?"

Tanner was shocked, but kept his composure, "Where is the grease cutter or floor cleaner? I need to get the spill up outside before it makes the entire trash bin area a permanent skating rink from all of the grease that will likely get embedded into the pavement. Every time that surface gets moist, it will be a really slippery, dangerous place to be, especially while trying to lift a heavy barrel, that's almost a certainty."

Diego pointed to a closet, "In that room you should find what you need."

Tanner opened the closet, found some cleaner, and headed back outside to clean up the mess he'd made. Still no hose. He went back inside, "Diego, do you guys have a hose out back?"

"Hose? What the hell do you need a hose for?"

"I spilled the bottom juice out of the trash all over the place, and it was full of grease, so I want to scrub the area with grease cleaner, then hose it away to finish cleaning it."

"Forget that. Get your feet clean, we can't have you smelling like that walking around inside the building. No one will eat here. Hurry up and get it done, now! We're going to need you back in here pronto. Lunch has begun. Don't let us down when we need you the most."

Tanner was mortified. He was a college graduate, a former supervisor, a once wealthy, self-made millionaire, and a sixty-year-old man. He looked at Diego and said, "I have to go and clean my shoes. I can't get rid of the smell without doing so. I can't be in two places at the same time, so bear with me. And, if you ever speak to me like a child again, I will walk out of this door and never come back without saying a word as to why I'm doing it. I'm not your child, and you will not talk to me that way ever again, got it?"

Diego looked at him, holding a gaze for a brief moment, nodded, then looked away without saying another word. He was pissed off. He slammed the stainless steel spoon in his hand back into the pot of beans, and walked to the back storage area. Tanner went back to the cleaning closet and retrieved a bucket, filled it partially with warm water, then put some of the cleaning solution in. He took the bucket outside with a folding chair and took his shoes off. He dunked his shoes in the bucket to let them soak for a couple of minutes. After a few minutes, he reached into the bucket and began scrubbing his shoes with a small scrub brush. Luckily, the nasty stuff that was already drying on his shoes came right off in the warm water cleaning solution mixture. His shoes now actually looked better than they had in a long time. He took the bucket inside and dumped the water down the deep sink in the cleaning closet, and then rinsed his shoes with clear water. He went into the bathroom and plugged in the hair dryer he'd seen in there earlier, and started blow drying his shoes. Pretty quickly, he saw that it was going to take too long to dry them, so he shut off the blower, and put his partially dry shoes back on.

Now, at least the vomit smell was almost completely abated, unless he stood in one place a little too long, like a minute, then the foul odor would slowly permeate the immediate vicinity, allowing anyone within about six feet to enjoy the fragrance all over again. To add insult to injury, his shoes were still pretty wet, and they now both made a distinct *varunk-varunk-varunk* sound with every step he took, making him extremely self-conscious.

Diego looked really annoyed, and stressed-out when Tanner finally came back out of the cleaning closet, and the shoe noise added to it. Tanner could see him clenching his jaw all the way across the room, tightly trying to hold his anger in check and get through the rest of today's lunch without any more problems.

Six more people came in. Already, the small dining room was nearly full, and there were more coming down the hall. Tanner opened the kitchen door a crack, and looked out at them. Some were already eating, and he couldn't help but notice how happy they all looked. Tanner felt excited about being a part of serving people good food and watching their day get a little brighter, even if only for a short time. He thought, *Something about eating good food always seems to bring out the best in people—for the most part.*

Tanner felt someone pulling him back into the kitchen. He turned around. Carmen was holding three plates of food she was trying to hand off to him. "Table 2, please, right away. Then take note of who needs water, and fill them up while you're out there. Please seat anyone coming in where available, give them menus, and tell them that someone will be right with them. Finally, continue going back and forth between the kitchen and the dining room. Bring menus, food, fill water glasses, give out silverware rolls, and clean up at tables already used as fast as possible. Got it?"

Tanner nodded affirmatively, took the food from Carmen, and walked them to table 2.

"Chile relleno plate?"

"Right here" the young man in the white shirt said.

"Two-taco plate?"

The mid-thirties lady with green lipstick, purple hair streaks, and three-inch-long finger nails answered, "Oh, right here. That's mine. Ummm. Looks yummy!" she unfolded her napkin and placed it across her lap.

Tanner set a three taco plate in front of a tall, young, black man with very short hair, and a distinct part on the left side of his head. He looked at Tanner and smiled, "Thank you, sir. Looks good."

Tanner smiled back, "Just raise your hand if you need anything."

Just as Tanner turned to head back to the kitchen to get the next order, the front door opened and Steve Caldwell and Sophie walked in. Tanner felt his heart rate instantly quadruple, but he simply smiled, and grabbed two menus, walked over to them and said, "Hello, Steve, Sophie, great to see you both. Follow me please. He walked them the ten feet or so to the last table available, waited for them to get settled, then handed them their menus.

Sophie smiled in her usual alluring way. "Hello, Tanner. What are you doing here?"

"Well," Tanner said, "I'm doing just what it looks like I'm doing, I'm working the lunch shift at Es Picante restaurant."

Steve's big ego couldn't stand not taking the lead. Looking perplexed he said, "So, this is the job you turned down my offer to train you in real estate for?" The only thing Tanner could see at that moment was the glaring white teeth in Steve's mouth, and his smarmy smirk.

Tanner decided to milk this one for all he could. "That's correct."

Steve looked both perplexed, confused, and a little angry now, "What the hell for? Do you know how much money you could be making right now?"

Tanner looked at him with confidence, "Oh, not really, but I don't really care. I don't need all that money; this job suits my purposes better than yours did, Steve."

"How's that?" Steve asked.

"Well, this job is a no-brainer, the hours are static, and I needed that, and I make enough to live on."

Steve looked at Sophie and said, "Do you believe this guy? He could be making six figures—"

"—Hocking overpriced, poorly built houses on people," Tanner injected, "Who will likely become so stressed from working their asses off in order to pay the bank back with the bulk of their hard-earned money, just for the privilege of having a house and living in California, that they're almost guaranteed to end up divorced in less than ten years. No thanks. I'm working on finishing my PhD in Nuclear Physics at Laurence Berkeley Labs, and this job works perfectly for me to be able to do that now."

Steve and Sophie looked at each other, then back at Tanner. They seemed impressed, and a little shocked. Steve, still sounding a tad skeptical said, "Wow, that sounds important. What are you trying to work out?"

Tanner said, "You wouldn't understand any of it, Steve. Nothing personal, but you really wouldn't."

Not to be outdone, Steve said, "Try me anyway. Tell me."

Sophie leaned forward chiming in, "Yeah, tell us, Tanner. Please?"

Tanner took a deep breath, then slowly let it out, "Okay, but then I have to get moving. Today is my first day and it hasn't gone great. Now, I'm talking to you too much. Anyway, I'm working on mapping out the required quantum distance that opposing black hole singularities can be, proximal to one another, without causing a catastrophic incident, such as the universe as we know it, inverting itself."

Steve gasped, "Seriously? Come on. It's incredible that stuff like that can be measured or even known at all."

Tanner smiled at him, "And, I really love it. It's my life's passion, and mission. But thank you anyway, Steve." As Tanner moved away to go to the kitchen, Sophie looked right at him and mouthed *Call me,* as Tanner moved away from their table.

He went into the kitchen to get more food for some of the other tables, barely able to keep from laughing. Diego pointed to the clock, then pointed to his mouth, then made a gesture like he was zipping his mouth closed. Carmen walked by and said, "He's saying don't talk to one table so long."

"Got it!" Tanner replied. He grabbed the next two plates for table 4. As he left the kitchen he saw Steve and Sophie laughing and talking up a storm. Tanner thought, *Shoot, I was glad that they were together. I thought I was off the hook. Didn't look like it when she said to call her.*

Tanner dropped the plates off at table 4 and felt Steve and Sophie drilling a hole in his backside as he retreated into the kitchen. Luckily, the drama was over, and the rest of the shift went without further incident. Once Carmen locked the door for the day, she looked at Tanner and said, "Over all, you did good. Points off for the spill out back though. Diego wants you to go and clean it up now."

Tanner nodded, and immediately went to the cleaning closet to get the degreaser again. "Carmen, do you have a hose somewhere? I see a hose bib to hook it to for water out back, but no hose."

Carmen said, "Oh, right. Sorry. Yeah, we keep it in the trunk of Diego's Cadillac. We don't have room for it in the cleaning closet, and we've had two stolen in the past when we've left them hooked up. It's a pain, but it's our reality. I'll get the keys."

A few minutes later, Carmen came out of the office with the keys, then had Tanner follow her out to her father's car. She opened the trunk, and Tanner saw the hose right away. It was lying right next to an open duffle bag which appeared to have at least four different types of rifles inside it. Tanner wondered what they were for, but decided to keep quiet, and not say a thing. He could tell from the way she looked at him that Carmen was grateful that he hadn't asked her anything about them. She slammed the trunk closed, and handed him the hose. "Come get me when you're done so I can put this back in the trunk, and don't forget to drain the hose out first. I don't want it draining in my father's trunk."

"No problem. Thank you."

"De nada."

Tanner hooked the hose up first, sprayed the degreaser all over the mess by the bin, letting it set for a couple of minutes. He began scrubbing the mess with a stiff bristle brush. As he moved the hose back and forth to move the mess towards the drain, his mind wandered back to his encounter with Steve and Sophie.

Steve reminded him of one of those rich, smarmy kids that went to Northgate High School. The school was built for all the kids who lived in the really big houses on the side of Oak Grove Road—after crossing Ygnacio Valley Road—and turns into Castle Rock Road, up by Boundary Oaks Golf Club, back in the late 1970s. You know them. They're the kids who got brand new cars for graduation from high school, and the same ones who got into really good universities because their parents were wealthy enough to be able to make a proper donation to the right person, even though their kid had marginal grades at best, and were basically complete idiots most of the time.

Tanner hated economic class division while going to high school. More than once he managed to get invited to the houses of some of the friends he'd made from being on both the tennis team and the wrestling team. Many of them lived in that upscale neighborhood. When Tanner went to visit them, he had been astounded by their huge, lavish houses with swimming pools.

Once he saw how some of his classmates lived, he was envious and ashamed that he lived in a small, rented, three-bedroom ranch on the poorer side of the school district. His entire house would easily fit inside the grand foyer of some of the homes his friends lived in. Some of their bedrooms were bigger than Tanner's living room and kitchen combined. Somehow, he always found a way to not say or tell anyone where he lived. He was petrified that, someday, the tiny house that he lived in, along with his dysfunctional family, would all be discovered and he would lose his friends and become a laughing stock.

Tanner flashed on what he had told Steve and Sophie at lunch about working on his PhD in Nuclear Physics and laughed out loud. He couldn't help it. Every time he played the scene over in his mind, it made him laugh all over again. He laughed hard, and kept chuckling the rest of the time he cleaned, while replaying the look of surprises on both of their faces when they realized that Tanner was working on something that went well beyond selling houses. Something important for science. He thought, *I always could do that bullshit routine well. It's so fun delivering some outlandish story that might be true, but not likely to be true, and then delivering it really well, with a straight face, maybe letting them down later by telling them that you were just kidding and that none of it is really true.* But this time, Tanner wasn't sure if they would ever know it wasn't true. He didn't plan on seeing either of them again anytime soon, anyway.

After cleaning, Tanner went in to get the last of his personal stuff, but stopped short before leaving when he saw Diego standing by the back of his car with his trunk open. Three guys with bandanas around their heads were talking to him. All three wore black, wraparound sunglasses, black t-shirts, jeans, and black steel-toed boots, with black leather vests, like they were part of a gang.

Tanner could see an insignia, but it was a Spanish name. He tried to burn it into his memory so he could look it up later. *Los Guardianes de la Paz* in a circular stamp embossed on the back of their jackets. The shorter Hispanic man in front presented Diego with a small canvas bag with a shoulder strap. Diego took it, unzipped the top and looked inside. He nodded, and gave them a Mona Lisa smile, then reached into the trunk and hoisted the duffel bag full of rifles up and out, and set it on the edge of the trunk. All three men moved in tighter for a closer look at the hardware. A couple of the rifles were brought out and examined closely. The men seemed pleased. They stowed the rifles and left. Diego got into his car and drove away.

Tanner went into the dining room. "Is your father coming back tonight?"

Carmen stopped wiping tables with disinfectant for a second, looked at the clock on the wall and said, "No, I doubt it. I think he's going to the bank, then home for dinner, why?"

"Well, I went inside to get the rest of my stuff to leave and your dad was doing some kind of transaction with some men. When he finished, he just got into his car and left. I had laid the hose out to drain while I went in to get my stuff. I guess the hose won't be able to be stowed in your dad's trunk tonight if he isn't coming back."

Carmen said, "That's okay. Just for tonight we can stow it in the cleaning room."

"Perfect! I'll leave it there, then I'll go. See you tomorrow."

"See you tomorrow, Tanner."

Tanner rolled the hose up, getting the last of the water out in the process, then left it inside the cleaning closet.

That night, Tanner kept getting muscle spasms in his inner thighs and his calves from all the standing and walking back and forth all day. He took some Tylenol, and smoked some Indica, then hit the sack right after eating another premade meal. This time he was determined to not let himself fall asleep in front of the television and wake up at two in the morning again.

So far, he hated the job. He loved seeing people get happy while they ate the food that he and Carmen and Diego had prepared for them, but his first day had seemed to never end. All the standing had physically taxed his older bones, and now his pain just made him want to sit down. The thought of another day like that was the last thing he wanted to think about.

He told himself that he would adjust, and that he should just give it time, but it wasn't really what he thought it was going to be—just like almost every single job he'd had since he was a teenager. Right now, he needed to stop depleting his savings, and make at least enough doing something to allow him to start slowly recovering financially. This sucked, though. He needed another gig, and soon. Then he thought about it some more, *Maybe I'll like the food truck better. At least I'll be out and away from one spot, and Diego.*

The next morning, Tanner decided to drive to work, despite the short walk, so he could go straight over to Tammy's again after work, but the Camry didn't want to start. He decided to deal with it later, and hustle to work. Unfortunately, by the time he got there, it was 7:10 a.m. As soon as he walked in the door, Carmen said with a straight face and a flat voice, Diego will see you in the office now. Please close the door behind you when you go in." She walked over to the work counter and began chopping again. Tanner went to the office door and knocked.

Diego's stern voice said, "Enter."

Tanner entered the office and closed the door. He moved forward and began to sit down in the chair in front of Diego, but Diego stopped him.

"I said enter, but I never said it was okay to sit down."

Tanner stood, already feeling annoyed. *Here we go again with the, 'you've been a bad little boy, Tanner and now it's time for your punishment,' routine again. Jesus, I don't know what poor Carmen might have gone through while growing up with this guy.*

"You're late!" Diego half shouted.

"Yes, I had a car problem this morning."

"I know where you live, Señor. You could've been on time."

"I wanted to leave directly from here after work, but my car wouldn't start this morning and, trouble-shooting it ate up the time I usually spend walking to work. In the end, I had to walk to work anyways. Now, I have to go home later and try to figure it all out, then, instead of now, and I won't be able to get any parts if I need them because my car is broken, and around we go." Tanner could feel himself winding up, his insides getting tighter, and tighter.

"I can't have it. I'm putting a note in your file. Get two of them, and you won't get any raise when the time comes. Get three, and I'll fire you. Understand?"

"I understand. Sure. You're a tyrant who wants to be Napoleon Bonaparte when you're here bossing the help around. Is that why you had a sign out front for help wanted? I'm betting it is." Tanner leaned in towards Diego's desk for emphasis. He noticed Diego tense and move his chair back a little from the desk, "It's a two-way fucking street, mister. I need to earn some money, but not if it means putting up with a tyrant who likes to micromanage others and be a bully. No way. Not at my age. Next time I'm late, go ahead and put anything you want in my file. Hell, put an enchilada in it for all I care. I'll work for you, but not if you're going to be a prick like this. You need me, you need my help, just as much as I need to earn some money. If we can both just be reasonable human beings to one another, I think we'll be all set. Oh, and by the way, this is your second notice in your file. I warned you yesterday about not talking to me like I was your child. Three of those, and I quit on the spot."

Tanner abruptly turned and walked out without another word, closing the door firmly behind him, but without slamming it.

Later, just before they opened for lunch, Diego came over to him asking about the class Tanner needed to take. "Did you sign up for the class you're needing to keep this job?"

Tanner looked apologetic, "No, I haven't. I'm sorry. It's no excuse, but it slipped my mind."

"It's the law, Tanner. Please sign up online tonight at Diablo Valley College's website. Culinary arts. You can sit for your food safety certificate after completing the first semester of that program because they cover food safety first."

"Thanks, Diego."

Diego smiled at him, a first for Tanner, and said "De nada," then walked away.

The restaurant wasn't quite as busy today, so Diego took Tanner behind the grill and showed him how to cook the meats, and get them ready. He had the hamburger on one side of the big square grill, sizzling, and he chopped at it with a large, stainless steel spatula. He also had a bunch of white breast and thigh chicken meat on the other side. Together, they finished cooking the meats and getting them into the containers by the prep counter. Tanner finished chopping the veggies, and made sure the dining area was ready to go. A short while later, they opened Es Picante for lunch. Tanner was grateful to have a slower day today. He was still sore from his first day, and he was still getting periodic whiffs of vomit floating up from his shoes. He focused hard, trying to remember everything both Diego and Carmen had already taught him. He wanted to impress them by doing things just right today. He felt like he'd gotten off on a bad foot, and wanted to get back in good graces with both of them.

The shift proceeded without incident. Tanner stayed the whole day today, and watched and helped with all the closing and cleaning procedures. He disinfected all of the tables, and made sure all dishes were run through the auto sanitizer. After he was done for the day, he asked Carmen if there was anything else she needed before he left, but she only shook her head no without looking up at him while she continued counting the money. Just when he was almost out of the door, she said, "Thank you, Tanner. Good job today. See you tomorrow."

"I'll be here bright and early. Have a good night, Carmen."

Just as promised, the next day Tanner was there at 6:50 a.m. ready to go to work. By the fourth day, neither Carmen, nor Diego had any criticisms or negative comments about his job performance. He'd found a private company that trained him online with all the information he needed to know to pass the exam, and gave him practice exams. Once he felt ready to pass the actual Food Safety Certification exam, he clicked the button and took it, passing with a score of 92/100. Diego had been happy about it and congratulated him. By the end of Tanner's first week, he felt like he knew enough to be able to open and close the restaurant if need be. Carmen was extremely happy with him, and had even started to tease him, and act a little playful towards him.

He was twenty years older than her. Tanner thought she seemed like a very kind and caring person. Quiet more than noisy. Thoughtful. Careful. Kind. Loving towards Diego. One morning, while they chopped vegetables together, she shared with him that her father was a widower who had lost his wife in a car crash when she was a little girl of only six years old. She said, "He raised me single handedly, and never flinched."

Friday finally came. "Do you need me for anything else before I head out, Carmen?"

Carmen was very focused on counting the money for the day and reconciling the receipts. She stopped and looked up at Tanner, locking her eyes on his. She continued staring without a word for almost a full minute, then smiled and said, "Sorry, I mean, no, thank you. Have a great weekend, and I'll see you Monday."

Tanner thought it a bit odd that she'd stared at him for so long, but the vibes he got from her while she did it were intense, and good. "You, too, Carmen. See you on Monday."

11

MENTAL SHIFT

Tanner flipped the channel to local news. Shootings, shootings, and more shootings all the time around the Bay Area. He flipped it right back off again. Right now, it felt great to be alone, in his own place, even though his money was flowing away as fast as a high mountain stream in the spring.

Tanner needed to feel that there was still hope for him to be able to finally live his best life. He wanted a positive life, with caring friends who helped others, and reinforced, supported, and affirmed others while they traveled through life. He wanted that more than anything now, even more than a bunch of money.

His only true regret in life was never finding someone to settle down with who really wanted to be a mother and have children. All those years with Sheila yielded nothing. In the end she'd told him that she just didn't feel maternal and had discovered that she didn't really want to be a mommy, but had been too afraid to tell him. She'd really wanted a career and money. For her, motherhood would've become a boring nightmare. If she'd only been honest with him sooner, he might still have been able to find someone else to have kids with.

Sheila had always been about money, money, money, and regarding her career, he knew better than to get in her way. But, more was always better with her, especially since she spent the money she earned as fast as she made it. Tanner paid for all the bills.

Her six-figure salary went to jewelry, make-up, massages, tennis lessons, endless shopping for clothes, and dining out. Girls night out—Sheila's night out—more often than not. Looking back, he can't believe he didn't see the party girl who was there right in front of him all along, instead of the mother she claimed she wanted to be.

Tanner would have been satisfied to have a much simpler life with a happy wife, and two or three beautiful, healthy children, and just enough money to provide properly for them without too much stress to acquire it. In other words, a more normal, far more balanced life.

Right now, the best Tanner could throw together into some semblance of the life he imagined for himself was to have a steady job that involved being a part of bringing joy or happiness into people's lives, while also earning money.

Tanner finally went to check on his car and, hopefully, figure out why it wouldn't start that morning. He lifted the hood and looked around for anything obvious, but saw nothing. He grabbed each one of his spark plug wires, one at a time, finding nothing. After one last look around, he slammed the hood back down, and slowly began walking around the car looking for anything external that might prevent his car from starting. As he moved around to the trunk, his eye caught the sight of something protruding from his tail pipe. He knelt down to get a closer look and right away saw the problem: someone had pushed a potato up his tailpipe, which was now blocking his exhaust and preventing his car from starting. He pulled out his pocket knife and whittled at the potato until he dislodged it, then got into his car and tried starting it. It started up immediately. *Phew! That could have been really expensive when I don't have any money to spare right now,* he thought.

Tanner knew that he needed to find a less risky place to live as soon as possible, or at least a place where he didn't have to wonder each morning what someone might have done to his car during the night to ruin or devalue it, or prevent it from starting. Don't the idiots know that they're picking on poor people just like them?

He headed over to Tammy's. He hadn't seen her in a couple of days, and wanted to pick up some of the stuff he'd left over there after their mushroom experience. Traffic was thick, but Tanner's mind was preoccupied. Like so many times before over the past several decades, he was imagining himself happy, fit, married to a babe, with zero money worries. Kids? Why not, but only if he would have begun fathering them in his late thirties. Job? A best-selling author, more like a *New York Times Best Selling Novelist* with books everywhere. At the bookstore, at the grocery store near the cards, at the airport bookstore, any library, as well as university bookstores and, of course, online at all the venues. *Okay, but I'm already sixty, so why do I imagine my life as if I am a younger man? Perhaps for my next life? Nice try.* Coming to that realization angered him for a second, and he thumped the dash hard with the bottom of his right fist. If only he'd had half the insight, then, while he was still young, that he had now.

Halfway over to Tammy's, Tanner purposely changed his mental station and focused on thinking about things that are more possible, than not, regarding his future. As he pulled in front of her house, there was a chopped motorcycle parked right in the middle of her driveway, forcing him to park on the street. He decided to enter through the side door of the garage; he wanted to throw a few things away, and he knew that Tammy kept the trashcan just inside the door. He opened the door, stepped inside the cluttered garage, threw his trash away, then continued into the kitchen. Once inside he didn't hear anything, so he figured they were likely out back on the patio.

Tanner got himself a cold water out of the fridge, then went through the great room and looked out towards the patio. He noticed some movement under the pergola, then he saw them. Tammy and her friend were both completely naked. Tammy was lying across the hammock under the pergola. Her friend was standing behind her. He gripped the hammock on either side of her body tightly, and instead of using his hips, he used his arms to minutely control the rhythm, cadence, and force by tugging repeatedly on the hammock. They both appeared to be in a deep state of ecstasy, and Tanner found himself fascinated by what he was witnessing, but he also felt intense frustration. Then jealousy sliced through him like a sharp meat cutter as he continued watching them. It irked him knowing he had just had sex with her less than two days prior, and her new friend wasn't even using a condom. *What? Does she still think it's the 1970s?*

Tanner left his bottle on the window sill, grabbed his backpack from the bedroom, and made his exit. He hit the highway and drove around, imagining the elements of his new self, and his new life, letting it play like a slide show in his mind. Driving became his form of meditation. He drove not caring where he ended up. He knew the Bay Area, he wouldn't get lost for too long.

He now knew that his new life didn't include Tammy, unless she would be willing to change and become an exclusive couple with him. Maybe then. Maybe. He'd always had a thing for her, but never figured out why or thought about it too much. Yes, they clicked a lot, but most of the time, she was too unfiltered and impulsive for his liking. Thinking about her more, he knew he didn't want *that kind of person* in his life anymore, if he ever really had. Sheila had many of Tammy's same qualities, and vice-versa. Tanner wanted a partner who moved a little slower, was a little more conservative, refined, careful, thoughtful, and mindful. He didn't want crass, careless, reckless, mindless, or aggressive. Then he thought, *Damn, I was pissed off after seeing Tammy getting it on with that other guy.*

He decided to grab some Chinese food then stream a couple of old Kung Fu movies while zoning out for the rest of the night. Tomorrow, he would take a trip over to San Francisco. He'd have some clam chowder at Fisherman's Wharf, then take a walk across the Golden Gate Bridge, something he hadn't done since taking Sheila across it back in the 1980s. It was something to look forward to.

Tanner sat and ate his General Tso's chicken and house fried rice while contemplating a loose improvement plan in his mind. Bruce Lee was kicking ass in *Enter The Dragon,* but Tanner barely noticed. He was too preoccupied imagining various ways of achieving his own goal to become more physically and mentally fit.

Saturday morning, Tanner got up and did pushups, sit ups, several stretching exercises, and used some small free weights to do some curls and overheads for his triceps. He made himself a bowl of Greek yogurt, with granola, blueberries, blackberries, and raspberries, and drizzled a little honey across the top for breakfast. After breakfast, he grabbed a light jacket, his keys, and the bag of vegetables and dip, fruit, and some mixed nuts, then got on Highway 680, south. When he got to the highway 24 interchange, he took 24 west to San Francisco. He remembered driving on it as a young man.

Today, right after exiting the Caldecott Tunnel, heading down the hill towards Berkeley and Oakland, Tanner was still at a high enough elevation that he could see right over the top of Oakland all the way out to San Francisco. The morning sun illuminated the eastern approach, making the city look stunning, and monolithic. The hard-edged skyline stabbed at the nearly sapphire blue sky surrounding the entire city like a well-fitting glove.

More than once in the past Tanner had felt coolness from outside fog slowly seep into his vehicle's cab while squinting to see while driving across the Oakland Bay Bridge to San Francisco. Fog that is legendary for leaving airline passengers stranded for half a day, forcing them to miss all of their connections. Today's early sun was a small miracle. It was a gorgeous, sunny day, and it was only nine thirty in the morning—an extremely rare morning event for that area. He got off the bridge at the Essex Street exit, and found his way over to the Embarcadero.

As a boy, he'd loved his parents driving him and his sisters along that stretch to see all the piers and ships pointing out towards San Francisco Bay. The majestic Golden Gate Bridge in the background and wind-driven white caps everywhere. Later, he enjoyed driving himself here when he was in high school, and as a young man. Now, here he was again, only this time much older, but still loving every second of it.

The area looked cleaner and more modernized than he remembered it being back when he was young; the constant smell of the salty Pacific Ocean remained front and center. He parked in the big lot, mainly for people who are taking the ferry over to Alcatraz Island, and walked towards the restaurants and Fisherman's Wharf. Once inside the covered complex, he bought some crab cocktail, a clam chowder with some crackers, and some coffee.

He found a seat on a bench and ate, watching several people carefully control their multi-colored, high-performance kites, making them dance around in the sky and other amazing acrobatics. He was sitting only a couple of miles away from the entrance to the Golden Gate Bridge which loomed large. He had walked across that bridge several times with classmates on field trips, and again on a visit in the mid-1980s. Now, as he sat alone looking at that mysterious, magical bridge, he was also able to see different parts of his past, reliving some of the experiences in his mind and feeling them again in his heart, remembering who he was then, and wondering what might lie ahead for him now. Somehow, he knew this time period was his last leg in life before really declining and dying. He also knew that if he could manage to carry on as well as he had been most of his life, he'd still have another couple of decades, maybe more.

Tanner finished his food, and began walking. He followed the sidewalk, and soon he was on the Golden Gate Bridge. Halfway across, he stopped to marvel at the sight before him: looking out at Alcatraz Island, Treasure Island, Angel Island, and countless sailboats, ferry boats, and speed boats—all doing their best to carve through the white caps. Tanner felt the warm sun on his face, and the cool Pacific Ocean breeze filtering through his hair, and continued to the other side. He marveled that anyone had ever jumped off this bridge, famous for its numerous suicides over the years. Two hundred twenty feet to the water was a really long time to wish you hadn't jumped off.

Looking out across the gorgeous water and surroundings, he started thinking about all the hungry people who came and ate tacos everyday at Es Picante, leaving with full tummies and smiles on their faces. He flashed on the many successful parties he'd been to over the years; they all involved full tummies. Sharing good food seemed to be one common denominator that results in people coming together to enjoy a shared meal or a party gathering and getting happy in the process. The whole idea around food and happiness struck him as an almost universal precept. Globally, millions of people gather to share food, and leave happier for doing so.

All the thinking around food left Tanner feeling hungry, and by the time he finally got back to Fisherman's Wharf, he was starving. He decided to double down and get the exact same thing that he'd eaten earlier, but this time he added a big hunk of buttered *Boudin's* sourdough bread, a local favorite. He ate on the same bench as earlier, and became mesmerized by the view of San Francisco Bay all over again.

Tanner felt grateful that he'd gotten a good night's sleep. He'd eaten light, and exercised a lot today. Walking just the bridge length is a two-mile round trip, not counting the long lead up to where the bridge actually leaves the ground, and rises up over the water. He figured he'd easily walked four, maybe five miles today. At 60, his legs—especially his knees, were feeling every inch of that walk, too.

Unfortunately, he still had a couple of miles to go before getting to the Alcatraz Ferry parking area where he left his car, so he got up, and slowly started heading back in that direction. Without any warning whatsoever, Tanner felt something hit the back of his head really hard. When it hit, he heard a loud, hollow, pop sound, followed by nearly deafening ringing in his ears in almost the same instant. He turned, just in time to see three guys in their twenties wearing hoodies. Two of them were white, the third was black. The black guy looked like he was pointing a pistol at Tanner, but under his sweatshirt. The taller white guy, with the gold hoop earring and a tattoo of a small lightening bolt over his left eyebrow gripped a little league bat. The shorter white guy was ultra white and his eyes were so black that, with his gray hoodie on, he looked a little like a blown-out lightbulb, or a mutant shark. The tall guy finally spoke with a raspy voice, "If you don't want another one of these to your head, you'll hand over your wallet, now." He held up the bat for emphasis.

Tanner was on the edge of passing out, and invisible to the public; they had backed him into an alley between two businesses.

Tanner was scared, but also very pissed off. "If you three presented yourself to me face on, eye-to-eye, I would have just handed it over to you. You might consider that before risking going to prison for life, or most of it, because one day you hit some poor schmuck a little too hard and kill him."

"Shut the fuck up and hand it over!"

Tanner took his wallet from his right rear pants pocket and handed it to the blown out lightbulb. Short guy quickly snatched it, and immediately began ripping into it. He took Tanner's three credit cards and his $66 in mixed bills and threw his wallet back at him. The wallet hit Tanner in the chest, before ricocheting onto the pavement and off to one side. Tanner stood still, not saying a word. The three of them took turns looking at one another for a minute, before tall guy suddenly thumped Tanner hard in his stomach with the little league bat, making him double over. Once he did, black guy snap-kicked Tanner, hooking his chin with his foot, causing him to become lifted straight up, and ejected backwards. Luckily, some of the boxes he'd fallen onto had prevented him from going directly down onto the pavement, likely saving him a fracture or two. Just as he began getting his bearings, he looked up and vaguely saw movement before a warm stream of liquid began hitting the side of his face. Before he could react, a second stream began hitting the other side of his face. Tanner tried hard to get up, but the boxes kept moving around, causing him to continue slipping, and tripping him when he tried to get up. The three thugs were laughing, having fun pissing on him. Before they left, they yanked Tanner's pants down to his ankles, and pulled his shirt up and over his head, locking his arms straight up, while covering his eyes.

Tanner finally heard them leave, laughing and talking as they walked away. He could feel the icy air coming off the Bay and every one of his movements to right himself, resulted in the semi-sharp-corners of the boxes he was lying on poking into him hard everywhere. Eventually, by moving his arms around as much as possible, he worked his shirt back down and freed them so he could pull his pants back up.

Tanner finally stood up and looked around. They'd forgotten his credit cards. They were lying off to the side, near where shorty had stood. A few feet away, farther back, and up against one side of the alley, lay his wallet. The whole incident left him extremely frazzled. He could hear his heart beating fast and hard in his head and ears, and the blood coursed through his veins at a life threatening pressure, giving him a potent headache. The worst thing, was the itchy feeling on his face and neck, caused by the strong, still drying urine they had hosed him down with.

Tanner got up, and brushed himself off. He put his wallet back together, and walked back to Fisherman's Wharf, going into the *Boudin's Sourdough Bakery* and using the mens room to wash up. Luckily, he was okay. Twenty-seven years in Massachusetts without being victimized once, even when going to Boston numerous times. Now, he'd already been mugged twice in less than a year. Recently, right outside his apartment in Concord, a forty-five minute drive from here, and now here in San Francisco down at the piers and Fisherman's Wharf area, a popular tourist destination. He already knew better than to not to bother with any police reports, they would just end up at the bottom of a pile containing hundreds more. *But isn't that feeding the problem while starving the solution?* he thought.

Tanner was finally ready to hit the road, but now he felt extremely paranoid. He hadn't been present, and he was caught off guard while his mind was preoccupied planning or daydreaming about his future. He felt sad. His otherwise perfect day was now tarnished by another violent, criminal act. At least he was able to drive home, still in one piece, instead of ending up at San Francisco Memorial Hospital barely alive, or at the coroner's office.

He was also sad that, just when his positive engine was beginning to fire on all cylinders for a change, some horrible, bad, life-threatening, incident had come along to try and ruin it. *Well, don't let it,* he thought.

Once he was finally on his way, he was glad to be on his way back to his apartment—that is, until he hit some traffic going up the hill towards the Caldecott Tunnel. Stop and go, stop and go. It drove him crazy—it always had, no matter where he experienced it. It struck him as so wasteful and counter productive. He tried to let his mind wander towards happier thoughts.

After finally getting through the tunnel, Tanner got off at the next exit in Orinda. He couldn't take driving while feeling so anxious and rattled any longer. The attack had completely shocked him and put him in a state of hyper-vigilance. His was body shaking from all the fearful thoughts that were keeping him adrenalized as he pulled into a parking space. He jumped out, slammed his door, locked it, and walked away. He walked away as if he were in a trance. Flashbacks of the warm piss hitting both sides of his face, hearing the evil laughter, and feeling deep humiliation and additional fear blinded him to all else. Then, flashbacks from his abusive childhood began intermixing with the images of what had just happened. He realized that he knew these feelings well and he'd been living more or less in a state of hyper-vigilism his entire life.

Feeling dizzy, he sat down on a picnic table that had been placed under an oak tree in front of a western attire store. He felt like such a loser. He gazed out at highway 24, and watched the other rats zipping by, racing to fulfill their agendas. Tanner was sick and tired of dreaming about what he wanted only to have some person, or some unexpected thing, come along and somehow prevent it from happening. *Things happen when you move in the direction you want to go,* he thought.

It was hard to understand because, most of the time, he kept focused on what he wanted, rather than on what he didn't want to have happen in his life. He was a firm believer that, whatever someone focuses on the most will eventually manifest into reality, so he tried hard to keep focused on what he wanted for himself, more often than not.

Tanner heard his mother's voice in his mind saying, *Life's not fair,* when he'd object to not getting something he wanted, but it had literally became a self-fulfilling prophecy for his life. *Goddamn right life isn't fair,* he thought.

Tanner got back on highway 24 east, and about fifteen minutes later, got off at the first Concord exit and headed straight to the Safeway grocery store. He bought some Pillsbury pop-n-fresh cinnamon buns, a six pack of microwave popcorn, two frozen pizzas, a two-liter bottle of ginger ale, another 2-liter bottle of Coca Cola, and two pints of Ben and Jerry's ice cream—*Chunky Monkey* and *Cherry Garcia*. Finally, he stopped off at The Sky's the Limit cannabis dispensary, and bought a quarter ounce of some Gorilla Glue. Nearly all indica, this strain was guaranteed to give him the four things he both wanted, and needed: the giggles, the munchies, arousal, then rock solid sleep.

As soon as he got back home, he put the pizza in the oven, poured himself a ginger ale, then fired up a big bowl of Gorilla Glue before turning on the television. Clint Eastwood in *High Plains Drifter* was coming on in a few minutes and Tanner couldn't wait.

12

CARMEN

Tanner always managed to straighten himself out in time for Monday mornings. He'd get up early enough to shower, give himself a close shave, eat a good breakfast, think about exercising, make excuses why he couldn't, and show up at Es Picante with a smile on his face, ready to go to work.

No matter how he felt, it had always been important to him to put on his best face for the world. It was something he'd learned over the years. Life runs more smoothly when the high road is taken, the best face is worn for the world to see, and your kindest, most understanding self is presented. If you smile, most other people will respond in kind. Like Mahatma Gandhi said, "You must be the change you wish to see in the world."

Carmen was no exception. She'd see him smiling at her, and would smile back every time, often with obvious curiosity. While chopping the lettuce, he looked over at her shredding the cheeses. She looked content and happy to be at work and busy. She felt him staring at her again. Without looking up, she smiled, "What? Why do you keep looking at me and smiling so much? Is there something I should know about?"

"No, not at all. I was just observing you while you work. You're usually so quiet, and stay busy constantly. Now that I've been working here a little while, I guess I am a little curious to know a little bit more about you, that's all."

"Why? I'm your boss, and I don't date the help, so more information about me won't get you anywhere."

Tanner looked surprised. "Whoa. I never said anything about dating. I am just a little curious about you, but never mind. I apologize."

Tanner kept chopping the lettuce in silence, not looking up at her anymore, but now feeling her gaze on him. Finally, she said, "What do you want to know?"

Tanner thought for a moment and without looking up said, "Are you married, and do you have any children?"

"Does it matter?"

"No."

"Then why ask?"

Tanner was silent for the next few minutes, not sure how to answer her counter questions. "Family matters have been a big issue in my life, and I've been doing a lot of thinking about marriage, family, and children, trying to figure a few things out. I guess because that's been in the forefront for me so much lately, that it came out effortlessly as a conversational starter, even though it's pretty personal."

Carmen looked up from her shredding, "Care to share? It's kind of your turn, I think."

"You haven't answered my questions yet, now you want me to keep talking?"

Carmen said, "Okay. No, you're right. I'm not married and I never have been and, no, I don't have any children, even though I still want some. Your turn."

Tanner played along now. "What do you want to know?"

Carmen smiled at him, then teasing said, "Are you married, and do you have any children?" She looked over at him again to see the impact.

Tanner smiled and chuckled, then said, "Fair enough. No longer married, no children, but always wanted them." He looked down in concentration to avoid Carmen seeing the hurt come across his face.

More silence except for the sound of chopping and shredding. Then Carmen said, "My parents came here looking for a better life. After the accident that killed my mother, my father and me, and his brother, Ernesto, managed to cobble a hard, but decent life here by opening two restaurants, my father opened this one. There is another one not too far from here, El Toltec, and they are what my grandparents entire life savings combined bought. Someday, I will inherit this place. After all, I'm my father's only child. Trouble is, it's not the only thing I want. Like I said, I want children, at least two. If not, who will I leave this place to?"

Tanner looked surprised. He could tell that Carmen was being serious and didn't really know what to say. "El Toltec? I had some food from there not too long ago. It was great. A friend knew about it and stopped there and we bought some to take home. I'd eat there again, for sure," he said smiling at her.

Carmen smiled back, "I'll tell my uncle the next time I see him. He'll like hearing that." He smiled back at her, again, then quickly finished chopping the lettuce and filling the prep bins to the hilt with the pieces. The more he could fit in the bin now, the fewer trips to refill it. He put the rest of the lettuce in the walk-in refrigerator, and grabbed the meat to get it ready for the grill.

Today, Diego was out running errands and it was Tanner's first day grilling the meats and putting the meals together for serving. He was confident, but a little nervous too. He put the meat bin on the counter next to the flat grill. He turned the gas on, and heard the flames ignite and begin to heat up the giant slab of stainless steel.

Once the grill was hot, he put on his gloves and using two large spoons, dug into the hamburger meat. He scooped it out onto the grill. Once it hit the hot grill, it began sizzling instantly. Tanner couldn't help but connect that sound to his feelings. Now that he and Carmen had been talking about children again, his anger about Sheila not wanting them brought it close to the surface again, and broke his heart every time he thought about it.

He looked up and watched Carmen make a couple of round trips to the dining room getting things ready for opening. He loved her hair, her shiny brown eyes, her beautiful smile, and her height. She was shorter than him, but not by very much and, for whatever reason, he liked that.

He really liked her peaceful, steady way, too. She never freaked out, or panicked, or got angry, even when customers got upset at her for having to wait for a to-go order, all while dealing with a full house of guests, and answering the telephone.

Today, everything went smoothly. No mistakes by him or Carmen. No upset customers. A nice steady flow of customers perfectly timed—some leaving, just as others were coming in— for about two hours. It was just right. Once the doors were locked, the money counted, and the kitchen cleaned, Tanner was ready to leave for the day.

As he was walking out Carmen said, "Tanner, nice work today. I felt like I had a veteran chef back there. You did really good. I couldn't believe it. Every time I came back with a new order, you had a previous one ready to go. They all looked really nice, and the portions would have made Diego smile. Thank you, and keep up the good work."

Tanner looked down at the floor for a second before raising his head and looking back at her. He could feel himself blushing. "Thank you, Carmen. That means a lot to me. I tried hard to ensure a smooth sail for both of us, and I'm glad it worked out that way."

Carmen stepped a little closer to him while they talked, and looked deeper into his eyes, "Me too. Hey, are you doing anything right now?"

Tanner hesitated, a little unsure of her intentions, "Ah, um, no, not really. Why?"

"I don't want you to think it's a date, because it's not, but I like talking with you. Would you like to come over and visit for a while?"

"Ah, sure. When?"

"Now."

Tanner felt his heart pounding in his head, and it was already starting to give him a headache. He looked at her smiling at him playfully, not sure what to say.

She looked away. "Okay, I get it. Not interested in being friends with me. That's okay."

Tanner reacted immediately, "No. I'm interested. Very interested, I mean, yes, I'd love to come over for a visit now. Thank you so much for inviting me."

Tanner followed Carmen to the house she shared with her father. It was a cute, three- bedroom L-shaped ranch, built in the 1960s on San Simeon Drive in Concord, only a few miles from the restaurant, and from Ygnacio Valley High school, where Tanner had graduated almost fifty years ago. After parking, he got out of his car, immediately noticing the impeccable landscaping in the front and side yards. "Nice landscaping. Did you and your father do all of this, too?"

"No, Diego's cousin comes once a week and keeps things mowed and trimmed up really nicely. You haven't met him yet. His family eats for free twice a week as payment. He has six children. I put together a bunch of food and take it over to them every week on Tuesday and Friday nights." They walked the rest of the way to the front door. Carmen unlocked it and stepped in, then held the door for him. "Welcome. Please make yourself at home. What would you like to drink? Before you answer, let me just tell you what I have. Water, both still and sparkling. Iced tea, coffee, beer, wine, and soft drinks."

Tanner didn't hesitate, "Coffee, please."

Carmen gave him a big smile, "Perfect. I was hoping you'd say that. I want the same thing. I need a little pick-me-up after being on my feet today." Tanner followed her through the small living room walking on plush wall-to-wall carpeting. The room was filled with quaint, overstuffed furnishings that were obviously rarely sat on, all carefully placed. There were a few nature pictures on the walls, and a large crucifix hung on the wall next to the kitchen doorway. The entire house had a faint but constant pine odor, and everything seemed to be in its place. They entered a small, brightly painted kitchen. Tanner sat down at the kitchen table and began watching Carmen set up the coffee pot.

He said, "I'm still getting used to standing for hours at a time again. I used to stand a lot before I got into stock investing full time, but I've been sitting a lot more for the last year or so, and now I've been paying the price. But, like I already said, I'm getting used to it again, and it's not necessarily a bad thing to stand a lot. It burns more calories, and keeps your core tighter than sitting does."

Carmen seemed a little surprised, "That's interesting. I didn't know that, and I hadn't really considered the calorie part. Gosh, if I'm this big standing all day, imagine how big I'd be if I sat all the time."

"You're not big."

She laughed, "I'm bigger than most women my height," she said with a huge smile.

Tanner said, "You're what's referred to as *a thick woman*, not big, or fat. It's just the way you're designed."

Carmen looked towards the coffee pot. It was gurgling and about half done. "Thick, fat, full-figured, call it different things, but most men don't like it. I get the vibe from them about it. They like talking to me, but it's never gotten serious in any way. Not that I'd want it to get serious with most, if not all of them."

Tanner agreed. "No surprise there. And, I hate to say this about my own gender, but it's what I believe: most men are idiots. Most don't know what they want until it's too late. Men who are only about looks when it comes to women are fools. I know I'd hate to be with a drop-dead, gorgeous woman who had no intellect or conversational skills. That would be my worst nightmare. If I had to choose between a model with no brain, home skills, or maternal instincts, against a woman with less than perfect looks, but who has a nice appearance, is smart, and conversational, and has home skills, I'd pick the latter every time. No question about it. Looks, for me, are only a very small thing. The huge thing, nearly the only thing, is how the person is. What they say. How they say it, and how they treat others. If she is strong, and positive, and wants to be healthy, that's the person I want in my universe, for sure."

He gave her a long look after that. She didn't avert her eyes whatsoever. "Wow. Are you for real?"

Tanner laughed and pinched himself, "Ouch. Yep, I'm for real."

Carmen stood up as the coffee finished up. She strolled over to the cabinet where she kept coffee mugs and pulled out two ten-ounce mugs. "Cream? Sugar?"

"No, thank you. I love the subtle flavors from different kinds of beans and roasts, which I can only taste when I drink coffee black."

Carmen nodded, "Exactly." She poured both mugs full of black coffee and returned to the table. "Can I get you a little something to eat?"

Tanner smiled. "No, I'm only a little hungry. But thank you for offering. Please just rest now, and let's visit."

"I have a cherry pie I made last weekend, and I was hoping my father and our cousins would eat most of it, but they didn't. I only eat sweets once in a while, so I have half a pie left."

"Well, if you put it to me like that, I'd love a big piece, please. That just happens to be my favorite kind of pie. That, and peach. I just love fruit pies." Tanner rubbed both hands together and licked his own lips in a gesture of appreciative anticipation.

"Cherry is my favorite pie too. I love pie more than cake or most any kind of dessert."

Tanner nodded, "Same with me." Carmen had just talked herself into a big piece too.

They ended up chatting for hours about everything while eating pie and drinking coffee. Tanner was impressed. Carmen had always worked extra hard to excel at every task she'd ever undertaken. She learned English quickly, and became the family interpreter. She earned straight A's in school, and had graduated with an AA degree in restaurant management from Diablo Valley College, which is where she learned about the bookkeeping side of restaurant ownership.

Her parents, seeking better lives, brought her to America illegally from Mexico. They worked under the radar as produce pickers. One day, her mother, Angelina, was riding in the back of the produce truck she and the other pickers had just finished filling up. A front end suspension failure caused the truck to veer off the road and overturn in a drainage ditch. Her mother was crushed by over a ton of watermelons and the weight of the truck. Carmen was only six years old when it happened. Apparently, Diego had crumbled, and started drinking heavily. She quickly had to learn to take care of herself. She thought she might end up homeless, or have to go with her aunt Mimi who had made her own crossing into the U.S. years earlier, and lived nearby. Luckily, Diego's brother, Ernesto, stepped up and began intervening. It worked, and her father managed to get sober. Ernesto, who owned another restaurant, got him started and Diego eventually bought him out to own Es Picante himself.

She grew quiet for a bit. Tanner wasn't sure how to respond, or whether he should respond at all. She continued, "If I left him to his own devices, he'd likely start drinking all over again, and put himself into an early grave. I'm not entirely okay with that, but it's my duty. That's how I see it. It's my culture and my heritage. We look after our family, especially our parents and siblings. But, between that obligation, and all that's involved in keeping the restaurant going, I don't have time to really enjoy life, go anywhere, or meet anyone to marry and have a family with." She chuckled a bit, "But, I'm very aware that my time to have children has been ticking all this time, and now it's almost midnight."

Tanner was deeply moved by Carmen's sense of duty to her family. No deep sadness and giving up, or bitter about how it might be impacting her chances to have a life of her own. She still wanted a family and wasn't giving up; She still had hope about achieving that.

"So, other than the restaurant being yours someday, and still wanting kids, is there anything else that you want to experience or accomplish in your life?"

Carmen looked right at Tanner, "Love. I want to know the joy and power of real love with another human being. Hopefully, with someone who will want to be a father and have a family with me."

Tanner felt stirred by her words. It was as if she were speaking directly to the unfulfilled part of him that had always wanted the same. He completely identified with what she was saying, and in that moment, even though he was old enough to be her father, he wanted more than anything on earth to be able to be that person for her.

Carmen sensed a change in him. "I'm sorry, did I say something to upset you?"

Tanner was surprised by her question. "No, not at all. It's just that I think it's sad—tragic even—how few people end up experiencing what they're looking for."

Carmen thought for a moment. "Have you known it?"

I should have known that was coming next.

"Yes, and no. I felt like I had arrived in heaven for the first five years of my former marriage. Then, she began to spend a lot more time at work. Then, well . . . long story short, she fooled me for a long time about not being able to conceive. The truth was, she didn't want kids. In the end, she traded me in for some rich guy.

I've been trying to make sense of how she could lie to me so well and so often. Now, I'm trying to regain my own sense of worth. Her exit made me feel like I was a defective human being for a time." He smiled at her, adding sarcastically, "Since then, I've been validated enough by others to know that, indeed, I'm just fine."

"You never had the kids you wanted."

"No, and I spent thousands of dollars on fertility doctors for ten long years of my prime adult life. Waiting. Wanting. Hoping. I'm mostly past it and no longer bitter or angry. I've almost entirely let it all go. It's over, and I'm okay. But, I resent having to go back to work again. She took just enough of my retirement fund to make that my new reality."

Carmen nodded. "You've been through a lot in recent times. Now, it's time for healing and a new life." She held up her coffee mug, "I propose a toast, To Tanner and his new path. May he finally know peace and find true love."

Tanner smiled and looked at Carmen with gratitude written all over his face. "Cheers!" They tapped their mugs together, leaving their eyes locked, never blinking. As that continued, he felt his heart begin racing, while the butterflies in his stomach frantically searched for the exit. *What is happening here? She is too young for you. Don't ruin this with any advances or improper suggestions.* He finally forced himself to begin getting up, "Carmen, can you please point me to the restroom?"

"Through that door, down the hall, second door on the left," she said pointing to the doorway to the hall.

"Thanks." Tanner quickly found the bathroom, locking the door behind himself to ensure no one would be able to easily walk in. His mind was racing, and he was having trouble processing how much he and Carmen wanted the same thing, and how tragic it was that he was too old for her. He tried to calm down. He relieved himself before returning to the kitchen, but once there, Carmen was nowhere to be found. "Carmen?" Tanner called out.

"I'll be there in a minute," she shouted from one of the bedrooms.

"No need to hurry. I'm going now, Carmen. I'll see you tomorrow. Thank you so much for your hospitality, and for the nice conversation. I really enjoyed it."

Out of the corner of his eye he saw a flash of movement. It was Carmen. She had popped her head out from the bedroom near the end of the dim hallway. "I enjoyed it too, Tanner. Thanks for coming over. We'll have to do it again soon. I'm changing as fast as I can, if you want wait a minute."

"I'd love that, I mean, I'd like that very much, getting together again. I'm going to go for now though. I'll see you tomorrow."

Carmen waved from down the hallway, "Bye, Tanner. See you tomorrow."

All the way home, Tanner couldn't stop thinking about Carmen. He really liked her a lot. He thought she was a beautiful younger woman, and kept trying to figure out how the universe would decide to suddenly be bringing a seemingly perfect woman to him now, in a cruel twist of fate now that it's too late and he's too old.

Sure, he was aware that some older men marry younger women. Some women prefer older men. But she was his boss, and one of the owners. The other owner was her father, and Tanner had a hunch that Diego would never stand for it.

Nevertheless, Carmen remained in Tanner's mind nearly non-stop, even hours later while brushing his teeth before bed, and he was shocked by his attraction to her. Knowing what she wanted almost perfectly matched his former desire to have a happy family, but now that he was older, he wasn't so sure. He'd slowed down quite a bit, despite being relatively fit. But, a child or two children? Two children wanting to play all the time, screaming at the top of their lungs with excitement, needing mommy and daddy's attention ninety percent of the time? He knew in his heart that the answer was still a big yes.

Tanner hadn't been thinking about marriage, or kids, or anything like that at all. He was still recovering from his painful divorce, and readjusting to life in California. He decided to work at *not thinking of it as a real possibility*, and to see it for what it really was, just a passing fantasy, posing as a possibility.

He thought of Tammy. The two of them had always gotten along and managed to find things to do together that were fun. He'd missed her a lot over the years, and now that he'd reconnected with her, he didn't want to just snub any possibilities of a relationship with her, perhaps even a long-term one. He wondered how it would be living with Tammy day in and day out. He wasn't sure why, but he had the strangest feeling that they might only be compatible as friends, and for short-term experiences. He feared that any more time spent together than that would likely result in them arguing all the time, leaving one or both of them living in misery.

Tanner smoked a big bowl of indica, and finally managed to slow his mind down enough to be able to fall asleep. He lay back in bed staring at the darkness. He closed his eyes and imagined Carmen with a little boy and a little girl. He pictured them moving in slow motion, smiling and giggling, blowing fuzzy dandelions, backlit by glorious sunlight. He could see Carmen's features, and his own in both of their faces, and felt his heart soar knowing that they were his and Carmen's beautiful children. He joined them and saw himself put his arms around the three of them, hugging them all tightly. They all closed their eyes in a silent prayer of gratitude, for the beautiful day, for having each other to love, for all the gifts they enjoyed together as a family.

13

COMPETITION COMES FOR LUNCH

The next morning, Tanner woke up feeling remarkably rested and optimistic. He vaguely remembered the beginning of a dream about being in a family with Carmen, which by now had faded enough that he wondered if he'd even had the dream at all. After relaxing with Carmen, he felt like work would be more comfortable and that made him happy.

Today, he arrived fifteen minutes early. Carmen had arrived a just a few minutes before, but Diego was still out. "Ola, Carmen."

Carmen smiled at him, "Ola, Tanner."

"Thanks again for having me over last night. I really enjoyed myself."

"Me too." She winked at him and added, "We'll do it again, soon. I promise."

Tanner smiled back at her. "I can't wait." He walked to the refrigerator and began getting all the produce out for the daily chopping and prepping. Carmen put on some unusual Mexican rock music that Tanner found himself moving to while he chopped.

"Who is that?" he asked.

"Aliento Ardiente."

"What does that translate to?"

"Burning Breath."

Tanner heard the back door slam hard, and turned just in time to see Diego walking in. He was already shouting a bunch of stuff in Spanish that Tanner didn't understand. Tanner noticed Carmen take a really deep breath, slowly let it out, then walk over to the boom box and turn off the music.

Tanner glared at Diego, "Ah, why did you have to go and do that? I was just getting into it."

Diego shrugged without saying a word, then began quickly looking around as if trying to find something he'd misplaced. All of a sudden, he turned around and, without making eye contact with either of them, quickly walked into his office, slamming the door behind him.

Tanner looked over at Carmen who was busy shredding cheeses. He could tell she was really annoyed that her father had shown up acting like such a sour puss first thing in the morning. After a few minutes went by, she stopped shredding and put the cheeses together in a large bin near the food prep part of the kitchen.

She washed and dried her hands, then went into the office, quietly closing the door behind her. Tanner couldn't hear a thing —for a moment. Then, like a train leaving the station, their voices grew loud enough to be heard a fair distance into the kitchen. Eventually, their shouting grew so loud it was now really disturbing. Tanner thought, by their tone, that they were both giving each other ultimatums and he was beginning to get worried for both of them. Diego had a temper, and Carmen was his daughter. He might think he still has a right to hit her. Diego might also have a cardiac arrest at any moment.

Tanner couldn't believe the ferocity of his shouting. He couldn't fathom how Carmen could stand being that close to someone so loud, and obviously unhinged. Then, sudden silence. Thirty seconds later, Carmen emerged, walking fast to nowhere, shaking her head in disgust. Diego slammed his office door behind her. Tanner knew better than to say a word to either of them.

About 10:30 a.m., a half-hour before opening, Diego came out of his office cussing in Spanish, and left just as abruptly as he'd arrived, averting his eyes from Tanner as he walked past him grumbling. *Well, I guess he's not going to stick around to give us a hand today,* Tanner thought.

Carmen didn't waste any time deciding that Tanner should be the prep chef, again. She would take the orders, drop them off to him, and pick up any completed plates ready to be served to hungry customers. "Go ahead and finish setting up the tables, I'll get the food ready to go for you back here, then we'll change places," she said with a smile. Tanner smiled back at her. It was a welcome break from the negative vibe that Diego brought with him that day.

Tanner went back out to the dining room and began setting the tables. He saw a movement and looked up to see Sophie in the front window. She smiled at him, then pointed to the door knob. Tanner shook his head no to her, pointing to his watch. She insisted, doing a little stomp with her right foot, making her eyes bulge out and pursing her lips tight, almost commanding him to let her in by pointing at the door knob again, but this time with more intensity.

Reluctantly, he let her in, while nervously looking around. For now, Carmen was still in the kitchen, but she wouldn't be for long. Sophie looked like she was either going or coming from a wedding. She wore a dazzling, short-sleeved, off-white dress embroidered with sequins, with matching off-white gloves. For the final touch, she wore a beautiful light pink pearl necklace, and matching light pink pearl stud earrings. Her outfit went together perfectly, while contrasting flawlessly with her red hair, and blue eyes.

As soon as she stepped into the restaurant she smiled at him, and said, "Hi, I was in the area and thought I'd stop in and say hello."

"Hi. Thanks. That was really nice of you but, unfortunately, I really can't talk right now, I'm trying to finish getting ready for opening in half an hour, and I still have quite a bit to do. I don't want to push you back out, but I really can't talk."

Carmen, hearing their voices had quietly come out of the kitchen to investigate. She was still wearing her apron and had been chopping onions for almost twenty minutes straight. She had onion tears streaming down her cheeks on both sides, and she looked intense. "What are you doing?" she said.

Tanner looked over at her, "I'm getting things ready for our opening."

Sophie jumped in. "Hi. I'm Sophie. I was asking Tanner if I could just come in and sit until opening. I promise I won't ask for anything or interfere. I really didn't think about how busy you probably were. I was just in the area and thought of Tanner, so I thought I'd stop in and say hello. I'll just get a menu and have a seat. Please just pretend I'm invisible."

Oh yeah, pretend you're invisible. Right. Not only will everyone will see you. Everyone will have a really hard time taking their eyes off of you, Tanner thought.

Carmen stood still. Tanner could see her wheels turning, never taking her eyes off of Sophie. "Is she a friend of yours, Tanner?" She said as if Sophie wasn't standing there.

"Ah, well . . . yes. She's a friend."

Carmen came closer, stopping about ten feet from them and looked directly at Sophie, "You can sit and wait for us to open if you're planning to order lunch. Otherwise, you'll need to leave and contact Tanner during his off time. It's only the two of us, and we're opening very soon and need to be ready. Now, if you'll excuse me, I have food prepping to finish."

Before Carmen could turn away to leave, Tanner hastily said, "Sophie, this is Carmen, she is co-owner of this restaurant."

Carmen looked annoyed. She immediately shifted her intense gaze at Tanner and, before Sophie could say a word, Carmen said, "Nice to meet you, Sophie." Then turned around and headed back into the kitchen.

Sophie smiled while loudly whispering, "Wow, not very friendly to customers now, are we?"

Tanner shot her a dirty look, "She's under a lot of pressure right now about a lot of things. She's doing great, considering." He filled a glass with iced water for Sophie. Then, without a word continued setting the tables, making sure to put a few flowers in the vases at each one. He tried to focus, and managed to work with intention fairly well, but he could feel Sophie's eyes on him the entire time he worked. He looked over at her briefly. Of course, she was right there, and her eyes met his instantly, but she managed to beat him to the punch with a smile.

Tanner went back into the kitchen. He glanced at the big clock on the wall over the exit. 10:51 a.m. Tanner made a final check on the meats, beans, and rice. Everything was hot and ready to be served up. Carmen kept avoiding looking at him. He watched her for a few seconds, and saw her clenching her jaw, her muscles flexing in her cheeks, almost like she was chewing.

Not being able to stand it, she finally said, "That's a good-looking friend you have out there. Where did you meet her?"

"I stopped in at Penny's Roadside Cafe not too long ago. She's a part-time server there."

Carmen kept busy arranging things, and putting things away that had just come out of the dishwasher, but Tanner could tell she was listening with both ears.

"Well, somehow you must've made a really good impression. Why else would she come looking for you? She certainly doesn't look like a server or someone who would do that type of work."

"She came in with Realtor Steve Caldwell not too long ago, and saw that I worked here, that's how she knew I'd likely be here today. She wasn't looking for me, per se, just knew that I was working and thought she'd come in for a bite and say hi. No big deal."

Carmen, trying to act like nothing was bothering her said, "I can clearly see that. No mixed signals whatsoever."

"Carmen, if I were a woman, you wouldn't think much about her being my friend, so can you extend that acceptance to include me?"

"Sure. No issues. It's not my business, until it comes into the restaurant and becomes my business."

"Yes, ma'am. But, just so I'm clear. Are you saying I'm not supposed to tell any of the friends that I make to come here to eat when I'm working?"

Carmen stopped working for a second, and looked right at him, "No, of course not. I trust you to be professional and put your priorities in their proper place. That means work before pleasure when I'm paying you to work."

"Understood. I'll go open up now. Yes?" Carmen nodded.

"Please just stay back here and get ready to prepare the orders that I bring you."

Tanner was glad that he had an excuse to not have to go out to the dining room and get distracted again. He couldn't really understand Sophie's attraction to him. *She is so beautiful, why would she want me when she could have almost anyone? Am I just imagining her obvious attraction to me?* Tanner put on his chef's apron and got behind the grill and prep area.

Carmen went out front, unlocked the door, and put the, *Yes! We're Open!* sign in the window. When she'd entered the dining room, no one was at the front door yet, and Sophie was gone. She was glad. She went over to where Sophie had sat, and collected her water glass. Thinking about Sophie again, Carmen felt a mix of anger and curiosity pass through her. It was so strong, it took her totally by surprise. She was shocked at how jealous she felt, and how inadequate she imagined herself as compared to Sophie.

Carmen knew that on the looks front, she could never compete with Sophie. As she walked back into the kitchen to grab some more menus that she'd left there, she felt a little like she was floating. She was worried and anxious, and didn't know why. Tanner was a nice man, and a good worker. He'd seen a lot in his life, and recently suffered a lot of heartache. She felt bad for him. He seemed sharp, and even somewhat good-looking to her.

She knew she was his employer, but after spending time together last night, she felt she had also made a new friendship, one that she already valued, and hoped would continue. She was always so darned busy managing the restaurant, and managing Diego. She rarely got out, never had dates, or enough off-time to make friends. She really had fun with Tanner last night, just sitting and talking about random things they thought to talk about, and she'd actually felt herself genuinely relax for a change. It was a pleasant surprise, and one that she hoped she'd have again.

She definitely didn't need that beauty queen coming around here, chasing after the only man she felt she could really talk to and share things with. After seeing Sophie, Carmen couldn't understand what she might want with Tanner, not that he was hard to look at either, but she looked like she could get almost any man she wanted, so why Tanner? Why not Steve Caldwell?

She went back into the kitchen and got the menus she needed. She was so busy in thought, she didn't even notice Tanner before returning to the dining room to greet the first customers of the day.

14

STORIES, EXCUSES, CONFESSIONS

Thursday night, Tanner came home completely exhausted. He'd been constantly busy at work the entire week. For whatever reason, Diego was gone most of the time now. When he was there, he was quiet and contemplative. He would sometimes leave without saying a word to Tanner or Carmen; they would discover his absence and have to start doing double and triple-time to make up for his part. Tanner knew better than to ask Carmen anything about it. He might have if Diego wasn't her father. He could sense that something was definitely wrong. Not sure what, if anything, he should be doing about it, he decided to leave it alone.

He showered, then heated some leftovers in the microwave for dinner. He smoked a bowl of indica before setting his alarm, looking forward to feeling his heavy head hitting the soft pillow. He got up, grabbed the remote, and clicked off the television. He grabbed his plate, still sporting the remnants of his two-corn-dogs-with-mustard-and-pinto-beans-with-ketchup dinner, and put them into the sink. He was almost into the bathroom, when there was a loud knock on the door, only a couple of feet from him. Tanner stopped moving. His heart, now racing, mainly because he wasn't expecting anyone and the knock startled him. Luckily, he was still dressed.

Note to self, talk to the manager about getting a peep hole installed sometime soon.

Tanner listened intently, but didn't hear anything. "Who is it?" He asked with authority.

"Oh, you are home. Let me in, guy, it's Tammy."

Tanner opened the door. Tammy stood there smiling at him. He'd missed her, but lately, whenever he thought of her, he would flash on seeing her with motorcycle man, doing the deed on her hammock out back. Yes, it was kind of erotic, but he was *having unprotected sex* with her, and she had let him. "Hey, Tammy. Come on in. But, I can't really hang out right now, I was just getting ready to brush my teeth and call it an early night."

Tammy looked at her watch, then looked back up at him, "Wow, I guess you're calling it an early night. It's only 7 p.m. Why are you so tired?"

Tanner didn't really want to make small talk with her right now. He was somewhat stoned, and exhausted. "Can we do this another time? I'm fried, Tammy."

"Sure thing, Tan man. I just wondered what happened to you, and why you suddenly cut me off. I've called you three times, and texted you numerous times each day, but they're all being ignored. Why?"

Tanner looked at her, "Still having fun with motorcycle man from last week?"

Tammy looked shocked. "How'd you know about that?"

"I stopped by to get my things that I'd left behind from spending the night with you. I came in through the garage to

172

throw my drink bottle away, and then went in through the kitchen. I called your name out, but you didn't answer. I went to the sliding glass door, and that's when I saw you with him. I felt jealous, and I felt angry that you let someone have unprotected sex with you after you gave me such a hard time about wearing protection. After that, I left angry. I've been hanging out with my boss, Carmen, some, and just staying to myself."

"Tanner, no one ever said we were going to be exclusive. I apologize for not insisting that my lover of the moment wear a sleeve, but it's not the end of the world."

"It might be the end of my world if you end up with something. Not only could I end up with it too, but even if I didn't, I wouldn't be able to bear living my new life without you in it."

Tammy blushed a little. "Aw, Tanner, that's so sweet. I love when you talk to me cooingly."

"Well, Tammy, it's true. You know, now I'm waking up a bit. Let me take your coat and then come and sit with me. I'll pack us a bowl."

"Are you sure? I don't want to interfere with what you need to do for yourself, like getting some extra sleep."

Tanner smiled, "No, I'm good now. Come on in." He took Tammy's coat and hung it up in his tiny hallway closet, and had her go into the living room while he fumbled with getting his bowl and weed together."

Tammy looked at him seriously, "Carmen? Who's Carmen?"

"My boss at Es Picante Mexican cuisine, just down the street in the little strip mall. Hey, what would you like to drink? Can I can get you some tea or coffee or something?"

Tammy looked a little surprised, then smiled and said, "So, what's up with that? Are you guys sleeping together too?"

"Give me a little credit, will you? No, I'm not sleeping with my boss. That would be complicated, for sure. My other boss, and hers too, . . . sort of, is her father, Diego, although I'm not sure how much longer he'll be around."

Tammy pretended to not hear the part about Diego. "What's she look like? Is she pretty? I'll bet she's a stone-cold fox. You always did have a hunter's eye for them, even if you never really did that much with your instincts."

Tanner contemplated her comments. "Yes, she is pretty, in a wholesome, mother-Earth kind of way. She is all natural. No dyes, perfumes, or additives for Carmen. She works hard, is a woman of few words, has a happy disposition and a kind heart. She's made her whole life the restaurant. She wants financial security, and is willing to work hard for it, but . . ."

Tammy looked interested and confused. "But what?"

"I don't think I should say anything more. It's personal, and you two have never met."

"Oh, come on, Tanner. Tell me. What? You really think I'd go over there and say something to her or tell anyone about any of her business? Give me a little credit."

Tanner thought about it, then said, "She and I have something in common, but her dream is still possible, mine isn't."

Tammy sat up and looked straight ahead. She took the pipe Tanner handed her and drew hard on it, holding the smoke in for a few seconds before slowly letting it out, and finishing with a cough. She looked over at Tanner and smiled. "This is good weed."

Tanner nodded in agreement. "You see, we both very much want a family. A spouse, a couple of kids, happy marriage. That's what we have in common. She's still young enough, but she needs to find a way to go out dating."

"Well, there are lots of different dating sites and apps to put on your phone, you know."

"Yeah, I know. And, if I know at sixty, then she'd know in her thirties. I like her a lot. She's kind and fair. I wish her well, but I'm worried for her. I don't want her to suffer my fate. Putting it off just long enough to miss the boat entirely. I mean, she's got a biological time clock. She can't wait forever, and nothing happens just thinking about things. You have to implement and move towards something you want by moving away from the dreaming and finally start the doing. She's doing fine on the money front, but terrible on the personal front."

Tammy looked down at the ugly carpet for a second, "Poor lady. In my case, I didn't want to be tied down for the longest time. Once I did tie the knot, I grew into a new me that I didn't even know existed before then. Since Rodney's passing, I've had a lot of time to think about our relationship, and I really think that, over time, we would probably have gone ahead with having children too. That would have left me with a living piece of him. Someone, or more than one person alive that has his DNA, and, through them, a way to still catch glimpses of Rodney, like a certain look they would give me, or the way they might laugh. I wish, now, that I'd gone ahead with that sooner, rather than thinking that we had all the time in the world."

Tanner said, "To be honest, it's a little more than coincidental, and quite a bit frustrating to me that, after all these years of wanting children and trying with the wrong person, I meet someone, out of the blue, who I get along with, admire in many ways already, and after only one evening spent visiting with her for several hours, feel like I know that she would make an outstanding mother and wife. But, she's my boss, and she's young enough to be my daughter."

Tammy was attentive but, judging by the look on her face, Tanner could see that she was a bit alarmed by what she was hearing.

"You're in love with her, Tanner."

Tanner's eyes grew wide. He looked at Tammy and said, "No, I'm not. I can't be. I'm only feeling these things because of how long I've wanted a family, and here is an opportunity right in front of me, but I can't do anything except get over myself. It's just not going to happen because I won't let it. It wouldn't be right to go down that road, then die when the kid is still young, and leave Carmen a widow."

Tammy said, "Well, I'm glad to see that you're trying to think all of this through. Points for that, but it seems to me that you're deeply affected by these new circumstances, even though you've come to the conclusion that none of it is a real possibility. Am I right?"

"Yes. Yes, you're right."

"And, thus my conclusion about your feelings for Carmen."

Tanner shook his head no. "Tammy, I haven't known her long enough to love her. I barely know her at all."

"Doesn't matter. You feel what you feel."

"True, but what strikes me about this whole thing is that having a family is something I'd given up on entirely. A big part of me still wants to just move forward and get over the fact that I missed the boat and become more realistic. Then this comes along, popping up out of nowhere. It's like the universe is trying to tell me that I may still have a chance at that dream, even at my age." He looked at Tammy with confusion and wonder in his eyes.

Tammy smiled at him, then got up and went over to him, and knelt down in front of him, forcing her body between his legs, and turning her head to the side, finally wrapping her arms around his torso and hugging him tightly. "You'll figure it all out, my friend. No worries. Let it all go for now."

Tanner felt Tammy's warm embrace, and he could feel her love penetrate him to the core. He closed his eyes in response, and let it seep into his heart, and his bones. After several minutes of their silent embrace, Tanner gently pulled back from her. "Hey, you remember me telling you about my trips over to Muir woods?"

"Yes."

"What do you say we take a day trip together this coming Saturday. I'd love to show it to you."

Tammy's eyes lit up bright, "Sure. I'd love to. That sounds fun. Hey, we missed you last week for the jump. How about coming over to my place after work this Friday, and I'll drive us out so we can keep the tradition going."

"Sounds great, Tammy. I will admit, I thought about you guys last week and missed going with you."

"Then that makes two dates." She paused, thinking. "We can grab a steak after the jump, go back to my place afterwards, and we can leave from my place on Saturday to go to the woods."

Tanner loved it. "Actually, that's three dates, if you count what happens when we get back to your place," he said with a wide smile.

Tammy tickled his sides and got up to leave. Tanner rose to see her out. They looked into each other's eyes, and Tanner said, "Thank you, Tammy."

"For what?"

"For this. For coming over. I feel so much better, and now I have something to look forward to for the rest of this week."

Tammy reached up and pulled his mouth to hers. She kissed him passionately, probing his mouth with her tongue. "Thanks for having me. When you didn't answer me, I was concerned. I wanted and needed to know that we're okay. I'll be home and ready to go when you get to my place on Friday."

"I'm looking forward to our time together." Tanner leaned down and kissed her again, this time taking the lead and exploring her mouth and lips ever so slowly and gently.

"Should I stay?" She whispered.

"No, not tonight. I'm too tired, but I promise I'll be ready to go on Friday."

"Fair enough."

Tanner closed the door quietly behind her and finally went to brush his teeth, feeling closer to Tammy than he'd ever felt before.

15

REVELATIONS

The next day, Tanner showed up at Es Picante sporting an ear-to-ear smile and a Skydive Byron T-shirt. Carmen took notice almost immediately.

"Ola Tanner. Que Pasa?

"Ola, Carmen. Nada. Todo bien." Tanner smiled and went to put his apron on. When he returned, he laid everything out on the counter, and began his chopping and dicing with focus. Carmen glanced over at him every minute or so. Finally, not being able to stand it, she asked, "Where did you get that T-shirt?"

Tanner looked down at what he had put on, then looked up at her, "At Skydive Byron, in Byron. You know, Byron, California, not too far from here?"

"Do you actually skydive or have you?"

Tanner nodded, "Yeah, almost every Friday I go up with a few friends. I love it, especially going at dusk or sunset."

Carmen seemed surprised, even a little stunned. She stopped grating her cheese, "How high up do you go?"

"Usually a couple of miles, but lately nearly three miles so we can all float for a bit longer."

Carmen gasped, "Float? Aren't you falling?"

Tanner chuckled a little. He stopped trying to chop and dice while explaining skydiving to Carmen. He was afraid he'd slice the tip of one of his fingers off. "Yes, falling at about 120 miles per hour, but there is so much wind buffeting against your body at that speed, that it offsets the feeling of falling, supplanting it with a sensation of floating. You just have to keep glancing at the distance to the ground, confirming your actual distance by looking at your altimeter in order to make sure that you pull your ripcord and deploy your primary chute at 5,000 feet. That way, if it doesn't deploy for any reason, it still gives you enough time to realize that it didn't and enough time to pull your reserve chute ripcord. It's too bad that only one, singular possibility is what keeps most folks watching, forever thinking about going, but never actually doing it. They let the fear of what *might happen,* stop them from going and being able to enjoy the experience."

Carmen almost cut him off, "And, count me in that crowd. The one that never goes, because I know myself well enough to know that I never will. I can only imagine doing that, but I could never actually do it. I could not get out of the plane and let go with only a chute and a prayer." She chuckled a little. "Heck, going up on a ladder to fetch my neighbor's frisbee is about as far up from the earth as I ever want to be. I can't stand heights. Two, three miles up, then just letting go and falling? *NOOO. NEVER.*"

Tanner thought about what Carmen said for a moment. "That's exactly what I said once-upon-a-time, thirty years ago in Massachusetts. Then, I watched a sports special on television about skydiving where these guys went all over the world and documented all different kinds of skydiving. From traditional and simple static-line jumps, to free falling, and even becoming part of a large formation of skydivers—they showed video of all different variations of skydiving. Next, they moved on to the newer types: jumping off of the world's highest buildings, peaks, and cliffs, using flying squirrel suits, or wing suits as they're called. They showed a jumper leaving the top of the tallest building in the world. This guy free jumped Dubai's Burj Khalifa, which is almost 2,800 feet tall. Then they showed cliff jumpers, again using wing suits, this time in tandem with parachutes for softer landings. After leaving a tall peak in the Swiss Alps, they would fly all the way down to the town below, then deploy a small, high-performance chute to allow the jumper to steer themselves to a nice, soft, stand-up landing."

Carmen was all ears listening to Tanner talk about skydiving. "At the end of that show, I knew that I had to overcome my personal fears about it, and experience it for myself. And, I knew that if I didn't, I would regret it for the rest of my days. I looked at it as a growth experience, and it sure became one. It's taught me about my own strengths, and made me less fearful about almost everything."

"That's amazing, Tanner. I had no idea, and I would never have imagined you doing something like that. You just strike me, at times, as a non-extreme person. No, that's not it. Um, you seem to me to be strong, but also a very mellow, thoughtful, and kind person. Not that people who skydive aren't those things. I'm having trouble expressing myself about this, and I'm not sure why." Tanner listened attentively, wanting Carmen to speak her truth. "Okay, here goes again. Simpler this time. You simply don't strike me as someone who would jump out of an airplane. That's it. I don't know how I got that impression, but I stand corrected."

Tanner laughed, "No worries, Carmen. I get it. Well, now you've learned something about me that you didn't know before."

Carmen smiled while nodding, "Indeed. I have. Apparently, you have nerves of steel when necessary. That's good to know." She was shredding away, and seemed to be deep in thought, but Tanner noticed that she had a faint smile on her face.

Tanner played it up a bit now, "That's right. Nerves of steel, gumption beyond belief. Able to chop four heads of lettuce, dice up a dozen tomatoes, twenty onions, and two dozen green chiles in thirty minutes flat. Un-aided by anything except a couple of chef's knives and a big chopping area. That's right, folks. Bring it. I'll out-chop you, and you, and you over there," he said, pointing to Carmen while giggling.

Carmen laughed and shook her head, "Oh my gosh. You're crazy, *and* silly, Tanner."

"Why not come over to my place tonight and I'll show you just how silly I can be?" He waited a second for effect, then looked over at Carmen. She was looking at him with a surprised and curious look on her face. Tanner, speaking through his laughter said, "Nah, just kidding. I can show you some video clips of some of my past jumps."

"Sounds great, and I wish I could, but I can't. Not tonight. I have to drive Diego to a church meeting in Walnut Creek. He's a deacon at Sacred Heart Catholic, but he can't see well enough at night to safely drive himself."

Tanner didn't even hesitate, "Then how about Thursday night? If you care to, and are free, that is." Tanner saw Carmen blush. Tanner had noticed that when she was embarrassed, her normally light brown cheeks filled in ever so slightly with a pinkish hue, while she tried to control herself, and act like nothing was up.

Carmen looked over at him, "Thursday sounds great. I'd love to see those videos, and any pictures you might also have lying around of you, when you were younger. That would be fun." She looked at him, searching for any sign of apprehension in his face. But, there was none.

"Sure. I have quite a few pictures of me in the past. So, it's a date." He said it with a finality even he wasn't expecting. He didn't look up right away.

Carmen said, "Cool. I'll bring some easy dinner things. Not any hispanic food. How about some extra crispy chicken tenders with dry-rubbed spices, some sweet potato fries, and sweet'n hot baked beans?"

Tanner was already salivating as she verbally listed the food she was planning to bring. "I absolutely LOVE sweet and hot baked beans. I haven't had those in years. I always forget to buy them. That sounds perfect. I'll pick up a deep dish apple pie and some vanilla ice cream for dessert."

"Oh my gosh. I can't believe it. I was thinking the exact same thing," Carmen said. "I love that combo."

"Me, too."

The rest of that week flew by, and the two of them worked wonderfully together as a team, even with Diego's sporadic appearances, which were completely counter-productive. Tanner and Carmen would get in a groove, and figure out a smooth way to get everything done during lunch, then he would show up out of nowhere, wanting to do what he always did—man the grill and meal prep table—something Tanner had grown used to doing. That, in turn, would cause Tanner and Carmen to have to suddenly reconfigure how they did things, on the fly, and things would be forgotten.

Sometimes, he'd come in acting like the old boss again. He'd bark out orders here and there, to both of them, but they'd both learned to just take it with a grain of salt, keep their mouths shut and their heads down, and answer deferentially with either a *yessir* or *yes, chef* whenever he got like that. Tanner quickly learned that nodding and saying *right away* was his best response. It minimized the potential for further drama, making Diego's tantrums as short as possible. In the end, Diego would just walk away shaking his head, mumbling in Spanish.

That Thursday, Tanner and Carmen hardly said anything to one another, mainly because they were so busy. They both knew that they'd have time to relax and talk at Tanner's later that evening, but still smiled at one another every chance they got. Once everything was cleaned and put away, and the door locked, Tanner said, "See you at six?"

"Sounds perfect. I'll bring the sweet and hot," she said, giving him a wink.

"Ice cream and apple pie are waiting to be conjoined with your hot and sweet," he said winking back at her.

Tanner went right home and did a final check around the apartment. He was glad that he'd already done a deep cleaning the day before. After ensuring that everything was the best that it could ever be, he put on some Bon Jovi, and waited for Carmen.

Carmen knocked precisely at six. When Tanner opened the door, he couldn't believe his eyes; she looked amazing, and seemed really happy and animated. Tanner took half the bags from her and set them on the counter in the kitchen. He knew Carmen was nervous. When he turned to say something, somehow she was right there, only an inch remained between them. They locked eyes. Tanner felt her positive energy rapidly combining with his.

She reached up and wrapped her arms around his neck, then slowly and gently pulled his mouth to hers, delicately kissing him. Tanner let it happen without any protest. Her lips felt extra soft and plump. He loved the way they cushioned his mouth. He felt her body heat and felt himself responding. He felt both exhilarated and repulsed at the same time. Somehow, as much as he felt flattered that she wanted him and seemed to enjoy him, he still felt weird about their age difference. He hadn't thought it would be a big deal. In fact, for a brief time, he'd been aroused by her youth. However, she was twenty years younger, and young enough to be his daughter. That, somehow, seemed more sobering to him contrasted against any excitement or desire he felt borne out of her flattery.

He gently pulled back, not saying a word and smiled at her. "Thank you, Carmen. That was really nice." She smiled back at him. Tanner could tell by her look that she enjoyed their embrace as much as he had. He turned away from her so she wouldn't be able to spot his physical response to what just happened. Once he finished his about-face, he opened his refrigerator, "What can I get you? Wine, beer, fizzy water?" He stood back again, and turned and looked at her. "Hot tea," he said, snapping his fingers and pointing at her.

"That would be perfect. Thank you." She looked as relieved as he felt. While he opened the cabinet where he kept his teas, Carmen looked around at his tiny kitchen, then went over to the opening leading to the living room.

Tanner glanced over at her, "Tiny, right?"

"Indeed."

"Well, it's what I can afford around here right now. But, it's really all I need. A small place to have simple meals, relax a little, and lay my head down when I'm tired. Besides, I've got wanderlust and I'm hardly ever home. I'm either at work, at a friend's, or cruising around looking for new and fun places to visit. It's the single person disease. Well, for most of us singles it is."

Carmen looked a little perplexed by Tanner's somewhat abstract analogies, but got the gist. She nodded, "I understand completely. Although, for me, I've slowed that down quite a bit. Mainly because I'm at work so many hours of my day, that once off, it's time for rest for a couple of hours before sleep, and then getting up and doing it all over again. It's not much of a life, but it's my life right now, and it feels like it has been for too long, if you ask me."

The tea pot signaled that the water was at the ideal temperature for white tea. "White, green, oolong, gun powder, or black?" Tanner asked.

"Um, black sounds great. I always have green. Wait, it's not Earl Grey, is it? I hate that bergamot they add to it."

"No, it's not. I have Irish breakfast tea. You'll get a very energizing boost from it. My personal favorite any time I feel like I need a lift. For me, it works better than coffee for a lift."

"I'll try that. It sounds great. Do you do straight tea, or add milk and/or sugar to it?" she asked.

"I love the natural flavors of all the different teas, so I never put anything in mine."

Carmen seemed pleased. "Me, neither."

Tanner tapped the button on the tea pot that said, BLACK (Boiling). "It'll only be a few minutes now. It's already warm enough for white." He started getting plates and mugs out of the overhead cabinet. He handed them off to Carmen, who took them over to the dining room table. Tanner followed behind her with silverware.

Once again, they just seemed to click. This time Tanner really noticed it, about midway through them getting dinner ready. They would both go into motion, each one taking care of one or more things, while the other seemed to intuitively know what other things to tend to, all without saying a word. Somehow, at times, they could silently communicate with one another so seamlessly, that they didn't even realize that they were doing it. Tanner had never known silent communication the way that he and Carmen could convey things to one another. He'd noticed it at work a few times before and then it became obvious.

"I know, right? I don't know how we do it either. But I've noticed it more than once now too."

Tanner's eyes bulged out of their sockets for a second. "What? How did you know what I was . . ."

"I don't know." Carmen said matter-of-factly. "It's both disturbing and fascinating. It's like we be—"

"—Belong—" Tanner added,

"—Together." Carmen finished.

They hugged, and then kissed passionately again. Both of them noting how good it felt, but not sure which thoughts were safe to think in the presence of the other. It was both thrilling and scary at the same time. At times, Tanner felt a little overwhelmed, and felt like he was no longer in control of his own destiny anymore. He couldn't *truthfully* deny his feelings for Carmen, any more than he could *truthfully* deny the age difference between them. It was almost as if he had put so much intense energy into *willing the future* he'd always wanted, that he'd finally succeeded in getting the universe to sit up and pay attention.

Lately, he'd noticed himself getting a lot of attention from different women, and he wasn't sure how or why that was happening. He knew he would never marry again, and that was a non-negotiable item in his own mind ahead of having inevitable encounters with women, and having women friends. He knew his most asked-for wish, of wanting to have a happy family, needed to start with the right mate, despite his advanced age for any type of new family beginnings.

"Tanner. Tanner, did you hear me?" Carmen had her hand on his arm and looked concerned.

Tanner had heard Carmen's voice, but it had sounded like she was still a mile away in the woods. Slowly, her voice grew louder, until he realized she was talking to him. "Oh, gosh, I'm sorry, Carmen. I was thinking about how things have been going lately, and just sort of zoned out. I'm really sorry. I apologize."

"Are you okay?"

"Yes. I'm fine." He smiled at her and began putting food on his plate. The spiced tenders looked amazing. "Where did you get them?" he asked.

"Over at Popeye's."

"Oh, yeah. I always forget to think of that place when I'm trying to think of what type of fast food to get, I don't know why. Maybe because when I lived here, there weren't any. The only places I've seen them were down in the south, and the mid-Atlantic. Later, they came to New England."

They ate and made small talk at the little table. Tanner felt light and free inside. He loved Carmen's company. She was so pleasant away from work, one-on-one. After they'd had their fill, and several cups of tea, Tanner stood up and stretched. Then, with the best British accent he could manage, he said, "Would her ladyship care to adjourn to the living room for continued festivities?" He shifted his arms in a formal way towards the living room to indicate the direction, then offered his elbow to her ladyship.

Carmen seemed more than pleased, and played along, "Why, thank you kindly, sir," she said as she stood and took Tanner-the-butler's hand, letting him formally guide her into his most comfortable chair in the room.

Carmen said, "Okay, I'm really wanting to see some pictures of you when you were younger. You're pretty darned handsome, in a boyish sort of way, so I'm betting you were a real cutie pie when you were in your twenties." Carmen laughed at herself. She looked playfully at Tanner. He chuckled too.

"Cutie-pie. Ha! Well, it just so happens that I spent a little time last night going through my box of pictures looking for the best ones for you to see. The ones with me in them, and not the old us, my former wife and I."

"Sheila? I think I remember you mentioning her name to me once before."

"Yes. Anyway, here they are." Tanner handed her the photo envelope. Carmen opened it up carefully and took out a small stack of pictures.

"I took the liberty of putting them in order: youngest to oldest. I don't have too many of me as a kid, but right there, that picture on top, is me in my cub scout uniform when I was six years old. I have a toddler picture, but I couldn't find it. It's here somewhere though.

"Wow. It's you, I can see you . . . you . . . look like a mini-you. I like you in a uniform."

"Thanks."

"Oh, how old are you in this one?" she said, fishing another one out of the box.

Tanner leaned in closer to look at the picture. "Twelve."

"Wow. I can see the difference and how you thinned out moving into your teen years." He was standing next to his old newspaper delivery bicycle, the one his step-father had taken apart, painted, greased, and put back together—even installing chrome fenders on it to protect both him and the newspapers from rain water splashing up off the tires, along with a heavy duty rack for mounting the saddle-style canvas delivery bag onto.

Carmen seemed to thoroughly enjoy looking at his pictures—hearing the stories about how old he was for each one, and what was going on during that time. Her favorite one was a picture that a friend of his had taken of him shaving when he was in his early twenties. The friend stood in the doorway, then zoomed in on Tanner's naked upper torso and face. He was pretty fit and slender at the time, and had the darkest tan of his life. The sun had bleached his strawberry blond hair nearly blond, and Carmen thought he looked *hunky as hell*. Tanner blushed when she said that.

He excused himself to use the restroom. When he returned, he looked through a small pile of videos and picked one out to start with. He showed her clips of his static-line jumps, and told her the story of how ultimately unfulfilling they were, but how they'd led him to begin free falling. She saw him being taught, while falling 120 mile per hour, by two jump masters signaling him to get certain parts of his body positioned better. She saw his first on-his-butt landing, and his first soft, professional-looking, stand-up landing and his total exhilaration afterwards. She listened to him with utter fascination as he talked with lots of animation, description, and theatrics. His excitement was obvious. After showing her the clips he had, and sharing the stories that went along with them, he felt really energized, "Talking about this always makes me want to go again."

Carmen smiled. After looking deep into his eyes, she already knew that. His eyes told her everything she needed to know about his feelings around skydiving. She took a deep breath, then let it out slowly. "I'm impressed. I would never be able to do that, but I can sure see the appeal, definitely. I can also see, from how it affects you, why you continue doing it."

Tanner said, "If you came along, you could observe from the landing area. You'd be able to see us exit the plane. We'd be tiny, but binoculars are a great equalizer."

"I think I'd like that a lot, but please don't ever try to convince me to go up with you, then act all indignant when I won't do it. I'm telling you right now, I will never skydive; for me, it isn't worth taking that risk, nor is it something I think I would enjoy. I think it would be more akin to something that I would be enduring while doing, and feeling lucky afterwards to have survived it, while wishing I hadn't done it."

Tanner heard her seriousness and said, "Understood."

Carmen stayed serious. "Tanner, I'm sorry, but I don't have this kind of alone time with you at work, and I need to change the subject if that's okay?"

"I'm all ears," he said.

Carmen continued, "I know you've noticed how my father has been lately, and I'm very worried about him. He's just not himself. He acts like he's in his own little world lately, and he's always either mad as hell, or worried sick, but he won't share what it's about with me at all."

Tanner paused. He thought about the weapons he saw in Diego's trunk, and the Mexican motorcycle gang members showing up to buy them. "Is your father in any kind of trouble? Does he owe someone money, perhaps?"

"He might. He likes to bet on the horses over at *Golden Gate Fields*. I don't know. He doesn't tell me anything. He has mentioned to me that he's really wanting to get the food truck started up, but he needed a little more time. I'm betting that he's been moonlighting, selling things on the side to pay for it."

"I'm looking forward to giving that a go. I'm just not certain that we can do both with only three of us. I think we'll need to hire another person, at least for a little while."

"Probably. Let's not talk shop tonight. Not here at your place while we're off. She looked at her watch. Shoot, I had no idea it was already ten. My 5 a.m. alarm will be waking me up before I'm ready if I don't get to bed soon." She rose to leave. Tanner stood and smiled at her.

"Thank you for coming tonight. I had a really fun time."

Carmen smiled, "Yes, I enjoyed it too. I've really learned a lot about you in the last few days, and you're really starting to grow on me, mister." She leaned in for a kiss, but Tanner, not wanting to get carried away with that again, pretended to not have noticed before turning around and walking towards the door. Once at the door he began to open it a little as he turned to look at Carmen.

She had a concerned look on her face, but Tanner wasn't going to ask her about it. He hoped she had, perhaps, figured out that he was having mixed feelings about being intimate with someone so much younger than himself, and he also suspected that she wasn't sure what her own intentions were. He'd noticed that she seemed to have picked up on his quiet desperation around not having children while being married all those years, and saw an opportunity to, perhaps, fulfill her own need and desire to become a mother. Perhaps, with him involved. He wasn't sure if that was the case or not, but right now he wanted to think before making any grievous errors, or do anything that would disrupt his already tenuous financial situation.

"Good night, Carmen. Thank you for coming over. It was fun showing you my jump video clips."

"Yes, it was. Thank you, Tanner." Tanner leaned in and gave her a gentle, but firm kiss on her lips, without escalating or using his tongue. She met his gentleness with her own, then pulled back and looked at him one more time. "See you in the morning."

"See you, Carmen."

When Tanner opened the door the rest of the way, he almost stumbled backwards; Sophie was standing at point blank range directly in front of him.

"I was just getting ready to knock." She said with a big smile. She was wearing a tight, mauve skirt, with an off-white, low-cut blouse, and two gold necklaces, with impeccable make-up and hair. In short, she looked fantastic, like she was ready to go out on the town.

16

UNEXPECTED VISITOR

Between the surprise of Sophie showing up unexpectedly, the timing of her sudden appearance, her stunning outfit, and the awkwardness of these two coming face to face, again, jolted him. Instantly, his heart jumped ship, escaping to his head to safely pound away there, even though he'd done nothing wrong. "Uh, hello, Sophie. What are you doing here, and how did you know where to find me?" Tanner tried to act normal, but he was shocked and wondered what was going on.

"I saw your information on Steve's desk. He'd written down some preliminary information that you'd given him, like your name and address so he could get set up for you when you came in, but then you changed your mind."

Carmen said, "Excuse me, I was just leaving." She pushed past Tanner, and Sophie stepped aside to let her out. Tanner noticed her tight, pursed lips, and the death stare she gave Sophie."

He watched her leave. Once outside, she kept walking towards the parking lot without looking back, picking up her pace as she went. Tanner felt bad, but he didn't know any of this was going to happen. He felt a surge of anger. He looked at Sophie, "How about calling first?"

"Why haven't you called me?" She snapped right back.

"What? Why would you think that I would be calling you at all? It's not like we're a thing."

She looked hurt by that. Tanner didn't care. She tugged on his man genes; just looking at her was an enticement in real time, but he didn't trust her. Something about her always seemed to be fake, or plastic—deceptive. Yep, that was it. He didn't trust her because he sensed that she always had an ulterior motive for doing everything, while keeping her cards close to her chest. That secretiveness was what Tanner despised. It reminded him of Sheila. There was no way he was getting involved with this woman. Maybe not even as a friend. He knew that his life would somehow be ruined if he spent any serious time with her.

"Uh, because you said you would call me after we had dinner at my place but, so far, you've reneged on our deal."

Not wanting the neighbors to overhear what they were saying or be disturbed, Tanner finally said, "Come in. We should finish our discussion inside, but you can't stay. I was just getting ready to hit the sack. Tomorrow comes early."

Sophie immediately did her best by pleading with her eyes *why won't you just loosen up and entertain me. I only want to be entertained. Please?* Once inside, Tanner showed her into the living room. She turned around and faced him and was just about to say something, when Tanner let her have it.

"Sophie, what the hell do you want with me, anyway? Really? I'm a relatively healthy sixty-year-old, and I need viagra to keep it going. I'm broke, and I'm fairly broken inside too. Why the hell do you keep bugging me about calling you, and seeing you? I don't get it. Look around. Look at this place. Is this what you want? A guy that managed to work his ass off his whole life only to end up here, in this god-forsaken shit-hole of an apartment. This misery-magnet of a nest that I find myself living in again. You're just the opposite. You have the looks to attract damn near anyone out there, including that jock strap, Steve Caldwell. Why do you care to bother with me at all?"

Sophie threw her purse into a chair and abruptly sat down. She pulled out a cigarette and lit it, then exhaled long and slow. "You mind?" she asked.

"Go for it." Tanner said, before getting his bowl and packing it with some weed. Afterwards, he sat on the opposite end of the couch. He fired on the bowl, took a huge hit, and set it down on the coffee table without offering her any. Somehow, he had figured out that Sophie wasn't a partaker of cannabis; she was more of an alcohol lady. Then, before he could blink, Sophie snatched the pipe, taking her own big hit, then exhaled while smiling wide at him and with no cough at all. Not being able to resist her beauty, Tanner smiled back at her. He really did like her, and found her attractive beyond belief, but something about her made him wary, something he sensed, but couldn't put his finger on or figure out.

Sophie looked like an attorney ready to convince the jury of her client's innocence. "Why? I'll tell you why. It's because I know you're a good man. A decent man. Someone with morals and a few decent values, other than making lots of money." Tanner was all ears. "You know, I sometimes wish I wasn't a pretty girl at all. It's not as fun or as exciting as people think. I have to constantly be on guard, and on the lookout for people who would kidnap me, rape me, or kill me, or all three. Always looking over my shoulder. Always vigilant when someone wants to pick me up and take me somewhere, about the possibility of being taken somewhere to be drugged and made into someone's sex slave. I have to ask myself, do they really like *me*, or do they just want a pretty face and a set of tits to be seen with? Am I your trophy girl, and for how long? Do you really care about me, or do you just want to have sex with me?"

"I can see how that might be a real issue for you. You are gorgeous, and I'll admit, your next-level appearance makes me more cautious than normal."

"See?"

"What?"

"Well, I know you're not going to believe this, but good looks equal loneliness." Tanner gave her a skeptical look through another cough. She continued, "Yeah, I know that sounds crazy, but it's true. Good looks help you become more popular initially, but extremely good- looking people are the loneliest on the planet. They are the outliers, the extremes on the looks spectrum. Everyone either doesn't trust them, or they don't feel that their own looks are good enough to be able to hang out with that person, or date them. Whatever the reasons, they don't feel worthy enough to go for what they really want—the good-looking person. They've already concluded that the person they're interested in is simply out of their league. So, the hot girl, the super good-looking dashing guy, or the woman who looks like a playboy model, often ends up eating alone, watching movies alone, traveling alone, and ending up childless. Then there is burnout from being used by others—for sexual gratification, for being someone's trophy for a night, a prop for some man's ego."

Tanner locked eyes with her. He could see her eyes were swollen, heavy with a full load of unreleased tears, as she fought to hold back from crying. The longer she spoke about the hazards of being born beautiful—which she had no more control over than someone born with a horrible facial disfigurement—the more Tanner connected with her, while recognizing his own sensitivity around matters of the heart. He could see her humanity behind those perfect, plump lips, stunning diamond blue eyes, and her long, wavy red hair flowing down over her right shoulder. She was scared a lot, and more vulnerable than he had imagined. She was still innocent about so many things.

"I gave you my best shot when you had dinner with me that night a while back. You held. You are the only one who has ever done that, and you made it look kind of easy. I haven't stopped thinking about you and remembering how polite, yet firm, and in control you were about being honorable. That is so rare these days, it's like finding a flawless diamond lying in the gutter while taking a walk. You are what I've been looking for and have been unable to find ever since high school, Tanner."

Tanner offered, "I understand better now. I felt like you were kind of stalking me. Now, I get it. I was only doing what I thought was right, and I had an early day the next day, and we'd just met. I will say this, too: you might want to rethink leading with so much personal, somewhat explicit information when you first meet someone. I wasn't sure how to take that. I was more than a little weirded out by your candor, even though I appreciated you trusting me with it."

Sophie exhaled loudly, then stubbed out her cigarette in the big stone ashtray that Tanner kept on the coffee table. She looked at him with a neutral expression. "Can we start fresh, then?"

"What do you have in mind?"

"How about a regular date?"

Tanner thought about Tammy, then how just a short while ago Carmen had been sitting in the same chair watching him sky-dive on his television screen. He saw Carmen's smiling face, and how her eyes seemed to light up whenever he entered the room or walked towards her. It was obvious how she was beginning to feel, and he'd begun to realize that soon he would need to be making some serious choices, otherwise he'd risk losing his friendship with Tammy, his newly made friendship with Sophie, and his friendship with Carmen—maybe even his job at Es Picante.

He smiled, "I'll call you to set it up. Fair enough?"

"That sounds good, Tanner. Thank you. I don't care that you're older than me. For the record, I'll just go ahead and get it out of the way now, I'm fifty and I can't bear children. I want you to know that I've been thinking that, while parenting may have been important to you before, now that you're a little older you've realized that you likely won't be a father. You're not looking for a wife as mommy partner anymore. No, this time, a more serious, monogamous companion-mate would be perfect. Am I right?"

Tanner looked away, a million things racing through his mind, "I don't know what I want right now, other than stability and peace. Let's just try and become friends, first, and see where that takes us."

"Agreed. Call me then," she commanded. She rose, and came towards him, and he could see that she was looking forward to another make out session. He managed to dodge to the side, then give her a short kiss on her right cheek, before quickly turning away and heading towards the front door.

"Can I get your number?" he asked as he started opening the door for her. Sophie fished inside her purse and handed him her card. "Here you go. I'm really looking forward to hearing from you. It's simple. I have a good feeling when I get around you, and I want to feel that way more often. Sorry. I'm selfish." She smiled, then kissed his cheek and walked out. As she walked away, she periodically looked over her shoulder waving and smiling at him. Tanner finally closed the door to block the foul odor that began coming in the minute he opened it to say goodnight to Sophie. He went to the front window and looked outside. That's when he saw the big truck near the corner. Three men. One directed traffic around the truck, the other stood watch over the man in the hole who was using the vacuum hose to suck out stench-filled, built up muck in the bottom.

He started to shut the curtain, and stopped, doing a double take while looking towards the parking lot. He saw Sophie standing next to a car talking with someone. She looked tall next to the car. She looked to be smiling, but serious. Tanner couldn't make out the person in the car. He decided to let it go and head to bed. Maybe someone she knows from the diner? He started to close the curtain again, but noticed that Sophie was now looking and pointing towards his apartment periodically, while also appearing to become more agitated. Tanner watched her point at the sky, then stomp her foot to emphasize some point she was trying to make. Now he was curious.

Against his better judgement, he got out his spot light he used to use in Massachusetts when taking his dogs out for their last pee-pee before bedtime. He turned it on while aiming it at the sky, then rapidly lowered it down, intentionally moving it to mimic the motion of car headlights, but letting it stop for a split-second on the face of the person in the car. Yep, it was Carmen.

What are they arguing about? He thought. This is exactly why I made up my mind on the way out here to do everything that I could to prevent myself from getting caught up new bullshit with another woman. Look at the two of them. I know for a fact that under different circumstances, they'd get along stupendously. How'd this even happen?

When the light passed over them, they both looked around a little confused, but Tanner was quick to point it at his kitchen floor and turn it off. He peeked out of the bottom of his curtain, in the dark. He wanted to make sure they left things civil. He didn't want to have to break up a fight, or call the police or anything like that.

He wasn't sure what to expect now that he'd seen Carmen and Sophie arguing, but figured he was likely in for a little crap about it at work tomorrow. He hoped Carmen would rethink everything in the morning and just let it all go.

17

THE FUN CONTINUES

Tanner was already awake when his alarm went off. It had taken him at least two hours before he finally drifted off into a restless sleep last night. He'd been ruminating yet again about his earlier life and what went wrong. He thought about his role in the divorce. Could he have been far too focused on his own need to be a father, while also not being sensitive enough around her need to pursue a career, and that's what ultimately drove her away?

Probably. But, don't forget, she also shared with you that she just didn't feel like a mommy. She didn't have maternal instincts or a maternal desire to have a baby. Especially while also having to depend on another person to take care of the financial end. Unfortunately, for a woman, the prime time for career building is also the prime time to have children.

He thought of Tammy and how much he enjoyed being around her and how happy he felt in her company, but it was always unfocused humor and kidding around with her, she was never very serious about anything. In fact, it was almost as if she were simply uncomfortable talking to him, or anyone for that matter, at least about any serious stuff.

He was starting to see that he enjoyed her more as a buddy, rather than a romantic partner. Someone to hang out with, party with, explore with, have sex with, travel with, skydive with. Not marry, not commit, and not to have children with. He was beginning to realize that his love for Tammy was for one human to another, not romantic love. He loved her, and would do almost anything for her, but he wasn't sure if he'd ever be able to live with her. He liked having her in his life, but noticed that his feelings towards her peaked when he hadn't seen her in a few days or a week. Then they would always begin to slowly deteriorate once they'd been together for more than two days straight.

When things got tense between them, Tanner would make haste, retreating back to his own apartment (*Good thing he'd kept it*). They would stay apart for a short while, then the civility would return. It oscillated like that, and the oscillation was consistent, and chronic. Tammy was great, as a pal, buddy, or friend, but not someone Tanner would want to be married to. Now, he knew he would never ask her to marry him, and the real answer had always been never. He now felt foolish, having spent so many years trying to make things work right with Sheila, while at the same time fantasizing about being with Tammy, and beating himself up about it. It was an amazing and valuable revelation. He was surprised by how much lighter he felt inside, now that he was liberated from pretending that someday he and Tammy might actually tie the knot.

Since it was still early, he got up and shuffled into the kitchen to make coffee, eggs, and some toast. He was vaguely aware of how much of the night he'd spent thinking about, and processing, memories around wants, desires, fantasies, and regrets, not only about Sheila, and Tammy, but also around Sophie's reappearance, and her disclosure about her feelings for him, and her emotional pain and issues with *beauty loneliness.*

He sat still, eating his eggs in silence. Off in the distance, he could hear the highway roaring in pain from the weight of thousands of cars going to work. Tanner wanted simplicity and peace more than anything. He was tired of complexity. Now, the minute things become complex, he headed in the exact opposite direction as fast as possible.

When he walked into work, the radio was on. Not loud, but on. It was a welcome distraction. He couldn't read Carmen's mood, but he didn't want to try and figure it out either. She made a little small talk with him, but much less than usual. He wondered what truth or lie Sophie might have told Carmen last night. He finally decided to let it go. He wasn't prepared to get into anything with her, and anything they shared was none of his business. He kept working and minimized his conversation with Carmen. Diego was in the back today, whistling.

Hearing Carmen suddenly speak, startled him; he'd been deep in his own thoughts. "Diego didn't come home last night. I woke up this morning and saw that his bed wasn't slept in. I went downstairs to see if he was on the couch, but he wasn't there. Just when I was about to call the police, I saw a car pull up. He was in the passenger seat. He leans over, kisses the woman driving him, and then comes inside, whistling the entire way. He said her name is Rosita. Can you believe that?"

Tanner smiled. "Believe what? That her name is Rosita?" Without waiting for an answer, he said, "So, you think he—"

Carmen started to giggle, "—Yes, I do." She started laughing, then it became almost uncontrollable, something Tanner had never seen with her before. Tanner started laughing too. Diego heard them all the way in the kitchen, and came out to see what was going on. His serious look made them laugh even harder.

He looked at Tanner and with a smile and a friendly tone said, "You, señor, in my office, please." Tanner complied. Once in the office, Diego looked directly at him and said with a serious tone, "Are your intentions with my daughter honorable?"

"What intentions? We're just new friends."

Diego shook his head. "I know how it goes. First it's jokes and laughs, then it's dinner and candles. Next is soft music and wine or cocktails, followed by sex. Then come the kids. Am I not right?"

"Yes, and no."

"Explain it to me, then."

"Yes, that all can be true, but the sex may, or may not happen. Some people don't drink, I'm one of them, and I hate candles. The scented ones tickle my nose constantly, and I get fatigued from sneezing all of the time. I no longer drink, so that would not be offered. Sex is something I no longer take lightly or participate in like it's some kind of recreational activity—although, I wish it were that simple. Finally, I'm too old for her, too old to be a full-time father, and I do not date or have sex with the people I work with."

"That's too bad. I was hoping that you might be on track toward becoming my son-in-law and the future co-owner of this restaurant."

"What? What do you mean?"

"Carmen has told me she adores you and doesn't care that you're older. I do, but if my little girl's heart is with you, then I will not stop her, or you from pursuing happiness in any manner you deem necessary. I like that you've learned a lot in a short time. You show up on time everyday. You work hard without complaining. You're great with the customers, and you seem to be just as talented at making my Carmen happy; I don't think I've seen her smile as much as she has been lately in a decade or more. She wants a family. I want her to have one. She has told me of your long history of wanting one, but never having one for yourself. Mr. Dalton, I can tell—"

"—Tanner, sir. Please."

"I can tell you, Mr. Tanner, that I respect you, and if you want, or think you want, to have a family, then Carmen is waiting for you. She will welcome you with open arms into our family, and I will too, and so will our extended family. *La Familia es muy importante. No?*"

"Yes, about as important as it gets, sir."

"I never said to you any of this, señor. Si?"

"Si."

Tanner nodded at Diego and smiled, "Thank you, sir. I appreciate your consent very much." When he stood, Diego put his hand out. Tanner shook his hand with a firm grip, but not too firm. He nodded and turned to leave, feeling Diego's eyes on his backside all the way to the door. He felt self-conscious and wondered when the roller-coaster ride would finally end, but he already knew the answer to that. It would end when he made up his mind about what he wanted, and what he was going to do about what he wanted. In other words, it would end when he ended it.

Tanner had been stunned by what Diego said. He was green-lighting his relationship with Carmen, telling him to take his daughter as his wife and have a family with her. Tanner had not thought of that as a possibility, but now found himself feeling somewhat intrigued, and very honored.

18

WEEKEND WITH TAMMY?

Tanner went for a jump after work just as they'd planned. He showed up at her place ready for another weekend of skydiving, good food, and good sex. Well, at least that's what the norm had been up to now. But, unbeknownst to Tammy, or Sophie, or Carmen, Tanner had decided that he wasn't going to have sex with anyone right now. He wanted to spend time with his new friends, and get to know all of them without sex. Besides, since coming to the conclusion that he and Tammy would never be more than buddies, his desire for her, or his thoughts about making love with her had gone from red hot to barely luke-warm. The sex was always amazing, and he knew this would be a hard plank to walk, but he was determined to let things quiet down a bit, hopefully revealing even more useful things about his new friends.

Today, Tanner noticed for the first time how Doug always seemed to have a real *arms wide* policy with Tammy. Whenever they went skydiving, Doug was always the eager beaver offering her a hand, helping her pack her chute, but not with Tanner or Stanley. *Maybe that's the way I should go. Encourage Doug. Encourage them. Maybe drop it to him that Tammy wishes he'd make a move or some-thing along those lines, then get out of their way. I want Tammy to be happy.*

Today, they all had fun. Even Stanley, their usual pilot, jumped today. Stan's friend, and fellow pilot, Christian, piloted the plane. Christian was looking to gain some additional experience, specific to small skydiving groups, and also wanted to be able to log some hours.

As they ascended into the sky, the visible death of the day, the last sliver of multi-colored light lying across the horizon, sank fast. The vast darkness and stars above seemed to mercilessly press downward, squeezing and forcing the light to the other side of the planet for a much needed half-day break.

They exited at 28,000 feet, almost three times higher than a normal free fall height, or 5.3 miles up. Once they were all in a circle, they took turns crossing the circle to the other side. After only a few seconds, they became pretty well synchronized, with each of them taking a turn. When one person would start across to the other side, the person directly across from them would also go. They started high-fiving each other as they crossed paths in the middle. It was fun to start and stop, turn one way, then another, all while falling at terminal velocity against a nearly dark sky. Over time, Tanner really began enjoying these jump experiences. For him, they provided the internal reset that he sometimes needed by the end of a long week.

It was silent for the most part on the way back to Tammy's after the jump. At some point, Tanner looked over at her. "Tammy, have you ever thought about having Doug as a partner for sex or a permanent partner?"

"What the hell, Tanner. What do you mean by that? Have I ever had sex with Doug? Is that maybe what you want to know?"

She sounded pissed off already. "No, that's not what I meant, and if you have, it's not my business. What I do mean, I guess, is have you ever thought about being romantic with Doug? Or, have you felt interested? I only ask because I see how he is around you. He seems to be kind to us, but extra kind to you, if you get my drift."

"No, not really. Why would you ask me such a thing? Are you worried or jealous or something?"

"No, not at all."

"Then what the hell is it? You've never asked me about anyone in our group before. Why now? I don't get it."

Tanner wasn't sure how to reply, but he knew that honesty, while capable of being brutal, often clears things up nicely once everyone knows how everyone else feels. He had seen many times how, once the air is cleared with the honest truth, things can be better put where they really need to be. "I ask you because I want you to be happy. That's all."

"Happy? I'm as happy now as I've ever been. Especially now that you and I have reconnected and have developed a sort of understanding or, I guess the beginnings of a relationship of a more serious nature. Right?"

"Well, I guess I'm just going to have to come out and say it."

"What? What are you going to say to me? You better be careful if you still want a chance in hell of still having a fun weekend with me."

"Tammy, it's just that, well, I've thought a lot about you, and us, and our past, and . . ."

"And? And, what? You've decided you're really gay at age sixty, and you don't know how to tell me? I don't like where this is going at all. Just say it, Tanner."

"Fine. I think we should just stay friends. Permanently. Friends that hang out, skydive, smoke weed, go to the movies, take a trip to San Francisco to see a show or have a fine dining experience, but not sex pals or marriage partners or friends with benefits. There. That's it. I said it. I said what I believe is my truth about us."

Tammy was stunned. She kept driving normally, but she didn't say a word. She didn't cuss either, and she didn't pick a fight or argue. At one point, when they passed under a street light, Tanner thought he spotted a tear on her cheek. After he looked away, he saw her quickly wipe it away while watching her out of the corner of his eye.

"That's a damn shame, Tanner. I was actually considering changing my mind about the whole, I'll-never-get-married-again routine, because I feel myself beginning to fall in love with you. Real love, for you, for the first time in my life. Now that I'm there, you're not. Fucking great."

"I'm sorry, Tammy. But you've seen how we get after a couple of days being together non-stop. I truly believe we'd need

God's help and some kind of an intervention if we were ever to do something as foolish, as say, take a road trip across the country and back, together. I have a feeling that only one of us would return, and you know it's true."

The rest of the trip was quiet. Tammy was obviously plotting how she could murder him without getting caught, and various ways to dispose of the body afterwards. When they got to her house, he said, "I'll just get my things and be on my way, then."

"No. Please stay. If that's the way you really feel, then that's something I'll need to get used to. In the meantime, I do not plan on ever letting you out of my sights again, as far as being friends. I want to be your friend for life. If that's what you want and need me to be, that's what I'll be."

Tanner felt so relieved, "Thank you, Tammy. Thank you for understanding and not bailing out on me. I want to be your friend for life, too, and that's exactly what I'm going to be from now until the day I die."

"Sure thing, Tanner. But, I am a little pissed off that I don't really have much of a choice. I either accept your terms, or I no longer have you in my life, and I don't want that. So, I accept it." She started getting out of the car and paused, turning and looking at him again. "And, by the way, Doug is gay, so that ain't gonna happen, between him and me. At least not in the way you may have envisioned it, my man. Trust me, his niceness alone was enough to make me sit up and take notice about him a long time ago." Tanner nodded and smiled back at her, then looked away feeling a little ashamed of himself.

They both went inside and took turns showering. She made dinner while he took his, but she wasn't that hungry, so he ate alone while she took hers. Afterwards, she ended up eating a little food, and they both drank some wine, and smoked some good weed. Then they talked about everything imaginable and it felt good.

Tanner slept on the couch just for good measure. Before going to sleep, he thought about his life some more. He felt that he needed to spend more time with Carmen and Sophie strictly as friends in order to sort out his true feelings about them, and about his future. After what he'd just finished going through with Sheila, he was in no rush to lock himself up in another cage, and he felt just fine living on his own for a change. But, he understood loneliness, and he also understood the benefits of being monogamously partnered with someone that you're deeply in love with, or deeply care about.

He'd begun to realize at a deeper level that, these days when someone comes along that is nice, decent, and meets other baseline criteria for mating and procreating, or for companionship and monogamous sex, it's best to keep them, if possible. If you don't, someone else will. Like the saying, all the good ones are already taken. The minute someone becomes available because of death or divorce, all the lonely bachelors or bachelorettes give it their best shot, each in their own way. Their briefly perceivable freedom is only an illusion. He chuckled about that.

The next morning, the sky was gray, and so was Tammy's mood. Tanner was already up and the coffee was brewing. He'd shaved, thrown on some comfy clothes, and started breakfast. Tammy shuffled out from the bedroom mumbling, "Thank you," without making eye contact with him.

After giving her a moment he asked, "So, do you want to go to someplace different today? You've talked about how much you enjoy going to places you've never been to. Ever been to the Lawrence Hall of Science in the Berkeley Hills?"

"No, I can't say that I have."

"Want to go?"

"Whatever you want to do is fine with me," she said flatly.

Tanner stood and looked at her while she stared into space, acting as if he were invisible.

"Hey, Tammy. Look at me. Please." Tanner waited, but she kept staring straight ahead, not saying anything, periodically sipping her coffee.

The smell of scorched scrambled eggs filled the room. Tanner looked over and saw smoke rolling out from under his formerly fluffy eggs. He grabbed the pan off the stove, and turned off the burner. He scraped the egg into the sink, flushing it into the drain, and flipped on the garbage disposal. After the eggs were ground into oblivion, he filled the pan with soapy water, dried his hands and left the room.

He gathered his personal things up and left without a word. *Let her stew in her own juices,* he thought. Starving, he decided to head over to Penny's Pantry and have breakfast, and figure out the rest of his day and weekend while eating. He knew Sophie was off, and knew that by eating there he'd be thinking about her the whole time. Hell, for that matter, he already was. He was more than a little curious about what she'd said to Carmen that night out in the parking lot, and thought it would be nice if Sophie just happened to mention it, or brought it up and then talked about it a little without him having to say anything.

Once he got to the restaurant, he decided to give her a call. He sat in the parking lot and found her number in his contacts. When she'd given him her card, he made sure he put her mobile number in, along with her address since he already knew it. He dialed her number and heard it begin ringing. On the fourth ring, Sophie picked up. "Hello?"

"Hi, Sophie, it's Tanner."

"Hi, Tanner, what are you up to? I was really hoping to hear from you this weekend, I'm so glad you called."

"Oh, not much. I didn't figure you'd be working this morning because I remember you saying that you were strictly weekdays, afternoons, part-time only. But, I neglected to go shopping yesterday, and I woke up starving. So, I decided to go to Penny's Pantry this morning for breakfast, and when I got here, I was already thinking about you, so I decided to call you and ask you if you'd like to hang out with me today? If you're not doing anything, that is."

There was silence for a long moment, "Sophie, are you still there?"

"Yes, I'm here. I'm sorry. No, I didn't have any plans today. I wasn't sure I was going to do anything beyond the New York times crossword puzzle that I'm working on right now."

"Care to meet me here for breakfast? I'll wait in the parking lot for you and we can go in together."

Sophie said, "Come here. I'll cook you breakfast this morning. How about that?"

"You cooked for me last time. I want to treat."

"Then treat me to lunch later, and dinner after that and we'll be even."

Tanner smiled. "I'll be right over."

19

WEEKEND WITH SOPHIE INSTEAD

Tanner found himself at Sophie's quicker than he thought possible. It was still early, and traffic was light. He parked in the visitor spot and found the passageway that led to the elevator lobby. He took the elevator to the third floor, walked to her door, and knocked softly.

Expecting him, she opened the door on the third knock. When he stepped inside he immediately felt welcome and at home. Her radiant smile, her welcoming greeting. The smell of sausage and eggs cooking. The open space and modern furnishings added a nice ambiance. To him, it was almost as if she'd pulled the design for her place, furniture and all, straight from his personal dreams.

"Thank you for having me over on such short notice, Sophie."

"Not a problem. I was hoping you'd call me this weekend. I'm delighted. Come in. Have a seat at the counter. Your eggs and sausage will be ready in minutes."

Tanner walked over to the kitchen and sat on one of the bar stools at the counter across from the huge Viking gas stove she was using to cook his breakfast. She had inserted a flat grill onto the stove top. It was so big that she was cooking his entire breakfast on it. Pancakes in the back, then the eggs, followed by the sausages in the front.

Tanner watched her cook. He admired her petite frame, her long hair, her stunning diamond blue eyes, and her equally stunning figure. He was impressed by the way she seemed to effortlessly glide back and forth between the sink, the refrigerator, the coffee machine and back again. There was a graceful quality to her that he wasn't used to, but found absolutely fascinating.

She spoke, startling him out of his trance. "I spoke with Carmen the other night. I spotted her while I was walking to my car."

Tanner sat up a little taller on the stool. "Oh? I wonder why she was still there when you left?"

Sophie looked at him. She seemed surprised. "Well, it's not rocket science. She was probably wanting to see how long I stayed. Maybe she wanted to see if I stayed all night."

"Were her headlights on and the motor running, like she'd just come back because she forgot something?"

"No. She was just sitting there looking right at your apartment. So, I decided to go over and talk to her for a moment. It was a little surreal. I think I startled her. She kind of acted like she hadn't noticed I was leaving."

"What did you guys talk about?"

"I just asked her what she was doing there and she said nothing, that she was just doing some thinking, and that she hardly ever has a chance to do that. She said she is always so busy that sometimes she has trouble slowing her mind down enough to fall asleep."

Tanner was contemplative for a moment, "It's true. I haven't seen anyone as busy as her in ages. She has herself to take care of, she is half-owner of Es Picante along with her father, Diego, but she is also managing him, too. He's slowly losing his mind. I feel bad for Carmen. She seems like such a good person, but always ends up as the sacrificial lamb. She has no siblings to help her with him or anything else, and everything is on the line financially with the restaurant. If she says enough, and leaves, then the business folds, leaving her father high and dry. If he passes away or loses his cognitive abilities, then she's kind of in the same boat, I think, but it's not really any of my business."

Sophie finished cooking their breakfast by piling it all up on four plates, two each with the eggs and sausages, and the other two for their pancakes. She had already set two complete places for them at the counter. Tanner noticed she'd made sure that no matter what he might want on his cakes, he would have it. There was a split glass bowl with two sections. She'd filled one side with granulated sugar, the other with powdered sugar. There were two squeeze bottles next to the sugar. One had maple syrup in it, the other honey. Finally, she'd filled a little three-bowl caddy, made of chrome plated, stainless steel bowls joined at the center, each filled with different jams. Strawberry, peach, and marmalade.

"Dig in," she said as she finished refilling his coffee mug.

"This looks amazing. Thank you, again, Sophie. You certainly are quite the chef."

"Thanks. It's only breakfast, nothing fancy. The first meal I ever learned how to cook on my own. I tiptoed downstairs to the kitchen when my mother turned thirty, determined to give her breakfast in bed that year. Well, I did it, but not well. I made her two fried eggs and three pieces of bacon. I started the eggs too soon and over cooked them. Then, while peeling an orange, I forgot to turn the heat down on the bacon and it got really kind of burned and had a bunch of black charring on the pieces. Nevertheless, I buttered the toast and put grape jelly on it, put the over-fried eggs and charred bacon on a plate, and I took it to her on a tray to her bedroom.”

"How'd that go?” Tanner said.

"She woke up and acted surprised and very happy. She ate her breakfast and drank her coffee while I watched. She told me I should be proud for being such a grown up girl.”

"How old were you?”

"Eight. I had no idea that morning that by showing my mother just how much I knew and could do in the kitchen, that I would now be cooking for myself, more often than not. It seemed like, after that, she always had excuses about how she wouldn't be home until late and *would I be okay* figuring out something for myself for dinner.” Tanner kept eating, while listening attentively.

"At first I didn't mind. But after a while I got tired of eating alone and watching television by myself. I started spending more and more time with friends, and spending the night with them as much as possible just so I wouldn't have to feel so lonely all the time. I wanted someone to talk with. When I was over at a friend's house, I had people to talk to, play and study with. So, I made it my job to always have a close group of friends. I also read a lot. Who knew, when our first grade teacher, Mrs. Staunton, took us to the library on our first field trip away from the classroom, that it would become such a big part of a push back on the blues and loneliness for me. That's how I made it through my childhood. I had no brothers or sisters. My father died young from an inoperable brain tumor, and my mother never quite seemed right after that. She was always distant. Looking back, I think she'd become addicted to brooding."

Tanner shook his head. "That's really sad. I'm glad you managed to figure out a way to get what you needed, albeit the hard way around. But, nevertheless, you figured it out and survived it all."

Sophie smiled tightly and looked away. "True. I survived it. One other bitter irony about it is that I also managed to do well in school and I got good grades. I was set to get a scholarship to San Francisco State University and my mother didn't have a clue. By then, she was a wrinkled up old alcoholic who could barely keep her job at Safeway as a checker. Her boss threatened to fire her more than once after getting two complaints about her boozy breath from customers. Later, there was a rather large discrepancy with her money drawer at the end of her shift. Turns out, after looking closely at the overhead video surveillance footage, that she wasn't stealing. Instead, likely drunk on the job, she'd given some customer change for the equivalent of a one hundred dollar bill when all he'd given her in actuality was a ten dollar bill. Somehow, she hadn't noticed, and the dishonest customer, likely sensing her condition gave it a try, and when it worked, he didn't say anything.

She checked out seventy some odd dollars worth of stuff, then took his ten and gave him back almost thirty dollars in change thinking that he'd handed her a one hundred dollar bill. Later, when they closed her aisle and went to count her drawer, not only was she short, but there was no one hundred dollar bill to be found anywhere, even though she swore she remembered getting one that afternoon at some point."

Tanner looked shocked. "And she didn't get fired for that?"

"That's what I wondered too. She didn't come home until late that night. I remember it because she told me all about her mistake after getting home. I was tired and wanted to go to bed. She was drunk, as usual, and I was mostly tuning her out. I knew if I told her I didn't want to hear it, I'd hear the extended version, and likely a lot more on top of it. Later, I remember thinking to myself that she likely had relations with that nasty man just to keep her job. I hate to say or think that about my own mother, but I really think that's the kind of situation my mother began finding herself in more often as her drinking escalated. That's the situation I believe she found herself in that day." She shuddered afterwards, still imagining the things she'd left unsaid.

"Is she still around?"

"No. She died ten years ago. The alcohol never stopped, and it eventually caused a cascade event in her body. All her organs began shutting down, one-by-one. Each shutdown compounding the toxic effects to her system. Once it started, she was gone in a week. Everyone who knew her, knew she wouldn't be around long if she didn't lay off the booze. They saw her death coming, but no one thought it would be that soon, or that quick. What they didn't realize was how long she had been drinking. From adolescence to her death. Essentially, her whole life. Over time, with each passing year, she'd kept steadily drinking more."

Tanner was speechless. He had finished eating and had been sipping his coffee, listening. He stood, then moved in close and wrapped his arms around her, hugging her and holding her tight, gently rocking her back and forth without saying a word. After a while, he felt her push her face into his chest so he wouldn't hear her loud sobbing. He kept rocking her so she could just let it all out.

After a few minutes, still crying, but quieter now, she pulled back and looked into his eyes. Her mascara ridden tears had left both cheeks streaked, giving her the look of a warrior who'd painted her face while getting ready to raid the enemy's camp.

"I'll never forget the night when I told her I wish she would get some help. I begged her to stop and try going to AA. I even looked up online where there were meetings close to her. I found three within a two-mile radius from where we lived. But she wouldn't have any of it. She said AA was for losers. Can you believe that? I think she wanted to die to protect her ego, even though the entire world already knew she was a raging alcoholic. She still believed that she was fooling people about the true level of her massive dependency on alcohol."

Tanner stayed quiet, and continued holding Sophie for a long time. Eventually, she grew silent in his arms, and they separated. Tanner smiled at her, then leaned down and gave her a kiss.

"Thank you for breakfast, Sophie. Ready to start the rest of our day?" She chuckled and grabbed a napkin to blot her eyes. When she saw the mascara, she looked a little embarrassed.

"Yes, I'm almost ready. Excuse me, I'll be right back after I finish freshening up."

When Sophie came out of the bathroom she said, "Hey, do you play any sports?"

Tanner thought for a second, then said, "I used to play tennis a lot, and racquetball. I haven't played racquetball for decades now, ever since leaving here. I love both, but pickleball is likely the only thing these old knees would be able to handle now. I've never played it. I've seen others play it. And, I like to still say that I golf, but I haven't golfed regularly in years. Now, I skydive every Friday; I went up yesterday as a matter of fact."

Sophie raised an eyebrow, "You skydive? Seriously?"

"Yes. I love it. It's the one thing that always breathes life energy back into me and, at least temporarily, makes me feel young again. I never saw myself as a regular skydiver, but I am."

"I've always wanted to try that. At least I think I do."

"Why haven't you then?"

"I don't know. Well, yes, I kind of do. I haven't gone yet mainly because I've never know anyone else who skydives or any-one who is even willing to try. My friends would all say I'd be crazy to do it too."

Tanner smiled. "Of course it's scary. That's half of it. Fear is the fuel for the firehose of adrenaline that gets pumping and it feels amazing, almost addictive. As soon as you finish your first jump, you'll either want to go right back up again, or never want to go up again for the rest of your life. It's very definitive. Kind of like eating raw oysters: you either love them, or hate them."

Sophie looked at him. She seemed impressed. Tanner was glad. It had been a long time since a good-looking woman in his company seemed impressed by him in any way whatsoever. An unexpected, but welcome, dividend from continuing to skydive, thanks to Tammy.

"How'd you get into doing that?" she asked.

"Growing up, I saw skydiving with the old fashioned parachutes on ABC's Wide World of Sports, and I was mesmerized. I watched World War II movies growing up, and always thought the paratroopers were the bravest men on earth. Then, one afternoon I watched a movie with my father and grandfather about Joseph Kittinger's historic skydive on August 16, 1960. As part of the U.S. Air Force's Project Excelsior, Kittinger jumped from a gondola suspended beneath a helium balloon at an altitude of 102,800 feet (31,300 meters/19.5 miles)—the edge of space. He was trying to help generate data for perfecting high-altitude ejections from aircraft, and for future space travel. After that, I knew I had to skydive. Then, I thought I'd really like to be a regular Naval aviator flying off of aircraft carriers, seeing that as a possible springboard into becoming a commercial airline pilot and traveling the world for free while earning a really good living."

Sophie sat wide-eyed, listening without interrupting, and seemed really interested in what he was sharing with her. Tanner loved having the conversation. He felt heard for the first time in years, and it was really nice for a change to be speaking to someone who actually seemed interested in him, and what he had to say.

Years later, after watching another skydiving special, I decided that I would never forgive myself if I didn't fulfill my dream of skydiving at least once in my life. So, I set my fear aside and did it anyway. I realized that if it were my day to die, that there was nothing that I could do about it, otherwise, I had nothing to fear. I turned the whole thing on its head. I realized that the odds were in favor of me not having a fatal incident while skydiving. I started looking forward to it, instead of letting my fear of what might happen get in my way any longer. Yes, it's still a gamble, but so is life. Every day, we face unseen and unknown dangers that might end our lives. We just never know. Besides, what are the odds that the day you decide to go skydiving is the day you die? Really? When the jump-masters that you're going up with have logged over 1,500 jumps or more, doing high-altitude formation dives with large groups, all of them going out of the back of a large aircraft—highly unlikely. So, after coming to that conclusion, I called down to the local airport and asked around about a good place to learn how to skydive. I learned about Skydive Turners Falls, in Massachusetts, where I lived at the time. After basic training on getting in and out of the plane and how to assume the correct free-fall position, I had to memorize the hand signals I'd be given in lieu of the spoken word. Over the next year, I did two static-line jumps from 3,500 feet, and three free-falls from 10,500 feet."

Sophie gasped, "Oh my."

"The most intense part is getting out on that wing strut facing into a ninety-mile-an-hour wind, then nodding at the pilot that you're about to leave and then finally letting go."

"Wow. I just pictured myself doing that, and got goosebumps."

"Good goosebumps, I hope," Tanner said with a smile.

"Not sure. I think so. Then what happened?" Sophie asked.

"After my third jump, I was thinking about going again when I read in the paper that the jump-masters that I'd gone up with died while going up on a group formation skydive. Their Queen Anne plane took off fine, but barely five hundred feet up the plane malfunctioned and ended up crashing, killing all twenty-two people aboard. At only 500 feet, there isn't enough time for parachutes to open successfully."

"My God!" Sophie gasped. She seemed horrified. "I hadn't even considered that possibility."

Tanner tried to lighten the mood a little, "I know. It's always something, right?" he said through a chuckle.

"When did you start skydiving again?"

"Oh, my old high school flame, Tammy, got me back into it fairly recently."

Sophie smiled, and with a voice of inquisitiveness and concern she said, "Oh? Old flame, eh?"

"Well, yeah, kind of. We were inseparable for a while during high school. Like a close buddy relationship, but also with benefits. We split up when I left to move to southern California. Then, the rest of our lives happened, with me on the east coast, and her still here in the Bay Area. She never wrote back to me when I wrote to her after moving to Huntington Beach. That was it. I wondered about her off and on during all those years, I wondered what happened to her and if she ever got married and had a family, that kind of stuff. When I moved back here after my divorce, I looked her up and she was still around. I was surprised that she was still local because she always talked about moving to Paris someday. I thought she'd dreamt about doing that so much that she'd have no choice but to give it a try, but she didn't. During a fairly recent visit, she said she was going skydiving that afternoon, and invited me, thinking I'd turn her down cold, but I surprised her. That's when my previous jumps came in handy. I agreed, and ended up going with her that day. She was really surprised, and happy, that I knew my way around skydiving enough to suit up and go out the door with her and her friend that day. Now, we go every Friday, right after I get off of work. If you'd like to come sometime, I think I can make that happen."

Sophie looked down at the floor for a second. Tanner could see her processing all kinds of things. Finally, she looked up, "Count me in. Can I go next Friday?"

"I'll set it up."

Sophie screeched and squealed with glee. She jumped up and said, "Oh my God. I can't believe I just said that. I'm actually going to do this. Finally. I'm so excited. I can't wait." She threw her arms around Tanner and began kissing him passionately. Tanner let her for a minute, then stopped her.

"Let's wait. Please?" Sophie nodded, then without hesitation asked, "How about we go and play some pickleball? I have two racquets and a whole bunch of balls."

"You're on!" Tanner was happy to hear that she wanted to go and do something. They stopped by his place. He went in by himself and changed into some shorts and swapped his suede loafers for some running shoes.

When they got to the pickleball courts over at Concord Community Park, Tanner flashed back to when he and his sisters and step-siblings used to get dropped off with some money to go swimming at the public pool here. After admission, they had enough change left for a couple of hot dogs and a drink for lunch. It seemed almost surreal to him how long ago that was. He looked over at it. It had hardly changed. It looked like most of the trees were still there. Some had grown enormous. It shocked him to think that it had been half a century since he swam in that pool, and forty years ago since he regularly played tennis on these same courts.

Sophie was really good at pickleball. She maneuvered well, was quick on her feet, and seemed to have an intuitive sense of where the ball was going next. Tanner could barely keep up with her, and she easily won the first set. The game turned out to be slightly harder than Tanner had anticipated, but he liked how it was compact and confined to a smaller area, making it a little easier on his knees than tennis, but only a little. After three sets, Tanner called uncle. His knees were almost bone-on-bone, and all the running and sudden starts and stops weren't doing either of them any favors.

After they stopped, they decided to take a stroll around the park and enjoy the greenery and chirping birds. An entire army of white puffy clouds had filled the sky. As they talked, Tanner found out some more about her. He quickly learned that if you wanted to know more about anything, just ask her a leading question and the rest would follow.

"So, what else do you like to do in your spare time? Do you like watching news or sporting events, maybe listening to music?"

Sophie thought for a moment, "I like to watch the news mainly for the weather. I've learned that the rest is usually only going to be a verbal police log for the area, or just information designed to make me feel afraid, so I avoid watching it as much as possible."

"Politics?"

"I hate politics. I vote for who I think the best candidate is at the time. I turn it off the rest of the time." Hearing this was music to Tanner's ears. Finally a good-looking woman with a brain. Someone who is thinking, and doing, what she needs to in order to stay physically and mentally healthy. What a breath of fresh air. He was already starting to think that he had misjudged her. There was a lot more to her than her beauty.

Before, he thought she was narcissistic and all about manipulating men by being sexually playful and provocative to get what she wanted. Now, he was beginning to see a much brighter, more interesting person in front of him. He was beginning to feel lucky to be in her company, and even luckier to have her taking an interest in him.

"As far as music goes, well, I used to listen to tons of music, all different types. But, then it seemed like the field became so saturated with different artists that, at first, I lost interest, then I just gave up trying to keep track of any of it." She stopped strolling and looked at him directly. "I know this might sound a little strange to you, but now I like streaming instrumental ambient and space music. Music that doesn't get stuck in my head. I don't care for crowds either. I don't think I ever did, I just went along with what others wanted to do in going to concerts and the like."

Tanner was amazed by how much they seemed to have in common. He felt himself grow more excited inside with each new revelation. He also hated crowds, hated noise, and hated music that would get stuck in his head, and he voted independent. They both read more than they watched television. They both enjoyed suspense, thrillers, science fiction, and well-written romance novels. They both shared that Stephen King was their favorite overall author, but Tanner said it was a tie between King and Ken Follett for sheer breadth and talent.

They had lunch at the International House Of Pancakes. Tanner loved going there and getting crepes of some kind or cheese blintzes with fresh strawberries and real maple syrup.

"Thanks for lunch, Tanner. I appreciate it. Not being at Penny's is nice for a change. The decor here is all different. Much sunnier and more welcoming in my opinion. This is nice."

"You're welcome. I'm glad you like it. Have you eaten here before?"

"No, I've been wanting to for years."

Everything was outstanding, including the coffee. Feeling better now, Tanner asked, "So, did you just decide at some point that you weren't going to have any children of your own? I know I shouldn't ask you such a personal question, but I have been curious about that. Mainly because you're so good looking, and I can totally see many men wanting to court someone with your looks, if only for your genes. I'm sorry to put it so bluntly. That sounds horrible, doesn't it? I shouldn't have said or asked you anything that personal yet."

Sophie was visibly taken aback by the question. Tanner regretted asking her after seeing her tense up. She regained her composure and looked Tanner directly in his eyes. "Yes. I absolutely did. I wasn't about to have to endure a pregnancy while I was being drugged and pimped out to other men. I certainly wouldn't have married the asshole just because I was carrying his child. I also didn't want to have to risk getting pregnant by him or a stranger, so I went ahead and had my tubes tied as soon as I could. I really didn't think I was coming out of that situation alive. The last thing I wanted to do was leave a child behind in the care of that psychopath who brainwashed me while abusing me to no end.

Do I regret it? Yes, and no. I really do have maternal instincts, and likely would've made a great mother, once upon a time, but not after all my scary and bizarre experiences with men after high school. It took secretly getting my tubes tied to squash my worry of having children by that bastard, or any of his so-called friends. It also took years of psychotherapy for me to realize that not all men are sexual demons who see women as objects for their own personal pleasures whenever they want them. You validated that revelation for me the night I made you dinner. I think if I'd had children I would've worried excessively about them, especially if I'd had a daughter. I would have never wanted to think, or know, that my daughter was being sexually used, or abused, like I was. Just the possibility of that would've driven me crazy." Sophie paused for a moment while continuing to sip her coffee.

She continued, "I have no idea if I would've been able to cope with being a mother 24 hours a day. In retrospect, I have a feeling that I also would've likely filled my daughter's head full of my own baggage. I know that sounds awful, but I think I likely would have—no, I know I would have, because that would've been before I got away, and before having therapy." Tanner was surprised by her continued introspection, candor and honesty. It was refreshing to see someone espouse their truest feelings about something so intimate, without hesitation, and with such surety.

"So, despite my sense of having built-in and learned maternal instincts to love and protect a child, I had so much going on around motherhood, psychologically, that it probably wouldn't have worked out well even if I hadn't gotten my tubes tied. I've even asked myself, what I would've done if I'd had a little boy instead of a girl? God, I have no idea how that might have gone either. I know I would've needed to read up on how to be a mother to a boy, to make sure that he turned out to be a proper man, because I think I'd have been clueless about how to raise one. Now that I've seen how fragile the psyche of a young person is, I would be petrified as a parent about maybe making too many mistakes that would end up warping a kid or something."

Tanner listened attentively. He felt her angst, and his heart felt heavy after hearing about her past, her experiences being denied a normal transition from high school graduate into full adult womanhood. He also knew she had to struggle for a long time to learn how to cope with being denied her ability to become a mother out of self-protection. He said "I'm so sorry for what happened to you, Sophie. For whatever it's worth, from what I've seen from you, so far, I think I'd be fine growing up with a mom like you. You seem less intense and edgy than my own mother was. I could totally see you as a mother."

"Thanks for that, Tanner. And, you're right. It was worth it for me, at the time. When I remember how things were back then, I realize that I really didn't have a choice. I did what I had to do. So, no regrets. Things happen in life, and all we can do is make the best choices possible under all kinds of varying conditions and situations. I did what I had to do."

Tanner stayed quiet for a bit, sipping his coffee, contemplating what Sophie had just shared with him. He looked over at her, "I think you were brave, and still are." Under the table, she reached over and laid her hand over his, gently giving it a squeeze while looking into his eyes, silently thanking him for his understanding. While he had her attention he asked her, "Do you mind if I call it for today? I'm really tired, and want to drop out early tonight. I'm really sorry. I had a great time, but I think maybe the pickleball took a lot of my game out of me. I'd definitely like to go with you again, though."

Sophie looked genuinely disappointed, but quickly resumed her upbeat attitude. "Oh, shoot. I was hoping for dinner with you later, too. I thought we might go to a late afternoon matinee, then to dinner, but I understand if you're really tired. If you are, you are. I know how that can feel, so no problem. We'll save that stuff for our next date, right?"

"Right. Thank you, too, for being understanding. I appreciate it."

Tanner was tired, but he also wanted to throw Sophie a little off, which he'd just done by suddenly changing the game plan. He felt that, for now, such tactics were necessary in order for him to honor his own desire to not fog up his lenses with sex, and he had a strong feeling that it was in her cards to attempt that with him again, likely tonight. At this point, he knew that if she did try to seduce him, he would likely give in. She was so attractive, and they had so much in common. His own intuitiveness informed him that their love making would be incredible, and he had also sensed her desire. It seemed to leak out of her all the time with little comments, and that look she could levy at him, it made his knees wobbly. It was hard to ignore.

The thought of making love with Sophie was as enticing as she was mesmerizing. Sometimes, while in her sphere, he felt magnetically drawn to her. It was as if the closer he was to her physically, the closer he wanted to be. Her scent, her softness, her feminine glow, her dazzling eyes, and her amazing physique. It was a lot for Tanner to manage, but he was determined to wait, and postpone sexual activities, knowing that when they did make love, it would be amazing.

20

SUNDAY

The next morning, Tanner woke up already thinking about Sophie. He had initially thought she was someone to be avoided at all costs. His plan was to avoid her completely, while also conveniently forgetting to call her until she simply gave up, and left him alone. Then she'd explained herself more, and that had helped quell his fears around her mental state or general stability. He had agreed to a first, *normal* date, and it had gone very well. So well, in fact, that he had become a little obsessed about her.

He had been stunned to learn about so many of her likes, dislikes, and preferences. The amount of similarities between them seemed implausible, but undeniable. He couldn't help thinking about what might have been had he met Sophie all those years ago.

All the years wasted with Sheila, when he could have had a wonderful life with Sophie, and Sophie wouldn't have had her natural maternal instincts trampled on and ruined forever. He thought about how tender her lips were when they'd kissed, and how his body seemed to respond, revving up instantly, almost on contact, when she touched him. And, she touched him a lot. Sometimes, she would gently put her hand over his, or she'd give his hand a quick, reassuring squeeze. Other times, she'd pat one of his knees, then leave her hand lying on his thigh until she needed it back for something. Out of the blue, she would put her arm around his waist and pull him in close, sometimes with an additional kiss to his neck and cheek which always gave him goosebumps. Often, she would lay her head against his shoulder after laughing or while resting and being quiet with him. It made him feel loved, desired and cared for, and he loved it. Who wouldn't? He thought, *feeling loved, wanted, and cared for easily wins out over acquisition of money and power; what good are they if you're alone and unloved?*

Sheila had been most affectionate when they first began seeing each other, and he'd enjoyed her enthusiastic touching and teasing towards him. They used to enjoy the thrill of doing it outside, even in broad daylight. More than once, they'd gone into a public restroom together, locked the door, and had a quickie.

Tanner couldn't remember when her physical affections towards him began to wane. Only later, did he finally recognize that she wasn't used to his intensity or his anger, and that she had been unprepared for it. He knew that her feelings about him had grown darker after seeing him get angry. Unfortunately, and even worse, she'd never thought getting angry about anything was justified, but merely a waste of time. That sometimes infuriated him. To her, nothing mattered except that he'd gotten angry. It shocked him that she could be so selfish and uncaring, and lack so much perceptive capability. It was a turning point in their relationship for sure. The kind that drives couples to therapy, divorce court, and extra-marital affairs. All three seem to interact in prolonging the inevitable breakup.

During their marriage, he and Sheila had always had regular relations, but as the years went by, their lovemaking sessions were shorter, far less intense, less playful, and had become less loving. She was willing to (do her wifely duty she used to say) have sex, reluctantly, but their sex had become much more perfunctory, passionless, and utilitarian. That had become a sort of unspoken language that Tanner thought communicated a lot about Sheila's true feelings. Once he realized her true feelings about having sex with him, sex in general, he hated how unloved he felt. Tanner had craved feeling loved by her. Over time, he had begun craving being touched. Sheila would only touch him when he complained and pointed out to her that she no longer did. Her desire for him had waned enormously, and it was obvious. During that time, he still hadn't made the connection between them not having sex, and how that meant less likelihood of a pregnancy. He was too caught up feeling sorry for himself, and doing a hell of a lot more jerking off to make up for it.

Back then, he was still very young, and testosterone still coursed through his veins at a high level, making it difficult for him to think about much of anything else. He'd hated that aspect of their relationship. He'd hated craving a woman's touch, while married, denied what he wanted and needed physically, while honoring his own beliefs of remaining faithful to her.

Not being touched, or having a willing partner during sex, left him fantasizing about many other women for years—wanting them, at times lusting for them, wondering what it would be like to have sex with them—while many had let him know that they were available, and willing. All he had to do was call them—but he never did. He hated Sheila for denying him what he'd wanted and needed for so long, while giving it all to the rich dude she just married.

For Tanner, that was the single hardest thing about being married to her. He thought, *If she had only touched me more. But now I know why she didn't. She associated touching with sending me a signal that she wanted sex or would be okay with it. That, in turn, increased the likelihood of her getting pregnant, which is something she secretly did not want. She wanted her career and freedom, while also enjoying all the perks of marriage. By not touching me, she could minimize the amount of sexual activity and, for her, that was mission accomplished.* But, Tanner was a firm believer in karma, and believed *what goes around, comes around.* He thought, *By not touching or making love with me, she could save it all for future hubby number two.* What a contrast between Sheila and Sophie. Polar opposites. Maybe now I'm getting mine. Maybe Sheila will be getting hers, too, but not necessarily the way she wants it. I don't know why I stayed with her for so long. *I should've cut the cord with her ages ago. But that's on me.*

He'd slept in because he could, and now he craved something spicy instead of the usual breakfast fare. He rummaged around in the fridge and came across some Es Picante rice and beans and a chicken taco from two days earlier. *Perfect,* he thought. Heating the food, he began to smell it, and the smell reminded him of the restaurant. He pictured Carmen wearing her food safety cap, gloves, and apron while chopping and shredding the food before opening each day. He deeply admired her ability to put smiles on people's faces; Turn hungry people into full, happy people; Grumpy, frowning faces into happy faces.

Every time he thought of Carmen, he couldn't help but think about how she wanted to have a child almost more than anything. She knew her biological time clock was ticking so loud now, that she could hardly get to sleep at night anymore. He felt bad for her. *That's quite a quandary.* I can relate to how it feels to want a child and not be able to have one while you're watching yourself grow old, knowing that soon it will no longer really be an option, he thought, but I cannot imagine it from a woman's perspective. That pressure they must feel. How awful for them. How awful for Carmen. No wonder Diego is trying to do his part to help secure a man for his daughter. But how is she supposed to do that? She's caught between a rock and a hard place. *She needs more of the time she never has, to be free to date, and spend leisure time with men of her choosing, not just thinking that it will happen—someday.*

When he thought about Carmen, he honestly felt intrigued about the last chance possibility at, perhaps, still having a family, complete with a much younger wife, and finally, a child. That fantasy had a lot going for it and always got him excited when he thought about it. Then he'd flash on his own age, knowing how much things had already begun to change for him physically. More pain being felt everywhere, less overall energy, less stamina and endurance than just ten years prior. He knew he'd never be up to full-time parenting. Maybe, with some help. If only he could be a part-time dad, instead of a full-time one. Was that even a real possibility? Then it hit him, of course it is. Rich people do it all the time. They hire nurses, nannies, house cleaners, landscapers, shoppers, and everything else they might want or need, on demand, as needed or desired.

Tanner knew that unless he had those kinds of resources, he wouldn't realistically be able to father a child. He felt profoundly sad about that, but knew it to be his truth.

He thought, *I waited too long.* Stayed too long. Just give up the family fantasy, and finally feel better. You know you would feel better if you just let it go. You didn't do fatherhood, boo-fucking-hoo. *Get over it and have fun while you still have your freedom.*

21

CONSIDERATIONS

Things between Tanner and Carmen had recently begun to cool a bit. He'd been leery to pursue her further, or even be too nice to her, due to all his recent revelations about fatherhood. He knew he likely couldn't be with her unless the child option was also activated, but he'd decided that he didn't want to stop something potentially really good by getting ahead of himself mentally about any of it.

The next couple of weeks went by with nothing odd or out of the ordinary going on between Tanner and anyone. Carmen seemed fine. She greeted him cheerfully every morning, just like always. Tanner felt guilty that he'd not followed up their first date with an offer of a second date. He hoped she had not thought too much about it. He didn't want to hurt her, or give her false impressions about his intentions. He wished he could just date her and enjoy her company without all the baggage around having children.

After his shift was over on Wednesday, Tanner spoke to Carmen, "Saturday morning, would you like to take a drive over to Muir Woods and hike through a silent cathedral of massive, thousand year-old trees, then sit up on a ridge that offers a view of the Golden Gate Bridge, and San Francisco while we picnic?"

Carmen looked surprised, but pleased. "Wow, it sounds really nice. I'm in. It sounds like you've been there before?"

"Yes, semi-regularly when I still had enough money to drive over for a hike. I love the place. I feel a spiritual presence there that I've never felt anywhere else, except Stonehenge in Great Britain. But even that was different. I'm somewhat convinced that what I feel and experience at Muir Woods comes from the trees and the ground itself. I can't decipher the messages being put out and carried away by the wind, but I feel the energy from them, just as much as I feel the sea breeze in my hair and the sun on my skin while I'm soaking it all up."

Carmen's eyes grew wide, "Wow. I've never had an experience like that before. I hope to, someday."

Tanner went on, "When I was younger, I used to discount similar experiences I'd had, chocking them up as just my imagination. Then, starting in my twenties, I opened not just my mind, but my heart to the possibility that I might be privy to a very special, natural form of timeless communication. So, I just stayed present, and decided to not judge what I was feeling intuitively while experiencing the communication. I know it sounds crazy, and I hope you won't judge me harshly now that I've shared that with you."

"How long have you been aware of this phenomenon?"

"Since childhood."

"Has it ever changed?"

Tanner looked away for a few seconds, then said, "Yes, when I'm there, it comes more often and the energy seems stronger, but I'm clueless about the content."

Carmen answered, "What does your intuition tell you?"

"I'm picking up on some kind of warning, like there is something about to happen or something is coming, something good . . . or bad is coming . . . or about to happen . . . I don't know. But I know that it's different, more urgent and powerful than it used to be, and I don't know if it's trying to tell me or warn me, personally, or I'm reading something for everyone."

Carmen stayed silent for a few minutes, then said, "I'd love to go with you. I'll put some food and drinks together for us to take, and can be ready for ten, if that works?"

Tanner smiled, "Perfect. I'll pick you up at ten on Saturday, then.

The next day, Carmen and Tanner had little to say to one another outside of work-related things, but she smiled, her eyes twinkled, he even detected a blush once. He understood. If he was deciphering her signals correctly, he felt the same way. They were both looking forward to having some time alone and away from work.

Finished for the day, he went straight home for a change. He was hungry tonight, but didn't want to go to the store. Luckily, he found one last pre-formed hamburger patty in the freezer, and decided to make a simple meal of a turkey burger with eggs. He gently microwaved the burger back to room temperature, then threw it onto a hot, oiled skillet. The room filled with hissing and sizzling, then the rich aroma of cooking turkey. Tanner's watch thumped his wrist. He looked at the notification. Tammy had texted him. He turned his patty over, added some salt and pepper, and turned the heat down considerably, then read her message.

Hey, I'm not up to skydiving this week, but I'm sure Doug would love being able to have someone to go out with. I'll catch up with you soon or see you next week for a jump. Tanner responded with a thumbs up and a smiley face with sunglasses on.

It was obvious to him that she was still upset from having her romantic aspirations dashed on the rocks. Tanner really thought she'd actually be relieved, not upset. He hadn't realized how much her feelings for him had changed. He felt bad about that, but he knew his decision was the right one. They would always be able to be great friends, but he knew trouble would likely come for an extended stay if, and when, they tied the knot or moved in together. He could never be her Rodney, and he was glad that he'd finally realized that.

He cracked a couple of eggs and dropped them into the turkey fat and caramelized butter from the burger on the opposite side of the pan. The yoke broke on the second one, pissing him off a little. He liked yokes unbroken and half hard. Then, with sudden, unexpected anger all the suppressed little things that had angered, annoyed, irritated, or poked at him over the last couple of weeks, all seemed to join hands at the same time. The feeling was powerful. So powerful, that he had to clamp shut his impulse to grab that pan and sling the whole thing—pan, meat, and eggs—really hard across the room. He couldn't believe how angry he felt—over nothing. He took a huge breath, letting it out very slowly before grabbing a knife and a fork and frantically cutting and slicing the ground turkey meat and eggs in the pan. Once chopped and sliced up to his liking, he angrily mixed the whole mess together, restraining his impulse to turn the heat up high and watch it all turn to crispy charcoal.

Tammy would just have to get over herself. And she would, but not before going out into left field, then right field, prolonging his punishment for being honest with her about his true feelings. A gift that many people never get from their friends, partners or spouses—real honesty.

Tanner pushed his breakfast amalgamation onto a plate, generously squirting ketchup over everything, then sat down and focused on eating, which helped squash his anger and his sadness about the situation with Tammy, at least a little—for the time being.

He wondered if it would be too awkward to bring Sophie with him to skydive, then immediately decided against it. That would add fuel to the fire, for sure, and he really didn't want Tammy to feel any worse than she already did. Instead, he decided he'd wait, then introduce the two of them, and gauge from that. If they got along okay, perhaps then he would broach the subject.

Right now, introducing either Carmen or Sophie to Tammy would not be a good idea at all. Tammy needed time to process her feelings about him, and come to the same conclusion—that the two of them should remain friends, but nothing else—on her own. Once that happened, he thought she'd have a much easier time accepting any female introductions from him.

He felt tired, and hit the sack early for a change, skipping the bad news machine on purpose. When he woke up, he felt fantastic. He did some stretching, took a shower, had some cereal, and went to work with a smile on his face.

Today, he planned to come straight home after work and do some laundry and clean his place up instead of waiting until Sunday. He'd only have food shopping left to do, and he was really looking forward to having a nice, low-key, relaxing day on Sunday. *Gosh, looking forward to down time, solitude, and quiet . . . Uh oh, someone's getting old,* he thought.

He shook his head and chuckled. He had been thinking about his age a lot more these days. When he made his decision to move back to California, he hadn't expected that he would become involved with three different women at the same time. It was a first. Carmen, his direct boss, Sophie, a stunning beauty he met at Penny's, and Tammy, his trusty friend with benefits. Now, just like things were before leaving all those years ago, for whatever reason, he seemed to be able to effortlessly attract women—in California.

He'd been completely monogamous and honored his marital vows for nearly thirty years while married to Sheila, and he'd learned well how to live at that end of the spectrum. She ended it. He was free again, but just now really understanding that fact.

He thought, *I'm lucky as hell that things are going this way again, I think I'm going to stop resisting it, and start enjoying it. Besides, this is likely my last gasp with romance, sex, dating, the whole thing, anyway. What the hell. I'm going for it.*

Once he left the house, the entire day seemed to accelerate, and before he knew it, he was checking in with Carmen one more time about their date on Saturday. She seemed very relaxed, and was expecting his question. She looked up at him and smiled as he approached, and before he could say anything she said, "Yes. I still want to go tomorrow and I'll be ready at 10 a.m. I've been looking forward to it for a couple of days now." He'd also really been looking forward to having Carmen with him in Muir Woods.

"Okay. I'll see you tomorrow, then. Have a good night."

"See you in the morning."

Tanner decided to hit the grocery store that night. For some reason, it wasn't very crowded for a Friday. He'd taken a quick, visual inventory last night, and hadn't needed as many things as he'd thought he did. He'd get his shopping done and go home and take care of the cleaning and laundry, then heat up something for dinner. Tomorrow would be wide open for him and Carmen, and Sunday would be a completely open day to relax. *Perfect,* he thought.

It was Friday, and it felt strange to not be driving over to Tammy's to go skydiving. He thought about going anyway, but didn't feel like it. It would be strange to go to Byron and skydive without her. He would go, but only if she went too. Otherwise, he'd simply give up going at all. Skydive Byron reminded him of both Skydive Orange, and Skydive Turners Falls, in Massachusetts. Both of them were small outfits with a couple of tight groups that regularly skydived.

It was nice to have the extra time on a Friday afternoon. Tanner found a parking spot right up front at the supermarket, which was rare, and the aisles were as uncrowded as he'd ever seen them. This time, he remembered to start with produce, and end with frozen and refrigerated stuff so they wouldn't get too warm on the way home.

He opened one of the freezer doors to get two bags of frozen broccoli out, but he couldn't grab both at the same time. He threw one in his basket, then reached back in to get another. While backing out, he happened to look through the glass of the door and saw Tammy at the other end of the aisle. She was looking at the ice cream, which was where he'd planned to go next. Now, he wasn't sure if he really wanted to see her, here, when it was obvious she needed some space.

He looked back out through the door, and saw that she was strolling towards him now, very slowly, as if window shopping, looking at everything inside each of the freezer door sections carefully. Tanner quickly turned his back to her, controlling the closure of the door, so it wouldn't slam and attract her attention and began walking away from her. He headed directly around the corner as soon as possible, barely slowing down enough to grab the milk and eggs he needed and hustling to the checkout aisle. If she saw him, then what? She might think he was upset and was maybe stalking her? Who knew. All he knew was that he wanted to avoid her, and so far, had managed to accomplish that. He walked out to his car in a hurry and got the groceries stowed away. He half-walked, half-ran to put the cart away, and hastily pulled away from his parking space.

He was sitting at the light, waiting to exit the parking lot, when he saw her come out of the store in his rearview mirror. He felt his tension ease a bit, until he saw her looking in his direction.

She stood just outside the store exit, leaning on her cart full of groceries, looking right at him, staring at him without looking anywhere else. He knew she'd seen him.

Now, he felt bad for not saying anything to her. If she'd seen any part of his haste in getting out of the store and off the premises, then she was probably shocked and still trying to figure out what that meant. He felt a bit guilty and very petty. Guilty for not assuming the best and going over and speaking to her, even if nothing more than a simple, *Hi, how are you? Are you feeling a little better now?* But he had been sure that doing so would have only make her feel worse. Now that he'd seen her shopping, he doubted that she felt sick at all. He'd already assumed that she'd called to say she wasn't going skydiving to prevent him from coming over to her house after work. But, it was still early. Normally, they wouldn't leave for another forty-five minutes or so, and he wondered if she was going anyway, without him.

He decided to let it all go and just let her have the space she needed. She would come around to either make up, or break up, with him when she was ready. He wanted her to be the one to call him. It was hard for him, but he was determined to leave it alone. At least for now.

Tanner put it out of his mind and drove home. He cleaned his apartment while baking a boxed pizza. After dinner, he cleaned the bathroom, then gathered up his dirty clothes and walked over to the laundry room on the corner of his building. One washer going, one dryer going, and no one in sight. Three more machines available.

He despised doing laundry outside his home, and he'd had clothes stolen out of machines before when he'd left them unattended. Now, he babysat them in order to prevent another pair of pants or a good shirt from disappearing again. He resented the hell out of it and he missed having a washer and dryer at home where he could sit and read, or watch television while the machines washed and dried his clothes.

The next day he got himself together, and left at 9:45 a.m to pick up Carmen. The world had awakened hours earlier, but it was an easy drive to get to her place only a few miles from his apartment. He was excited. It was going to be another gorgeous day. The kind of day that is so beautiful that, if for no other reason, you can't help but smile.

When he arrived, she came right out carrying a large picnic basket, a light jacket, and her purse. "Ola, Tanner," she said smiling wide. She looked happy and comfortable. She wore well fitting bluejeans and walking shoes, and her sweatshirt read, *I'm the boss* screen-printed over a picture of a Chihuahua with the caption, *Don't make me show you,* underneath.

"Ola, Carmen. You look great."

"Gracias." She said, still smiling. She handed him the picnic basket and her jacket, which he put in the back seat.

Tanner felt compelled to apologize for his ratty car, "I'm sorry you have to be seen in this beater, but it's pretty reliable, despite the rough appearance."

She looked over at him as she buckled her seat belt, "Don't even worry about stuff like that with me, Tanner. I don't care how this thing looks. I'm confident that you feel that it works well enough to be driving me to Muir Woods, you said?"

"Yes, Muir Woods. You know, over by the ocean?"

Carmen said, "It's strange that I've lived here for decades, and you've only recently moved back out here and it seems like you know more places and ways to get around here than I do."

"You should get out more often, my dear." Tanner said with a big grin.

"You're right! I should. I have my little closed-in life at the house, managing my father, and the restaurant. I don't go any-where." She looked over at him. Her face showed a mixture of sad-ness and surprise, as if hearing her own words had suddenly made her realize what a shuttered existence she'd been living all of her adult life. "I never have." She looked away.

Tanner tried to stay positive, but that testimonial was downright depressing to him. Trying hard to stay upbeat, he said, "Well, then, we're going places as often as we can, I hope. It'll be fun. I can show you a lot. I've lived in both northern and southern California, so we'll have plenty to see and do."

Carmen smiled at him. She seemed a little better, or at least she was going to give it a good try. "I love it! I'm going to have my very own personal guide to show me around the state that I've lived in for 36 years. That seems so odd to say 36, I can't believe I'm that old now. I can't believe that I've never been to Muir Woods before. Heck, I've only been over to San Francisco twice in my entire life! Once to the zoo with my father when I was 10, and again for a mu-tual friend's birthday party at the *Benihana of Tokyo* restaurant."

Tanner was mildly stunned by this revelation, but wanted to stay upbeat. "Well, then, like I said, we're going to have to start taking lots of little day trips. In fact, let's make a pact that once every other week, or more, we pick out a place to take a day trip to, and then go there. Sound good?"

She looked over at him excitedly, "I love that idea. Can we start with going to Golden Gate Park next time? I've heard little things about the gardens, the aquarium, and the live snake collection."

Tanner said, "That's definitely a place I'd like to see again. We could go to Golden Gate Park, eat at the House of Prime Rib, go to Fisherman's Wharf, get ice cream sundaes at the Ghirardelli chocolate factory, walk across the Golden Gate Bridge—all of it."

Carmen looked excited. "I love that idea." She leaned across the center console and kissed his cheek, then slowly pulled away from him, stopping only inches out from his face. Tanner could feel her looking at him. He tried to keep his eyes on the highway, but he could still feel the wet from her kiss drying on his cheek, and he could feel her breathing on his neck. After a few seconds, she said, "Where have you been all of my life?"

Tanner felt a jolt of energy pulse through him and felt himself becoming aroused. He never answered her, and the rest of the ride was quiet. Tanner put on a playlist of oldies from the 70s and 80s and he could tell that she liked it. Sometimes he could see her silhouette bobbing up and down to the beat of some of the songs, while tapping her foot on the floorboard, and her fingernails on the armrest. Here and there, he'd glance over at her. She'd immediately notice him doing that, and would instantly look right at him, smiling back.

Once they arrived, they got out and began walking into the park. Carmen seemed both amazed and awed by the size and grandeur of California's Giant Sequoia Redwoods before her. "Wow. I never . . . I have never seen anything like this in my entire life," she said.

Tanner let her take it in a little longer, then said, "No one can imagine this beauty. It has to be experienced first hand. I'm so glad to be a part of you seeing them, and now you know where they are."

Carmen felt a little dizzy trying to walk while looking up, trying to find the tops of the trees (without luck), while listening to Tanner. She said, "The quiet here is remarkable. Even my steps are cushioned enough by the redwood needles so they can't be heard." Tanner continued slowly walking in front of her, in order to give her plenty of time to take in one of nature's finest cathedrals, Muir Woods National Monument.

Slowly they made their way to the ledge where Tanner liked to meditate and spend time alone. A barely visible trail rose steadily up a small slope, veering off from the main trail. Tanner led the way. They hiked in that direction for a short while before ending up on a grassy knoll high above and facing the Pacific Ocean. They stood still while taking in the vast view. The coastline stretched out in both directions, seemingly to infinity. Looking southeast: a commanding view of the City of San Francisco, the Golden Gate Bridge, Alcatraz Island, Treasure Island Naval Base, the Oakland

Bay Bridge, and the Oakland/Palo Alto peninsula all stretched out behind it off in the misty distance. A full 270-degree view.

Even after extensive travels with Sheila, Tanner considered this place to be one of the most spectacular places to visit anywhere on earth. Somehow, like magic, the amazing view, combined with the positive energy emanating from the woods, always put him into a much better mood.

Tanner stood still, his eyes riveted on Carmen. Her natural beauty sometimes left him speechless. He watched her taking in the vastness before her. The way the cold wind pulled her hair nearly straight back at times, tugging at her clothes and forcing them taut against her, outlining her athletic figure.

One day, not so long ago, she had made him promise to never call her *Chica* because she wasn't a little girl, and to please promise to not ever point out her shortness, because she already knew she was short, and didn't need a constant reminder about her height. She found jokes about her height annoying, because she'd heard them her whole life. Enough already. So he did a little research and came up with *Mi Mujer* by googling how to refer to your wife or woman in Spanish. She loved it.

"I will always remember this place, Tanner." She looked over at him with penetrating sincerity, then came to him for a hug. He wrapped his arms around her as she turned her head sideways hugging his chest tightly. They hugged one another for a long time. They were completely alone, and for that moment, Tanner felt like they could've been the only two people in the entire universe. He closed his eyes and felt himself connect to her. They shared their loving energy. He felt it swirling around inside him, and all around both of them like a breeze swirling in different directions, forming an eddy as it pushes around an object.

Periodically, he would pause and pull back to look at her. Her brown eyes and soft complexion looked so vibrant. He smiled, "Ah, mi mujer, Carmen, es muy bonita!"

She laughed, "You can be so cute. I'm glad you think I'm still very beautiful. I have a hard time taking in all the changes that I see in the mirror now, but I can't do anything about it."

"Changes? What? Changes in the mirror? Maybe. But your face? Nah. You look very youthful. Besides, having to deal with watching yourself age is still better than the alternative."

"Thank you, Tanner. I appreciate that."

"De nada. Besides, you deserve something extra for all your toiling. Youthful appearance and, hopefully, extra longevity to go along with it is a great start."

They sat for over an hour taking in the view, talking about growing older, and the shock of watching the world change in ways that they both found scary and disturbing. They made out a little, and they almost worked themselves into a thermal emergency by the heat they generated from their passion. Determined to not let his arousal cloud his thinking by going all the way with anyone right now, Tanner stopped short from progressing any further, even though he wanted to. He wanted to so badly, that he'd barely been able to listen to his own internal voice and make himself stop, which he did. Now, calming down, they both sat and meditated without a word.

At one point, Tanner sneaked a peek at her. She was sitting facing the ocean. Her eyes were closed, her hair was blowing backward, and she had a *Mona Lisa smile* on her face. He was glad. This place had the same impact on him, and he'd hoped it would for her too, as she'd never had a chance to get out and see the world and breathe some fresh air.

"This place is healing for sure, Tanner," Carmen said unexpectedly. "I can see why you make the trek." Her voice suddenly cutting through the silence had made him jump. "The energy and vibrations here are amazing. So vibrant compared to the edginess that I feel in the inner valley. I think it's the heat and the brown hills that stay that way for months. The whole scene often makes me feel flat inside, like I'm only surviving while living in an inhospitable place, rather than thriving. You know?"

Tanner was amazed. He thought, *to hear her describe her experience as being able to feel the good energy and vibrations, and how certain places make her feel inside. Not everyone is that aware or even capable of feeling anything, especially to that degree. Perhaps only ten percent or so, at best.*

"Yes, I do know. Here's an example. Forty-three years ago, my apartment used to drain me of good energy. I felt like a total loser living there. I was only seventeen, still in school and it was a safe haven away from my crazy mother. It was really very touch-and-go financially. Now, after all these years, to find myself not only in the same apartment complex, but the same exact apartment that I lived in when I was seventeen, is bizarre. Even though it's all been updated, it's still strange.

Carmen seemed to understand. "I get what you're saying completely about how some settings—homes, offices, places in the woods, certain cities, *feel different,* and the feelings aren't always good, or bad, but they exist, and they impact those capable of detecting them. Like us. Which brings me to how I'm feeling right now, which is very close to you. I want to ask you something."

Tanner sat up taller and looked right at her, "Sure. Anything."

Then, changing her mind, "Well, hold that thought. I'm not certain *anything* is necessarily an appropriate response. But, thank you. Maybe we should eat first? Or, at least have a snack. I'm very hungry all of a sudden. Do you mind?"

Tanner was starving, "No. Actually, I was going to suggest the same thing. How about we find another spot, inside the woods, and away from the wind?"

"That sounds great," she said enthusiastically. Tanner led the way, heading back towards the main trail. "It's like walking into a really quiet library, isn't it?"

"Yes. The quiet really captivates me," he said. "The steadfast solitude of these giant timbers stretching upward almost to infinity. The ocean breeze. The view. I wish I could build a small house here, and live like a semi-hermit. It's really strange to hear myself say that. I love being around others in a social way for short periods of time, and need that regularly. But, in-between I'd prefer to be in a place just like this."

Carmen smiled. "You wouldn't get any argument from me about living here. That's for sure."

"Yeah, it sure would be amazing wouldn't it? It's too bad that moving here would mean that others would want to do the same. Hell, some would even go to court to argue for their right to do so. In the end, it wouldn't be quiet here anymore, and the pristine quality would be lost forever. Good thing this place is a national landmark which protects it from just what we've been talking about doing. Rich people would grab it up instantly."

Carmen said, "Yes, they would, and they'd also put gates and fences up around all of it to keep everyone else out. I've seen that my entire life. Rich people doing whatever the hell they want to, and always getting away with stuff that only they can get away with by paying for expensive lawyers, and sometimes even paying off law enforcement, and judges."

Tanner joined in, "It's as if our truest fantasies, our fondest dreams, are forever doomed to remain just that. Nothing more than electrical activity between neurons in our brains. Like a permanent carrot that the universe holds out in front of you. Here you go, come on and get it, here it is, almost within reach. Just work a little harder, and you'll get it, *someday, maybe.*"

He looked over at Carmen. When she felt his eyes on her, she turned and looked right into his. She smiled at him and nodded. He nodded back, then came closer and put his arm around her. They continued strolling, looking for a good place to sit and enjoy lunch together.

After another half-mile or so, there was a small trail that branched off heading towards an area that seemed much brighter. They decided to take it. After hiking for a couple of hundred more yards, they emerged from the trees into a large, flat, grassy field. The beauty was stunning: a mountain meadow tucked away between three ridges in the coastal range of northern California, abutting a thousand-year-old redwood tree cathedral.

The field at the bottom consisted of three-foot-tall grasses heavily infused with wild flowers: pink, red, yellow, blue, and purple flowers of various sizes, all swaying in the gentle breeze. The faint scent of perfume teased the air. The sound of wrens and blue jays could be heard occasionally, as could the breeze rustling through the grasses. Their surroundings gave them both a feeling of safety and solitude. Tanner looked at Carmen, "What do you think? Good place to have lunch, or what?"

"Tanner, this is the most beautiful place I've ever seen in my entire life. I'm not just saying that, I mean it."

"It is stunning. I've thought so every time I've been here."

Together, they laid out the blanket and sat down. Carmen opened up her picnic basket and took out all the goodies she'd packed for them. Tanner was surprised, and very grateful. He knew that she'd packed a good lunch for them, as judged by the weight of the basket that he'd been carrying for them since their arrival. He loved the lunch simplicity of sandwiches, chips, a fruit, an energy bar, and a water.

They were very hungry and ate in silence. While peeling an orange, Tanner couldn't stand the suspense any longer, "So, what is it that you want to ask me, Carmen?"

Carmen finished chewing the bite of apple she'd just put into her mouth, and lowered it into her lap. "Well, okay. I put it out there. Here goes, and please don't be upset or weirded out by this, please. I don't want you to quit."

"Carmen, just say it. Please?"

She looked right at him and then suddenly, almost as if spitting, she said really fast, "Tanner, will you give me your sperm so I can have a kid?" Tanner tried to play it cool, but he was stunned. "But, before you say anything, I just want you to know that I've sensed you holding back, hesitating during our make out sessions, except maybe not during that last one just a little while ago. So, I figure that you're not into me. That's okay. But—"

"Wait," Tanner interrupted, "I am into you and that's the problem. For some reason, I'm having a harder time than I thought I would getting past the fact that, currently, you're my boss, and, secondly, that you're so much younger than I am. I think our age difference is just too far apart. Plus, you still want a baby, and I've always wanted one too. I love being with you, but I don't think I can be a full-time father anymore. I'm just old enough that I think I'd be exhausted all the time. I would still like to be a father, but only if I could be a part-time one. I think I could do that, and would like it. But, you're right. I have held back, on purpose. I didn't want to let my penis do the talking and deciding for me, and I didn't want to risk getting you pregnant, when I wasn't ready to back it up by marrying you and/or being a full-time father to our child."

Carmen immediately responded, "I understand now. Thank you for that. One more thing, if you say yes, and I hope you do, Diego won't like it, but he won't have a choice, and he'll come around."

"Well, that's a big incentive." Tanner wondered if Carmen had heard a word of what he'd just said. She seemed a little desperate now. He could tell she sensed he was close to saying yes.

She acted like she didn't hear him, "It's just that I don't get out, ever. I can't. The online dating thing is crap, and I don't want to waste my time with that."

"I'm flattered, Carmen. I've never been asked by anyone for my sperm before. Don't worry, I will never share our secret with anyone, unless we first both agree that it's okay to tell others."

"I was hoping you'd say that. You're a good man, Tanner. You have a good heart, good manners, and real decency. Plus, I like your looks. You're a good-looking man, and I think we'd have fine looking children." She stopped, and they both stayed quiet for a moment. Tanner stared off towards the trees again, his mind racing. She continued, "You don't have to marry me, support me or the child, or raise the kid. Hell, you don't even have to spend any time with our baby at all if you really don't want to, but if you started to and later changed your mind, I might have a hard time with that."

Tanner looked at her and said, "Now that I've thought a little more about it, I just want us to be clear: If I give you my sperm and you become pregnant, I most certainly would want to help you and spend time with both of you, and I'd be able to be a part-time father finally, wouldn't I?"

"Yes, you would." She smiled affectionately at him, and reached up and gently laid her hand on his left cheek, "So, you'll seriously consider it?" she said while nodding and smiling at him. Her eyes danced playfully, taunting him. Trying to telepathically convey to him that if he still wanted a child, like he'd said to her while they were prepping at work, then here was your chance—likely, your last chance. Her eyes were magnetic now. He could feel his heart and his soul being pulled towards her. He stood still. Feeling it all. He closed his eyes and absorbed her energy, taking it deep into himself. When he reopened them, he was sure.

He looked deep into Carmen's eyes, "Absolutely. Yes. In fact, I don't need or want to think about it any longer. I'm in. Hell yeah." After that revelation, they hugged for a very long time. Neither of them wanted to let go. Tanner thought Carmen had been extremely brave to just come out and ask him for something so personal and intimate. But now he was ecstatic that she had. In doing so, she'd just given both of them the opportunity to finally realize a dream that they'd both had for most of their adult lives.

When they pulled apart, they looked at one another with new eyes. A deeper connection had been made, and in his core Tanner knew that he'd just made a very consequential, but great, choice.

They decided to have a celebratory dinner. After leaving Muir Woods, they stopped at a wonderful little bistro and enjoyed some crab cakes, corn, and southern hush puppies, and then they shared an ice cream sundae.

The drive home was uneventful and traffic was minimal for a change. They talked a little about Diego. Carmen was more concerned than ever about him. He always seemed to be gone mentally, and always going out, somewhere. She said that even when he was physically in the house, he was still gone mentally. Apparently, she'd been noticing his forgetfulness increasing for quite some time.

She told Tanner that Diego hadn't ordered any supplies in nearly a year, that it was just her running everything now. Meanwhile, he still liked to act as if he were in charge, getting mad at her for nothing then storming off and disappearing for another two days or so. "He never asks how the bills get paid or how the food just magically appears. He just stays in his own universe now while he walks amongst us with a smile on his face, oblivious to any of it, including why he is smiling."

When they got back to Carmen's, Tanner walked her to the door and helped her in with her picnic basket. The house was quiet, except a television could be heard coming from the den. "Well, there you go. He's home. Probably asleep in his chair. All I'll need to do is make sure his shoes are off, cover him with a blanket, turn off the television and the light, and go to bed."

"I had a really fun time showing you my favorite place today, Carmen. Thank you for coming with me and allowing me to share that with you."

"The pleasure is all mine, Tanner. I thoroughly enjoyed myself. Thank you very much for a wonderful time. The woods totally exceeded my expectations. I had no idea about that place. I can see why you like going there."

Tanner stepped forward and hugged Carmen, then pulled back and leaned down and gave her a nice, soft kiss on the cheek and said, "I'm so amazed by what transpired between us today, Carmen. I still cannot believe that I'm actually going to become a father after all."

Carmen had to suppress her urge to squeal with delight. His mentioning the baby brought it all to the forefront again, instantly perking her up. She smiled at him. "I know, I can't believe it either. I was petrified to ask you, but now that I have, I have no regrets and I'm so excited I can hardly stand myself."

"Is your father coming in on Monday? Wait, don't answer that. I'll get up with him real soon and tell him about our plans. I'll let him blow up a bit; it's to be expected by any father that finds out his daughter is going to be pregnant without wedlock in the picture. He may even want to do a shotgun wedding with me in it anyway. Who knows. I'll talk to him soon."

"Thank you, Tanner. When I asked you at dinner if you'd speak to him, I was worried all over again, because of the look that came over your face. You don't hide your dread very well," she said with a smile."

"Sorry about that."

"I don't blame you one bit. I've had that feeling off and on my entire life as his daughter. I hate having to go to him about anything serious. He always has to blow up and he doesn't listen and doesn't hear a damn thing anyone says. It's an awful, knee-jerk reaction and I've always hated it."

Tanner nodded. "I'll see you on Monday. Have a good day off tomorrow. Try to take it as easy as possible. The word has gotten out about Es Picante, and I'm sure you've noticed the increase in customers at lunchtime, so it promises to be a busy week for sure."

"I will, Tanner. You, too. Thank you."

"Thank you, Carmen."

Tanner felt really good for the first time in a long time. He was truly excited to have one last shot at being a father. His genes were going to be passed on after all. He went home tired, but very happy.

22

GONE FISHING

On Sunday, he slept in a little, waking up naturally around 9 a.m. hungry and alert. He took a shower, shaved, and made breakfast. As he cooked his eggs and French toast, he thought about the previous day with Carmen—how mystical, magical, and surreal the time they'd spent in the woods had been for him. The way they'd connected spiritually and how they seemed to be able to feel each other's feelings. Just a fraction away from being able to read each other's mind. He'd never experienced that before with anyone else. It was special, just like her proposal.

He picked up the current copy of *Wired Magazine* to finish the article he'd started a couple of days prior about the chip technologies powering artificial intelligence. He could hardly believe what the article said about how many terabytes per second some of these machines are capable of—There was a knock on Tanner's door. He put the magazine down and went to see who was knocking. He opened the door to see Sophie standing there smiling at him, all dressed in weekend casual, looking like she was up for just about anything. "Hi, mind if I come in?"

Tanner stepped to the side, "No, come on in. This is quite a surprise. What brings you here?"

"Boredom, and intrigue about what two, good-looking, bored people might figure out to do on a quiet Sunday afternoon," she said as she strolled into the living room.

"Well, I wasn't planning on doing much of anything today. I'm tired. I could use some down time. Work comes early tomorrow."

"I can respect that. But, there are many things that can alleviate boredom, while also promoting relaxation."

Tanner gave her a sideways glance. He had a half-smile on his face. "Like what?" he said.

"Um, I don't know. We could— "

Tanner snagged the chance to end it well "—Go fishing, for example."

Sophie's eyes grew big. "Okay, you got me. That's a mixed one for me. It's certainly something to do, but I've been bored with that before, too."

"Fishing means I'll really be able to relax." He smiled at her. "Have you done any fishing?" Tanner wasn't sure what to expect for an answer.

"Yeah, when I was eight years old, my father took me to some river and we fished. I don't remember how to though. Why?"

"Let's just do a completely spontaneous thing and go over to Walmart and get us a couple of inexpensive poles, one tackle box to share, and some hooks, and a few lures. I know a couple of lures that will work well to catch striped bass. We'll pick up some night crawlers and blood worms on the way. Once we get our gear, we can head out to a spot I know of near Crockett, not too far from here, it's right on Suisun Bay. We'll get some sandwiches and something to drink on the way. Sound good?"

"It sounds . . . interesting, I'll say."

"Really? You don't think it sounds like fun?"

Sophie rolled her eyes, "Not really. I say that only because the biggest thing I remember about fishing was how bored I was that entire day. My dad mostly stayed away from me—down river—that day. He stayed quiet, and so did I. It was awful."

"Did you catch any fish?"

"Nothing. When we went to leave, my father came over and told me to reel it in. When I did and he saw that I had no bait left on the end, he laughed and told me that's why I didn't catch anything. I asked how I was supposed to know if the bait is still there or not, with the line in the water? Then he told me that even an idiot would know to pull the line in once in a while to check for bait. I was so mad at him for that. I didn't know what I was supposed to be doing, I'd never been before. After that, I never wanted to go again."

Tanner said, "Wow, I get it. I wouldn't have wanted to go again either. At least not with that dickhead. Oh, sorry. I shouldn't have called your father a dickhead. I apologize."

Sophie smiled, "No worries. He was a dickhead. For sure. He died shortly after that trip. The only thing I miss about him is the way he would give me the most loving, caring look and smile— out of the blue. But, over time, I learned that I couldn't trust him, despite that look. Most of the time, he treated me like shit. He would never show affection, or look at me most of the time, not even when I spoke directly to him; he would continue looking at his newspaper while I spoke, sometimes he would answer me, but it always came from behind that printed, monotone veil. I was sad, for a brief time, after he died, but I never think of him anymore, really, and that's just as sad to me."

Tanner sat, sipping his coffee, listening attentively. He could tell that she needed to be heard right now, so he stayed quiet. She continued, "Weird how my mom never said much or looked happy either. She was just barely able to bear living, doing her duty, unwilling to complain, knowing it would do no good if she did. What about you? Your parents? Care to share?"

Tanner shook his head, "No thanks. We all have our mommy and daddy issues to some degree. Maybe someday I'll share about that stuff with you, but right now, I'd really rather go fishing. Please?"

"Okay. I'll give it another whirl. But only because it's you asking me."

Tanner smiled. "Perfect—and your jeans, sweatshirt, wind-breaker, hiking boots, and hat are absolutely perfect for today for where we're going. How'd you know?" He chuckled. "Let me get changed, I'll only be a minute." He started towards his bedroom, then turned back towards her, "Oh, one more thing. I'll guarantee you that, today, you will have the pleasure and know the thrill, of catching a live, struggling fish."

A short while later, they went to Walmart and bought their gear. For Tanner, having a pole and some gear in his hands again felt really good. He was anxious to catch a couple of striped bass.

When they were only a mile or so away from the turnout that Tanner used to take, he was pleasantly surprised to see that the little bait shack where he used to get his bait was still there. He pulled in.

"Come on, you won't believe this place, if it's the same on the inside as it was back in the '70s, well, you'll see." Going inside was like stepping back into a time capsule. All of the old photographs of people standing on nearby docks next to the huge, 250- to 400-pound sturgeons they'd just caught, or striped bass that weighed 50 pounds, were still plastered all over the walls, and the support beams that held up the roof. Tanner was shocked. The place hadn't changed at all in 50 years.

The prominent odors of worms-in-wet-dirt, beer, tobacco, and heavy dust were so strong, Sophie whispered "I'll be right outside," before rushing out. Tanner bought a large cup of blood worms and a large cup of night crawlers, but changed his mind on the live minnows. The worms always seemed to work fine anyway. He badly wanted to go down memory lane with someone, but the only other person in the store was a young, high-school aged kid at the checkout, so he didn't bother. It was obvious that the kid was new, and hadn't even been born when Tanner used to come here.

The fishing spot was only a couple of miles away. Once they parked, Sophie helped Tanner carry their gear over some railroad tracks, then down a small embankment comprised of grasses, small shrubs, and rocks that gently sloped down to the small strip of sandy beach no wider than three feet at the water's edge. They carefully made their way down to the little beach and set their gear down.

It was a gorgeous view on a bright, sunny day. The late morning sun was now high overhead and the water looked dazzling and only slightly choppy. The faint scent of salt was in the air. Dozens of nearby seagulls and sandpipers were frantically scavenging. Sophie stood and looked out across the bay, and smiled. On the other side, she could see hundreds of mothballed navy vessels tied together, floating in unison. The light breeze coming off the sparkling water gently blew through her full, red hair, lifting it slightly away from her shoulders adding to her beauty and revealing another part of her delicate, petite frame to Tanner for the first time.

Tanner began unpacking the gear from the store. Without thinking about what he was saying, he began telling Sophie all about buoyancy, positive displacement theory and other scientific oddities, until he saw her roll her eyes. He'd forgotten. It was Carmen who loved science, science fiction, astronomy, and other kinds of science and spirituality. After spending time with Carmen recently, he'd just spoken automatically. Sophie seemed content to just have fun. She didn't care about how something was invented, how it worked internally, or anything about the electronic theory underlying the circuitry. All she cared about was whether it worked or not, whether it did what it was supposed to do, and the price.

Seeing the look on his face, she changed her tune, and tried to sound a little interested. "Honestly, I have no idea where you get all of this information from, but I like learning new things so, please, continue."

He'd already thought a little about what it would be like to live with her or marry her, and had already concluded that the only way he could manage that would be for him to have rock solid alternative outlets for his need to intellectualize. She was smart, but in a more utilitarian way. He would need to have someone available to have more scientifically oriented discussions with. She was capable of discussing, but not interested in discussing many things he would enjoy talking about. Without that, he could envision how they might stop talking to each other completely. She'd want to talk about her day at the mall and show him the new designer purse she'd bought on a whim that had been on sale, while he would want to talk about the implications of ignoring global warming, and the things that could be done to improve mankind's odds of survival.

Tanner got Sophie all set up for fishing. He patiently showed her how to hold her rod, how to use the reel properly and explained the purpose of *drag* and how to use it. He then had her set the drag on her own reel. He demonstrated casting and was surprised how well she learned. She casted farther than him within minutes and playfully stuck her tongue out at him, taunting him. Tanner said, "Oh yeah, watch this!" He pulled his rod back, and gave his next cast everything he had. Afterward, he began looking all around and said, "What happened? Where's my rig?" Then he spied Sophie, looking at him with her hand over her mouth concealing her laughter. Finally, not able to contain it any longer, she laughed out loud. She told him that he'd casted so hard, his heavy rig had stretched his line out to its limit and it snapped off just before he'd let go. She said she saw it fly away fast, straight towards the horizon.

"Are you laughing at me? Again?" Tanner was smiling wide. "That's it!" He dropped his pole and ran towards her. She shrieked, dropped her pole, and ran down the beach with Tanner hot on her heels. She was laughing so hard, she could hardly see where she was going. She tripped over something and fell down, still laughing. Tanner landed next to her a second later.

He looked at her and smiled. She looked back into his eyes before reaching up with both hands and pulling him to her. She began probing his mouth with her tongue. Seriously aroused now she said, "Tanner, please. Right here. Now. Please. I don't want to wait any longer." She pulled back from him and tried to move away. He jumped up thinking she had changed her mind. He moved aside so she could do what she needed to.

She quickly undressed from the waist down, turning her clothes inside out, then eased down onto them. She lay back, propping herself up slightly with her elbows and looked directly into his eyes. Tanner never broke their gaze while quickly shedding his clothes. He knelt down in front of her, then eased down onto her body and began kissing her. He could feel her moisture and feminine warmth. A second later, he was deep inside her. Their bodies became one, and their writhing, moaning, and eventual screams of pleasure were a testament to their passions finally being released as they allowed themselves to finally have what they'd both wanted from the very beginning.

When they finally stood up, Tanner couldn't help himself from watching Sophie get dressed. Her natural, naked beauty went well beyond what he'd already imagined. Now, seeing her beauty close up and in bright daylight temporarily made it very difficult for him to put his pants back on.

He admired her in so many ways. "I love your sense of spontaneous adventure," he said. "I'm not sure why, but being out in nature, especially at the beach makes sex a lot more exciting for me, and it always has." Tanner was glad that he'd gone with the flow this time. He was more than ready for it. He had been saying no to her, no to Tammy, no to Carmen for quite some time. He was beginning to discover a lot more about why he was here, and why he'd met the people he had since returning to California. *The universe heard me on my way back here,* he thought.

"Glad to be able to help you with that." Sophie said with a big smile. "Just like you said. It's something about being outdoors, fresh air, I don't know. It often makes me horny as hell too."

Now that their physical and psychic tensions had been released, at least for the time being, they both felt more easy going. Tanner was grateful that it had gone the way it had. It was great. Fun, spontaneous, fantastic. He felt so much better now, and Sophie seemed happy and relieved too.

They spent the rest of the afternoon seriously fishing and ended up catching two dozen striped bass. They took some pics of a few of them, and Tanner got a nice video of Sophie reeling in the biggest fish either of them caught that day. They threw all of them back so they could someday fight again. Sophie had never imagined that fishing could be so fun. She was really glad that she'd decided to come. She was both disgusted and fascinated while watching Tanner put the worms on the hooks, and she'd screamed with delight when the first decent-sized fish grabbed her line that she managed to wrestle in successfully. They'd both gotten a little sun and it looked good on them. After a few hours, the bait was running out, some dark clouds were beginning to work in from San Francisco Bay, and the wind was picking up. Tanner could tell it would be raining soon, so they packed up and left.

Back at his apartment, they lingered over tea, watching the rain come down in droves outside. Tanner was grateful that Sophie didn't seem put off in the least by the modest surroundings of his apartment. He'd worried about her reaction to it. His place was a huge step down from her place, and he was delighted when she seemed fine. They ended up talking about some of the strange people they'd met or seen over the years. She spoke about some of the odd characters that had come into *Penny's* at times while she'd been working, and he let her in on some of the characters he'd noticed in the public sitting areas at Sunvalley Mall.

They talked about having dinner together, but Tanner said he'd like to take a shower and have some alone time for the rest of the evening. She agreed, she was feeling tired too, and now that it was raining, she just wanted to head home. She thanked him for a wonderful afternoon and they made arrangements to have dinner together Tuesday night. She gave him another passionate kiss, and then left happier than he'd ever seen her.

Tanner was energized by the day's events. He knew what had happened between them today had taken things to the next level. He thought that their physical intimacy was something consequential, and somehow felt right, but now he needed to figure out how he was going to transition to becoming a father while still keeping Sophie in his life.

23

LATE AFTERNOON RAIN
STRIKE ONE

After Sophie left, Tanner wanted to totally relax. He loaded up his bong with some top-shelf Indica and took a massive hit. He held it in as long as he could, then coughed it all out, feeling the cannabinoids hit his system like a welcome freight train.

Reflecting on the events of the day made him smile. All of it was utterly unexpected, but had thrilled both of them. He was glad they'd had sex. Once it began, he'd realized just how much he'd needed it, and now he could hardly stop replaying their lovemaking over and over again in his head. He could see her naked, lavishing his body with her tongue, gently and skillfully giving him pleasures he had forgotten were possible to experience. He'd been scared at first, but then she'd taken off all of her clothes and gently laid back, spreading her legs for him, never taking her eyes off of him, as if she were looking directly into his soul—that slight smile, that devilish glint in her eyes—his pleasure was just as much hers.

She loved the power she had to control him with a simple yes, or no. And he loved that she had that power over him, to entice him, make him lust and yearn for her. Make him want to penetrate her, pleasuring himself inside her until giving her his last possible gift.

He could feel the tide beginning to turn. He saw that Sophie was an extraordinarily funny and fun person to be with, not to mention a perfect physical mate. She was someone who still had physical desires and would likely become someone he would be able to have as much sex with as he wanted, and Tanner knew better than to take that gift lightly.

But, at a spiritual and emotional level, he felt far more connected to Carmen. Tanner knew that sex could quickly get boring if that's all there is, and connections, at a spiritual and emotional level, tended to almost *demand some physical bonding,* especially if quite a bit of sharing and time spent together have already elapsed without any physical gratification.

Tanner thought, *Sophie is super fun to be with, but so is Carmen in her own, more youthful way.* Sophie has a sophistication that Carmen lacks, but she isn't nearly as happy and content as Carmen. Carmen seems much more content overall, and she absolutely knows who she is, where she is heading, and what she wants. Sophie doesn't know who she is, or who she wants to become. She only knows who she has been. She lucked out and escaped her horrible situation, but now she is nothing more than a little lost sheep looking for someone to latch onto to protect her. She is someone to strictly have fun with. Only two things are bothering Carmen now: not having a child without having to adopt, and Diego's worsening mental state. Carmen, wants a child from me. *Sophie wants me, but only so she can continue having fun.*

He wondered what would happen if he said no to Carmen. Would she play it off as if nothing was up? Or, would she be really upset and, unable to control her rage, fire him?

When he really thought about it, he knew in his core, he wanted to father a child before he died. He wanted more than anything in the entire world to have a child with his genetics. As weird as it may seem, or sound, the need to procreate is a powerful instinct in human beings, and Tanner had felt the pinch of that need for decades now. He had given up long ago on the opportunity to become a father and thought he had come to terms with it long ago, and put it to rest.

Now, he was finally being offered a chance to fulfill that dream, with someone that he felt was not only a fantastic human being, but someone he knew would make a great mother. He knew he had to do this. No doubt whatsoever.

The teas had worked their magic on his bladder. As he stood over the toilet relieving himself, he heard his phone begin to ring in the other room. After five audible rings, it finally stopped, and went to voicemail. Tanner wondered if it was Tammy, Carmen, or Sophie. He said it aloud, kiddingly, trying to sound very British, *Hmmm, I wonder if it's Tammy, Carmen, or Sophie? My, aren't we in high demand these days, hmmm.* He chuckled and washed his hands, feeling a little like a *swinging bachelor*, and went out to see which of the three ladies he was going to be speaking with next.

When he picked up his phone, he saw a voicemail notification from a number that he didn't recognize, and wondered if it was just another spam call. Then, he noticed the little red number 1 next to the voicemail icon. He tapped the icon, then tapped the message, "Tanner, it's Doug, from skydiving. Please give me a call right away. I have some news." That was it. Nothing more. Tanner almost panicked, thinking something happened to Tammy, then he realized that it could be something as simple as Doug letting him know that no one would be going skydiving or the plane would be inside for maintenance that coming Friday, or any number of other things, so he relaxed for the most part.

Tanner tapped the call back button and heard the phone ringing on Doug's end. After four rings, he connected to Doug's voicemail. He left a message, "Doug, Tanner. Hey, got your message, I hope all is well and I hope we're still going to be able to go up this coming Friday. Call me back soon, okay? Thanks. Peace." Tanner began pacing the room trying to calm down. He was having trouble controlling his thoughts and not imagining the worst outcome. He went over to his bong and fired on it, taking in another massive hit, then letting it out slowly. He wanted to kind of zone out, relax, and be able to take bad news more calmly, should the need arise.

He was getting hungry, and wanted to take a shower. He began getting undressed and went into the bathroom, but he took his phone with him in case Doug called back. He was just about to get in and his phone rang. It was Doug, just as he'd hoped. He shut off the shower and connected. "Doug, hey man, how's it going?"

"Tanner, glad I finally caught up with you. Hey. Yeah. Um. Hmmm . . ."

"What is it, Doug? Just tell me, man . . . TELL ME, MAN!"

There was a pause so long that Tanner thought they'd been disconnected. "Doug, you still there?"

"Yes. I'm here. Okay, here goes. Tanner, I'm barely able to tell you this. I witnessed the whole thing and I've been speechless until now."

"What is it?" Tanner was sure it was Tammy, but he was holding back until he knew for certain.

"We went up late on Saturday. Me, Tammy, Alvin, you know, that weird dude that pilots part-time at Skydive Byron?"

"Yeah, I know Alvin."

"Well, we all went up to 20K for a sun setter, and it was off the scale, dude. I mean, every color imaginable could be seen right when we went out. It was so fucking awesome. All was well, and we all sailed down to the danger zone with shit-eating grins on our faces until Tammy's parachute decided to fail."

"WHAT?"

"Yep. Her chute didn't deploy, dude."

"What about her reserve?"

"Deployed, but it was too late. By then, she was only at 800 feet. It definitely slowed her down, but . . . ." Doug was sobbing now. Tanner listened to him. Finally, Doug coughed and took a drink of something and finally finished, "She died on impact, man. I'm so sorry, dude."

Tanner couldn't say a word. He was speechless. He tried, twice, to say something back to Doug, but nothing came out. After failing on the third try, he simply hung up.

Tanner shuddered in silent remorse. He cried harder than he'd ever cried in his entire life. He pictured Tammy falling with that smile on her face that she always got when she jumped. He did too. He got it. She got him. They were besties, for sure, and now, they were besties no more.

He shook for an hour, rocking back and forth in his chair, picturing her, picturing them together, talking, kissing, making love, exploring new horizons together with psilocybin mushrooms. He remembered being inside her again. How good it had felt. How she'd gasped with pleasure as he'd entered her and they'd made up for lost time, finally able to express all that they'd felt, unimpeded.

Now, she was dead and Tanner would never see or speak to her again. He'd never hear her laugh, cry, or chuckle at one of his stupid jokes, ever again. The finality of it kept grabbing him, shaking him with grief, making him want to be able to see her, talk to her, kiss her once again.

He drove over to her house. It was dark. No lights had been left on. Someone, likely Doug, had left her truck in the driveway. Tanner parked next to Tammy's truck. He went around the garage to the side door. Sure enough, it was unlocked. He slipped inside and found his way into the kitchen. When he closed the door behind him. He stood still, listening to the silence. He went into the great room and walked over to the sliding glass door. He looked out at the landscape that Tammy had created out of thin air, and flashed back on her having sex with motorcycle man on the hammock. He walked down the hallway to the bedroom.

He turned on the small lamp near the door, and looked at the bed. He remembered the night he'd taken his first mushroom trip and she'd led him in here and made crazy love to him. He remembered how she'd felt like a silk mannequin to him that night.

He broke down again, standing there in her bedroom, picturing her sleeping, the two of them making love, her bending over to pull up her stockings while getting dressed later, and him taking advantage of the position knowing that she had all the time in the world. He already missed her. He felt her now, watching him. He knew she was there in the room with him. Somehow, he knew she was crying with him while he cried. Tanner could feel her the entire time he was in her house, in each room, in each thought, and in each feeling. He loved her deeply, and had for his entire adult life. Apparently, their destiny was always as friends. Eternal friends. He silently prayed for her soul, and verbally thanked her out loud, "Thank you, Tammy. Thank you for being my friend for all these decades. Thank you for loving me after all these decades. I'll always love you. I miss you already, and still cannot believe you're gone. I'm sorry for anything I ever did that hurt you in any way. I NEVER wanted that to happen."

Tanner stuck around for an hour or so. The entire time, he walked from room to room, speaking telepathically, and verbally to Tammy. He knew she heard him. He knew she felt him, and what he felt inside, and understood his messages. He needed to feel that way. He was glad he'd come. He knew that very soon, lawyers, courts, and thieves alike, would all descend upon this place, and Tanner didn't want to be anywhere near here when it happened.

After kneeling in Tammy's living room and closing his eyes, he said a prayer for her soul, asking the power of the universe to accept her and love her for all eternity. Afterwards, he left quietly, locking up behind himself.

24

NEW BEGINNINGS

Judging by the crowd at her funeral, it was obvious that Tammy had known a lot more people than Tanner had met, or known about. Close to three hundred people showed up to pay their respects, and at least a dozen people got up to share something about her. Tanner felt a lot of pressure to do the same. Quite a few people he'd met at Skydive Byron were there and knew about his close friendship with Tammy. But Tanner froze. He had so much to say, but no idea how to say it. Besides, most of what he would want to say would be pretty personal and he wasn't going to talk about his personal stuff in front of strangers.

He'd loved her. What else was there? Anecdotes to make the funeral attendees laugh, turning the whole thing into a stand-up comedy routine, then maybe say *Tammy's watching this right now and loving every minute of it?* He only came out of respect for Tammy, not to entertain, enlighten others, or inform on his sincerely missed friend.

Carmen sat on his left, Sophie on his right. Neither of them seemed bothered in the least by the other, and Tanner was grateful for the support and company. After the formal ceremony, there was a gathering in the basement of the church which doubled as a classroom, or a dance floor, or what ever else they might need it to be. The three of them sat together at a small table near the food and drink. Lots of people paraded past, giving weak smiles and nodding. Tanner had no idea who they were, but they were there to pay their respects, just like him, so he nodded back respectfully.

Tanner glanced between them as he spoke, "Tammy was a free spirit for sure. She loved challenges and enjoyed hard work. But, more than anything, she enjoyed skydiving. She had a love of heights and flying and being on top of mountains. Skydiving was the next, natural extension, a combination of all those things rolled into a single experience that she could repeat over and over again, each time getting the thrill of a lifetime. I'm glad she got me back into it, too. Now, I'm not sure I'll keep going. It would seem really strange for me to go with the people she introduced me to, but with her always gone from the group."

Sophie looked frightened. "But how did this happen again? I'm still not clear on what happened."

Tanner answered, "She descended to a dangerously low level before deploying her chute. At least that's what her jump mate, Doug, confirmed. He went out with her. He said she fell normally. She even did a few full circle turns, a backwards somersault, and a brief nose dive maneuver, and appeared to be having a blast. He pulled his chute at the recommended 5,000 foot level, but she kept falling. When he saw how low she was going, he said he screamed at her to pull her ripcord, that he'd felt compelled to do it even though she couldn't hear him. Doug estimated that when she pulled her primary chute ripcord, she was just under 2,000 feet. Right away, it wrapped itself up and she'd frantically tried to unwrap it the rest of the way down. She hastily pulled the reserve, but it was already too late. She'd exhausted all the buffer she would've had if she'd just pulled at 5,000 feet instead of waiting so long. She died trying to get just a few more seconds of free fall in, and the double-thrill of cutting it so close, which turned out to be a fatal decision."

Sophie looked horrified. "You said I'd love it and I should come. I thought about it and thought it sounded fun. It doesn't sound fun anymore."

Carmen couldn't stand it any longer. She looked right at Sophie and said, "Oh my gosh you're so right. That night, when I was leaving Tanner's apartment and we met, I'd just spent the last couple of hours looking at videos of him skydiving. It looked fun, but also scary as hell. Me? I'll stay on solid ground, thank you. I will not go up in a small airplane, then get out on the wing and let go. I will not fall at 120 mph and hope that my canopy deploys and stops me from, well . . . from ending up like poor Tammy." She was still shaking her head no, trying to get the gruesome images out of her head.

Carmen changed the subject, "Tanner mentioned that you work, or used to work at *Penny's Roadside Cafe?*"

"Yes, four to six hours a day during the week. I go in after the morning rush, and leave before the evening one. Why do you ask?"

"Have you been doing that long?"

"About ten years now, why?"

"I'm asking because I need to hire another person. My father has become unreliable and he is failing mentally. He used to come in and do certain things every day. Now, I never know when I'll see him. I cannot operate like that. I need a certain amount of help that I can count on. My family and I are going to be taking his driver's license away from him soon. We're not sure how he'll take that event, but we're certain it will not be easy, or pretty.

Sophie thought for a moment, then said, "I'm so sorry to learn about your father. That's got to be scary, hard, and just awful. I would welcome a change away from *Penny's.* Would you be willing to match my hourly wage?"

Carmen looked excited, "Yes, I will, if you'll be flexible about what I have you do. I might even have you take my father to an appointment so I can keep the restaurant open, would you be okay with doing that occasionally?"

"That would not be a problem, unless he tries to paw me or be inappropriate with me. He's not like that, is he?"

"So far, no."

"Good. But one more thing, you realize that Tanner and I are in the beginning stages of becoming a couple? I'll let him disagree with me if it's not true." She looked at Tanner, "If it's not true, please nod no, now. No nodding? So, it's true." She smiled and laughed. "There you have it then." She gave Carmen a hard look, "So, that wouldn't bother you?"

Without hesitation, Carmen fired right back, "I expect you both to do your jobs while I'm paying you to work. Tanner can vouch for how we can suddenly get very busy. I can only offer you part-time hours, but it sounds like that's all you want anyway, am I right?"

"Yes, you are."

"Well, think about it. If you can be professional and keep your hands to yourself and keep things respectable and leave the groping at home, then I could use your help." She took a sip of her coffee, then a small bite of a little triangle shaped sandwich consisting of two pieces of white bread with the crust removed, stuffed with deviled egg. She looked at Sophie calmly and confidently, chewing. Then she said, "Oh, and you do realize that Tanner and I are planning to have a baby together, don't you? I'll let him disagree with me if it's not true. Tanner, if it's not true, please nod no, now. No nodding?" Tanner sat still, like a statue looking straight ahead. "So, it's true."

Both Tanner and Sophie were stunned. Tanner was stunned because she'd not spoken with him about telling Sophie or anyone else about it first. Sophie, because Tanner had not even mentioned it to her.

"Oops. Did I say something I shouldn't have?"

"You could have talked to me about this first, Carmen. She's my friend and I was planning to tell her, but then Tammy died. I just haven't gotten around to it yet. I don't appreciate being outed like that."

Sophie was staring at Tanner. Her stare was saying a lot of things, none of them good.

Carmen said, "All right. I started this, and I'm sorry. Sophie, it's like this. I run a busy restaurant and it takes up all my time. I haven't been out on a real date in years. Most of the men I have dated I didn't want to see again. I just don't have time to play that whole dating thing. Meanwhile, my biological clock is running out and I very much want to have a child. The short of it is this: instead of going to a sperm bank, I've asked Tanner for his sperm. But, without having sex with him and without marriage, monetary support, or anything else he doesn't want."

As she listened to Carmen explaining herself, Sophie's expression softened considerably. "Tanner and I had a couple of dates and they went well. I think we could easily be a couple too, but he's let me know that he's uncomfortable with our significant age gap, and would prefer to be a part-time father."

Tanner took over. He looked at Sophie, "It's true, Sophie. We've gotten to know one another while chopping up food every morning and it's come out that we both want children. Well, I really wanted them when I was younger, but when Carmen just recently made me the offer to father a child with her egg and my sperm, I knew, deep inside, that I still did want to pass on my genes, but I also knew I couldn't do a full-time commitment being a father, I'm too old. Then, as attractive as she is, she's young enough to be my daughter, so I knew I also would never feel right being romantic or sexual with her, no matter that she's a legal adult. It's just not who I am. It just makes more sense doing it this way. It gives Carmen the baby she's always wanted, the child that I've always wanted, and makes for a little bit of a family unit, too. I'll be able to come over as often as I can or want to, and spend time with my child or to help Carmen out by watching the baby when she has to be at the restaurant or just needs a break."

Sophie was quiet, but still being open. She looked at Carmen and Tanner, and smiled at each of them. "You know, you might actually be on to something. Sure, it's an alternative existence, but it might just work. Maybe better than you think. I still think both of you should iron out your preferences about religion, baptismal choices, rules around food, television viewing, how old before they get a smart phone, all that kind of stuff."

Carmen chuckled, "You're right, but some of what you're talking about can happen as it needs to happen. Every child is unique. There is no way to make some decisions in advance. The child will write his or her own story and we should just be there as supportive witnesses."

Sophie said, "True, but perhaps an attorney should be consulted to ensure that both of you are on the same page. Things might come up. Having some things set up in advance might be a good idea. For example: what if someday, Tanner gets some kind of really lucrative offer and now needs to move to another state or even another country. What if the child is closer to him because of the amount of time they've spent together. Now what? Does the child relocate with Tanner, or stay here with you?"

Carmen looked frustrated. "Thanks for trying to help us cover all our bases, Sophie, but I think we'll be fine. We'll figure things out in a comfortable and equitable way. If we can't, then we might think about getting an attorney involved. There really isn't a need for one at this point. We're really doing well working things out between us organically. We have a way of doing that. We have a rare, strange kind of connection. We feel each other, and that's the only way I can describe it."

Sophie looked down at the table, then back at both of them but she didn't add anything more, she just nodded and smiled at them. Tanner was hopeful that everything would work out. So far, everything was. Sophie now knew about their plan, and was still here talking and trying to help them cover all their bases. Sophie looked at Carmen. "I've decided to take the job. I accept your offer." Tanner and Carmen were both happy to hear this. Now, not only were they getting an experienced restaurant worker, but also someone they would have a personal connection with.

"I'll be able to start in a couple of weeks. I want to give proper notice. I've been there for ten years and they count on me. But, I'm so ready for something different. This is a really great co-incidence."

Both Carmen and Tanner looked at one another and laughed.

"What? I don't get it."

Carmen answered her, "It's just that there are no such things as coincidences. Tanner and I thought the same thing when you said that. This change was needed, so it manifested into reality."

Sophie rolled her eyes, "Whatever. Personally, I've never subscribed to mystical beliefs, any more than organized religions or other spiritual venues," she said with surety.

Tanner came right back with, "Not wanting to debate you, but ancient Hinduism and Buddhism both posit that the karmic path of our existence will interact with us continuously throughout our lives, independent of our willingness to embrace, or recognize any of the spiritual concepts or spiritual experiences we may have already had or not, and what they might mean." A minute ticked by without a word. Tanner's gaze wandered, but when it returned to her she was giving him a skeptical grin. "What can I say, I read some," he said. She shook her head in disbelief and looked away.

He looked at Carmen and in a more serious tone he said, "I'd like to help you with getting your father re-situated someplace."

Carmen looked a little surprised. "Oh, thank you, but that won't be necessary, Tanner."

"Are you sure?"

Carmen nodded. "Yes, but thank you, anyway."

"Let me know if you change your mind."

"Sure. Thank you. I'll definitely keep that in mind."

"It's just that I remember my neighbor got violent when they tried to put him in a similar place. Same reason, too."

Now, he had Carmen's attention. "Did he hurt anyone?"

"No. Luckily, the EMT's got there in time to help his wife calm him down a little bit. At least long enough for them to give him a shot and put him to sleep."

"My cousin, Vincent, said he'd come over. He'd take the day off and help me with Diego. After hearing that, I'm glad he is coming now."

Tanner nodded. "Perfect."

Sophie, sounding eager to contribute something, looked at Carmen and said, "Well, since I'm going to be seeing Tanner, and I'm going to be working at your restaurant, and I'm also getting to know you at a personal level already, I'd like to offer my assistance with the baby when it arrives." Now, she had both Carmen's and Tanner's attention.

"Tanner already knows about this, but when I was of child-bearing age, my circumstances were such that a pregnancy would have made things a lot worse for me, so I avoided getting pregnant at all cost. Now, it's too late for me to have any children of my own; I've already gone through the change. Anyway, I didn't mean to make it all about me, I just wanted you to know a little bit about where I was coming from with that offer. I'd love to help in any way that I can, while also having the honor to witness the child growing up. Who knows, maybe I can even become *Auntie Sophie* at some point."

Carmen and Tanner both smiled. Carmen reached over and put her hand on Sophie's. "It is I that am honored by your offer to help. Of course, you can definitely help and be a part of the baby's life. I've always said, it takes a village to raise a child." Tanner put his hand over Carmen's. Sophie put hers over Tanner's. Now all three of them were physically connected. Carmen closed her eyes. Tanner followed suit. Slowly, Sophie closed her eyes, too. The sound of the other people at the funeral shifted to a murmur. Carmen felt the goodness of their connection coursing through her body, partially emanating from within herself, but also passing through her as if she were a conduit for the entire group. When she reopened her eyes, Tanner opened his, and looked right at her with a smile on his face. He'd felt it too.

Sophie looked at both of them and smiled. "Thanks, you guys."

Tanner stood up. "Group hug. Come on, bring it." Carmen and Sophie both stood up and moved in closer. Tanner wrapped his arms around both of them the best that he could. He could instantly feel their warmth. He smelled a hint of Sophie's expensive French perfume contrasting with the faint aroma of tacos coming from Carmen, and he felt oddly comforted.

25

LIKE A WELL-OILED MACHINE

Now that the three of them knew how things were going to be, they all managed to relax a lot more. At work, there seemed to be a new, light, carefree feeling. After three additional weeks of working the restaurant with only the two of them, Tanner and Carmen almost cried with joy when Sophie walked in at 9 a.m. sharp that following Monday.

Carmen showed Sophie everything the same way she'd shown Tanner when he'd first started, and gave her a space of her own right next to Tanner's. She showed Sophie where all the supplies were and let her know that her primary duties would be to come in, set all the tables up with a flower, a candle, placemats, and silverware for the maximum that each of the small tables could hold. Carmen wanted her to open the door at 11 a.m. sharp for lunch, and close at 2 p.m. for the day. She was to greet the customers, get them seated or inform them about how long the wait would be, give them menus and something to drink, then get their order in as fast as possible.

Sophie said, "Don't worry, Carmen. I understand what you need me to do. Meet, greet, seat, feed and water, clean up after them. Repeat. Right?"

Carmen smiled and said, "Not bad, but you forgot about the part where you take payment and collect tip money."

"Well, that goes without saying," she said with a quick wink.

The difference she made was immediate, and fantastic. Carmen, could now spend full time in the back chopping and prepping with Tanner in the morning then, once the restaurant opened, Tanner stayed by the grill putting together the plates for Sophie to pick up. For the first time since Diego started going AWOL regularly, Carmen was finally able to spend time in Diego's former office ordering supplies, paying bills, counting the money, and making the daily deposit to the bank's night drop on her way home after work each day.

Once the door was locked at 2 p.m., Tanner and Sophie each cleaned for an hour, calling it a day at 3 p.m. He'd sterilize the grill and the counters, then mop the floor and take out the garbage in the back. Sophie would clean all of the table tops and mop the floor out in front. While at each table, she'd collect the flower, blow out the candle, then spray the whole table with disinfectant and wipe it clean. She also watered the plants in the windows along the back wall, collected anything left in the seats of chairs, and did the first drawer count, before taking the drawer back to Carmen for final count before deposit.

Tanner loved the way things were now. He could only re-member a few other times in his past where, at least for a while, everything seemed to proceed like a well-oiled machine. He thought, *but eventually, something always happens along to ruin it. But I remember a couple of times in my life that I cruised with good luck, good health, good friends, and a great income, only to have it all change from other people who came into play.*

The three of them were really become synchronized with one another. Sophie was already beginning to intuit a lot more—somehow communicating and understanding things mostly unspoken. He also enjoyed how well Carmen and Sophie were getting along. He was really surprised how much they both seem to care about each other already. No suspicious attitudes, no jealousy, no competition. He knew that Carmen was satisfied at the thought of finally being able to have her child, and he planned to be more than just the father, he planned to also be the child's dad, and all that encompasses. He liked that Carmen knew that he and Sophie had become lovers, and that she had been fine accepting that she would never know Tanner's physical love. Once that issue had been settled, things had grown much easier and become far more relaxed all the way around.

Later, she shared privately with him that she felt mixed about his choice, but that she ultimately understood why he'd made it. She said that she had been fully prepared to sleep with him and try to get pregnant conventionally. She added that she had even been a little curious about what it would be like to make love to him, but once she knew that wasn't going to be an option, she'd come to terms with trying to become pregnant using whatever methods the doctor told them would be the best to use. She said she was a practical woman and knew that she couldn't have everything she wanted, at least not all at the same time. She'd thought about it some more and realized the truth behind his decision and, in the end, she very likely would have felt strange about having had conjugal relations with him. She told him that she really enjoyed him and had a lot of respect for him, and that she definitely didn't want to do anything that would cause him to change his mind at the last minute. She was grateful to him for his donation and for agreeing to be there for her and the newborn once it arrived. She added that she hoped they could have a shot at having a regular family life.

Tanner had assured her that he wasn't going to change his mind. That he, too, had wrestled hard about his physical feelings towards her, that he'd found her extremely attractive, and for a while, couldn't believe that he was going to be able to sleep with her. Then he realized that, for him, it would be like sleeping with his daughter and he knew he wouldn't be able to do it. He'd thanked her for her honesty and candor, and had asked her to set a date with the clinic so that they could get started.

She promised she'd give him a date soon. He promised that he'd lay off sex of any type for two to five days before going in order to maximize his sperm count. She'd let him know that instead of watching a porn movie while self-gratifying at the clinic, that Sophie would be able to go in with him and help him obtain the sample in private. He thought that was both kinky and exciting.

26

DOMESTIC DISTURBANCE WITH FATALITY
STRIKE TWO

Since Tammy's death, life for Tanner seemed to have suddenly accelerated, at least in his mind. On Friday, he was nervous all day. He knew he would be skydiving later, but instead of looking forward to it, he was dreading it. A voice kept telling him that maybe he should sit this one out, but he knew he couldn't. This was the jump to scatter Tammy's ashes. He had been nominated to scatter her ashes into the wind above the eastern arm of San Francisco Bay from two miles up, and he was honored.

Tanner and seven other skydivers all went up in a Queen Anne and, once it was opened and angled downward, exited from the rear ramp. Tanner's heart was in his throat remembering how all of his former skydiving jump masters had been killed when their Queen Anne went down shortly after take-off. For a minute, he thought he might be having a heart attack, but it was his anxiety that had his heart jumping out of his chest.

They went up to 20,000 feet, and all eight of them exited within milliseconds of one another. Once Tanner settled into his free fall position, he quickly brought his hands together and opened the vessel with Tammy's ashes inside. He wasn't expecting himself to become overwhelmed with emotion while falling at 120 miles per hour, but he was. Now, all he could hear was his own breathing and his heart beating. Despite his high speed, everything around him seemed to morph into slow motion. He looked down at the vessel in his hand, and saw it had been laser engraved with a skydiver in the free fall position on the side of it. He popped it open, then resumed his free fall position, turning the vessel downward to make sure all of Tammy's ashes were scattered. He glanced up and saw them spewing in all directions. Minute particles vanishing almost instantaneously into the vast expanse around them, quickly blending in and becoming part of the sky.

The rest of the group had surrounded him in a wide circle. One by one, they saluted as her ashes were released. At about 5,000 feet, they all pulled their ripcords, leaving Tanner's sight instantly. He didn't notice. He was still falling at 120 miles per hour.

He was remembering his time together with Tammy. Their jumps together, their mushroom trip together. He stayed focused on the ground. He thought *so this is what is looked like to her. My God, the ground seems to be racing at me faster and faster by the milli-second.* Then he heard her voice in his head, *pull your ripcord. NOW.* Tanner snapped out of his trance just in time. A quick glance at his altimeter confirmed that it was now or never. He'd already fallen to 2,000 feet. He pulled his ripcord hoping like hell that it would open. It always had before, but Tammy's had just failed . . .

He was terrified. He'd just caught a glimpse of what Tammy had likely seen and experienced the last few seconds of her life and he felt horrified for her. As soon as he finished that thought, he felt his own body rapidly slow down; two-thirds of his speed yanked back by sudden, rapid deceleration. He looked up and saw that, indeed, his chute had fully deployed. Looking out towards the horizon, the rolling hills were riddled with houses that seemed to go on forever. From that high up, in high contrast to the surrounding landscape, they looked like garbage strewn across the earth, like someone had thrown their fast-food trash out of the car window while speeding through the area. As his descent continued, he began to smell the faint, but growing scent of cow dung as he descended into a dome of foul-smelling off-gas convecting from the farm next to Skydive Byron.

Because he'd fallen to such a low altitude before he deployed his chute, he ended up being the first one on the ground. He knew he'd hear it as soon as the others landed. *How could he be so short-sighted? Did he have a death wish, or secretly wish he were dead so he could be with Tammy, now?* No. He'd inadvertently fallen into a trance while watching the ground race up at him, and now he wondered if the same thing had happened to Tammy.

For Tanner, his jump was different. This time, as soon as his feet had touched the ground, he'd known with every fiber of his being that he would never go skydiving again. He'd loved the experience, but no longer wanted to take any more unnecessary risks for the thrill. It was pretty safe, overall, but he'd experienced enough of it. He'd already quit cigarettes going on ten years ago, and stopped the little bit of drinking he'd done a long time ago. He drove safely, and did everything else right. Indeed, he did everything that would maximize his chances of being able to grow very old except *he engaged in high-risk recreational activities.*

He knew that the mortality stats were far worse for motorcyclists and motorists, but after Tammy's incident, that jump was it for him as far as skydiving was concerned. Now, all he wanted to do was spend as much time as possible being the best elderly father he could possibly be for his new, future baby.

As soon as he got home, he took a lingering shower. He was glad he'd decided to quit skydiving. He'd grown pretty comfortable with it, and he enjoyed the experience tremendously—except, that is, the part of having to manage that ever-present fear of chute failure. Fear of the things that happen, like what recently happened to Tammy. It was the fear. Not death. That was the gist of it. It was fear about the pain you'd feel hitting the ground if both of your chutes failed or were rendered unusable. While drying off, he heard his phone buzzing in the other room. He hurried and saw that Carmen was calling. "Tanner, thank God. Please come over right now."

"Carmen, what's going on?"

"Just come now, please. I'll explain when you get here."

"On my way." Tanner threw some clothes on, grabbed his keys and drove straight over to Carmen's. When he got there, Carmen's Aunt Jasmine and her cousin Vincent were both sitting with her on couch in the living room. When they saw Tanner, they got up and greeted him, then excused themselves and went into the kitchen.

Tanner sat down next to Carmen. She'd obviously been crying. With a trembling voice Carmen said, "My cousin Vincent and I approached Diego earlier about his failing mental state. He was outraged and denied that there was anything wrong with him. When I told him that I had an appointment tomorrow to check out a really nice place where he could get the care he needed, he laughed at me. Then, he looked at Vincent and threatened him. He told Vincent that if he, or anyone else, tried to make him leave or move into some place where he would be forgotten, left to rot all alone until he died, that he'd shoot them."

Tanner looked surprised. "Shoot them?"

"Yes. Then, he pulled a gun out of his dresser drawer and showed it to us. Without saying another word, Vincent went into the other room and called the police. Then, all hell broke loose. When the police showed up, they were too aggressive. They came barging in and scared the hell out of him, and me. There was this one really big cop. He just barged right in and, in a big booming voice, ordered my father to put his gun down or face the consequences. Diego was so nervous. He kept looking at me, then at Vincent, then at the gun in his own hand, then at the big cop again, all the while shaking and trembling. The big cop took his hesitation as a threat and, when Diego did finally start to put it down, for a split second it was pointed in the direction of the big cop and that was it. The big cop tased my father. Diego dropped the gun as he slumped to the floor, convulsing. Within about thirty seconds or so, he went into cardiac arrest and died before paramedics arrived. It was already too late, and I can't believe I saw the whole thing happen. One second he was still here shouting at me, at us. The next, he was having body spasms and then died right in front of me and I couldn't do anything about it. Once my father went down, the big cop assumed the CPR stance and started performing it on him while waiting for the paramedics to arrive, but nothing worked. He was already gone. It was too late to save him." She stopped talking and began sobbing hard again. Still crying, but no longer sobbing, she managed to finish. "The sergeant who showed up a short while later looked at the body cam video, and determined that big cop had been justified in tasing him. They said there was no doubt."

Tanner wrapped his arms around her, and she buried her head in his chest, lifting her face up to talk and explain things to him, only to bury her face back into his chest again to cry some more. He felt the warm, salty drops saturate his t-shirt, and was glad he could offer her some support now.

She stopped at times, needing to regain her composure, then would start again. She was overwhelmed by grief while trying to explain everything that had happened. He vowed in his mind to be there for her, no matter if he had to sit there holding her for the rest of the night. "What a horrible thing to have had to witness. I'm so sorry."

He stayed with her until the early morning, listening to her and comforting her. A couple of times he'd gotten up to use the restroom and came back with warm beverages. The first time he brought a cup of chicken broth. Carmen had been surprised and grateful. A couple of hours later he came back with two big mugs of hot chocolate, one for each of them. He'd found some mini marshmallows in the cupboard, and a can of whipped cream in the refrigerator, and had added both to their drinks.

Carmen would be quiet for a while, until she remembered something funny or scary about Diego, then she would tell him the whole story. She was laughing one second, crying the next, and angry the one after that. After he finished his cocoa, he kissed her forehead and was just leaving to go home when Carmen gave him some more bad news. Unfortunately, *Es Picante* would be closed until further notice. She said she was sorry and would be in touch with him about everything later.

Tanner had started to ask a couple of follow-up questions but, under the circumstances, decided to leave it alone.

27

TARGET LOCATED

A week later, Tanner and Sophie both attended Diego's funeral. Tanner had never been to a funeral where so many relatives, and relatives of relatives, attended. They came from southern California, the central valley, from Mount Shasta to the north, even a cousin that hadn't seen him in thirty years from Arizona, all gathered at Ouimet Brothers Funeral Chapel for the viewing. Tanner and Sophie stood just inside one of the entrance doors giving tight smiles and nodding at strange faces. Most of the people did the same thing back to them before shuffling in to view Diego's body.

Tanner could just see Diego's body through the doorway to an interior room. He was against the far wall, lying in his casket with his arms bent at the elbow, then placed in criss-crossing angles across his chest. Even from that distance, he saw that the mortician had affixed a rested, yet serious look on his face and Carmen had given them his favorite suit for him to wear. The room had lots of chairs set up for people to sit and *view the body*. Eventually, he and Sophie went in and sat, briefly, but never went up to take a closer look.

Carmen sat in the front row, closest to her father, staring straight ahead at his casket. Her eyes bloodshot from crying, but for now, she was quiet. The first two rows of chairs behind her were occupied by a dozen motorcyclists wearing leather jackets

with the *Los Guardianes de la Paz* insignia on the back. Some of
them were also still wearing their dark sunglasses, even in the dim-
ness of the funeral parlor. Tanner recognized two of them. They
were the same two men he'd seen buying weapons out of the back
of Diego's trunk that afternoon when he'd first started working at
Es Picante.

He remembered looking up the insignia shortly after seeing
them that day, and he had been very surprised to learn that *Los
Guardianes de la Paz* stands for *The Guardians of Peace*. He remembered how it had changed his perspective and his thoughts a
little about those men and their weapons purchase, before realizing
that the change in perspective was intended. Mission accomplished
for the insignia. *Peace . . . my ass. Not through weapons,* he thought.

Carmen had decided to have the actual funeral service at
Queen of All Saints Catholic Church where Diego had become a
permanent deacon ten years ago. Once everyone was accounted for,
there wasn't a single parking space to be found within an eighth of
a mile radius from the church. The entire parking lot behind the
church, and the streets on both sides for several blocks, were
bumper-to-bumper.

Once the ceremony began, no one seemed to notice two
tall white men slip into the rear pew, near the door. They both
wore gray suits, black ties, black shoes, and they, too, were also still
wearing their sunglasses as they quietly slid into the pew. Their
dirty blond hair, blue eyes and blockish chins, along with their
thick arms, big chests, and identical attire made them appear both

formidable, and somehow genetically related, or part of an army of duplicates.

They scanned the people in the church independently. When one of them spotted Sophie, he lightly elbowed his partner, pointing her out by nodding while looking in her direction. His partner looked, then confirmed that it was Sophie by nodding back. No one had even noticed them, and they were glad for that. They both left just as quietly as they'd come in while the ceremony continued. They got back into their vehicle across from the church. A spot that gave them an unimpeded view of both the front and the rear of the church. They would wait for the service to conclude. Once it did, people would stream out of the church and begin walking to their respective vehicles and get a place in line for the motorcade that would snake through town over to Memory Gardens cemetery.

Tanner, and two of the gang members, spotted the blockheads sitting in their car. They immediately let the other gang members know. Afterwards, they all took turns staring at the two men from across the street. A couple of them gave them the middle finger as they roared by on their choppers. Tanner took note, but kept quiet as he guided Sophie to the car. They looked like a couple of detectives to him. *They're probably here watching what the gang bangers are up to,* he thought.

The men didn't react. Instead, they sat like wax statues. A couple of robots staring at the parking lot and the church. When Sophie had come out with Tanner, they'd started their engine to get ready to continue following her. One of them made a brief call, then nodded to his partner.

28

UNPLANNED VACATION

After the funeral, Sophie wanted to spend as much time with Tanner as possible. Since he wasn't going to be going to work everyday, at least for the time being, she suggested that they take this time to have some fun and play a little. But first, she had a few questions.

"Do you have any kind of a timeline for when you're going back to work? I'm only asking because I'm thinking you're likely not getting paid for this unplanned leave. Do you have any vacation or sick time available to you?"

Tanner gave her a deer-in-headlights look and said, "There was never any discussion about benefits like that. So, no. I do not have any accrued time to use as a buffer against income loss." Oddly, Sophie smiled—as if him not having any time or insurance or anything to offset his income loss was a good thing.

"Let's move in together." She said as she looked right at him anticipating something good.

"What did you have in mind?"

Sophie looked at him, "Move in with me at my place. We'll still have two bedrooms to spare to use as an office and a guest room. And, I have two full bathrooms, so we'll never have a logistics problem with that."

Tanner didn't have to think about it more than two seconds. "Done. When can I start moving in?"

"How about right now? We're both off and have the time."

"Perfect. It's the middle of the month. I can give the manager two weeks notice instead of a full month. He won't care as long as there is no damage and I'm all paid up. It'll give him a chance to rent it to someone else for even more money."

They had something to eat and then took both of their vehicles over to his place. The office manager's door squeaked loudly as Tanner entered. The space was stained beige, smelled musty, and the odor of over-baked coffee lingered. It was obvious that this particular part of the building had been overlooked during the remodeling project. The manager of the day was sitting behind the counter watching television when Tanner entered. He'd never bothered learning this guy's name; he was the third office manager in two years.

"Hello. I'm sorry to bother you, but could you please come to my apartment for a moment? I would like to have a brief discussion with you."

The manager looked put off, "About what? Who are you? What's your apartment number?" He rattled off like a bird ruffling its feathers. His voice had a peculiar nasal quality.

"If you don't mind, I'd really rather just have you come to my apartment so I can do a show and tell with you there. You'll understand once you're there." Reluctantly, the manager rose to accompany Tanner back to his apartment. He was a tall, skinny man with greasy hair, and bones that took turns presenting themselves briefly in multiple odd places while he walked, giving him a lurching, jerking gate causing his glasses to repeatedly slide down his shiny, oily nose. Each time, he'd quickly raise his right hand and push them back onto his nose and ears better. Enroute, Sophie caught up to them and was introduced to *Mr. Anderson.*

"Thanks for coming. The reason I asked you here is to show you all of my furniture, including the bed and small appliances—like the microwave, the toaster oven, and the blender." Tanner showed him his bed, his living room furniture, and his dining room table and chairs, as well as all of his pots and pans, spices, salt, and oils. "You could advertise for a furnished apartment, complete with everything. *Just move in with your clothes and personal effects.*"

"Nice idea, Mr. Dalton, but my hands are tied. This building is owned by a big company that owns apartment buildings all over America and their rules clearly prohibit me from doing anything like that. I'm sorry. The apartment will need to be completely empty, undamaged, and in clean condition in order for me to close you out as the tenant and return your $1,800 deposit to you." He paused to push his glasses up, and clear his throat. "Once it's empty and clean, come and see me again. I will give it a quick look over and promptly write you a check for $1,800."

"Will do. Thank you anyway. I appreciate your taking the time to indulge my idea."

"No problem at all, Mr Dalton. I think it's a great idea and, if I owned this building, I would've taken you up on that offer, immediately. It's a great deal, or would've been. I'll see you at some point soon?"

"Yes, I'm leaving and not coming back. This will be my last month."

"Very good. I'll wait until you're ready, then I'll come and inspect and return your deposit afterwards." He nodded, then turned and left. Tanner watched Mr. Anderson lurch and jerk back to the office. *That would be awful. I'm so lucky nothing like that has happened to me* he thought.

Sophie said, "Well, it was worth a shot. I had no idea you were going to do that. Why did you?"

"Well, I can't afford to pay movers, and I don't want to move into your ultra modern, super-clean place with this mostly dilapidated crap that I bought at second hand stores when I got here. I'm not going to contaminate your space with this crap. Your space is the space I always wanted—open and modern. Help me by going through my entire place and pick out what you want to add to your cabinets and can use at your place. I'll grab my clothes and shoes and personal effects for now and take that with me. The rest can go."

Sophie nodded and got to work right away. Tanner helped her gather up all of the kitchen stuff up that she didn't want, or couldn't use and tossed it all into a plastic bin that he usually stored clean sheets in. All the silverware, cooking utensils, oils, spices, plates, glasses, and pots and pans not wanted went out into the open area that most apartments faced on one side. Tanner wrote, *Free Stuff*, with a permanent marker on a big piece of cardboard left over from an Amazon delivery, and propped the sign up next to the bin.

He went back inside his apartment, and began moving his dining room chairs outside, one by one. He set them up in a semi-circle, then went back inside for the table. He took the center leaf out of his table and scrunched it back together into its smaller configuration as a circle. Sophie helped him carry it out to where the chairs were. Just as they set the table down, he heard a woman's voice behind him say, "Is all of this stuff really for free?"

Tanner smiled and said, "Yes, it is.

"Oh, how perfect! I'm over in 402, and I sure could use some new stuff. So, if you're really sure and don't mind?"

"Help yourself! I'm happy to see you taking anything you think might be useful to you. " Tanner said sincerely. He watched the lady, now a little giddy having found such good fortune today, start taking the chairs to her apartment, one-by-one. Sophie and Tanner helped her by carrying the table to her apartment for her. Tanner loved it that he could give his still useable goods to others who were happy to reuse or repurpose them. In this case, 402 was going to put the whole set in her second bedroom and use it as her poker table on poker nights. Tanner was thrilled that it was going to such a good cause.

Little by little, he put everything he thought someone else might want or would be able to use outside. A couple of people helped Sophie and him get the couch and two big arm chairs outside. By six o'clock that evening, about ninety percent of the stuff Tanner had put out for free, virtually everything he had owned, had already been claimed by their new owners and were all now safely tucked away in their new homes. What remained was either in Sophie's car, Tanner's car—which were both overflowing, or resting inside the big garbage bin behind the apartment complex. Tanner was pleased. He went through his apartment one more time, then vacuumed the place, leaving the vacuum out for free afterwards.

That night, they were too exhausted to cook and they were filthy from moving all day. They went back to Sophie's, leaving the stuff in their cars until the morning. They ordered a pizza and ate it with one eye on the comedy shows and the other on each other. Finally, Tanner looked at her and said, "I'm sorry, Sophie. This is where my age kicks in. I'm going to hit the sack now, I'm exhausted. I've been fighting to stay awake."

"I've noticed you almost nod off twice. I'm exhausted too. Tomorrow's another day," she said, winking at him.

The next morning, Tanner awoke earlier than usual. The automatic blinds were slowly opening as the new day dawned. He wasn't used to that kind of light first thing in the morning, but he found himself feeling refreshed, like he'd slept really hard.

He looked over at Sophie, still sleeping peacefully next to him. She was so beautiful. He hoped more than ever that they would somehow be lucky enough to be able to unravel the mystery of happy unions. He desperately wanted to be happy with her while they were together. She was so different. She was so many things he'd always wanted in a mate, and a wife. He now wanted to be with her, happy, for the rest of his natural life. He figured he might see another 25 years, if he lucked out. He thought, *lots of people are married that long. The long-term marriage group is actu-*

ally bigger than many might think. Sexually, she exceeded his wildest dreams and satisfied him like no one else ever had. He had no idea how all of this had manifested, but he was grateful that it had.

Now, it seemed that so many complex, long sought-after desires were finally being expressed and realized, not only by him, but also by Sophie, as well as Carmen. For the first time in his life, Tanner was seeing how growing old has a way of forcing a person to get to the heart of what it is they really want or are seeking because time is of the essence. And, even though the three of them were at different ages, and stages, in their lives—spanning 24 years—they had all grown old enough to crystallize desires that remain unfulfilled."

Tanner thought about all the suffering, yearning, wanting, and that awful, persistent nagging feeling that it's all impossible, and that, *it's-never-going-to-happen* thinking that he went through over his lifetime, is actually supposed to happen and life is supposed to be that way—a test. Tanner had gone through plenty of all of it. Call it generalized angst. Over time, he realized that it's simply paying dues and doing the necessary hard work. He had to prove to the universe that he wanted and deserved good things—and it was a work in progress. He and Carmen and Sophie had all been living their lives largely unsatisfied, while hoping for and working to have a better life over the long term. Now, the three of them were going to get something they've all wanted in their own way and never had. A parenthood role. A chance to be a living example by *living right* as a healthy model for the new baby.

Tanner could tell that Sophie loved and trusted him. She had intimately whispered in his ear that he was the best man she'd ever known in her entire life. He knew that she honored and respected him and Tanner felt her love and also felt extremely grateful to have her in his life now.

He loved feeling uplifted and feeling love in his heart and having love in his life again for the first time in years. He was also grateful to be able to offer to give Carmen the possible gift of a child, something she'd just about given up on ever being able to have. He was looking forward to sharing the parenting with Sophie and Carmen and knew the child would know love and caring at a level that he had never felt from his own parents.

Today, they unloaded Tanner's stuff out of both of their cars and actually managed to find perfect places for a lot of his things. After lunch, they decided to visit Carmen before taking a little break and visiting the summit of nearby Mount Diablo. Tanner phoned ahead; Carmen was looking forward to their visit, although Tanner thought she'd sounded a little reluctant.

When they arrived, Carmen greeted them at the door. She briefly hugged them and then they all sat in the living room. "Would either of you care for anything? Coffee or tea?"

Tanner looked at Sophie, then at Carmen, "Nothing for me, Carmen. Sophie?"

Sophie smiled, "No, thank you," she said somewhat apologetically. "We've just finished breakfast. I'm all set, thank you. So, are you feeling any better, Carmen?"

Carmen glanced at Tanner, then looked at Sophie, "I wish I could say I was feeling better, because I was. I mean, I am better, but . . . it's just that . . ."

Tanner leaned towards her and rested his hand on her shoulder. "Take your time, Carmen."

"Thanks. It's just that I found out that my father cashed his life insurance in for ten cents on the dollar to use at the race track to bet on horses. I contacted the insurance company and they gave me the bad news. Then, I double-checked all of the accounts. There were never any corresponding deposits made to any of our accounts. Next, I found a whole box of losing betting tickets under the work bench out in the garage. Most of them were dated after that cash out of the insurance. Some were hundred dollar bets, but a few were five hundred dollar bets." Carmen looked horrified. As if thinking about what Diego had done was like witnessing someone being brutally murdered. "How could he do that to me? Now, I've had the restaurant closed all this time, not able to pay you and I've been living on a small cash reserve savings account and was counting on the insurance money to replenish that account, to get the restaurant stocked up and ready to go again. Now?" She shook her head over and over, "I don't know how I'm going to come up with the money to reopen, and soon, I'll not have a way to pay the lease payment. At least this house is paid for. Luckily, my father paid it off after my mother died. So, I still have a place to live, but nothing coming in, and I still need a way to pay for the taxes, insurance, utilities, and for food. I'll likely end up having to sell the business and get another job somewhere, and so will both of you two. I'm so sorry, but I'm just not seeing how it's going to be able to go any other way."

Tanner was speechless. He took a deep breath and let it out slowly. "I'm sorry too, Carmen. I feel extra bad now knowing that once upon a time I had enough money to take care of this, but not any longer. I guess I'll be taking an unexpected vacation."

"I'm sorry, Tanner."

Tanner's mind was reeling, "Now that we know about this, give Sophie and I a little time too. Please. Just hang tight for a little longer and we'll see if we can't manage to come up with a way to make this work.

"Okay. Thank you both, so much. I can use all the help I can get right now. I'm glad you came to see me today. I've been missing you, Tanner. Our chopping time was more meditative for me than I realized. I miss that and our talks. Okay, ready for a little more bad news?

Tanner and Sophie both said "No," at the exact same time.

"I'm also thinking that, even though we were all in agreement about artificial insemination, now that I'm likely going to the unemployment office looking for a job, I, or we, should hold off on that too, at least for now. I can't think about having my first baby under this kind of stress and uncertainty."

Sophie nodded yes. "I understand, Carmen. I wouldn't want to have a baby while unemployed either."

Tanner felt crushed inside. Just when he'd convinced himself that he would still be okay to become a father as long as he had the support his friends had promised him, now it looked like this rare opportunity wasn't going to happen after all. As he listened to her, he felt his fatherhood chances slipping out from under him like dry sand leaking out of a pair of cupped palms.

"We'll think of something. We will," he said, forcing a smile. "Looks like you could use some fresh air and some exercise. Would you like to go up on the mountain with us while you actually have the time?"

The question caught her off guard. She said, "I'd love to, but I have a doctor's appointment in two hours. Rain check?"

"Sure thing." Tanner smiled at her. "Do you need anything else? Help with anything?"

"You're so kind. No, I'm good. Thank you. You know, I was thinking, and it's really sad to me to realize that if my father knew how we were going to have a baby together, he likely would have disapproved. I miss him dearly, but I'm glad we didn't have to go down that road with him. Anyway, I don't want to get started on that. Thank you very much for coming today. I've missed you."

Tanner really didn't have any response to Carmen's hypothesis about Diego. "You're more than welcome. We're going to figure something out. Just please keep your faith going about it. For now, try not to convince yourself that the restaurant closing is a done deal, okay?"

Carmen smiled and nodded. "I can pay for the lease and the utilities for one more month. So, whatever is going to happen, needs to happen soon. I've got to get going on alternatives now." When they got to the door, they hugged goodbye and Tanner promised he'd be in touch within a couple of days.

On the way up to Mount Diablo, Tanner's mind was racing about so many things, he felt like he was constantly playing *Wordle* or trying to figure out the answers to the *New York Times* mini crossword puzzle. They talked about Carmen's situation and they both felt bad for her. Tanner was livid that Diego had done something so selfish. After paying premiums for all those years and then turning around and cashing out the policy for such a ridiculous discount, only to lose it all at the track. That alone, would have been enough for someone to want to commit suicide or cause them to have a heart attack from the sheer stress of the financial implications. Tanner thought, *No restaurant, no job, no baby with Carmen, at least until she gets her life reconfigured.*

Mount Diablo rises to 3,849 feet, and can be seen off in the distance from a wide audience living in many cities surrounding it. In high school, Tanner used to cut school and come up here on a nice day to drink beer and smoke some weed and hike around.

One of his favorite things to do was to just take in the scene; seeing things off in the distance, like the massive mothball fleet of naval vessels tethered together on Suisun Bay. More than once, he'd seen the top of the Oakland Bay Bridge poking up over the western horizon at a straight-line distance of 25 miles. It was another *Bay Area magical place* for him. Lots of fun memories and the perfect place to go with Sophie today.

Sophie looked over at him, smiled, then said, "I can become an investor in Es Picante."

Tanner started to say, "You don't need to do . . ." But Sophie cut him off,

"Yes, I do. I have plenty of money. I can cover Carmen with what she needs and get the restaurant back up and running. Besides, I'll be there working too, remember?" Tanner kept thinking, not saying a word, while driving them the rest of the way up to the top of the mountain in contemplative silence.

Tanner was looking forward to feeling the warm sun and the nice breeze. He loved having all that silence and all that space. He was shocked that she'd never been up here before. She said she always looked at the mountain or happened to notice it off in the distance, but only in the sense of it being something on the horizon that she saw everyday and that it should be there; her mind's eye expecting it to be there.

They continued driving up the treacherous, winding Summit Road, enduring eighteen sharp, 180-degree hair-pin turns on the way up to the top. As they traversed, slowly and steadily ascending the mountain, each 180-degree turn presented them with continuous, stunning views.

Tanner was finally starting to enjoy himself. He felt at peace sitting next to Sophie, like they were meant to be. This minute, it felt right being with her. Periodically, she would glance over at him, smiling warmly. Once, she looked at him with the most loving smile he'd ever seen from her, which confused him, but he'd decided to just go with the flow.

Once they made it to the top, they pulled into the parking lot, parking a few spots over from the only other car there. They got out and walked over to the stairs leading to the lookout. The couple that came in the other car were leaving. They nodded and mumbled hello as they passed by. Once Sophie and Tanner were on the top deck, they slowly walked over to the edge, bordered by a thick stone wall. The wall surrounded the entire circular deck and tower, making it hard to accidentally fall or trip into the steep canyons surrounding the lookout.

They stood side-by-side facing northeast towards Benicia, looking out across the vast, developed tundra below. Squinting a little, you could just barely make out the tiny cars on the roadways that, from this far up, looked like blood vessels.

Tanner felt Sophie's positive energy grow as she moved in and stood closer to him on his right. She said, "Today, I'm seeing sides of you I haven't seen before. I must say, I really like the light-hearted, fun-loving, caring, gentle Tanner that I've seen a lot of today, and I have an idea or two that might improve things even further." Tanner kept looking at her, smiling. Suddenly, she moved in closer, hugging him like her life depended on it.

Tanner loved feeling her warmth, smelling the fragrance of her morning shower, while allowing their energy fields to meld together and become one. Once joined, he always felt whole, relaxed, and soothed. It was always good medicine.

Sophie said, "Tanner, please try to keep faith in your heart that good will always prevail over evil. Know that it always has, as sure as the sun comes up each day. Recognize me right now, standing before you, as a big part of the current good in your life. The good that will help heal you and allow you to finally become the fully integrated man that you were always destined to be. I would be honored to stand by you through it all, doing what I can to help you along that path, if you'll let me."

"Thank you."

"You're welcome." Sophie smiled back.

Sophie was in front of him, and moved in closer. Tanner spread his legs apart a little so she could move all the way up to the wall. Once she finished, he wrapped his arms around her and began gently rubbing her back. She looked up at him seriously, then placed her hands gently on either side of his face and pulled him towards her. He met her halfway and they began passionately kissing and lightly groping each other. After a few minutes of heated passion, Tanner pulled away, looked into her eyes and said, "I won't ever leave you, Sophie."

Her eyes danced back at him, "Promise me," she whispered.

"I promise."

"Come with me now. Follow me."

"Where are we going?"

"You'll see." Sophie held out her hand. Tanner took it and she led him down the long stairway from the upper lookout deck to the parking lot. Their car looked lonely sitting alone in the huge parking lot. Tanner had never witnessed this lack of people up here before. It was very strange, adding to his feeling that his life had recently become almost surreal. Sophie didn't walk them towards the car. Instead, she kept them close to the lookout, hiking around it to the side facing downhill. Luckily, the small trail they were hiking on stayed level. As they walked further around to the back, the trees and bushes grew thicker. Sophie spotted a nice, shady break in the shrubbery near the exposed wall of the building.

"Over here," she said with a devilish grin on her face. Once she got to the wall, she unbuttoned and unzipped her pants and quickly pulled her pants and panties down all the way to the ground in one swift motion. She bent forward some, turning so her backside faced him, then looked at him over her shoulder. "Tanner, please. I want you so bad." He was a little caught off guard, but not as much as he had been when fishing with her recently. He was entirely turned on now and quickly unbuckled and dropped his pants and proceeded to make hot, passionate love to her with complete abandon, allowing himself to become completely sucked into the passion tornado that had formed around them.

Just a couple of months ago, he wouldn't have been able to remember the last time he'd been naked outside, had sex in the woods or at the beach and this was the second time in a month that Sophie had offered him an outdoor pleasure excursion. It thrilled him to no end. Their mutual gestures of love and the sharing of loving feelings for one another heightened their lovemaking, giving both of them two, powerful, simultaneous orgasms. Afterwards, they continued kissing each other passionately, like they were a couple of hormone-filled teenagers.

The park ranger's voice cut through their passion like someone scratching a phonograph needle harshly across a record, "Uh, if you two are about through, I won't call the police or give you a ticket, but I will ask you to please leave. And, I shouldn't say this, but nicely done, you two!" He stood about fifteen feet closer to the main trail wearing a smokey-the-bear hat and khaki uniform with a patch on his left sleeve with *California State Park Ranger* embroidered on it.

After their initial shock, Sophie and Tanner worked hard to suppress their laughter and embarrassment. Tanner finally said, "Yes, sir. We'll leave. Thanks for being mellow about it. We very much appreciate it and, thanks for the compliment, but we're both quite embarrassed by having been seen."

"Ah, don't sweat it. We're all adults. We've all seen men and women naked before. That's the chance you take doing it outside, but isn't that the whole point? You guys aren't the only ones who have felt inspired by the scenic vista and decided to take a little side excursion. Not by a long shot." Hearing the ranger say this, they both finally let it all out, and ended up laughing so hard, they had a little trouble walking back to the parking lot.

29

THE OFFER

Two more weeks went by. Tanner knew that Carmen's lease payment would be due soon. He'd continued putting her off, trying to buy some more time, telling her that he was still actively working on something. Finally, he spoke with Sophie who assured him that she would be fine working out a payment arrangement with Carmen for a loan to keep her going for now. Sophie was also wanting to get started sooner, rather than later. She had begun feeling a little bored, despite all of their recent activities.

Tanner tried to follow up on his promise to take Carmen all the places she'd never seen, and honor her request to go to Golden Gate Park, but whenever he asked her to make a date with him, she'd make excuses why she couldn't.

Tanner started taking Sophie to many of the places he'd planned to show Carmen. She'd been to some of the places, but having lived a fairly secluded life herself, she also had not been to many of the places Tanner had discussed taking Carmen to see.

He took Sophie freshwater fishing at nearby Lafayette Reservoir. He showed her his special bait combo: a combination of red worms and salmon eggs; they caught almost a dozen lake trout casting from the shore. Next, they'd visited the Lawrence Hall of Science in the hills above the University of California, Berkeley.

Sophie seemed really interested in all the displays about physics, chemistry, and astronomy.

Another day they drove down to Santa Cruz to the boardwalk and ate fast food. While there, Tanner knocked over enough stacked bowling pins to win Sophie a stuffed bear, and they'd taken a long walk on the beach afterwards.

Finally, they'd gone to Walmart and Tanner helped Sophie pick out a complete starter set of ladies' golf clubs. They then went and played a round over at Buchanan Fields, a little nine-hole course over by the airport near the Sunvalley Mall. Tanner hadn't played in years, and Sophie had never played, but she golfed better than Tanner had ever seen someone play on their first round.

Now that they were kind of on a roll with outings, Tanner wanted to go to Golden Gate Park in San Francisco next. Sophie said that she'd never been there and she couldn't wait. She was enjoying all the excursions but—oddly, her wonderment seemed centered on how many different places were left to visit, not so much about the content within each destination. Like she was collecting travel tokens just to be able to say she'd been someplace.

Tanner enjoyed the company, and he loved revisiting all of the places they had gone to, so far. He was pleasantly surprised to see that many of the venues had expanded over the years.

Today, at breakfast, Sophie had said, "I'd really like to have Carmen over for dinner. As you know, I'm going to offer her a loan or a partnership, or both, to be worked out by our attorneys." Tanner took a deep breath, smiled and said, "I like that idea. I'll call her and make arrangements to have her over this coming Friday evening at, I don't know, 5 p.m.?

"Perfect. I'll surprise her with a steak dinner. Does she eat beef? Do you know?"

"I believe she does," he answered cautiously. He thought about it a little bit longer, then said, "Yes. She does. I remember her making a plate with two beef tacos, rice and beans for her own lunch one day."

"Outstanding. Then, steak dinner it will be. I want to make her feel special and pampered a bit, you know?" She said, her voice rising almost a full octave.

"Well, I think a dinner like that will be a fantastic start."

Tanner could tell that Sophie was excited about helping her new friend. Someone that she may still end up sharing mothering duties with. Tanner knew that Sophie had also felt utterly deflated upon getting the news that, at least for now, the procedure was on hold. She had privately expressed to him her excitement about being able to be a part-time mother to Carmen's, and his, child, albeit in a rather lukewarm way, which he found confusing. Now, they discussed their disappointment to each other about this turn of events, but no one else.

Tanner made the call. Carmen was thrilled to hear from him and ecstatic about being wined and dined on Friday. Tanner told her to not bring a single thing. Just herself would be perfect.

Friday at 5 p.m. Carmen arrived looking happy and well rested. She'd lost a little weight, likely about ten to twelve pounds, just what she'd put on from emotionally eating for a while. Now, she looked slim and pretty fit in her skinny jeans and bright yellow sweater top. Her smile seemed genuine and her mood was in a positive gear.

Tonight, it almost seemed as if she wanted to get started on regaining that weight that she'd lost; she'd brought an incredible, six-inch thick New York style raspberry cheesecake for dessert. Sophie had anticipated that Carmen would bring dessert because she knew that they didn't drink alcohol and wouldn't be bringing wine. Just in case, Sophie had bought stuff for banana splits as a fallback dessert. After Tanner set his eyes on that cheesecake, he almost wanted to skip the main course and have one large piece for dinner, instead of the steak.

Tanner grilled the huge T-bone steaks out on the deck while Sophie tended to the rest of the meal. Sophie kept the wine glasses filled with non-alcoholic, sparkling wine and the music at just the right volume. Tanner and Carmen shared a bowl of a new hybrid that he had just picked up down at *Rare Earth Cannabis* while he grilled the meat. Carmen seemed very happy to be there, relaxing and enjoying herself with friends for the first time in a long time. After smoking and talking with Tanner a little bit, she went into the kitchen to visit Sophie, and offer her assistance.

"Oh no, no you don't. Tanner and I are treating you. You always work and do everything. It's our turn to pamper you for a change. And, we're both in agreement about it, so don't think about complaining to him about it."

Tanner couldn't hear Carmen's response, but a short while later, he heard them chatting up a storm. Occasionally, a loud burst of laughter would explode out through the sliding glass door and onto the small deck where he was grilling. He was happy to hear them getting along so well.

Tanner brought the steaks inside and set the platter down on the counter. Sophie and Carmen put the rest of the food on the table. They each chose a steak and found a seat. The steaks were cooked perfectly, and were beyond delicious served up alongside Sophie's sautéed mushrooms, roasted red potatoes, and broccoli with cheese sauce.

Carmen groaned with culinary pleasure exclaiming, "Everything is so good. So perfect. Thank you both for this incredible meal."

Sophie said, "You're welcome. I'm glad you're enjoying it."

"Tanner, the meat . . . wow!"

Tanner smiled at her. "It is really good. I'll admit it."

Sophie said, "Carmen, I'm just going to get right to it, I want to propose something to you, and I don't want to make you uncomfortable with anything I might say, so please tell me if I need to stop at any point, okay?"

Carmen looked a little confused, but nodded. "Sure thing."

"I'm hoping it's going to be okay to write you a check for $10,000 to get you by, that is, until we can legally finalize our new partnership agreement that I had my attorney draw up. I want your restaurant to stay in business. I see how much it means to you. It isn't fair what your father did, but I will fund you or sponsor your reboot of Es Picante. I am also planning on being involved as a working partner."

Carmen set down her water glass. "Really? For real?"

"Yes. For real. I'll do a 55/45 split with you. Of course, you will have the controlling shares since it was your business to begin with. However, if you fail to pay back the initial $10,000 loan, as promised in our agreement, then the split will still be the same, but in that case I'd be entitled to take the 55% stake. Agreed?"

Carmen didn't have to think about it at all, "Agreed! Yes. Absolutely. My gosh, you guys are so good to me. I don't understand your friendship, kindness, and generosity per se, but I'm so grateful to both of you. Sophie, are you sure you want to do this? We barely know one another. I mean, it's a lot of money and a lot of trust."

"I've already seen how you are on the job. All business. I have a feeling that together, along with Tanner's help and input, we'll be better than fine. I know it as sure as I'm sitting here, and I'm willing to fund it and take the risk."

Carmen stood up and walked around to where Sophie sat. Sophie knew what was coming next, so she stood too, and they hugged like two sisters who'd lost touch with one another a couple of decades ago.

Tanner said, "I just realized, that means that . . ." Both Carmen and Sophie were still hugging, but had turned themselves towards Tanner, and were now looking at him waiting to hear him. " . . . that Carmen will still be able to have the insemination procedure. That is, if you're still wanting to. I mean, now we'll be able to work together as a team. I'll go and give my sample or samples, as needed down at the clinic, then we'll go for the fertilization together. We'll do it all together. And, why not? Carmen, when you are at the end of your pregnancy, you won't be able to stand all morning chopping food, not without a lot of pain, but Sophie can, and will. Right, Sophie?"

Sophie looked at Carmen, still halfway in her arms, "Absolutely. Teach me and Tanner everything we'll need to know to run the place while you're on maternity leave. We'll be able to see you and the baby regularly, and bring over groceries, cook for you if needed and be your safety net. We can take turns with the baby, too. That way, you get a break, while we get our fix. I'm saying this is a win-win, the more I think about it. Well, at least it has a strong potential to be one."

Carmen couldn't take anymore. She broke down and began crying, sobbing tears of joy for several minutes. Sophie gently held her, letting her cry in her arms. Tanner moved in closer and began gently rubbing Carmen's back, while looking lovingly into Sophie's eyes.

Carmen finally regained most of her composure. "Thanks for the support, you guys. Really. Thank you, thank you, thank you. Carmen motioned for Sophie and Tanner to move in closer and pulled them into a tight huddle. She looked at Tanner, then Sophie, smiling and very excited, she said, "Yes! If you're still in, I'm ready again. This is amazing. You are both angels sent down from heaven to help me. I can't believe your generosity and willingness to help."

"That's what families do for one another. We're there for each other. Right?" Tanner asked with certainty.

Sophie nodded holding a tight half-smile.

"Damn right!" Carmen said, smiling wider than she thought possible.

Not wanting to waste another minute, Sophie left a copy of the agreement she had her attorney draw up on the counter for Carmen to look over and, hopefully, sign at some point soon. There was nothing in it that she hadn't already said to Carmen, except this one was done in legalese, and only needed her signature.

They spent the rest of the night celebrating their rekindled union, and joint decisions. Lightheartedly listening to music, eating cheesecake and laughing about silly memories and other anecdotes. Tanner felt lighter and a lot more hopeful again.

Sophie had saved the day with her offer. It was truly an amazing and generous one too. He was proud of her for coming to all of it on her own, then without wasting any time at all, had contacted her attorney, outlined her plans, expressing that she wanted a contract that she could take to Carmen for her signature. He loved her pro-activity in getting not only what she wanted, but what *they* wanted.

At the end of the evening, they all agreed to meet the next day, right after lunch, over at Es Picante to look the place over and make a list of items to stock in order to get rolling again, along with doing some light cleaning.

After breakfast, Tanner checked the morning mail. Among the usual assortment of coupon pack advertisements for vinyl siding and replacement windows, there was a letter from a law office that looked pretty official. The law office of *Stephen and Stephen, LLC.*

Tanner slowly opened the envelope as he trudged back to Sophie's apartment. By the time the elevator reached his floor, he had already read the letter. They wanted him to call for an appointment to discuss Tammy's estate. Like an arrow, Tanner felt the guilt strike his heart first, then wedge into his stomach. He'd been meaning to go by Tammy's house to see what had become of it. She had never shared the details of her estate planning with him. Tanner always hated assumption, but in this case, *he had assumed* that another relative or a trusted individual unbeknownst to him, such as an estate trustee, would step in and finalize the distribution of all assets according to Tammy's final wishes.

Tanner phoned them right away and was surprised to be able to secure an appointment for 3:30 that same afternoon. For the time being, he decided to not share this information with Sophie. He tucked the letter into the pocket of his robe then went to find her. She was in the kitchen cleaning up after breakfast. Tanner looked at her and said, "I've been meaning to go by Tammy's house to make sure that it's okay. So, I thought we might take separate vehicles to our meeting at the restaurant today. That way, you can go grocery shopping afterwards, while I go check out Tammy's house."

Without looking up from the sink she said, "Or, you could come to the grocery store with me, and then we can stop by Tammy's on the way home."

Tanner had hoped she'd just say okay, but no. "Well, if it's all the same to you, I'd prefer to go alone this time. I have a lot of memories that go back decades with Tammy and, if possible, I was hoping to spend some time in her Zen garden out back doing some thinking. Don't worry, I won't be too long. In fact, I might make it back before you do."

Tanner could tell Sophie was intrigued, and more than a little curious about what was really going on with him, but she wasn't going to start something needlessly to satisfy that curiosity. "Okay. I understand. I'll see you when you get home or you'll see me when I get home after our meeting. No big deal," she said turning away from him to leave the room, working hard to control her voice.

Later that morning, Sophie followed Tanner over to the restaurant. Carmen was ready for them. They all gathered inside Diego's old office. Carmen reluctantly showed them the account books and how Diego had drained the money and cashed-out the insurance policy. She had been keeping the lease payment going using her own personal savings account, the same way that Tanner had done after arriving in California, learning firsthand just how fast money can be depleted while living there.

Sophie was contemplative, then said, "How much to re-stock the food, ensure the lease is up-to-date, ensure the utilities are up-to-date, and leave us with a two-month cash buffer, minimum, in case of no income?"

Carmen said, "Hmmm. Well, let's see. Give me a minute, please." Carmen looked over one of the spreadsheets, then quickly added up several columns of numbers. Once she had a total, she looked up at Sophie and said, "About $7,800, maybe just a little more."

"So, it looks like my $10,000 jumpstart money will be adequate."

Carmen smiled. "More than. I can put orders in for the food we need on Monday morning, send checks out when they invoice me."

Tanner didn't want to agitate anyone, but curiosity got the best of him. "You guys were operating in the black when you hired me, weren't you?"

Carmen slowly looked up at him, and shook her head no. Tanner was a little alarmed. "Did you ever operate in the black?"

Sophie stood back slightly, letting Carmen and Tanner have the floor. "Overall, no. Never. Well, we'd be ahead for quite awhile, then there would be these sudden lapses in customers. We'd spend more on advertising, see a little bump, maybe even break even for a month, but then not for the next two. Lapses in customers means bigger losses to food waste or money going right into the trash can. Between that, insurance for everything, taxes, utilities, and the lease payment, we were always hopeful for more customers, but couldn't afford any more for advertising. We were slowly sinking, and the rate of loss had picked up. What my father did was a fatal blow."

Tanner took a deep breath and let it out slowly, then looked over at Sophie. "Well, at least we know now. Were you ever going to mention this to us?" He glared at Carmen. Then, without waiting for her to answer, he continued, "It's kind of a critical thing and Sophie is trying to save your sinking ship."

Carmen hung her head, "I'm sorry." Tanner gently squeezed her shoulder.

"Apology accepted. However, I think we should reevaluate reopening your restaurant, don't you?"

"Yes. You're right. I can't ask you to invest in a sinking ship. That will be added to my total long-term debt and will be so big, I'll never be able to pay it off and I'll end up having to work for the rest of my life."

Tanner pictured the headline: *Ninety-two-year-old woman dropped dead while working 12-hour shift attempting to keep her bills paid.*

Sophie stepped in closer to them. "You know, I'm a little embarrassed that I was so busy trying to help, that I completely didn't think to ask any pertinent questions, or just ask you or your accountant for a straight profit and loss statement. Look, I still want help you, but an analysis of what has happened over time and a detailed plan about turning this place around is really going to be needed now. There are multiple ways to achieve profitable objec-tives. I really need more time to think about this project. I'm sorry. Let's take a step back for a couple of days, and then we'll revisit this. How does that sound to everyone?" She looked at Tanner who nodded yes.

Carmen mumbled, "Sounds fine."

"Good. Then that's settled. I'm going to go ahead and leave. I have to go grocery shopping, and run some errands. I hope to see you again, soon." She stopped close to Tanner on her way out and gave him a quick kiss, then left without another word.

Tanner looked back at Carmen. "I feel bad the way things have gone today, Carmen."

Carmen looked directly at him, "No. I'm the one who should be apologizing. I knew we hadn't been in the black, but I had no idea that my father was doing all that he was behind my back. If I had known, I'm not sure what I would've done, but I would never have entertained any offers like Sophie's." Only a short time ago, she would not have been able to say that without breaking down in tears.

Now, Tanner saw the anger and could hear faint hints of it in her voice. "I know a solution will present itself. Wanting to be able to bring a child into this world, one that will have three parents is a lot of potential good. The universe isn't going to ignore that, or us, only make sure that we're worthy. If and when it decides that we are worthy, we will be rewarded. We will get to form, and we will become, a brand new family. I'm certain of it. I'm going to get going now, Carmen. Today, both Sophie and I have quite a few errands to run. Do you need anything?"

Carmen stood up. "No, but thank you, Tanner." She hugged him tightly. "I'll see what I can come up with regarding ways to save money here." She tried to take it all with her head held high, but now she looked gravely disappointed, and had a very worried look on her face. Tanner kissed her gently on her cheek, and left.

30

STEPHENS AND STEPHENS, LLC

After leaving Carmen at the restaurant, Tanner drove over to Tammy's house. He was curious about how her place looked, yet at the same time, he dreaded going over there.

As he pulled up in front, he saw no other cars. Tanner barely recognized the place. It was as neat as could be. The yard had been professionally modified back to one that not only fit in better with the surrounding neighborhood, but now even exceeded many yards, adding an additional layer of desirability to her former property. All the junk that could be seen in the garage windows had vanished. The shrubs that had covered the bedroom windows had been trimmed, and all of the bedroom windows facing the front were so clean, they looked brand new.

Tanner parked his beater in back of Tammy's truck. He got out and, as usual, went around to the side of the garage. This time, the door was locked. He continued along the side yard to the backyard fence gate. Luckily, the gate was unlocked and he let himself in. Peering through the window on the side door to the garage, he could see that the only thing left inside it was a brand new lawnmower, with a gas can sitting next to it. Tanner couldn't make out the brand, but he could see how shiny and new it was; the tags were still hanging off of it. He turned to face the backyard and it was all exactly as he remembered it.

There was no doubt that someone was taking really good care of the place, and he was really relieved, and happy. *Tammy would have liked the way they're taking care of the place for her,* Tanner thought. He took a quick look in the windows to the kitchen and part of the great room, and saw all of Tammy's furniture still there, sitting right where it was when he had stayed here briefly. All of her paintings and photographs were hanging right where she'd hung them. It was as if Tammy were still living here, and had hired a maid and a professional landscaping company to tend to everything for her now.

Tanner sat under the pergola where he and Tammy had shared tea when they first rekindled their friendship, reminiscing. He flashed back to their time together in high school, and then as skydiving buddies. He could see her smiling at him now, and he could hear her laughter, too. But most of all, *he could feel her sitting there with him, trying to talk to him.* Whatever it was, it felt good, and felt comforting to him. He'd missed her edginess, her sharp tongue, and her adventurousness. He'd enjoyed seeing her, and Doug, and the others every week while they were all skydiving together on Fridays. That had started to feel a little like a family to him, something he'd hoped he wasn't wrong about. Now that she was gone, skydiving no longer seemed worth the expense or the risk. For his entire life, whenever he thought he was part of a close family, or thought he might become part of one, something had always come along and ruined it. He looked at his watch *Time to go,* he thought.

Tanner arrived ten minutes early to his 3:30 appointment. The pretty receptionist acknowledged him, and politely asked him to have a seat. Less than five minutes later, she rose and escorted him to Mr. Stephens' office. A tall, slender man about Tanner's age, with blue-gray eyes and thinning white hair, rose from behind his desk and came around to greet him. "Mr. Dalton? Tanner Dalton?" He said holding his hand out as he approached Tanner. He was dressed in a light gray suit, white shirt and a checkered tie of black, white, and red squares making it look three dimensional, "Yes, and you are—"

"Joseph Stephens, senior partner here at Stephens and Stephens, LLC. Pleased to meet you, Mr. Dalton," he said, pumping Tanner's hand enthusiastically, and smiling just long enough for Tanner to catch a glimpse of his badly yellowed teeth, and a whiff of his foul breath.

"Pleased to meet you also. I'm curious about why I'm here."

"Please, have a seat, Mr. Dalton."

Tanner sat down across from Stephens. *Thank goodness for big desks,* he thought.

"Well, Mr. Dalton, I'm certain you don't remember me, but I was at Ms. Delgado's funeral, and I remember seeing you there, now."

Tanner nodded, "Yes, I was in Tammy's skydiving group for a while. We went up together every Friday, late afternoon. Tammy and I knew each other all the way back to high school.

She's kind of *the one who got away,* but we had reconnected recently."

"I see. Well, Mr. Dalton, our firm drew up Tamara's final documents. When she was first married, she had her estate documents drawn up listing you as the sole beneficiary of her entire estate upon her passing if you should outlive her now deceased husband and still had no one else, like children, to leave it to. She never had any children, her parents were both already deceased, and she was an only child." He smiled wide, but it seemed so forced it appeared more as a grimace, "She told me she couldn't think of anyone better than you to spring the surprise of a lifetime on. Isn't that incredible? So, if you don't mind, I'll spare us both the pain of me reading all the legalese out loud to you. If you would please be so kind as to provide us with some basic information, and your bank details, we'll wire the money directly into your account. Or, if you prefer, we can always draft you a check. We do prefer electronic deposit for ease, convenience, and security, though, but, either way, your preference will be honored."

Tanner sat stunned and speechless. He looked at Stephens across from him. The afternoon sunlight had slowly crept onto his desktop, brightening and outlining his most pointed facial features from the bottom up, accenting their sharpness, giving him an almost ghoulish appearance.

"She left her entire estate to . . . me?"

"Yes, she did. After fees, and taxes, not counting the house or truck—which are also yours now— she left you . . ." He moved a page off the top of a small pile sitting on the right side of his desk,

"Oh, yeah, I meant to mention that, per her instruction, the stocks were all liquidated, so she left you $5,236,141.36, in cash, plus the house and the truck, both of which are paid for, and both are yours as well, Mr. Dalton."

Tanner sat, shaking his head in utter disbelief. Slowly, an ear-to-ear smile began attaching itself to his face. He quickly filled out the forms and showed his driver's license for Mr. Stephens, who'd said to look for the money to come to his account in large chunks over the next ten business days. He handed Tanner his business card, reminding him that their specialties were both retirement and tax planning, and they said their goodbyes.

The solution came to Tanner slowly, at first. Then, it seemed to catapult forward through his mind to a logical conclusion as fast as lightening, and he now realized the gravity of what had just taken place: he had gone to the lawyer's office full of nervous trepidation, arriving in a car that barely ran, an unemployed elder on the verge of homelessness, and then left a multi-millionaire.

31

THE OFFER 2.0

The *Arroz con Pollo (chicken with rice)* came steaming-hot, along with a little drama to their table. Carmen's uncle, Ernesto, came out of the kitchen surrounded by servers, balancing the entire meal on an enormous platter which he set down in the middle of the table. He introduced himself to everyone, kissed Carmen on her forehead, then announced with a booming voice, "Arroz con Pollo—enjoy!" The only thing missing was fire. Afterwards, he checked in with everyone to see if they needed or wanted anything else, then commanded the server to "Take extra good care of this table," before turning and heading back to the kitchen.

Customers were really starting to fill the place up and Tanner could see Carmen taking pleasure knowing that Ernesto's restaurant had become so popular and successful for him.

Tanner said, "Thank you for bringing us here, Carmen."

"When my grandparents died, they left my father and my uncle, Ernesto, their life savings. They never went anywhere or spent a dime on themselves. They stayed in Mexico, but wanted their sons to know a better life. Luckily, their gift, combined with what my father and Ernesto had both managed to save, was enough for Ernesto to start this place and for my father to start Es Picante."

Sophie looked around. "I love the old world decor they've chosen."

Except for the groans of satisfaction with the food, the table grew quiet as they dug into the delicious chicken and rice dish that Ernesto had just prepared for them, "Just the way Mama would've made it," he'd said, after setting it down in the center of the table. Tanner saw an opening and decided to take it.

"So, other than the pure joy I'm experiencing right now, having another fine meal with my two most favorite people in the universe, I will admit that, this time, I did have an ulterior motive.

"Oh?" Sophie asked first.

Carmen looked at him, and knew Tanner was being serious, or trying to be. "What did you have in mind? Did you figure out a way to make my restaurant solvent again?"

"No, although that is still a possibility. Actually, it's a little more than that." Now he had their attention. "I went and saw an attorney today." Sophie suddenly looked very interested, even though they weren't married. "They had sent me a letter, something about Tammy's estate, so I called and they saw me today."

Sophie gasped, "So, that's what all that strange behavior was that day. Next time, just tell me the truth, I can take it."

Tanner gave Sophie a smile and nodded. "Anyway, she left me her estate."

The two women looked at each other, then at him, both at the exact same time.

Carmen said, "What?" Just when Sophie said,

"Seriously?" Then Carmen followed quickly with,

"For real?" Finally Sophie finished by adding,

"Holy Mother of Jesus."

Tanner waited momentarily for their reactions to subside. "About half of the money has already been electronically deposited into my primary account. The rest will be coming in chunks over the next ten business days, according to the lawyer. Bottom line: I no longer have to work for anyone ever again. Similar to your situation, Sophie." Sophie looked impressed. Carmen said, "God bless that woman."

Tanner looked at Carmen, then Sophie, "So here is what I propose. I propose that the three of us become a family. A co-parenting one. I stopped by Tammy's place on my way to the attorney's office and it's in mint condition. Four bedrooms, two bathrooms, large kitchen, double garage, large great room. Excellent landscaping, and a meticulously kept Zen garden in the fenced backyard. The sliding glass doors from the great room lead out onto a large cement patio, partially covered by a pergola, with a hammock and a picnic table underneath. In case I had declined it, the trustees were prepared to sell it on the open market and had some landscapers straighten the yard up. They also just painted the inside, and thoroughly cleaned it. Now that I am accepting it, we will now benefit from all that fixing up.

Both Carmen and Sophie stayed quiet. They were more than a little surprised, but not shocked, by any means. They'd all talked about a co-parenting arrangement of some sort, and now it looked like it might actually happen if, that is, everyone still wanted to do it.

Now that he no longer had any money worries, Tanner had briefly let some second thoughts enter his mind, *To hell with dia-*

pers and spit up. I could move to somewhere a lot nicer than this and live happily ever after . . . but knew better than that. Yes, he could move to Hawaii, or anywhere else he wanted, but that wasn't what would make him happy, and he knew it with every cell in his body.

"Carmen, Sophie, why don't you both sell your existing properties, and move in with me at Tammy's old house. There is good Mojo there. I can feel it. No need to reopen the restaurant at all. Now, we can focus on Carmen getting pregnant and having a healthy child, and we'll all have the luxury of being able to finally be parents, but between the three of us, none of us will ever be overly burdened with baby duties, except for Carmen while she is breast feeding."

Tanner waited for some excitement and was very disappointed.

"Well, I'm not sure I'm ready to give up my place just yet," Sophie retorted, looking slightly annoyed.

Tanner looked at Sophie. "No worries. If you don't want to sell your place, then hang onto it. I figured you might be at my new house more often than not, once the baby is born, and you said it was against the rules to rent in your building. I was just trying to save you the expense of keeping your place when you might hardly ever be there to enjoy it.

"Thank you, Tanner. I really appreciate that. And, thanks for coming up with a rather elegant solution, too. I have to hand it to you about that. Very efficient and logical and, you're right, it would be a perfect solution and an entirely different story if I needed money, but I don't. The longer I own my condo, with its exclusive location, and private, gated features, making it an almost ideal investment, it will be worth a lot more as time marches on. Trust me, now that you're into some money, you'll be shifting gears soon and begin seeing things from your new, no-worries perspective. Besides, having an extra house can come in handy, especially when other friends or family come for a visit."

Carmen seemed a little skeptical, "So, if the three of us are living together and raising our child together and a group of people from my family want to come for a visit, maybe even an extended visit and I've sold my house, you wouldn't have a problem letting them stay at your place?"

"Sophie looked right at Carmen, and said "No." Shaking her head for added emphasis. "I would assume that they would respect my property and treat it as if it's their own. If they didn't, then I'd have it fixed between the insurance company and you taking care of the damages."

Carmen seemed satisfied for now. She looked over at Tanner who had been watching her, "I like your idea. A lot. I'd be just fine selling my house to my cousin and his pregnant wife. They can't find an affordable place to buy anywhere that is decent to live. He's got a great job and has a bright future, but they're stuck in an apartment complex with a landlord who's a real dick and keeps raising their rent every six months. So, yeah, I'm on board. I love the idea of co-parenting."

She turned towards Sophie, "Although I agree with you in principle, or at least I agree with the economic and profit imperative part of your argument, it seems like a cop-out. Like, you're not really in all the way. You're keeping your bags packed and ready to go at the door. It just strikes me as, you, wanting the perks of having a cute baby experience, while leaving yourself an escape hatch that neither Tanner nor I will have at our disposal. You know?"

Sophie looked at Carmen indignantly, "Well, that's just perfect. I totally plan on doing my share of diaper changing, and bathing, and I'm actually looking forward to bottle feeding the baby with your breast milk, too. I will also help by doing some cleaning, cooking and shopping as necessary. I don't know why you think I'm not all in."

"Because you're not putting your money where your mouth is. Talk is cheap. Would you, for instance, sign a legal agreement swearing to the same level of commitment and contribution?" Carmen continued looking at Sophie, waiting for her to quickly say yes. But that didn't happen.

Sophie's face was getting pretty red now. Tanner could see her trying hard to control her anger. Finally, she looked at Carmen, then Tanner, and said, "I'll go you one further, and then we'll see who's in. I'm going to propose that we not only sell our places and move in with Tanner at his newly inherited house, but also put all of our assets into one big, legally-codified, jointly-owned pile. Part of the pile goes into a trust for the baby's future. The rest goes into two piles, short term, and long term. The short term will be spendable cash for everyday expenses, emergency funds for car and house repairs, unexpected medical incidents, and vacations. The long term will be more deeply invested and allowed to grow so that we'll be able to make large purchases, like for a new car or to pay for long-term care for one of us." Carmen was riveted to Sophie while trying to process everything she was saying, and Tanner was all ears too.

She continued, "My money, my house, into the pot. Carmen, your money, your house, into the pot. Tanner, your newly acquired house, and money, into the pot. We all become legal guardians of the child, and we all share our assets as if they are one household. We vote in case of conflicts. The total will be *our assets, the family's assets.* That's what I'm willing to do."

Both Carmen and Tanner glanced at one another after hearing this. Tanner said, "She's right. If we're in, then we should prove it and get all the way in, or leave now." Tanner already knew he was in for good. He didn't want to spend the rest of his life alone, looking out of a window at a world that he no longer participated in. Especially not when he finally had one last chance at becoming a father. "I'm all in. For sure," Tanner said with as much conviction as he had in him. He looked at the others.

Carmen said, "For sure, I'm all in, too." Sophie seemed pleased.

"Okay, then. That's more like it. All in, all the way, or I'm not in, at all." Then, just like Tanner had seen in a movie, maybe the *Three Musketeers,* Sophie stuck her right hand out towards them at waist level. Quickly catching on, Carmen followed suit, adding her hand on top of Sophie's. Tanner smiled, and put his on top of both of theirs. They left them together like that for few seconds before retracting them, finally losing the serious face and succumbing to some giggling, and much needed laughter.

Almost as if on cue, a three-person mariachi trio wandered close to their table, intrigued by the show of solidarity they had just witnessed. They stood at their table and sang a happy, festive song, none of which Tanner or Sophie could understand, but it was enjoyable nevertheless. Tanner thought the timing was uncanny. Curious about the translation, he looked at Carmen, "What were they singing about?" He asked after the band slowly walked away, now going from table to table.

"They sang a short wedding ballad that is usually sung at wedding receptions and it wishes the couple a happy, healthy life together. Wasn't that nice?"

Sophie nodded, "Loved it," she said stiffly, then looked away. Tanner thought that was odd, the way she referred to her emotion as more of a factual statement, rather than anything remotely like her truly describing herself as happy or in a loving state of being.

Tanner nodded and looked at Carmen. "I liked it a lot. Some day, I'd still like to learn more Spanish, just enough so that if I hear songs like that, I'll at least have a little bit of an idea as to what is being said. I find it frustrating not being able to do that."

Carmen said, "Are you kidding? I think now we'll have so much time together that I will be able to teach you. We can do it while I teach the baby Spanish, so he or she will be bi-lingual and have that speech advantage, effortlessly, later in life."

Tanner and Carmen were enthralled and excited about the possibilities for the newborn. Carmen didn't seem to notice, but Tanner caught a glimpse of Sophie rolling her eyes, then looking away and shaking her head after watching the two of them. Not able to watch any longer, she said, "Ah, hey, you guys, you know, all of a sudden I don't think I feel too well. Do you think we might be able to cut this a little short so I can get home in time to puke?"

Carmen glared at Sophie, who pretended not to see her. Tanner summoned the server who took his credit card and the food to box it up for them. Now, with their sudden lack of conversation, the loud restaurant noise seemed to move in and engulf them. When the server returned, Tanner signed the slip and picked up the boxed food. They thanked Ernesto and left.

Their silence followed them outside to the car and all the way over to Sophie's. Tanner felt like it would've taken a welder's torch to cut through it. After pulling up, he started to get out to see her in and tell her he'd be back after dropping Carmen off, but before he could Sophie had already gotten out and was already halfway to her building without so much as a word. She was walking fast and it was obvious she didn't want to talk to anyone, or say goodnight.

CHANGE OF PLANS
STRIKE 3

After Tanner dropped Carmen off, he decided to drive around for a little while before heading back to Sophie's place. He thought, *note to self, move into your new house right away so you'll have your own place to go to when things like this happen.* Now, he was a little mad at himself. He suddenly remembered a lecture he'd had in beginning psychology class about the inherent dangers in *triads,* and how they never worked.

Someone, usually the one whose gender is in the minority, such as when a mother and daughter bond in an exclusive way, the dad or husband gets ousted or is placed in the *outsider* position. Mom and her are close, dad is just dad. Dad doesn't get the same level of confidence and sharing as mom does. Dad misses most of the intimate dialog. Same with a couple that has a boy that attaches to his father and mom becomes a distant memory over time. He knows he can go to her, if need be, but he prefers to confide in his father.

Tanner sensed Sophie's increasing resentment about Carmen becoming pregnant using his sperm. He'd felt strongly that she'd overreacted when she came up with that ultimatum of everyone being all in or all out. He knew her well enough to know that she really didn't want to, or would actually put her entire stake into a shared account with Tanner and Carmen, and Tanner no longer did, either.

Now, he would proceed with Carmen, and just stop speaking about it in front of Sophie for the time being. He was doubtful that any of this was going to work now, at least with the three of them. Seems like the possibilities for jealousy and other negative emotions would be high all the time. If the baby was a girl, he would be the odd man out. Three women and him? He thought, *Yeah, that's going to work well. My vote would always be overridden.*

He really thought Sophie was genuinely happy about their plan and was really on board. But he had been wrong. He thought, *maybe she was just wanting that to be the case so bad, and then today she caught a glimpse of our happiness about our child.* She knew that, for her, it would never feel like it would for Carmen, carrying the baby from conception to birth, breast feeding it, having that intimate connection with the child that she would never experience, and she didn't like it at all. I get it. I don't think I'd like it either. I don't think this is a good idea anymore. I will still give Carmen my sperm and she can move in with me if she still wants to. We'll raise that child together as we talked about, but with Sophie? That remains to be seen. *We don't know each other well enough to do this. It felt like we did, but we don't.*

Tanner decided to go ahead and stop and get some munchies, something to drink, and something to scrub his mouth with. He was going to camp out tonight over at his new house. He thought he'd watch a comedy or two on his device, then call it a night. He was tired. A lot had been happening in a very short period of time, almost non-stop ever since he'd arrived back in California.

Not that long ago, he'd been wondering what he was going to do for a job and how long he had left to live on his meager savings and how long he would be able to sustain his weed and frozen pizza habits. Now, he was living with a beautiful red head that made love to him better than any other woman had in his entire life, another good looking woman who wanted his genes and was open to him being a father to the baby, plus inheriting several million dollars, a house, and a truck, all in just under a year.

Even though he was the proud new owner, he felt like a burglar breaking in at Tammy's old place and had to use a flashlight to see to get in, even though he had a key. It was chilly inside and he made a mental note to call the utility company tomorrow and get power and gas turned back on. Now that the door was unlocked, he went back out and got his bag of stuff and the sleeping bag he always kept in the trunk.

He rolled the sleeping bag out, took a couple of hits off of his cannabis vape cartridge, and tore open a bag of chips. He munched away, starting to feel the weed almost instantly. *Damn! I'm a millionaire now,* he thought, *strange how, right now, it doesn't feel any different than being poor.*

Tanner suddenly awakened, not even remembering falling asleep. He'd never brushed his teeth or even got up to use the bathroom. He felt strangely disoriented and wasn't sure where he was for a couple of seconds. He sat up and looked around. He felt like he'd been abducted by aliens and dropped off at the wrong location. Through the sliding glass doors, the bright white moon and stars illuminated the backyard in a hazy, diffuse, blue-white glow.

He looked at his watch, 4:50 a.m. It would be getting light soon. He got up and used the bathroom, wondering why he seemed to suddenly have so much nervous energy.

While urinating, he felt himself finish waking up. Like a candle being lit, the energy stirred his thoughts. Momentarily, he had to fight off letting them turn into fearful thoughts when he became aware that the hairs on the back of his neck were suddenly standing tall, and he felt goosebumps travel down both arms at the same time. At that exact moment, Tanner knew for certain that something bad had happened to someone close and that's why he had awakened.

He kept calm, but jumped into his car wondering if it was Sophie or Carmen that he should be concerned with. There was nothing on his phone from anyone. He decided to drive by Carmen's on his way over to Sophie's. Ten minutes later, he was there, and everything was dark and quiet. No need to wake her. Approaching Sophie's building, Tanner's stomach did a deep dive that almost instantly left a sick, heavy feeling in the pit of his stomach.

The flashing lights of the emergency vehicles in and around Sophie's building seemed to be everywhere. Tanner pulled up in Tammy's, now his, Tacoma across the street, not wanting to be in the way of anyone and wanting to assess things before driving in. He sat for a moment trying to see what he could ascertain from a distance. One of the officers on scene noticed him sitting across the street and said something into a walkie-talkie. A minute later, Tanner heard a strong voice command, *Concord police. Step out of the vehicle with your hands up in the air. Now!*

Tanner was shocked, but did as he was told and got out of the truck slowly and carefully, with his hands held high in the air. He saw the hulking figure with the strong voice stepping towards him from his right side, but he was backlit by the sun and Tanner couldn't make out any details. "Officer, my ID is in my right rear pocket."

"Hold still and turn around and face the vehicle!" he heard a strong voice say. Tanner immediately complied, then felt the officer kick his feet farther apart. "Interlock your fingers with your hands still held over your head." Tanner complied. The cop pushed him hard into his truck. The man's hands fast groped him everywhere, searching for trinkets of guilt, trinkets that might tell it all. Finally, Tanner felt his wallet leave his rear pocket. "Why are you sitting out here in your truck this morning, eh? Let's see here, ah, . . . Mr. Dalton?"

"I live here. I just moved in with my lady friend who lives in 3A."

"I see. That still doesn't really answer my question, though. Why are you sitting out here?"

"Simple. I was coming home from spending the night in my new house. I saw the police cars and ambulance vehicles and there were so many people milling around, I decided I'd park out here since your vehicles are all around the entrance to the parking garage. No big deal for me to walk in and use the elevator. What happened, anyway?"

Tanner could feel his heartbeat pounding like a fist into his throat waiting for the answer. He had been worried that something bad had happened to Sophie, especially after having already gone by Carmen's house. He braced himself for what he was likely going to hear.

"Unfortunately, we're not at liberty to discuss this with you, but there was never any danger to anyone else, nor is there any extraordinary danger."

"Then why did you want to question me? I was just sitting here."

"Crime scene, for now. Until everything is crystal clear. You looked suspicious sitting and watching us from half a block away. Some of us thought, hmm, could be a perp, or someone involved somehow. So, we wanted a word with you while we still had the opportunity to speak to you. You said you just moved in here recently?"

"Yes, a few weeks ago. Now, I've inherited a house and I'm going to be moving in there today."

"We'll need that address from you, but here, who do you live with?"

"Sophie, well it's actually Sophia. Sophia G. DeLaurent, we live in 3A." The police officer held up a finger, then pulled the square mic he had attached to his walkie talkie up to his mouth.

"Ah, Captain McDonald, yeah, this is Officer O'Reilly. Please have someone verify ownership on unit 3-alpha. I repeat. Please verify a Sophia G. DeLaurent as the owner of unit 3-alpha with the property manager. Over."

"Roger that. Information forthcoming. Hold tight." Faster than Tanner could believe, the radio suddenly squawked, "A Sophia G. DeLaurent is the lawful owner of unit 3-alpha. Over."

"Ah, thank you. Captain O'Reilly out." He helped Tanner slowly lower his arms and helped steady him as he turned around. "Okay, Mr. Dalton. You're all set. Sorry to have bothered you. You have yourself a nice day now." Tanner watched him as he turned and fast walked back over to the crime scene thinking, *a crime scene, yet no danger to anyone . . . that doesn't really seem right or somehow even possible.*

Tanner locked the truck up and proceeded past the entire scene with relative ease. At one point, he spotted O'Reilly watching him, but once he passed into the parking garage it was over. At least he thought it was. When the elevator doors opened on the third level, Tanner could barely see his own door. There were police, coroners, medics, and forensic specialists coming and going. One of the detectives watched him as he passed 3B, looking in the door as he did, but he only saw the backsides of more police.

He used his key and let himself in. As he entered the great room, Sophie was standing over by the sliding glass door. When she saw him, she ran to him and threw herself into his arms. "Oh, Tanner, I'm so glad you're finally home. I was so scared. I woke up and you weren't here, and there were terrible noises next door."

"What kind of noises? Did you tell the police everything?" Sophie nodded yes, then said, I woke up and looked at the clock. It was—"

"—4:50 a.m.?" Tanner finished for her.

Sophie looked at him wide eyed. "How'd you know?"

"I slept over at my new house in a sleeping bag last night. I suddenly woke up at that same time, and had the most powerful feeling that something really bad happened to someone close to me. I threw on some clothes and swung by Carmen's on my way over here. What happened next door?"

"After I woke up, I wondered why I was awake, but I had to pee, so I got up. While I peed, I heard this horrible moaning sound like someone either in horrible pain or having one hell of an orgasm. Then, a few muffled shouts followed by a bunch of thumping sounds and then nothing. Silence. I finished up, then went to the sliding glass door to peek out in that direction. When I cracked the curtain a little, I felt my heart do a somersault in my chest. There was a white man with curly brown hair wearing a light gray suit coat and white shirt. By the way, I've already told everything to the police. Anyway, he was looking over the balcony at something and talking to someone else inside. I heard sirens off in the distance, growing louder by the second. Then, I saw the man quickly disappear back into the apartment. The next thing I heard is the door slam. I went to my door and looked through the peep hole just in time to see two men waiting for the elevator. The wavy brown-haired man, and the other guy. A really big, muscular guy with an almost square or blockish head, and muscles that looked like they were still growing by the second." Tanner listened and couldn't believe what he was hearing. It was the stuff of spy novels or mob activities. "After that, it was quiet for a while, before I heard a bunch of noise in the hallway and I saw the building manager letting the cops in next door." Sophie looked scared, confused, and a little angry.

Tanner asked, "What happened, do you know? I saw some people from the coroner's office."

"After they interviewed me, they said at first they thought it was a suicide, but after hearing my story, they now say the man next door was likely pushed off of his balcony on purpose. They aren't sure if he was still alive or already dead when he went over. I never heard a big scream or anything, I'm just glad that I didn't look out towards the balcony at that particular moment. Can you imagine?" Sophie broke down and began to sob. Tanner tried to comfort her by putting an arm around her.

After a few minutes, she pulled away from him, and said, "I'm mad at you. Did you just say that you stopped by Carmen's on the way over here?" Tanner nodded affirmatively.

"Oh, I see. Carmen first, again. Oh my God. I'm so sick of it. God damn it, Tanner! We were going along so good. I was sure that I had finally found the perfect man for me. You are perfect for me in so many ways. Why would I ever want to share you, especially with the likes of—"

"What—her? Who? Carmen? Why would you say that?" Tanner looked at Sophie for a clue, but there was none. "Wait, is it because she's a Mexican? Is that what this is really about? Is it having to share me with someone else, or that she's Mexican, or both?" Sophie struggled to say something, then just stopped trying and looked at him with a neutral expression on her face. "Well, you know what, Sophie? I'm done. If that's your real truth, then I'm done with you. I'm not sure what you are, or who you are, except now I know where you stand on immigration, and how you really feel about people of color, or am I wrong? Is it just the brown ones, or is it the black ones too?"

Still nothing. Sophie just sat a couple of bar stools away, her platinum necklace flashing in the morning light looking like someone who was paid handsomely to come over in her nightie to make someone feel better. Finally, she conceded. "Okay, you're right, sort of. Well, I don't know, I know that they're out there. They're everywhere actually. Every time I see one, well, a man version of one of them, I always feel like they undress me and have sex with me right there on the spot as I'm being introduced to them. It freaks me out, a lot. So, I try to stay away. And the women just annoy me always talking that gibberish. I mean, my God, if you want to be American, then try learning fucking English for a change, you know? Now, you and Carmen are so close and you're giving her your sperm for God's sake. That will mean that I will have to attend parties and events that will have lots of *her people* there and I'm not liking it. I'm sorry, but you want to know the fucking truth? Well, there it is. I just spilled it all over the place."

Tanner felt like he was about to vomit listening to Sophie's racist, self-focused rant. Then, shouting it at him with her eyes bulging out of their sockets, "They are messing everything up in our country, Tanner. You know I speak the truth. The Mexicans and their drugs and the gangs and the blacks and their gangs and the carjackings and the home invasions, and the smash and grabs. The filthy mongrels are filling up all the schools, filling up all the apartments, causing the rents to skyrocket for everyday Americans, who can't find an affordable place to live. I mean, it's got to stop. You know?"

Tanner looked down at the floor shaking his head no, while listening to her go on and on with her disgusting comments about people of color and immigrants. Finally, he looked up at her, "Yeah, I know. And, you're absolutely right. This shit has got to stop or the human race, not just white people, are going to be doomed by their own narrow mindedness. I'm really surprised, no, shocked by this, Sophie. You really had me and Carmen fooled. I thought you were so excited to become part of the birth of a baby and you were looking forward to finally being able to be a mother for the first time in your life. What were you really going to do once Carmen became pregnant?"

Sophie rolled her eyes. "Be a fucking mother to some hybrid child? Think again. I won't be seen pushing a stroller with the likes of that child in it. Not me. I was going to try and find a way to get you to change your mind, convince you of what a dead end it would be." Sophie's eyes were wide now and she looked hysterical and seemed as if she was just shy of becoming totally undone. "I don't give a shit if it is your sperm that makes the child, Tanner. It will still be contaminated with the dirty seed from that woman. The child will forever be contaminated. You'll see Carmen in that kid's face every time you look at the child. The skin will never be *truly white*. It would be like taking a rescued Heinz 57 dog to an AKC event, trying to pass it off as some sort of equal with the rest of the dogs there. Tanner, you know, they aren't really like us at all.

You know that, right? There's a reason they've always been called *minorities* or *a minority,* and it isn't about how many of them there are. You know what I'm saying is true. All white people know it's true deep down inside. Now, we've all been conditioned to say, and believe what we all know isn't true, that *they* are equal to us, to whites, even when all whites know the real truth, that whites are superior and all the other, colored people, *shaded people,* while worthwhile—in a utilitarian sense—are, well . . . *less than whites.*"

Tanner couldn't stand it any longer. Sophie followed him into the bedroom and became even more adamant once she saw him retrieving his two huge suitcases from the back of the closet and begin throwing clothes into the largest one. Her voice became even higher pitched, as if the different tone would, somehow, alarm him and make him stop so she could finish convincing him of her self-righteous message and teach him the error of his misguided ways.

Tanner wasn't listening any longer. His ears were still hearing her hysterical voice, but he was no longer listening to the words. He was actually grateful things had worked out the way they had. Now, he knew that Sophie was more than just a hard-core racist; she was utterly mad. Perhaps it had come from listening to her parents while riding in the back seat as a little girl, while they poked fun at, belittled and said disparaging things about *minorities* whenever they saw them from either a distance, or on television. Listening to their put downs of people they didn't even know simply because of their darker skin, as they'd driven through the poorer sections of various cities and towns while she had been growing up.

Perhaps some more of it came from that horrible night when the men wearing masks had all lined up to use her for their own pleasure. How many had been black or hispanic? She'd ruminated about that before, always finding herself hovering over a vomit filled toilet bowl afterwards. What had gone through her mind while all that was happening to her was only something that Tanner could guess at, but he knew it likely may have been the precipitating event that finally took her over the edge. The rage and disgust that was suppressed deep inside herself that night was now leaking out a little here and a little over there, every time she looked at or interacted with *a minority* (as she referred to people of color).

Tanner finished filling his two suitcases with all the clothes he owned and some personal items, the rest he didn't care about at all. Sophie hovered close, shouting, hissing, screaming at him. Bobbing and weaving from one side of him to the other, trying to figure out which side would let her in close enough to convince him to change his mind. "Wait now, Tanner. Tanner, where the hell do you think you're going? You think you're going to just walk out on me now? Just like all the rest of them? Yeah, that's it. You're nothing, just like the rest of them. Damn losers. All of you. ALL OF YOU!"

Tanner stayed silent, unable to process what he was seeing and hearing. He grabbed a jacket and slung it over his shoulder, then leaned forward and pulled the suitcases off the bed in one swift motion using both hands and marched towards the door. He stopped for a second without looking back, "I don't want anything except what I have in my hands right now. Keep or throw away anything else of mine that you find in here. I didn't bring much. Every time I relocate, I have less to move." He set his jaw, but was grinding his teeth and left as fast as possible.

He couldn't believe what Sophie had just said. The hatred, the conviction of her words. It was one of the most blatant, ugly examples of racism Tanner had ever experienced in his entire life and it shook him to his core. He'd seen and heard similar things in the past, but mostly from boys and men. Nowhere else and at no other time had he ever witnessed such a show from a woman, adding to the darkness that seemed to overshadow the room as soon as the truth had finally come out.

Tanner had grown up during his most formative years around Mexicans in southern California and later bought his first house in a predominantly black neighborhood out east. Racism wasn't something he had ever felt comfortable being around and this was, by far, the most vicious outpouring of it he had ever witnessed. Now, when he remembered making love with Sophie, he felt sick and wanted to vomit realizing that he had essentially slept with the devil, or someone very twisted up.

It was over. Nothing she could say, or do, would make him come back to her or stay involved with her in any capacity, now. He walked out and slammed the door behind him. He could still hear her screaming and shouting obscenities at him, pounding her fists on the inside of the door to emphasize her words as he walked away. But he continued walking away, and he wanted away from her so badly, that he took the stairs instead of waiting for the elevator, just to continue moving away from the crazy woman in 3A screaming at the top of her lungs.

EXIT WOUNDS

As soon as Tanner left Sophie's, he headed straight over to Carmen's house. When Carmen held the door open for him, she knew something was wrong. "Come in, Tanner. Please, have a seat with me out here in the kitchen. I'll put the teapot on, unless you'd prefer coffee?"

"Actually, coffee does sound better to me right now, thank you." She prepared an auto-drip pot and got it started brewing, then joined him at the table. As soon as she'd gotten comfortable Tanner said, "Sophie is out. She's not going to do any of this with us and I don't want her to."

"What happened?" Carmen said, sounding surprised.

"I slept over at my new house in a sleeping bag last night. I awoke early this morning certain that something was wrong with either you, or her. I got dressed and drove by here and all was dark and seemed fine, so I went over to her place and found cops, forensics, the coroner, detectives, ambulances, a real big mess happening. I sat out in front for a little while trying to figure out what might have happened, and almost got arrested as a *person of interest*. Then, after quite a hoop jump with Officer O'Reilly, I finally get upstairs to her apartment. Turns out, the guy next door took a skydive off of his balcony earlier this morning at the exact same time I woke up."

The coffee pot announced an end to its brew cycle by gurgling loudly, then beeping four times. Carmen got up and unhooked two mugs hanging underneath one of her kitchen cabinets, filling them both with fresh coffee. "Anyway, the next thing I know, Sophie suddenly zooms in on the fact that I stopped by here, first, before going over there. Can you believe that?" Tanner shook his head, then took a long sip of his coffee while Carmen sat patiently listening and sipping her own. "I don't want to tell you this next part, but you must know about it for your own wellbeing and safety." Carmen sat up taller in her chair.

"I'm not liking this already," she said.

Tanner looked at Carmen and with a deadly serious tone said, "Carmen, Sophie is a stone cold racist. Hard core to the point of being a disciple of Hitler himself. You would have been in tears hearing her going on and on about anyone with darker skin than whites. She has either finally lost her mind or more likely, she simply hid her psychosis really well until today. What she said to me was the most racist rhetoric I've ever heard from anyone—male or female—in my entire life. I threw all that I cared to keep into two suitcases and walked out. I told her we were over.

"My God!" Carmen said, stunned. "I had no idea whatsoever. She played along with us like she was just as accepting of our genes being blended as we were. At least I thought she was." Tanner stayed quiet, letting the new information float for a few seconds, letting it take its time finding the cracks and fissures to percolate into.

Carmen looked mad. "How dare that bitch go racist on me. Who the hell does she think she is anyway? I mean, nice-looking and big boobs get it all if she wants it, right? Bitch! Well, I'm just glad that it came out now.

Tanner nodded, "I agree. Her hate shook me to my core. I have no idea what might have happened at some point down the road, if this had continued going on undetected by either of us, especially if, say, we'd left the baby with her to have a night out for ourselves? Carmen looked at him with alarm, then elaborated,

"Oh, gosh, I hadn't even gone there yet. That's scary as hell. I still can't believe it. She should've gotten an Oscar for best actress, because she fooled me all the way, and that disturbs me now more than the racism itself. It tells me that she's not only a racist, but also a really good liar. That's plenty enough for all of my alarm bells to be going off."

Almost as if he had read her mind he asked, "Hey, let's get you moved over to our new house and get you settled in while we try to get pregnant. What do you say?" Carmen nodded enthusiastically and smiled at him. He had wanted a child his entire adult life; it was a dream he'd already given up on and, for some reason, the dream had decided to turn around one hundred and eighty degrees and grant him his wish. Now, with a willingness and an open mind towards modern medical science, he hoped that he would be able to finally father a child.

Over the next week and a half they made trips from the house where she'd grown up, to the house where she would be living when she became a mother for the first time. Carmen was a lot stronger than Tanner had realized and they ended up moving all the bedroom and living room furniture, as well as the books and bookshelves. They also moved all the paintings that different relatives in Carmen's family had painted and given to Carmen's parents as gifts over the years. Carmen's cousin and his family would be moving into her old house soon.

The first couple of days, Tanner couldn't shake the feeling that someone, perhaps Sophie, was watching them. He kept feeling a dark, earnest energy, enough so that he kept repeatedly looking over his shoulder, trying to see who or what it might be and he knew why. He had looked into the face of evil and then felt it knife through him ever so briefly—that lightning fast, icy-hot pang of darkness—always hunting for new recruits, particularly the weakest, victimizing them with their own fears. Luckily, nothing bad manifested and today the moving had gone smoothly for both of them.

They had fun decorating the house together. They ended up mixing her nice furniture with a few new items that they both picked out together after dinner one night, shopping at a nearby furniture store. They'd agreed that this house, with its bigger windows, single story, open floor plan design and brighter atmosphere, along with the private, fenced backyard, was going to be the perfect house for the three of them.

By the third week, Tammy's old place looked entirely refreshed with different decor, inside and out, and Tanner was pleased with the way the landscapers had reshaped the front yard into something to be proud of.

It was a new week and they'd decided they'd finally go together to the fertility clinic for the initial consult. They both walked in and sat quietly, playing games on their devices until being called in. They met with a kind female doctor who quietly explained the various ways that could be incorporated to facilitate Carmen's pregnancy, but that it would have to be with a sperm donor, not Tanner's sperm. The doctor explained that Tanner's sperm count did not meet adequate levels for total amount, and their mobility was also lacking. She kindly stated that, at 60, his sperm looked pretty good, but was inadequate for them to be able to proceed, which was not at all unusual, and sent them home to think about things, asking for a decision within a couple of weeks regarding using a known or anonymous sperm donor. Tanner was embarrassed and also surprised at the complexity and the expense, especially considering that the odds of viability were only 30 percent at best for someone already in their late thirties. Both he and Carmen were quiet on the way home, and Tanner sensed that she was, perhaps, beginning to have second thoughts about the whole thing.

Neither one of them said anything more about it for more than two days. Tanner noticed that the paperwork with all of the information, including website addresses for more information, were all still sitting on the kitchen table. They were right where Carmen had plunked them down before wandering towards the bedroom, mumbling that she was going to lie down for a while and take a nap. When she got up a couple of hours later, she seemed extra discouraged, "Tanner, I don't think I want to go through with pregnancy after all. It's too much money and it still might not even happen. I was hoping for better news about this today, but it's worse than I even imagined. I don't want to go through it now and I don't want you to have to go for that roller coaster ride with me either. Let's call this thing off before we end up hating each other. I've been giving it a lot more thought, I even dreamt about it a short while ago. I've been chained for far too long. To my father, and to the restaurant. If I have a child, I will be handing myself my next set of handcuffs. I want to explore for a change, at least for awhile. I don't have the luxury of waiting, so I saying that I'm good with not having my own child. I no longer want to be chained anymore." Tanner nodded in affirmation but still listening without comment.

"Now that I have you alone, I want you to know that, although I, myself, am not at all creeped out by the thought of us having sex the normal way, despite our age difference, I know that you are and you have tempered yourself around me in a way that I didn't think men were capable of. You've never made rude or lascivious comments in my presence, alluded to any secret desires to have sexual relations with me, or joked around with me in that regard. Not once. Many men would pay lots of money to have sex with much younger women, but you . . . you're different. My point is, I have a deep respect for you. For your restraint and the tenacity to live by your own moral code, all the while spitting in the face of temptation. I've noticed, and I'm impressed. Thank you so much."

Tanner had been looking at Carmen while she spoke to him. He took a deep breath, letting it out slowly and smiled at her, not even trying to hide the tears that had begun slowly making their way down his face while he had listened to her. "I have to do the right thing, what I perceive as the right thing, all the time. I'm incapable of living with myself comfortably any other way," he said, sounding a little bewildered. They hugged each other tightly for a few minutes. Once again, Tanner felt an amazing, positive energy flow from Carmen while hugging her. "You sure about this?" He asked her.

"Yes. Unfortunately, I think I am."

Without any warning there was a loud knock on the door causing them to jump for a second. When he answered the door, it was Officer O'Reilly. "Mr. Dalton, mind if we have a word with you?" Tanner could see his partner standing back from the porch, his right hand on his pistol for good measure. Tanner nodded, stepped aside and motioned them in. After O'Reilly entered, Officer Stanton stepped forward offering Tanner his hand.

Tanner took it, "Pleased to meet you, Officer." Officer Stanton briefly assessed him, then smiled.

"Likewise, sir."

Carmen sidled up to Tanner, "What's going on?" Before Tanner could answer, O'Reilly looked at her and said, "Can we all please sit, if that's okay with you?"

Carmen motioned them into the kitchen and had them sit at the table. She moved her New York Times crossword puzzle and her partially finished bowl of Cap'n Crunch over to the counter, then brought each of the officers a cup of coffee. "If you like cream and sugar, it's right there, help yourself," she said, pointing to the center of the table. A little caddie sat neatly in the center. Cream on one side, raw sugar on the other, with a little napkin storage slot in-between.

Tanner waited, determined to let O'Reilly break the ice. "I'm never sure how to say what I came to say." Carmen's attention spun to Tanner. "I'm sorry to have to tell you that your friend, your former apartment mate, a Ms. Sophia G. DeLaurent is dead, Mr. Dalton."

Tanner felt himself grow dizzy before feeling his body grow very light, as though it had begun melting away, starting with his feet. Now, it seemed like only his mind and a pair of eyes remained behind to hear the rest. O'Reilly looked at him, alarmed, "Are you okay, Mr. Dalton? Do you want me to call an ambulance? You don't look well."

Tanner remained sitting. So many people around him were dying, it was becoming disturbing to him. Diego, Tammy, the guy next door to Sophie, and now Sophie.

"We have witnesses that saw two men, just like when her neighbor took a dive over his balcony. The surveillance cameras corroborate that. It looks as if they tied her up and beat her badly. The apartment was trashed and completely torn apart. It was obvious they were looking for something. Any idea what that might be?" O'Reilly was watching him so closely that it felt like he could ascertain the tiniest wiggle, twitch, or color change in Tanner's face.

"Yes, they may have been looking for a large amount of money that Sophie took from her boyfriend when he overdosed, but that was years ago now. She told me that, for a while, she was a sex slave for him and others in his drug-and-sex-for-sale circle she found herself in. She'd seen where he kept all the cash and she saw that he wore the key to the safe around his neck. One day, her boyfriend overdosed and died. She took the key and all the money she could carry. She wanted all of it, but was scared and didn't want to make more trips back there to get anything else. She gathered up her things and took a little over half of the amount that was there, which she told me was over two million dollars, then she said she left for good."

Stanton bumped O'Reilly's shoulder with his knuckle to get his attention. "That makes sense with what we have found so far. She must not have realized that the money she took wasn't her boyfriend's money." Tanner felt goosebumps appear all at once on his forearms when he thought, *I would've been killed had I still been living there.*

"Who does the money belong to then? Do you guys have any ideas?"

O'Reilly answered. "Yes, we isolated the facial images from the surveillance video, then ran it through the usual security channels and had their computers scan for a match. Interpol turned up the information in seconds. Both men are known Russian mafia members. Her boyfriend was into a little bit of everything with some very bad people. You really dodged a bullet, Mr. Dalton. Had you still been living there, you would've—"

"—I know. I've already thought about it, trust me." Tanner said, cutting him off and glancing over at Carmen briefly, before returning his gaze back to Officer O'Reilly.

O'Reilly continued, "We think that the gentleman next door, the one who took a nose dive yesterday was also a victim because those guys had simply gone to the wrong apartment, and they weren't going to take any nonsense from him when he answered the door."

Tanner shook a little inside. If only he'd shown up a little sooner, maybe it would have gone a different way. Maybe he would've entered that hallway when the two men were still standing there and then they would've knocked on Sophie's door next to take care of a witness.

Tanner got up and brought the pot of coffee over and re-filled everyone's mug, then sat down and proceeded to tell them Sophia G. DeLaurent's entire story, as far as he knew it, and all that she had shared with him. Both officers sat and listened attentively, surprised at times by what was said, as indicated by the horrified facial expressions they made. They stated that they would be turning over all of this new information to the FBI and that there wouldn't likely be any further follow-up questions. Over all, Tanner felt better from the visit and Carmen felt the same way.

On their way out, Officers O'Reilly and Stanton both thanked them for their information and hospitality. Then O'Reilly stopped them in their tracks, chilling them both to their core, "We don't think those guys found what they were looking for, though. There was no safe, and they really turned that place over. They worked her over so bad that if she had been hiding what they wanted there, trust me, she would've given it up to them. No one could've withstood that kind of a beating without telling all."

SOMETHING BIGGER THAN OURSELVES

They'd both sensed continued danger lurking after Sophie's brutal demise. No longer concerned about money issues, they had thinned out their belongings even more and put the rest in a storage unit, then hit the road for a long vacation. First stop: the big island of Hawaii, then Maui, then Oahu, before heading down to Ensenada, Mexico to meet some of Carmen's relatives. Everyone wanted to know more about the mysterious, older gentleman accompanying her. Some seemed judgmental, but it didn't take long for everyone to warm up to Tanner, once they saw that he'd learned enough Spanish to hold his own pretty well in a bilingual or mostly Spanish conversation.

On their third day, Carmen got directions to a secluded beach her aunt Isabella told her about. After losing their way twice, they ended up driving down multiple streets of rundown houses. Finally, they got on La Bufadora, one of the main drags that terminates at the blow hole tourist attraction on the rocky coast, just north of Ensenada. Tanner finally spotted the little sign *Punta Brava* painted in white. A small arrow underneath pointed to the right direction. After that, they found the last right turn and it dead-ended at the *Punta Brava* trailhead.

They grabbed their day packs and began hiking a well worn, narrow trail through desert scrub that pocks the landscape for millions of square miles along the arid, southern desert belt stretching through Mexico and extending across the entire desert southwest of the United States. Tanner could already feel the hot sun radiating back up from the scorched ground crunching beneath his feet. Once they finished climbing to the top of the first knoll, he felt the cool sea breeze comb through his hair, taking much of his heat buildup with it.

The view stunned him. Scorched earth and desert scrub all the way up to the edge of drop-off cliffs that jutted out randomly from the peninsula, carving a path through the aquamarine liquid hugging its base. Swells rolled in from the ocean, coming towards the cliffs with clear intention. They hit hard, dispersing a massive amount of kinetic energy, forcing millions of tons of water to disperse into a quadrillion tiny water droplets that quickly found their way back into the liquid abyss. No palm trees or white powdered sugar sand here, this was a hardcore, *Mother-Nature-made*, wonderland. Arid desert next to alluring aquamarine liquid was one of the starkest contrasts Tanner had ever seen.

Punta Brava lived up to its name which, translated for the setting, would mean *Wild Point* or *Rugged Point*. It was beautiful almost beyond belief, but Tanner knew that once the honeymoon wore off, he'd never want to live here. For now, he was enjoying the heck out of it.

They hiked along the *Punta Brava* trail for a couple of miles. The trail began turning downhill and once they had descended a little more Carmen said, "Look, it's the little secluded beach my aunt told me about."

Tanner could see that the trail they were on wound around an inside corner of the coastline a little more, then rapidly descended to a very small beach at the innermost point of an inlet that had formed into a sharp, finger cove. The beach had some nice sand, and lots of driftwood littering it. Tall cliffs surrounded it on all sides, and the only trail that led to it was the *Punta Brava* trail that they were on.

They carefully made their way down to the beach and spread a blanket, anchoring it with driftwood and a couple of rocks. They relaxed and ate some of the fruit and crackers with different cheeses that Carmen had brought.

"I can't believe I'm here right now, Carmen. This place is so different, yet shares so many similarities to Hawaii. It's rather surreal here. The contrast between the land and the sea is so stunning, I can hardly take my eyes off of it."

Carmen nodded, but didn't say anything. Tanner waited, eating some more sweet pineapple. Finally he said, "Okay, what's going on, Carmen?" She looked over at him and smiled.

"I don't know. I can't believe I'm going to say this, but I'm bored. Are you bored?" Tanner thought about it for a couple of seconds, then said, "Hmmm . . . I guess, somewhat, yes."

Carmen went on, "I mean, yes, it's fun traveling to new places, but after a while, I get tired of suitcases, different beds, different food and water, shifting nutrients, too much fat and sugar in our diets. I feel so spoiled, and I keep telling myself that I should just be enjoying it all. I mean, I've never had this much money or time off before. It's every working person's dream. Yet, I'm really

starting to discover that, for me at least, beyond all the flights, ho-
tels, caviar, and champagne, lies a deep chasm of discontent, boredom, and lethargy. A lifestyle capable of killing someone faster than
a poor working person without health insurance. It's too easy to
put off exercising, reading, and giving to others. Where is the joy in
just sitting around and paying for everything to be brought to you?
I can't find it. And, *if this is all there is about being rich,* I'd rather
be poor again." Tanner sat up a little more, propping himself up on
his elbows.

"I'm seeing it too, Carmen, at least now I am. When we
first took off and left Concord and that whole San Francisco Bay
area scene, I know, for me, the longer we've stayed away, the better
I've felt. It's like I ascended into cool, fresh, pristine air after nearly
choking to death on smog. I've also spent some time reflecting on
how much things have changed. I feel virtually the same way as you
do. I'm getting bored too. We go over here, we go over there. And,
when we get there, what do we do? We do what we always do, we
eat and drink. We sit at this table, and that one over there. We go on
little excursions, we buy things just to have something to do while
there, collecting trinkets along the way to remember those places,
and then we move on to do it again, somewhere else."

Carmen was smiling now. She sat up tall, turning to look at
him directly. "Right! You know, I've always wondered why all the
rich people I've seen on television, in different shows, and movies,
so often seem miserable. I know I'd never want to be stalked all the
time by the paparazzi. The only time I see them smiling is when
they are being recognized for some great acting, or when they're

being envied by someone, and they're aware of it, then they smile. The rest of the time, they often look like walking dead people, despite all of their fame and wealth."

Tanner added, "Exactly. I've noticed that too. They often walk around in their expensive getups with that mannequin face of neutrality, hoping—no, *craving*—being noticed. The minute they are, they want to get away and not be bothered anymore, even acting like the person who noticed them is some kind of creep or something. It seems like so many people are becoming that way these days. Let me spend an unbelievable amount of time and money on myself in order to look as astounding as I can, so that others will do a double-take when they walk by me later so I can act put off when they do." He chuckled before trying hard to make his voice sound like an unhappy, whiney woman, "Let me tuck these double-D's into this little slinky dress with a push-up bra, then act indignant when I catch you looking at my massive cleavage. You know?"

Carmen laughed hard. "Good one. Okay, let me try one." She shifted to get more comfortable on the blanket. "Hmm. Oh, I know, I know. I'm going to walk around with a tricolor mohawk, wearing heavy purple eye shadow, thick mascara, and dark red lipstick. I'm also sporting long, dangling earrings that have little hummingbirds wiggling on their ends and I like waving my long, claw-like, silver sparkling nails around so everyone will notice me and remember me as the little chick with the big boobs and the squeaky little four-year-old-girl voice, sporting only a lavender, semi-lace bra and a pair of pink spandex pants that show off all of her cracks and crevices. And, for sure, I'll act all indignant when I catch you snickering behind my back while staring at those cracks and crevices, even though I've worked extra hard to make sure that's exactly what's going to happen."

Tanner cracked up at the absurdity of real life, *modern life*. They both kept going for a while, feeling lighter as they did, unloading years of wonder, anger, curiosity, and intrigue in a very fun, cathartic way. Once things quieted down, Tanner looked over at Carmen, "So, what do you want to do about the boredom?"

"Stay busy from now on. Just like I used to. I want to put smiles on people's faces again. But, this time, I want to do it more directly, in a way that truly matters to those who receive my efforts."

"Do you have any ideas about what or how you might get to that?"

"Kind of, maybe."

"Well then, my dear, please let it out. You know I'm all ears, and you also know that I'm likely going to be all on board with whatever it is that you're thinking of doing. You know I will." He winked at her.

Carmen looked out across the ocean, spotting a fishing trawler about a mile off shore pulling fishing traps up. A massive flock of seagulls swooped around the boat, just a few feet from where the fisherman stood. Carmen looked over at Tanner, "I think I want to help children who no longer have parents."

"That sounds like a really amazing thing to do," he said.

"You spent a lot of time in Massachusetts, didn't you?"

"Yes, why?"

"My cousin, Sabrina, told me about a program that she learned about from someone who left their kid behind while being deported back to Mexico. She called it the Unaccompanied Minors Program or something like that. Anyway, in Massachusetts, they created and passed this program that is a one-stop help station for kids with no parents, not just immigrant kids separated from their parents who were deported without them, but all children without parents for whatever reasons. Private companies provide many of the services. I think I want to be one of those companies, only on a very small scale. Limit what we do to a dozen kids without parents. We provide them with what they need and offer a safe place for them to grow up. We can make our place a safe place for them to live and learn about getting along with others, and being a family while growing up. All the usual kid stuff until they go to foster parents, or get adopted, maybe coming back for a while, maybe becoming permanently adopted by their foster parents. They come, they get a room, a place to call home for a while until they are ready to try out a new family. That's what I'd like to focus on, I think. It will put a smile on lots of children's faces, and I think it will do the same for us and be a really good thing for all of us."

Tanner sat up tall. "I absolutely love your idea at face value. I feel like I want to do it, but let me think on it for a bit? That's kind of a big order for me, moving back to Massachusetts where my ex-wife and I lived together for so long. I love that state, though."

They spent another week with Carmen's relatives. On the last day, Tanner woke up and knew with every fiber of his being that he wanted to help Carmen realize her dream. He got dressed and quietly went to her room. He woke her with a kiss on her forehead and smiled at her. "Good morning, Carmen. I want to start a group home for kids with you in Massachusetts. Let's do it. It's perfect. We'll be busy being a family, just not in the way we originally imagined." They both smiled at one another. Carmen laughed a little, nervously, then giggled some more. She knew it was the perfect next step and so did Tanner. He loved the way Carmen always aimed for good, positive, and healthy—a better world means a better quality of life for everyone. After making arrangements, they said their good byes and left Ensenada to start new lives in Williamsburg, a small town on the eastern side of the Berkshire mountains in west-central Massachusetts.

Tanner flew out to Massachusetts to check out properties in the rural, western part of the state, hopefully in or close to the Williamsburg, Massachusetts area. Carmen went back to California to arrange to have their belongings moved, and put the house on the market. Wrapping things up in Concord seemed almost too easy. Having plenty of money to pay for professionals to move them made it a simple thing to get their belongings out to Massachusetts.

Tanner had remembered Doug mention that he was sick of renting apartments, but couldn't afford to buy a decent house and got in touch with him about buying Tammy's former place. After meeting with Carmen who showed him around, Doug was thrilled with the place and let them know he wanted it, but wasn't sure if he'd be able to afford such a stunning property. Tanner made it happen by offering him seller financing. Tanner agreed to sell the house to Doug for half its current market value with zero down, zero percent interest for any term Doug felt comfortable with. They settled on a fifteen-year loan. Doug was thrilled beyond belief that he was not only going to finally become a bonafide homeowner, but in a nice neighborhood, in his old-pal's former place, and for such great terms that he'd own the place free and clear in a mere fifteen years was beyond anything he could have imagined happening.

Vincent helped Carmen move all of the commercial kitchenware and canned goods to her uncle Ernesto's restaurant, El Toltec. Ernesto was a little saddened by the news of their departure to the east coast, but loved hearing about their plans to help children.

<center>~~~~~~~~~~~~~~~~</center>

They lived like husband and wife, but without any physical intimacy, beyond tight holding and hugging. Over time, Carmen's feelings for him grew, seeing his kindness in action. He could sometimes feel her desire for him, but he wanted to keep things trusting, warm, and most of all, loving. Sex would change everything. He knew it would *feel* good, and *feel* amazing in real time; he was convinced that it would also ruin their close relationship. Tanner was all set just leaving things between them intimate—sans the sex.

They purchased a large colonial that came with a connected barn and some horse corrals. They had the barn refurbished right away, turning it into a small hotel, complete with an office at

392

the main entrance, and hired several certified child care workers to monitor the children and their activities at all times.

They decided to name it *Unity House.*

They hired two language instructors to teach the steady influx of immigrant children how to speak basic English, while also helping them with their school work, or playing games with them during leisure time. Over time, Tanner began documenting the children during their stay at Unity House, giving his notes, photos, and any videos he had made of the children to the parents who adopted them, if and when they were adopted. Nevertheless, just as in any other family, everyone enjoyed seeing his pictures and videos; they brought much joy to all who took the time to look at them.

Carmen spent lots of time in the kitchen cooking the meals, and teaching some of the older children how to cook and make different types of breads, including her now locally famous sourdough bread. Tanner enjoyed throwing a baseball, a football, or a frisbee with some of the kids, and he could occasionally be found running around the property trying to steal a soccer ball from one of them, laughing the entire time.

One afternoon, during an extremely rare break, they both had a chance to sit back in their favorite cushioned Adirondack chairs out on the front porch with a couple of tall glasses of iced tea, quietly gazing out across the sloping lawn to the tree line and the mountains beyond. They were happy. Happier than they'd ever been in their entire lives.

Carmen spied him looking at her out of the corner of her eye and looked back at him, smiling. He raised his glass in her direction. She nodded and raised hers up a little, then promptly clinked her glass against his.

Tanner took a long sip, swallowed, and said, "Mission accomplished."

Later that afternoon, Tanner awoke from an unexpected nap. He'd fallen asleep without realizing it. He looked around the yard and couldn't remember the last time it had been that quiet. A gentle breeze stirred the pine trees lining the back property line. A small army of different birds were all singing, frantically sharing the daily gossip with the other birds. Tanner felt completely alive and very comfortable. The fresh air had worked its magic on him again.

He felt himself beginning to doze off again listening to the sounds of the birds and the breeze. He closed his eyes and felt the beginnings of unconsciousness begin to slip in through the cracks of his mind. Just as the last remnants of consciousness vanished, he heard the drone of the mail truck out in front. He pictured Tom, the funny, outgoing postal delivery guy that came on most days, opening his mailbox.

Tanner sat up. He remembered that his lawyer said he was sending him "a pleasant surprise." Bright son-of-a-bitch, that guy. Tanner got up to go see what Tom had left for them today. He opened the mailbox and pulled out a medium stack of junk mail, envelopes that might be important, and two things that were undoubtedly important. Halfway back up the driveway, Tanner saw an envelope from his attorney. He opened it and pulled out the letter. As he read the letter, he felt anxiety turn to surprise and then pure excitement. "No way! Tanner started running around the yard like a student who had just opened a letter accepting them into Harvard. "Wow. Wow. I can't believe it! Wow!"

Carmen heard him screaming about something outside and moved to the window. She watched him running around the yard so happy. She ran out onto the front porch, "What is it, Tanner?"

Tanner ran over to her and handed her the letter. Carmen looked at the letter which read:

Dear Mr. Dalton, I have enclosed the handwritten letter sent to me by your ex-wife. Once you read it, please get in touch with me as soon as possible to discuss getting this transferred into your account right away. Best, Bob Davies, Attorney at Law. Sheila's letter said:

Dear Tanner,

I hope this letter finds you well and happy. My attorney kept up on your whereabouts in case we needed to have further contact with you in the future. Good thing! Congratulations on Unity House. Wow, I'm impressed that you would do that. Way to go.

Please have your attorney, Bob Davies, contact me so we can get $3,260,262 transferred into your account(s). It's the money I took from your retirement account when I divorced you. I had it reinvested and I've decided to give it back to you because I don't need it—at all—I married a multi-millionaire! This money has just been sitting in the market, earning like crazy. So, here you go. I'm sorry I lied to you and treated you so badly when we divorced.

With love and much admiration,
Sheila.

Both Tanner and Carmen looked at one another, then screamed with delight. They joined hands and danced in circles, laughing and giggling until they were both so exhausted they went inside and collapsed on the couch together in total euphoria.

Tanner's retirement fund that he'd worked so hard for and risked so much to have, had come back to him in the end after all. Unity House was already in good shape financially, and Tanner wasn't sure what would be the best thing to do with the money, so decided that he'd park the money in a savings account for the time being until he could figure it out.

A couple of days later, he was driving home after seeing Attorney Davies where he'd signed the paperwork for the transfer, and it hit him: he would start a scholarship fund to reward high academic achievers coming from disadvantaged backgrounds. As soon as the thought ran through to completion, he knew that's what he was going to do with the money. Why spend it? He already had plenty. What he didn't have, was a legacy with his name on it. He knew it was his ego, but he wanted to be remembered, some-how. Even if only in the form of a grave marker. No, that wouldn't do. He admitted to himself he wanted more than that. He wanted his name to live on in perpetuity.

He'd known what it was like to be really smart and not able to go to college, instead having to go to work because he was being kicked out of the house. *No college in that picture, unless . . . some-one like that had, say, earned a B+ or better average for their four years in high school despite their bad circumstances and now they could get a full scholarship to college, while working part time at the school or a nearby venue of some sort.*

Tanner turned around and went home. He called his accountant and set up a meeting with a representative from the University of Massachusetts Amherst Foundation.

With help, he set up the *Tanner Dalton Academic Achievement Scholarship Fund.* That year, at the Foundation's annual dinner in Boston he was asked to give a speech announcing the scholarship's formation and outline it for everyone.

"The Tanner Dalton Academic Achievement Scholarship Fund is for New England high school students coming from disadvantaged backgrounds who still manage to achieve a B+ or better grade point average. These are the young people I want to help and this scholarship will be that help. These kids somehow manage to swallow their angst and change their future for the better through academic achievement. These kids, who have everything stacked against them, many living through a hell most of us will never know, have managed to come through for themselves by committing to achieve their goals, showing tenacity and making their own good luck, they earned or nearly earned a 4.0 grade point average despite it all. Grace under pressure. They deserve my help, and this fund is my offering towards that end."

The applause hadn't been sought, nor was it necessary—but it was received with quiet gratitude nevertheless. As he made his way back to Unity House, the echo of it followed him, soft and steady, like a tide in his memory. He thought of how far he'd come, of everything he'd endured, and slowly, a smile spread across his face.

A Request

Thank you for taking the time to read my novel, Unity House. Please consider leaving a short review on Amazon, Goodreads, or your favorite bookseller's site. Your feedback helps other readers discover the story — and it means the world to me.

Thank you for reading.

—Keith

About the Author

Keith C. Milne is the author of *The Unlikely Angel of Casco Bay* and *Unity House*. Originally from California, he now lives in Massachusetts with his wife. He writes stories about connection, resilience, and the unexpected ways people can change each other's lives.

You can learn more about Keith and his books at: www.keithmilne.com

Amazon: https://www.amazon.com/author/keithchristianmilne

Facebook: keithmilne.com/fb

Goodreads: keithmilne.com/gr

Pinterest: pinterest.com/authorkeithcmilne

Acknowledgements

Many people helped bring Unity House to life.

To my family and friends — thank you for your support, encouragement, and belief in this story.

To my early readers and editors — your insights and feedback have made all the difference. Thank you for giving me another set of eyes and your subjective analysis.

And to every reader — thank you for giving Unity House a place in your heart.